secrets
in
the
SMOKE

LINDA
STEFKO

Secrets In The Smoke

Linda Stefko

ISBN (Print Edition): 978-1-09830-759-2

ISBN (eBook Edition): 978-1-09830-760-8

TABLE OF CONTENTS

CHAPTER 1

May 1890—Jack

Young Jack Quinn knew he was not supposed to be in the gardens, but the warm breeze and the scent of springtime air called to him. His ears strained to hear his mum's voice in the whispering wind. The previous winter had been fierce, even for Pittsburgh, and he was enjoying every little bit of sunshine as it filtered through the budding tree branches. The boy studied the carefully tended beds, the borders of buds and blooming flowers, the neatly trimmed shrubs, and the flat stone path that snaked through the gardens.

To Jack's nine-year-old mind the abundance of so much natural beauty in a place so close to manmade ugliness was almost unimaginable. The town of Hazelwood, part of the east side of Pittsburgh, where Jack had been born, consisted of buildings and streets that were dirty and gray, blackened by the smoke that spewed from the steel mill. Families depended on the mill for jobs—it was their lifeblood. So, the people tolerated the grime, no questions asked. The dark river bordered his neighborhood: the deep water ran gray and brown, full of shit…and who knew what else. He didn't think so much as a flower could grow near the riverbank, nor among the chunks of black coal scattered by the railroad tracks.

Here, up on the hill in this world of shade trees, he could forget all the suffering and sorrow. This serene place was Jack's refuge. He removed his wool cap, lifted his face, determined to feel her touch, her hand gently stroking his rumpled dark hair. Just like the old days. Before she was gone.

It had been two weeks since Mum's funeral and he had watched the pallbearers lower the wooden box into the ground at St. Stephen's Cemetery. He couldn't remember the words of the prayers....He had stood speechless and numb as the shovels threw dirt and the priest sprinkled holy water. They said prayers, and the words swirled in his head: something about "ashes to ashes" and "dust to dust." The soul of Annie Quinn. Departed. Eternal rest. Words that did not patch the hole in his heart.

Now all that was left were questions, and sadness. "Why…? Why did she have to die? Why did she have to leave him?" He sobbed softly.

His mother had been sick for so long, and now she was gone. His sisters said she was with the angels. Wondering if Heaven was like this garden, he tried to picture Mum in the sky with the holy angels, surrounded by bouquets of flowers. Tears were trickling down his cheeks. Jack wished there was a stone path he could follow to take him to her. *If only*, he thought.

"Mum always liked flowers," he whispered to himself. He remembered how he used to pick two or three and hide them under his shirt. When he went back home, he would put them in a tin cup of water, setting it on the table next to her bed. She would smile at him and say, "Thank you, Jackie… they're so pretty." And then he would hold her hand. Flowers smelled good. She liked purple flowers the best…tiny violets scattered on the ground in the woods, and the bigger lilacs from the bushes. He hoped that she had lots of flowers in Heaven. Another tear slid down his cheek and he quickly wiped it away with the back of his hand. He bent down to pick a small purple crocus. Just then he heard heavy footsteps on the stone path and a deep voice shouting: "You there, you little Irish shit, git on home! Go on now, git on home. You don't belong here! Damn dirty ragamuffin!"

Jack turned and took off like a shot down the hill. The old caretaker couldn't catch him, and never tried very hard, figuring it wasn't worth the trouble. The man chuckled, satisfied that he had done his duty by putting a little fear of God in the young fellow. He contemplated putting up a sign that said NO TRESPASSING but didn't know if the Irish children could even read. He leaned against a tree trunk and watched how fast the boy could run.

Young Jack Quinn was only nine, but he was tall for his age, with strong legs that had outgrown his thin cotton trousers months ago. His dark hair blew back from his forehead as he ran as fast as the wind.

The sky turned gray and cloudy as Jack crossed the intersection of Second Avenue and Elizabeth Street and raced toward the railroad tracks. Or was the dark sky just a result of the black soot in the air? The smoke from the smokestacks and the resulting grime permeated every inch of his neighborhood.

He slowed to a walk as he entered the dirt alley that ran parallel to the tracks and Second Avenue, wiping his runny nose on the frayed cuff of his gray shirt. He bent over to catch his breath, hands on his knees, and then stood tall and looked at the rows of wood-framed two-story houses. They had been constructed by the steel company for its workers. He quietly slid into the backyard of the fifth house in the second row, quickly passed by the wooden privy, and opened the kitchen door. Skipping school was getting to be a daily occurrence for Jack since he had decided two weeks ago he would much rather look in the shop windows on Second Avenue, throw rocks at the coal barges in the river, and sneak into the gardens of the big brick and stone houses situated on the hills overlooking Hazelwood. Jack's older sisters sometimes went to the big houses—*mansions*, they called them—to sew and clean for the wealthy families. Dad called the rich people *cake eaters*. Jack mumbled, "I like to eat cake, and my sister Mary can make really good cakes. So why aren't we called cake eaters too?" Nobody answered his question.

He had heard somebody call him a river rat once, although he hated the river. It was dark and smelled bad. Mum always told him, "Stay away from the water…if you fall in, there's no getting out; you'll drown and get washed all the way down to the Ohio River." He wondered if rats could swim. None of his friends knew for sure. Nobody wanted to find out.

Inside the house, fourteen-year-old Margaret Quinn was sitting at the table peeling potatoes. She glared at him. "Take your filthy shoes off, hang up your cap, and then you best wash those grubby hands." Margaret was awful bossy and frowned a lot, but Jack figured that she was always getting told what to do by Mary and Florence, the two oldest sisters, and that would make most anybody grumpy. Dad told Jack, "Let your sister talk. Margaret likes to think that she's all grown up. Just cause she's grumbling and bossing you doesn't mean you have to mind her. But you better listen to Mary, especially now with Mum being gone."

Mary Quinn was eighteen and the oldest of his three sisters; Florence was sixteen. They both usually worked at one of the big houses on the hill but came home around three o'clock in the afternoon. They would walk down Elizabeth Street and stop in St. Stephen's Church to light a candle for Mum, then cross Second Avenue and hurry along to one of the markets. Mary was determined to take care of her family now that Mum was gone, and she liked to look for the freshest meat, cabbage, and potatoes. Sometimes she brought home a bag of apples too. It was a good day if Mary had a big chunk of cheese in her bag. Always hunting for a bargain, she was friendly with old Mr. Holdsworth, the butcher, who saved her the best soup bones and, occasionally, some lean cuts of beef.

"It pays to be nice to people, especially where I shop for our food," Mary had remarked one day. "Jackie, remember…it doesn't cost anything to be nice, and if you add a smile, then that just sweetens the pot!" Then Jack overheard Mary tell Florence, "I know not to smile at that butcher man, Mr. Holdsworth, when his wife is hovering nearby. She gives you moldy cheese if she thinks you're winking at her husband, as if any young woman would want that grisly old man."

At six o'clock the whistle at the mill blew and ten minutes later Dad was home for supper, always hungry from working a twelve-hour shift. Sometimes he stopped at one of the bars along Second Avenue on the walk from the mill. Most of the men liked to wash down the dirt of the mill with a shot and a beer. The older Irishmen called their beer "stout" and would drink a pint or two, and they all liked their whiskey.

When Dad got home, Jack watched him take a swig of whiskey from a bottle that he kept in the kitchen cupboard. Especially the last two weeks. Jack studied Dad's solemn face and knew that he missed Mum. They all did. Dad, Mary, Florence, Margaret, Jack. The entire Quinn family.

Every evening Jack climbed the stairs after supper and fell asleep in his clothes. He had a recurring dream where he pictured his family drifting, lost at sea in a small boat, with Dad pointing up at the sky, saying, "Jackie, look at the stars. We're not lost, your Mum is up there, guiding us. Every star is an opening to Heaven, and she can see us. Aye, for sure, she can." His Dad's words always made Jack feel a little better, especially at night when he woke up and stood at the window looking at the night sky…trying to catch a glimpse of the stars through the darkness of the smoke and clouds.

Jack used to ask Dad about the old country, where he had come from years ago, before Mary was born; but Dad would get quiet and just say, "It doesn't matter where you've been, what matters is where you're going. I'm just happy to be in America—and this is where I'm staying until the day I die." Mum didn't mind spinning tales about their big adventure. She had told Jack many times that she and Dad, Annie and Sean Quinn, had come over to America from Ireland twenty years earlier. Her brother, Jack's Uncle Mike, came with them. They traveled on a big ship with other Irish folks; the journey had taken three weeks. Mum said, "That boat was rocking, the waves were churning, the wind blowing, and we huddled close asking the good Lord to have mercy on our poor souls."

Conditions on the ship were awful, according to Mum. Spoiled food was all they had to eat, and the stench of sickness permeated every deck. Times were bad in the old country. Mum said legions of hungry poor people came to America for a better life. Dad had been told there were jobs to be had in all the big cities, and entire neighborhoods of Irish people from Galway and Mayo were living in Pittsburgh; jobs were to be found on practically every doorstep. Mum said she and Dad were young, brave, and not afraid of hard times. It didn't matter that they were as poor as field mice, since they were full of hope and faith in God.

In their drafty little house in the wintertime, the Quinn family used to sit close around the warm coal-fired stove in the kitchen during the long evenings after supper. Mum and the girls would work on their knitting and mending, and Dad would talk about Hazelwood, which had recently become part of the city of Pittsburgh. Jack listened quietly as Dad told stories he had heard from the old-timers in the bars. Dad said, "Before the mill was built and the railroad had come to town, there were many fine homes and rich people in Hazelwood. The first settlers were from Scotland, and they had farms cut out of the wooded hills. There had been a lot of hazelnut trees up on the hills, and rows of apple trees too. A man by the name of John Woods built a stone house over a hundred years ago that he called Hazel Hill." That house was still intact; Jack figured maybe the man's great-grandchildren still lived there. Jack and his best pal, Johnny Finnegan, had seen the old stone house many times when they were out exploring the hillside. The boys liked climbing the hills and eating apples from the apple orchard.

Dad continued: "A river captain built a grand house right down by the river, and he surrounded it with all kinds of flowers and shrubbery...." Jack wrinkled his nose and commented, "That must've been before the river was so dirty and smelly." During Jack's time growing up, most of the shops and businesses lined Second Avenue, the main street through the town, which had been paved with bricks many years ago.

Small brick houses had always lined Chatsworth Avenue, and nice homes stood on Sylvan Avenue as well; both streets ran parallel to Second, on the upper side of the railroad tracks. The mansions and grand estates that remained stood farther up the hill, bordered by gardens and a variety of trees, especially those hazelnut trees. Dad was aware Jack liked to visit those gardens and couldn't blame him.

Last year, when they were exploring, Johnny Finnegan and Jack had cracked open some hazelnuts to see if they were good to eat, but the boys hadn't liked the taste and spit them out.

According to Dad, about thirty years ago, a wealthy businessman named Mr. Jones wanted to build the first line of railroad tracks through the area. Not everyone in the town favored the idea. The river captain who lived next to the river in the beautiful house, along with other landowners whose houses stood along the river, banded together and refused to give consent for railroad tracks along the riverbank. They didn't want their views obstructed.

The railroad ended up going right through the middle of Hazelwood, which divided the town into two sections. The people who lived in the nice houses by the river eventually moved away, not liking the noise of the trains and the smoke from the mill. Buildings situated "below the tracks" were closer to the river—the Monongahela River, which soon became dirty and smelly. Jack now realized that must be the reason people said he lived on the "wrong side of the tracks."

Jack remembered last year, when Mum had given him a peppermint stick as a reward when he finally learned to spell *Monongahela*. She had been so proud of him…and he never minded being bribed with candy. Hazelwood was only a few miles from downtown Pittsburgh. It bordered the Monongahela, which flowed downstream and met up with the Allegheny River. Mary said, "Over a hundred years ago, a fort had stood there, built by the French, where they traded with the Indians, and then the British built Fort Pitt." Dad added: "The great George Washington fought many battles in that area before becoming the first president." Jack had learned these facts in his history and geography classes at school, but he found them more interesting when Dad and Mary talked about them. He wondered where the Indians went, and tried to picture George Washington as a boy. He wished he could ride a horse and grow up to be a general in the army.

Jack remembered in school when the teacher had hung up a map that showed the Ohio River flowing all the way to the great Mississippi River. He wondered if the Indians used to paddle their canoes in the rivers. He thought it would be exciting to ride on a riverboat all the way to the Mississippi....

Dad explained: "When the railroad came to town, it brought lots of changes, with new jobs and hundreds of new people moving in looking for work. When Mum and I—and other Irish folks—came to Hazelwood, the iron and steel mills were taking up more and more space: they started to squeeze out the big old fancy houses that were right in town. Some of the great old homes were knocked down, and then they built the rows of cheap wooden houses that were rented to the workers. Like where we live. The rich families moved to other neighborhoods where there weren't mills and factories close by."

Jack understood why those people wanted to move...and couldn't blame them.

"During the last twenty years," Dad said, "Hazelwood has become quite a bustling busy place. Lots of jobs in the mills or with the railroad, or down by the river with boat building or river trade."

The Irish men that Dad knew all worked in the mill, tending the giant furnaces and coke ovens. He said, "Coke comes from coal, and the coal is loaded into the train cars outside of Connellsville. That's where there are a lot of coal mines. That's one job that is probably worse than working in the mills. The coal miners go deep into the mines and never get to see the light of day. Sometimes there are explosions in the mines...I've heard stories about men being buried alive." Mary added: "Connellsville is about forty miles from

Pittsburgh, and the best way to bring the coal here is by rail, so they built the tracks that go right to the mills. They use the coke to make steel, and steel makes really strong bridges." Jack sat quietly in his straight-backed wooden chair and contemplated all he was learning.

Most nights Dad read the newspaper aloud to Jack and his sisters; he thought it improved his speech, since he didn't like anyone to think he was right off the boat, with a thick Irish brogue, especially given his notable Galway accent. If he was tired, then Mary would read. Jack remembered that Mum was not a good reader, but she enjoyed listening. The newspapers usually carried a story about a man named Andrew Carnegie. Jack listened to all the stories about Mr. Carnegie. He was a very important businessman and had come to America with his parents from Scotland about forty years earlier. Jack knew Scotland was close to Ireland. The family was poor, and when his father became ill and then died, Carnegie had to get a job to help feed his mother and brother. He was only twelve years old when he went to work. Jack figured Andrew Carnegie maybe didn't like school either.

~ひこふん～

St. Stephen's Roman Catholic Church, a brick and wooden structure that the Irish immigrants had built thirty years earlier, stood along Second Avenue. Jack's dad didn't usually have to work on Sundays, so the family dressed in their cleanest clothes and went to Mass. They walked the same route every week: two blocks down Lytle Street, across the railroad tracks, then one block down Second Avenue.

Other Irish families always crowded into the church, and Jack and his family nodded to their neighbors then listened to old Father Donnelly. His raspy voice repeated the familiar Latin phrases and prayers, which were comforting to Jack in the way that familiar things give people a sense of peace and security. Like a pat on the head or a hug from Mum. He missed her hugs.

"*Kyrie eleison, Kyrie eleison,*" the priest chanted during Mass. Mum had told Jack that the odd words were not English but rather Latin; they meant, *Lord, have mercy.* She said, "Jackie, we pray to God for mercy and forgiveness…since we are all sinners." She put a stern expression on her face and looked Jack in the eyes. "Aye, sinners!"

Father Donnelly liked to give long sermons and talk about sin. Jack remembered how his sister Mary would pinch his arm when he would start to fall asleep. The old white-haired priest droned on and on. He always commanded his congregation to attend Mass on Sundays…so as not to burn in Hell. He preached about how the devil and the hell-fires would devour your soul, especially if you didn't say your prayers and go to Mass.

Jack figured Father Donnelly knew everyone's sins since the faithful churchgoers had to recite their offenses regularly in the confessional. When Jack had made his first confession, one of the prayers he had had to learn was called "The Act of Contrition": he had to tell God, *and* Father Donnelly, that he was heartily sorry for having offended God. He wondered if he was ever "heartily" sorry, or just "regular" sorry for his sins. He wondered if trespassing in the gardens on the hill was a sin. He also wondered if refusing to go to school, playing hooky, was a sin…he was not heartily sorry for doing either! And not regular sorry either.

Mum had told him, "Jackie, when we say prayers we're talking to God, and God listens to us. We can also pray to God's mother, Mary." Jack figured that Mum must have liked the name Mary, since she named her first child after her. A statue of the Blessed Mother Mary stood in a dark alcove in the nave at St. Stephen's. Mother Mary looked pretty, like his Mum, with long dark hair and blue eyes. Annie Quinn didn't have to go to Mass after she got sick; Father Donnelly would simply bring the Holy Communion to the house for her. He would sit next to her bed and say prayers, and he blessed her with holy water. Mary and Florence always had to empty Mum's bucket, which sat by her bed, so it wouldn't stink up the room, especially when Father

Donnelly visited. Prayers by the priest, medicine from the doctor, the love of her family; nothing had helped to keep her here. Not even Mary's soup that tasted so good. Mary called it her Lucky Irish Soup since it had lots of potatoes and green beans and onions. One afternoon when Mary was preparing the soup and Dad snuck a quick spoonful from the pot, Jack heard him say, "Nothing lucky about the Irish, who have more sorrows than all the shamrocks in Ireland." Jack figured that must have been why Dad was happy to be in America.

~◦∞◦~

Before Mum became sick, Jack liked to hear her tell stories, like the one about how Dad had carried Jack to the church to be baptized when he was only three days old. Mum said, "Since many babies died right after they were born, they had to have the waters of Baptism sprinkled on them right away, so they could go to Heaven and not have to stay in purgatory or Limbo, which is in-between Heaven and Hell." Mum knew all about the rules of the Catholic Church. "Babies don't suffer in Limbo," she said, "but it's better to be baptized so they can go straight to Heaven. Aye, you know for sure God doesn't want any babies suffering, ever. He wants those little wee ones close to him with the angels holding and rocking them."

One night the year before Jack's Mum passed, Jack overheard Mum and Mary talking while they thought he was asleep. Mum was telling Mary, "I wonder what the baby that died would have looked like. He would have been six years old now, if he had lived. I pray for his wee soul every day." Jack figured out that he must have been two or three years old when that baby was born. He would have had a brother! He thought that would have been nice, having a brother to play with. His brother must be in Limbo since he had died as soon as he was born, before he could be baptized. That probably made Mum sad.

He thought about Heaven and Hell a lot during the weeks after Mum died. He missed her; but Mary told him, "Mum doesn't have any more pain now that she is in Heaven and there are lots of angels to take care of her. Heaven has sunshine and bunches of flowers, so it must be a nice place." Jack wished that he could visit Heaven, but Mary said, "Jackie, you can't visit. Once you're there…you're there forever." He asked, "Mary, what about guardian angels? They walk around with us, right? Do they fly back and forth between Heaven and Earth? And what about the devils, the bad angels…can they go back and forth between Hell and Earth?" Mary sighed. "Jackie, you have too many questions, and you're making my head hurt."

Whenever Jack watched Dad coming through the doorway after work, he was black from the dirt and smoke of the mill. The boy wondered if there was a bit of Hell in the fiery furnaces of the mill, but he figured Dad was probably safe there: Sean Quinn didn't have any bad sins on his soul.

Every evening before Jack went to bed, Mary made him practice his handwriting on a piece of slate using chalk. As his handwriting improved, she allowed him to use a pencil and a piece of paper. Dad called it fist-writing. Mary called it penmanship, even though he didn't use a pen. Jack thought that was an odd name for writing.

Mary went to school until she was twelve and then had to quit to help Mum. When she was fifteen, she started working for several of the "big house" families. Mum always said Mary had a good reputation with the rich people because she was a hard worker. Mary could sew, clean, do the washing, or help in the kitchen. Many of the people she worked for complimented her on her talents. Looking directly at Jack, Mary said, "It's good to have lots of skills."

One evening after supper, when Jack was practicing his penmanship, Mary told him, "Mrs. Oliver and Mrs. Lewis are always talking about how one is judged by what we say and how we say it. So, it's important, Jackie, to use good grammar when we speak, and to also write legibly." Mary would pretend to speak with an uppity air, very prim and proper. Jack figured that must be how the rich ladies talked. "It is also required to be refined, neat, and clean." Jack wondered what the word "refined" meant but didn't want to interrupt. That would give Mary a reason to preach about good manners. "Of course," Mary added, "those women are not having such conversations with me, but that is what they say to their children and to the maids. I just listen."

Mary looked crossly at Jack as he wiped snot from his nose on his sleeve. "And their children are taught to use handkerchiefs for their runny noses, and napkins to wipe their faces at the table—not their sleeves! *And* they wash their hands before they sit down at the table to eat."

"And, Jackie," she continued, "Mum always reminded me to be clean and responsible, since some Irish people are not, and they are the ones who tend to give all of the Irish a bad reputation. Mum also said to speak clearly and properly, so as not to be looked down on. And remember to be proud that you are Irish. We are just as good as anyone else in America, even if we are poor."

Mary went on: "I'm just a good listener. You can learn a lot by keeping your ears open and your lips closed. I don't ever talk too much when I am at the big houses." Jack also learned to be a good listener. Ears open, mouth closed.

Another evening, Mary grabbed Jack's chin and made him look her in the eye as she quietly told him, "Oh, and Jackie, Dad says if you keep skipping school he's going to take you with him to the mill." Jack heard but didn't reply. He figured Mary probably thought her words would scare him. Jack knew his father might follow through with his threat. Dad often said, "Say what you mean, and mean what you say." And Dad always meant what he said. Aye, for sure, he did.

Now that Mum was gone, Jack was tired of going to school and sick of trying to be good all the time. When Mum was ill, he had promised God, and the Blessed Mother, and all the saints in Heaven, that he would be good forever…if Mum got better. But God took her away anyways. So, no more bargaining. No more promises. Jack remembered how much his mother loved him, and he didn't feel very lovable anymore. Who would love him now?

Jack knew in his heart that he shouldn't be angry at God, but he couldn't help it. He was just sad, and disappointed, and so very angry. And he wasn't sorry.

He might have to go to confession and ask Father Donnelly whether it was a sin to be angry at God.

CHAPTER 2

March 1891—Jack

True to his word, Dad told Jack, "As soon as you turn ten years old, you'll be going with me every day to the mill. You don't want to go to school, so now you can go to work. Beating your arse hasn't done any good, so we'll see what you're made of. Someday you'll wish you had kept going to school. Aye, you will." Jack wanted to scream, "I don't bloody care! I don't give a damn!" Of course, he knew better than to even whisper those words. Doing so would just put him on the receiving end of a slap to the head or a few whacks with a stick. Dad didn't put up with any backtalk from his son.

Two months later young Jack Quinn was an employee of the Jones and Laughlin Steel Company, commonly referred to as J & L Steel. Originally the mill had processed iron, but the processing and production of steel was gaining in importance. The mills were looking for all the employees that they could find, anybody who could walk, listen, and not complain. All Jack knew was that the mill was a hot, dangerous, dirty place to work. On payday Dad would give him a small part of his wages…for candy or cookies from the market on Second Avenue.

Hazelwood kept growing. More mills, more smoke, more jobs, more immigrants. It had turned into a booming industrial town, the major employers being J & L Steel and the Baltimore and Ohio Railroad. Steel was needed for the construction of bridges and buildings in downtown Pittsburgh, and the production of all this steel was the purpose of the mills on both sides of the river. The mills relied on the strong backs and sweat of thousands of immigrants who lived in the towns built nearby: first- and second-generation immigrants, which included all of Jack's Irish neighbors, his Dad, and now him.

"I don't care," whispered Jack, night after night, as he sat on his lumpy bed and stared at the dark sky outside his window. He knew there was a moon and stars up there, but all he could see was the eerie orange glow of the mill as he listened to the slow-moving railroad cars in the yards banging together, the tracks hissing beneath them.

It was almost spring, which used to be his favorite season. Now he would walk in the gardens only in his mind, when he dreamed at night. In his dreams he pictured himself running past the rows of tall shade trees and smelling the flowers. Sometimes he could even see Mum's face smiling at him and watching him with her calm blue eyes. He would pick a purple flower, reach up and offer it to her. Then he would wake up.

⁓ ᥱᥬᘓᥩ᷁ᥲ⁓

In the early morning Mary always served warm biscuits with butter, and hot tea for them to drink. Jack liked to pour milk and lots of sugar in his cup of tea as he rubbed the sleep from his eyes. Dad said, "Eat up. It's a long time before we get a break for lunch." Mary had their metal lunch pails ready, filled with bread and cheese—and, sometimes, an apple. He felt very grown-up.

On the way to the mill the sky was always dark and dreary, sometimes rainy, creating a misty veil that hung low over the town. The shops on Second Avenue didn't open until well after the sun came up; as they headed to work

Dad and Jack usually stayed on the dirt path alongside the railroad tracks, filing silently in line behind the other workers.

As soon as they stepped inside the mill the air turned hot, and most of what he saw was surrounded by the bright and blazing fire of the furnaces. He had never seen such huge flames: long orange tongues trying to leap out and lick anyone—or any*thing*. He didn't have to be told that those fires were hotter than hot, probably as scorching as hell fires, and that they could melt the skin right off a man.

Since Jack was only ten years old, the bosses gave him a slew of oily rags to clean machine parts. He swept the floors, ran errands, and delivered written messages between the supervisors. At least here nobody hit him with wooden rulers and sticks—unlike at school, where cruel, vindictive teachers, true arseholes, slapped his hands with rulers if he hadn't done his homework. Here, nobody laughed at him for having holes in his shoes or because he didn't want to join in their stupid pranks or schoolyard games.

His main job was to fetch and carry water all day long. The men were always hot and thirsty; sweat constantly dripped off their faces and arms. They were kind to him and generally pleased to see him, calling him "the water boy." He would make the rounds with his bucket and metal cup. Eventually he constructed a small wooden cart with wheels and was able to carry four buckets at a time. "Just keep moving, boy," he was told by the men, "and keep clear of the fires. Keep your wits about you." So, young Jack kept his mouth shut and did what he was told. Ears and eyes open. Lips closed. He thought Mary would be proud. Dad and Mr. Finnegan, Johnny's dad, and some of the neighborhood men would just nod at him and thank him for the water. There was no chatting and telling stories here in the mill. Everyone had to pay close attention to his job, so as not to get burned, or worse.

Besides the heat and flames, the mill was a noisy place, with huge engines moving with thunderous pounding and railroad cars rumbling in the yards. If the whistle blew that meant quitting time. If the whistle blew longer than normal that meant there had been an accident. If a chain broke, causing a ladle to tip over, a man could be buried under a ton of slag or burned by the molten iron.

It was dangerous work, and accidents happened. Jack's senses were constantly assaulted by sights and sounds resulting in nightmares about things he witnessed. One day old Mr. O'Reilly, one of the skilled workers who had years of experience, suddenly grew dizzy and lost his footing on a wooden catwalk twenty feet above the floor. The poor man fell headfirst into a smoldering vat of iron. Later that day, on his way home from the mill, Jack heard Mrs. O'Reilly, now a widow, wailing and crying as he passed by their house.

The man's awful scream still echoed in Jack's dreams. He remembered how he had stood paralyzed after O'Reilly's accident, until one of the bosses had finally poked him in the back. "There's no cure for dying, boy," the boss had said sharply, "so just keep on moving."

Jack often thought about death. If he died, he could be with Mum. One night, he had a dream: he saw his mum standing next to his bed, smiling at him. "Be brave, Jackie," she softly told him. "I'll always be with you." He opened his eyes, and she was gone.

⁓⊶⊷⁓

Dad rarely spoke of her, but Jack's sisters prayed the Rosary every day for Mum's soul. Jack didn't say prayers anymore, since he was still angry at God. He suspected that Dad was probably angry at God too.

Sometimes he thought about his Uncle Mike, Mum's brother. Uncle Mike had lived in their small house with them, since he had never married. He worked in the mill with Dad. Jack liked it whenever Uncle Mike played ball in the street with him. He died five years ago: run over by a railroad car on the tracks at night. Jack remembered how Uncle Mike always handed out candy to the boys and girls in the neighborhood. Everyone was saddened by his death. One evening when the family had finished eating supper, Margaret mentioned Uncle Mike. Florence snapped, "Uncle Mike shouldn't have been so drunk that he fell asleep on the tracks."

Mary flushed with anger. She looked her sister in the eye, "Florence, don't be so cruel! You shouldn't speak ill of the dead, especially family! When he had his tragic accident, it was pitch-black out and he tripped and fell and hit his head right there on the tracks." Tears welled in Margaret's eyes. She started sobbing and said, "Uncle Mike was waiting in Heaven for Mum when she died. He probably was standing at the gates with Saint Peter. I think they are both angels now watching over us." The conversation ended with all three girls making the sign of the cross and pulling out the Rosary beads. They kept their beads in their apron pockets, always ready to pray.

Soon after he started working at the mill with Dad, Jack began to be bothered by a recurring dream that would wake him and leave him sweating and afraid. In the dream, he was engulfed in flames: orange hot fingers reaching for him, flaming tongues licking him. He told Mary about the dream; of course, she immediately informed Dad. Mary and Dad both agreed about how Jack should respond to the dream. Dad told him, "It is best to face your fears, Jack." Mary said, "It is part of growing up." Jack was confused and didn't want to ask unnecessary questions.

A few days later, after supper, Dad instructed him to sit down at the kitchen table. "Jack, you're doing a good job at the mill," he said, "but you have to learn how to stand up for yourself, if you want to someday be a man. I won't always be around to look out for you. Aye, for sure. You must learn to fistfight, how to be tough and never quit. You can't be afraid of anything, no matter if it's a dream about fire and flames in your head, or real-life fire right in front of your own two eyes. You need to lick the fear or be licked! You hear?" Wide-eyed, Jack nodded.

Dad continued: "Or if another man is pissed about something and trying to get you riled up. Someday you might need to know how to put a troublemaker in his place. There's a lot of eejits in the world. Aye, that's a fact. You're a Quinn, and you come from a long line of proud men."

Jack sat solemnly staring at his father. That was the most Dad had said about anything in a long time. He straightened up in his chair and paid close attention.

"Always remember that a man can get his nose busted because of his mouth. So, watch what you say…how you say it…and who you say it to. And know when to just keep your mouth shut—or that nose will be getting broke. Aye, for sure." Then Dad laid several long strips of cotton rags he had prepared earlier on the kitchen table. "Give me your right hand," he said. He wrapped each of Jack's fists with the pieces of cloth. "These will help protect your hands from bruises and swelling."

His sisters went to the front room next to the kitchen, to work on their knitting. Jack could hear them giggling. "Don't hurt him, Dad," called Mary, always the worrier. "See, Jack," said Dad, "living with three women is making you soft. This'll toughen you up a bit. Aye, it will." So, Dad taught Jack to box, or fistfight, right there in the kitchen. The Irish, Jack knew, had a long tradition of solving problems with bare-knuckle boxing. Some men even considered it a sport; they would place bets, picking the winners and losers. Most of the matches took place in bars and saloons; but young men had already endured years of training under the watchful eyes of fathers, brothers, uncles, and grandfathers. It was the Irish way. Sean Quinn knew what he had to teach his son. Jack had to learn the necessary skills…how to stand, how to hold his arms, how to move. When to jab, when to swing, and when to duck. How to size up the opponent and how to look him right in the eye. And, most of all, how to protect his face. "God gave you that good-looking face, Jack, so you best take care of it. Be quick and fight smart." That was the first of many lessons. Years later, Jack realized what an effective teacher his father had been. After they finished sparring and jabbing, Dad took his bottle of whiskey from the cabinet and said, "I'd say you've earned a reward. Aye, you have, for sure." He poured himself a shot and then poured a half shot for Jack. The whiskey burned going down his throat, but Jack had a wide grin on his sweaty face.

Damn right, I earned it, Jack thought to himself. He slept well that night and every night after.

CHAPTER 3

December 1895—Jack

By the time he was fourteen, Jack had grown as tall as most of the men in the mill. Mary studied him one day and declared, "Jackie, you're almost six feet tall, and already taller than Dad. And you have been blessed with Mum's dark blue eyes and dark hair. I think the girls will be chasing you soon enough." Jack's cheeks grew warm as he looked in the small mirror on the wall. The reflection revealed a serious young man with sad eyes encased in an angular face. Even his voice was lower now: deep, sounding like the men that he worked beside in the mill.

His sisters all had nut-brown hair and blue-gray eyes, like Dad. They were tall, sturdy women, but Jack could tell that Mary was the prettiest, and the smartest. When she wasn't doing housework or cooking, Mary was always reading a book or a newspaper.

Jack remembered the morning years ago when his Mum had declared, "The Quinn children are a handsome bunch. The cousins we left in Galway would have been jealous of my brood. Aye, I'm sure they would be drinking a few pints to toast our good looks and our smarts. No eejits and thick heads in this group!" Mum had spoken these words with pride, admiring her family when they were all washed up for church. She loved to sing their praises.

Nowadays, Mary just said, "The Quinn family cleans up nicely and has good manners. Our wit has been tempered by the veil of sadness that surrounds our gloomy, bruised hearts. At least we are not drowning our sorrows in a pint or a bottle, which seems to be the Irish way." Although Jack knew his father liked to knock back a few every day. But Dad was no drunk, like some of the ones who staggered out of O'Shea's bar.

~⦉❦⦊~

Jack was not only tall but also strong; he had started to develop muscles from laboring in the mill. He had a slender build, but muscles now shaped his arms and shoulders. Thank God for his sisters, who were all good cooks. Consequently, every night when he and Dad returned from the mill, a hearty supper awaited them: meat and potatoes, or stew and biscuits, which was his favorite. Sometimes there was even an apple pie. Mary liked to serve the dessert with a cup of milk, even though they usually drank tea. She said, "Mrs. Oliver always gave her children milk instead of tea or coffee. Milk is supposed to build strong bones and muscles. So, Jackie, remember to thank God for good food. You didn't get those muscles just from your hard work!" And she would give his shoulder an affectionate slap. Jack realized Mary did a good job of taking care of the family, and Dad remarked, "Mary will be a good wife to a lucky man someday." He never said that about Florence or Margaret. Those two girls each possessed a mean streak as wide as the day was long; they both were lacking in patience and humor. Even Jack realized that no man would want to come home to their sullen and cranky dispositions, no matter how good they could cook. Florence and Margaret seemed to get satisfaction from complaining and arguing. Jack tried to ignore them, figuring that those two would probably just keep squawking at each other until the day they died, like hens cackling in their pens. He laughed to himself, picturing them pecking at each other, walking in circles.

~ ✵ ~

Every day on their way home Dad would buy a newspaper from the boy on the corner outside the mill. Then Dad would hand the paper to Jack as he turned to step into O'Shea's bar with the other men. Jack would tuck the paper under his arm, sometimes lingering outside the door, reading notices pinned on the wall. He liked hearing the workers' laughter coming from inside O'Shea's, especially laughter from the men who never spoke a word inside the mill.

While his sisters prepared supper Jack would read the newspaper. Mary helped him with words he didn't understand. The paper was called the *Pittsburg Press*. Mary and Dad were still annoyed that the spelling of the city's name had changed a few years ago. Mary said, "Back in 1891 President Harrison persuaded many cities in the country to eliminate the final 'h' when spelling their names. Pittsburg, which had first been named by the Scottish settlers one hundred years earlier, *always* had the 'h' at the end. Now, apparently, because of all the Germans who have settled in America, the city's name suddenly ends with the letter 'g.' So confusing!"

"It all seems foolish to me," Dad commented. "There's more important things for the politicians to worry about. They should be paying more attention to fixing the ruts in our bumpy streets, so the wagons aren't always getting broken wheels." Margaret, who was forever cleaning rugs, pots and pans, even the curtains, said, "They need to just make all the streets brick or cobblestone so that we aren't sloshing through mud every time it rains." Dad said, "I suppose all the German folks over in Allegheny are happy," steering the conversation back to the subject of the spelling of *Pittsburgh*. "It doesn't make much difference to us." Florence added, "Mrs. Oliver is always complaining about it. All the people up on the hill want the letter 'h' back. She says her husband is going to keep after his friends in Washington, D.C. about it. And she says that Mr. Oliver never gives up. He's a force to be reckoned with." "Yes, the cake eaters always want their own way," Dad said. He winked at Jack as he stirred a spoonful of sugar in his tea. Jack just nodded and smiled, enjoying the banter of his sisters, the cackling hens.

One warm Sunday afternoon in September, Jack and Johnny Finnegan were walking through town, relishing their day off from work. Johnny was now also working at the mill, since he was also fourteen and there weren't many fourteen-year-olds who stayed in school. The furnaces needed all the laborers they could find, including big strong young boys who wore long pants instead of knickers.

"Johnny," Jack chuckled, "what do politicians and old spinster ladies have in common? You don't know? Well, picture them both walking in circles, flapping their wings, feathers ruffled, squawking and pecking at each other!" Jack strutted into the middle of Second Avenue, knees high, flailing his arms, clucking, scratching the ground with his foot. Johnny laughed loudly. He had to sit down on the sidewalk, hands on his stomach, snorting so hard he couldn't breathe, as Jack widened his eyes, cocked his head and stared at him, bent arms frozen at his sides like wings. "Watch it, mister," Jack warned, "I can peck, too. I'll peck your eyes right out of your thick head!" Finally, Jack was unable to keep a straight face. He erupted with cackling laughter as he collapsed on the sidewalk next to Johnny. After that incident, Johnny would call Jack either Mister Pecker or Pecker Head; both names made them snicker and chuckle. It was their private joke they didn't share with anyone.

Jack enjoyed finally having his best friend work in the mill. There was a camaraderie among all the young men who labored together, and Jack was a bit of a leader since he had already been working there for four years: he knew every corner of the place and could speak to the newcomers with the confidence he had gained from experience.

Jack had grown taller and stronger by then, and he had been trained to perform more physically demanding jobs. He had to shovel coal into wheelbarrows, and since he was so slender, he could climb and squeeze himself into small spaces in order to oil parts of the machinery that were difficult for some of the larger men to access. Jack had a better understanding, too, about how things worked and the concept of cause and effect. Open-hearth furnaces produced the hottest fires, and the waste gases of the molten iron generated the most heat. The heat eventually burned out the impurities in the iron, resulting in the silvery white steel. Before the furnace was tapped and the steel poured out, the skilled workers checked to see if there was any water in the molds. If water was present, it could result in an explosion: molten metal would fly across the work area, causing painful burns.

There was no escaping the danger, but Jack knew to stay alert and be aware, to keep his wits about him, as several of the older men had repeatedly warned him.

Jack had plans. He wanted to learn more skills, he wanted to pull the levers that controlled the gigantic ladles and the movement of the cranes. Better to be a skilled worker than unskilled. Since he had gained a favorable reputation for his good judgement and calm demeanor, the foremen were starting to trust him to make quick decisions and follow directions.

The younger men listened to Jack and respected his knowledge, and they knew that they could count on him for advice. He always warned them about the dangers posed by the fires and the machinery, but he also cautioned them about dealing with some of the workmen, saying: "Stay away from that asshole Joe Murphy and his pals, and if you have a question or need help from a foreman, go to Mr. Finnegan, Johnny's dad." Receiving a paycheck was the only advantage to working, and most of the young men had to hand over their pay to their parents. Everyone was in the same boat, so there was no sense in complaining. Jack and Johnny were both fortunate to be given some of their hard-earned dollars to spend as they pleased; they liked having money to buy all the candy they wanted. Jack's favorites were peppermint sticks and flavored sugar wafers. He would always buy extra candy to take home, which was especially useful if he had to bribe his sisters. Johnny was crazy about licorice and packs of chewing gum. Jack had noticed that Johnny always chewed gum in the mill. He said it helped him stay calm when his hands and arms got shaky. Since they were now young men, as tall as some of the men in the mill, their attire consisted of long pants with suspenders and long-sleeved shirts and vests. When the weather turned windy and colder, they wore wool jackets. They looked dapper with their brown caps pulled down on their foreheads. All their shirts and pants were either gray or brown cotton, in every shade from light to dark. Their leather shoes were replaced only when their feet outgrew them; the soles were patched whenever a hole appeared. Jack's sisters knitted socks for him, and a sweater every winter. Mum used to call sweaters "jumpers." But Mary said, "We have to talk like other Americans and use the word *sweater.*"

Jack and Johnny had been friends for so long they could sit in silence and just watch all the Sunday afternoon activity on Second Avenue. The boys would find a vacant bench outside of O'Shea's, which was closed on Sundays, and sit down, counting the remainder of their spending money. They were content as they sat together, starting to take notice, as young men do, of all the girls and young women passing in front of them. Some of the girls would stroll by arm in arm, laughing and giggling. Everyone seemed to enjoy staring into the shop windows, looking at hats, dresses, shoes, and boots. It didn't cost a cent to wish for things that you couldn't afford. Even years later, Jack would remember that day in September…the first time he laid eyes on her. She had long reddish-brown curls and a sprinkling of freckles across her nose and cheeks. Johnny had called out to the taller, brown-haired girl who was walking with her.

"Hello, Alice," Johnny said. "How's school?" He didn't give Alice a chance to answer. "This here is my friend, Jack Quinn."

"Hey, Johnny," Alice replied. "How are you?" She turned briefly to Jack. "Hello, Jack. Oh, and this is my sister, Clare." She glanced over at the shorter girl with the red hair and freckles. Jack didn't want to be ill-mannered, but he could hardly do anything but blink and sweat as he tried to swallow the lump in his throat. Clare gazed at Jack with green eyes that seemed to sparkle when she smiled. Jack felt paralyzed and unable to speak, but finally he managed a small smile. He reached out his hand with a roll of his sugar wafers in it. "Want some?" he said shyly. He was embarrassed by the cracking of his voice. He lowered his eyes as his cheeks flushed.

The Murphy family had moved to Hazelwood about a year earlier. Alice's father and older brother Joe had immediately gone to work in the mill. Alice was fifteen; Johnny had known her a while in school. She said her sister Clare was fourteen, the same age as Jack.

Jack froze when he heard the name Joe Murphy. He was acquainted with the infamous Joe Murphy, apparently the brother of these two lovely girls, and he knew to stay away from him as much as possible in the mill. Murphy had a hot temper and was always spitting out obscenities. Jack thought about how Joe Murphy called everyone a dickhead; he thought nothing of telling you to feck off or go hump yourself.

Dad had often remarked that when Joe Murphy got rotten drunk at O'Shea's bar, he picked fights with other patrons. More than once, Brian and Jimmy O'Shea had to throw him out into the street. He had a few friends who were easily intimidated by Joe's obnoxious behavior. They usually managed to take him home and dump his drunken body on his porch. Even Dad, who rarely spoke ill of anyone, declared, "Joe Murphy is an idiot, an eejit. Just beware of his shenanigans." Dad always said that men who talked like Joe Murphy were just plain stupid and couldn't think of anything intelligent to say. They simply thought they impressed others. "A fool should keep his mouth shut and keep people wondering," Dad said, "because when he opens his mouth everyone knows for sure that he's a fool." Mum never put up with cursing and cussing. One time when Jack was a lot younger, maybe seven or eight, he got so annoyed by Margaret complaining about everything that he punched her in the back. "God damn it, Margaret!" he screamed. "Shut the hell up and quit your bloody talking, you stupid shithead!" Well, Mum didn't tell Dad about the incident, because he would've gotten the stick; she always protected her son. But Jack remembered getting his mouth washed out with soap. Mum could be stern, but never mean. Then, stupid Margaret told Dad anyways, and Jack ended up getting a couple of good whacks with Dad's stick.

The next day he threw the damn stick in the river.

On the fine, memorable Sunday afternoon when Jack had first laid eyes on Clare Murphy, he and Johnny accompanied Alice and Clare on a walk up to the middle of Chatsworth Avenue, where there was a small park with some shrubs and benches. The boys usually liked to go down by the river to throw rocks, but Johnny knew that these girls wouldn't enjoy that. And besides, there were too many bad smells by the river: all the waste from the town and the mills flowed directly into it. The sisters, Clare and Alice, both looked fragile and pale. Later, Johnny told Jack, "If we had walked down by the river, and the wind had blown in their direction, the foul stink might have made the girls faint. Then what? They would go home and tell their parents and Joe, and you know what that idiot would do." Johnny and Jack both knew. The young men didn't want that misfortune to befall them. Jack could picture Joe Murphy beating the shit out of him and Johnny and then throwing them both in the river. Joe was four years older than Jack and much stronger. Jack agreed that it would be smart not to make Joe Murphy mad.

They spent the afternoon sitting in the park, talking about school, the mill, and their mutual neighborhood acquaintances. Jack didn't mind sharing his candy. Clare liked the chocolate and cinnamon sugar wafers, while Jack preferred the orange flavored candies. Jack and Johnny tried to impress the girls by describing the important jobs they performed in the mill: how they faced fiery demons and climbed up to staggering heights every day. Jack figured it was all right to embellish the roles they played in manufacturing the steel. It made their lives more interesting. The girls talked about school, which was a distant boring memory for Jack.

Every Sunday after their first meeting the four friends agreed to meet in the park. Jack and Clare shared candy, stories, and secrets. By December the snowflakes started to fall, but they didn't care. They still walked outside and wrote their names in the snow that never stayed white for very long, and they made snowballs even though the snow was as gray and sooty as the air. When the weather started to get too cold Jack would hold Clare's hand and then walk her to her doorstep.

Clare never invited him in, which was fine with him, since he didn't want to see her brother Joe. Stupid, shithead Joe Murphy. It was bad enough that he had to work in the same building with him.

Jack didn't think so much about dying and death anymore. He still had to attend Mass on Sundays, but he wasn't thinking about Heaven, Hell, or prayers. Rather, when he was sitting in the pews, trying to make himself comfortable, he looked discreetly for the Murphy family and his pretty little friend Clare. He thought about her day and night.

He was more concerned with learning how to live now and tending not just furnaces of the mill but the fires awakening in his heart.

CHAPTER 4

December 1898—Jack

Exhilarating, stimulating, perhaps intoxicating…that was how Jack felt about the times he spent with Clare Murphy, when they would sneak into the woods and gardens on the hills above town. He had introduced Clare to all his favorite flowers: irises, roses, hydrangeas, the fragrant lilac bushes. Even his private hiding places nestled behind the high foliage. Her wish was his command. He climbed apple trees to find her the most perfect, ripe, unblemished fruit. He helped her pick violets that grew in the woods—she made small bouquets for her mother, who, in turn, made tea from the petals and leaves. Clare would braid long grass stems to construct twine to hold the bouquets together. They collected hazelnuts and acorns from tall oaks as they watched the squirrels scamper about, preparing for the cold months ahead. Clare filled her basket with flowers, apples, and nuts, although their shared goal was never about the bounty. It was the collecting of memories, the laughter, the experiences. Nothing that they even put into words at the time.

Jack had shared his dream with her: someday he would own a grand brick house on a hill, somewhere away from the city. He described a house with a big front porch, and a back porch too. He planned to have gardens where he would grow vegetables and flowers and plant an apple tree, a pear tree, a cherry tree, and maybe even a grapevine. There would be a big green grassy yard and a hedge around the border of the property. And there would be no river and no steel mill. No smoke and grime. No soot and black snow. Clare would close her eyes and see it too. Jack's dream. She admired how he held onto that dream, even though it was sprinkled with too many words like *someday*, *some way*, *somehow*. Once she even remarked, "I guess it's nice that you have a dream, but I can only think about today, and sometimes that's difficult. We must decide what to eat, what to wear, what chores Mum needs help with. I just do what I'm told, or Dad will get all angry—and nobody wants that. And then we must deal with Joe. It's just all so exhausting."

The couple always gravitated to the large weeping willow tree located at the far end of one of the gardens next to the woods. It was their favorite place to just sit and dream. On warm days they would sit under the willow, lounging on the thick green grass in the shade. When there was a breeze the long soft willow branches would dance across their faces. Jack would study her freckles, finding them captivating, and Clare would comment that her mother always said, "A face without freckles is like a sky with no stars." Jack thought to himself that was a strange thing to say. He considered her bright eyes to be more like stars, not her freckles.

During the past several years, Jack had spoken several times to Clare's mother and dad. They seemed quiet, not very friendly, and they always glared at him suspiciously. Johnny Finnegan said they looked at him the same way whenever he visited Alice. Jack figured parents of daughters have to be protective of them…Dad was like that with any men who were friendly with Jack's sisters. As they sat next to each other under the willow tree, Jack often watched the sunshine reflect off Clare's auburn hair and then off the shimmering leaves of the tree. In the autumn, it was the prettiest sight he had ever seen, the reds, oranges, and yellows of the leaves swirling around her, and her green eyes sparkling. Her eyes always twinkled when she looked at him…he wanted to know the secrets behind them.

Their willow tree was so majestic it seemed almost magical, sun rays streaming through its long sweeping branches. Jack was mesmerized, captivated by all of it. Especially by Clare. His pretty, gentle Clare. They usually sat under that willow tree and held hands, lost in their own private world. He caressed her fingers and arms, astonished at how soft her skin was, almost like rose petals.

This is where Jack first kissed her. She smiled sweetly. Her eyes sparkled then closed as she leaned in and encouraged him. Her cheeks, usually so pale, grew warm and pink. Their lips came together as one, and tongues explored as minutes turned into hours. This quickly became Jack's favorite activity. He and Clare would talk a while, kiss…and then kiss some more. His hands also loved to explore, touching her neck, her back, her hips, and those soft legs under her skirts. His fingers crept up her thighs, slowly pushing her stockings down.

When it became too difficult to maintain their composure Clare would adjust her clothing, then stand and smooth her skirts. They had to take a few deep breaths as they both lowered their eyes and turned away from each other, suppressing their inner desires. Jack would sit for an extra moment. He had to relax and focus on other thoughts. He did not want to explain it to Clare, why he needed a minute before he could walk comfortably. She predictably suggested that they head back to the park, and then on to her doorstep. The emotions they both felt were confusing. Clare discussed with him the story in the Bible about Adam and Eve…how Eve had succumbed to the temptation of the serpent, who was the devil in disguise. She knew she should avoid temptations of the flesh; and they both had listened to Father Donnelly's sermons about sin and eternal damnation. She didn't want to go to Hell, to be banished there forever….

Jack didn't know what to say. And then they would just fall silent, lost in their thoughts.

One Sunday afternoon as they were kissing under their willow tree, Clare whispered, "Jack, the devil is tempting us to do more than we should." Jack agreed that their physical intimacies were like playing with fire—and he understood fire. It could be useful, he knew, but the flames could inflict great damage. His body wanted to engage in so much more with Clare; but Jack realized that there was a time and a place for everything. And a Sunday afternoon under the willow tree was not the time and not the place. He loved and respected Clare too much.

He was seventeen, and he was certain that he needed to get out of the mill. He hoped that he and Clare would always be together. He hoped they could live the dream that he shared with her. Time would tell. He had heard that expression many times; now he understood what it meant. He didn't want to end up like most of the men who had been working in the mill for years. Always dirty, tired, and unpleasant…except for Dad, who was content and satisfied with his life. Sean Quinn had seen and lived in worse conditions when he was growing up in Ireland, and he possessed a happiness that Jack didn't understand. He wondered why his father didn't want more, why he was content to have only the small things in life….

Dad had loved his wife and children, and he didn't complain about people and circumstances he had no control over. He just wanted to do an honest day's work, have a drink of whiskey, and come home to his family. He always said: "A man only needs a good woman, a bottle of whiskey, and enough money to feed his family and keep a roof over his head. It's the Irish way. Aye, that's for sure." Then he would look Jack squarely in the eyes and say: "Do your best, Jackie, and the good Lord will take care of the rest."

Most of the men at the mill were only happy when they were having drinks in the bar. Then they would laugh and have another shot of whiskey. "Knock back another one!" they'd cry. And then: "Another one for the road!" Occasionally a fight would erupt. If the brawl spilled out into the street, Jack would watch it carefully; he could always predict who would win just by tracking the fighters' moves. Dad had taught him well, and Jack was confident that if he ever had to fight, his fists would be victorious. Sometimes he dreamed about punching Joe Murphy square in the mouth. Joe Murphy was the most obnoxious human being that he ever met. He couldn't figure out how Clare and Alice could possibly be related to him. He would love to just pummel his face until that asshole dropped to the ground, down in the dirt where he belonged.

"If you're quick and smart, you win," Dad always reminded him when they practiced boxing in the kitchen. "Slow, sloppy, and stupid…you lose. And if you're too drunk, you'll lose for certain." Jack had seen it happen over and over. Dad always said, "Keep your wits about you. Walk away from trouble. But if you're caught up in it, stand your ground and fight like a man."

Jack knew there was a hierarchy in the mill. Many of the older Scots and Irish had moved up to better jobs. There was an order to the way things were run—as there should be, he figured. However, it wasn't always *what* you knew but *who* you knew; he was a witness to the fact. He saw how things were not always fair, and that the best workers did not always get the best jobs. Dad was one of the more reliable and responsible workers, but he didn't buy drinks for bosses and foremen. He often said, "I'm not kissing anyone's arse. A man has got to have some dignity." Johnny Finnegan's dad was a foreman, and a fair one; not all foremen were as just. Jack knew that Johnny would probably end up as a foreman too. So of course, Johnny would stay in the mill forever, chewing his gum and dreaming small dreams. But Hazelwood and the mill did not fit into Jack's plans. His dream was to escape the town—but of course he had to figure out how. He needed a plan. Pittsburgh was a thriving industrial town with lots of industry, providing great opportunities for intelligent hard-working young men. He knew he had to meet new people and latch on to a wagon or train headed out of Hazelwood. ….

He could ride a railroad car to Connellsville and dig coal; but the coal mines were not an option. Hell no. Leave that to the Slovaks and Polish, the newcomers. He had heard that the coal companies were recruiting entire villages of young men from Czechoslovakia and Poland, spinning tales about the money and riches they could have in America. Then, once here, they would find out that the company owns them. The poor bastards coming to work the mines couldn't speak English and couldn't leave, clinging desperately to their fellow immigrants, their families, their religion....

More and more Italians and Poles were coming to Hazelwood—*and* they were working in the South Side furnaces across the river. Dad said, "Our wages will never get better with so many men needing jobs!" In the newspapers, Jack read about the steel company owners: Jones, Laughlin, Carnegie, and Frick. These men were incredibly wealthy but tried to pay as little as possible to their employees, enriching themselves, not caring about the welfare of their workers.

Even Jack remembered what had happened across the river back in '92, when workers at the Homestead mill attempted to strike for better pay and improved working conditions. Carnegie was out of town and had left Frick in charge. But Henry Clay Frick was ruthless. The men in the bars called him Frick the Prick. He hired private guards to force the employees back to work. The guards were armed; they fired on the crowds of strikers. Many died or were wounded...and that was the end of the strike. The lesson that day stuck in Jack's mind: it was hard to be rebellious if a loaded rifle was aimed at you.

The older men liked to talk about unions, higher wages, and better working conditions. Those conversations happened only in bars and taverns, or sometimes in backroom meetings. The men were fearful of retribution... The fear of being laid off or having their hours cut was like a cloud that always hung over them. They all understood that their families depended on their meager paychecks.

"Don't make waves," Dad often said. Like most of the other immigrants, Dad had seen worse situations back in Ireland. He had been bold when he was young, escaping injustice and poverty in the old country. Now, he was content to have a steady paycheck and a family.

One cold afternoon in December, Jack was walking home on Second Avenue after work. His thoughts were revolving around Clare, snow, and Christmas, when he saw a sign posted on the wall outside of O'Shea's bar.

APPRENTICE PLUMBERS NEEDED

Must be 18 and able to read and write. See PAT MCGEE inside.

Jack would soon be turning eighteen. He realized that this was the opportunity he'd been waiting for. Right in front of his nose, in black and white.

He ripped down the paper and walked into O'Shea's, looking for one Mr. Pat McGee.

CHAPTER 5

July 1899—Emma

"I like this house so much better than our old home," mused fifteen-year-old Emma Moreau to herself, as she touched the lace curtains that she and Mama had just finished hanging in the parlor and the dining room. The curtains filtered the sunshine and still allowed her to see the view of the yard and trees.

The three-story house had wood clapboard siding painted white and a huge wraparound porch. A back porch sprawled off the large kitchen, and the dining room was highlighted by a fireplace. The parlor had a fireplace as well, and two stained-glass windows comprised of beautifully colored pieces of glass arranged in a geometric pattern. Emma ran her hand over the damask wallpaper, feeling the texture and admiring the floral designs.

The parlor was large enough for a sofa, two upholstered chairs, a rocking chair, and bookshelves, as well as the upright piano that Mama loved. She had taught both Emma and her sister Estelle how to play, insisting that they practice for a half hour every day. Mama made sure that the girls were very careful with her treasured sheet music. On the opposite side of the room, by the windows, was their treadle sewing machine. Papa had purchased a new model shortly after they had moved. Mama wanted a Singer machine; she claimed it was the best on the market. It was housed in a beautiful oak cabinet that had six drawers to store supplies. There was a matching chair with a padded seat. Emma and Estelle had both learned to sew with a needle and thread when they were eight years old. When they each turned twelve years of age then Mama taught them on the sewing machine.

Using a soft cloth, Emma polished the oak handrail that led to the three bedrooms upstairs. The third floor provided a large storage and play area for the children. Best of all, there was a bathroom with a porcelain sink, a clawfoot bathtub, and a toilet set on a ceramic tile floor.

After finishing with the handrail Emma went downstairs by way of the back staircase that led to the kitchen—which, of course, also had a sink with running water, a myriad of cupboards, and a walk-in pantry. The Moreau family had moved only three blocks, but this was one of the nicer homes in Elliott, a mostly residential neighborhood with a small business section along Lorenz Avenue. The neighborhood was located half a mile uphill from the West End, an industrial area that sat next to the Ohio River, a mile west of downtown Pittsburgh. Emma's entire family was delighted to finally live in a better section of Elliott, where the streets were paved with bricks, just like the boulevards of the city. Some of the main roads had steel rails being laid for the trolley cars, or "streetcars" as Papa called them.

Emma Louise Moreau was fifteen, the oldest daughter of Margaret and Henry Moreau. She had finished eighth grade at St. Martin School, where two nuns taught all the local Catholic children. The school sat next to the church, about a quarter of a mile from Emma's house. Emma had always excelled academically; she had even helped the nuns teach the younger children to read and write. Sister Mary Dolores claimed that Emma had immense patience and a gift for teaching the little ones: she loved to read books, and she could write an article about almost any topic. Several of her short stories had been printed in the *Pittsburg Press*, in the Young Writers section. The school year had finished, and Emma knew she wouldn't be able to attend the public high school with her brother Albert: Mama needed her at home to help with her younger brothers and sisters. She felt fortunate she had been able to attend school for as long as she did. Most of her friends had gone only until they were thirteen. The Moreau family consisted of seven children. Emma was the second child; her brother Albert, the oldest, was seventeen. Her sister Estelle was thirteen. Fred, the next boy, was ten, followed by eight-year-old Edmund. The youngest girl, Margaret, who was nicknamed Monnie, was four. The most recent addition, the baby of the family, was named Harry. Emma's parents had worked hard to make a good life for themselves. They were both children of immigrants from Alsace-Lorraine, an area along part of the border between Germany and France. All her grandparents had come to America in the 1850s and settled in the Elliott neighborhood of Pittsburgh in western Pennsylvania.

Mama's family had been from the section of Alsace-Lorraine that was closest to Germany, and Papa's people were more French, culturally speaking. Papa had told Emma about the Franco-Prussian War of 1871, which occurred years before she was born. His parents and Mama's parents had lost contact with the remaining cousins during this time. Papa had remembered reading about that war in the newspaper when he was young, although the reporting had been sporadic at best. Germany had been victorious over France; their so-called "prize" was the area of Alsace-Lorraine. The region had a nice blend of French and German culture. Papa declared: "The best thing that came from Germany was beer and sauerkraut." He loved Mama's sauerkraut, which she served with ham or pork chops. Mama's parents, Emma's grandparents, had opened a small bakery shop in Elliott in the 1850s. Margaret Becker, Emma's mother, was born in 1860. She grew up working in the bakery with her sisters Sophia and Louisa, making strudel, bread, and pies. Papa always said he fell in love with Mama—*and* Mama's pies and cookies. They were married in St. Martin's Catholic Church in 1880 when Mama turned twenty years old.

From the stories Emma had heard from Aunt Louisa, her talkative aunt, the wedding celebration of young Margaret Becker and Henry Moreau was the talk of Elliott in 1880. Mama's parents had known the Moreau family since they had all first settled in Elliott. Emma's grandfather Moreau owned a tavern on Lorenz Avenue. So of course, Emma's father Henry grew up sweeping the floors and socializing with the patrons. When Henry's father became ill, Henry took over, managing the business at the age of twenty-five. Henry Moreau and Margaret Becker were married shortly afterward. Aunt Louisa, plump and good-natured, said, "All the loyal customers of the Becker's bakery and Moreau's tavern were invited to the wedding celebration, which was held at the tavern. We spent *weeks* making cookies. And from all reports, an unprecedented amount of beer, wine, and whiskey was served to the guests that day. The bride and groom and *everyone* at the party had a grand old time, drinking and dancing until midnight." Aunt Louisa always giggled, her face turning red, when she got to the end of the story: "Emma, your brother Albert was born exactly nine months later!"

Henry had eventually convinced his father to change the name of the tavern from Moreau's Tavern to Moore's Tavern. It sounded more American, and Henry reasoned that it would appeal to more people. With all the immigrants moving to the Pittsburgh area, Henry thought it was a good business practice to appear welcoming to everyone.

Emma agreed with her father. She had heard somebody say that America was one big melting pot of people who came from many foreign countries. She liked to think she possessed a nice mixture of French and German tastes and traditions, and she strived to be tolerant and kind to everyone. "After all, we are all Americans," she claimed.

Papa replied, "That is why I serve different kinds of beer, wine, and hard liquor—like whiskey and brandy. Something for everyone! Not all my customers have the same tastes, so it's best to offer a bit of variety." It made perfect sense. Emma admired her father for so many reasons, one of which was his business expertise. More recently, however, in the newspapers, she had read about the temperance movement. It seemed to be gaining support across the nation as a result of the surprising amount of alcohol consumed by Americans and the resulting ill effects, like violence and illness. Although Emma worried about the growing movement to curb alcohol consumption, Papa said it wasn't affecting his business. Down the hill, in the West End, which some people called Temperanceville, no bars or taverns were permitted. Papa told Emma that the landowner who held the original title to all the land that made up the West End wouldn't sell property to any man who drank alcohol. That was where the name Temperanceville had come from. "That's fine with me," Papa told Emma, "because the men who work down there can just walk up the hill to my business. Better yet, now that the streetcar tracks are being laid, they can ride to the tavern."

Papa particularly enjoyed serving the Irish customers who came into Moore's Tavern. They consumed large quantities of whiskey; some had a gift of gab and told entertaining stories. As a result, Papa had shared with his children the tales of leprechauns and the pot of gold, much to their delight. Mama, always practical, said, "It sounds like a lot of nonsense to me, and quite convenient for a young troublemaker to blame his misdeeds on some storybook character. Shenanigans by little elves…nonsense!"

Grandfather Moreau and Papa had both been friends with an Irishman named Mr. O'Leary, who had died about ten years before the Moreau's moved into their newest home. He came to America in the 1840s without a penny to his name. He had worked hard as a laborer, saving his money. After the Civil War he started a company with a neighbor selling lumber and coal on Main Street down in Temperanceville. The two men secured contracts for all manner of construction projects. Papa said some of those contracts had been signed right in the tavern.

In the 1870s, before Emma's parents were married, Mr. O'Leary built a fine home on Steubenville Turnpike, which bordered Elliott. Most people called that road Steuben Street. It ran from the river in the West End all the way west to Steubenville, Ohio. Emma walked that road for a quarter of a mile to get to school. On Sundays the family rode in their horse-drawn wagon up

Steuben Street to the church. They also had a carriage with a roof and doors that they used when it was rainy or snowy.

Mr. O'Leary had brought many Irish friends into the tavern. When the Irish had started pouring into Pittsburgh in the 1860s and 1870s, people had not readily accepted them, saying, "They are not like us." But Grandfather and Papa enjoyed their wit and humor and the stories they told. "Any friend of Mr. O'Leary is a friend of ours," they often said. The Irish of Emma's day were generally accepted; they blended well with the French, Germans, and English.

Since taverns and bars sold alcohol, they were closed on Sundays, as the city government had pushed for Sunday closings after realizing that Sunday was the only day the immigrants did not work. The mill owners and the politicians wanted to stifle discussion about politics, wages, or working conditions. Grievances, fueled by alcohol, were generally aired in the taverns and bars, so the men with power agreed it was best to force workers to stay home on Sundays.

So, every Sunday, the Moreau family ate a grand dinner early in the afternoon, and Papa told entertaining stories that he had heard in the tavern earlier during the week. This was much to the delight of Emma and her siblings, especially when Papa added a few salty details. Papa's favorite tales, which he heard from his Irish patrons, were about Irish boxers. Apparently Irish boxing was "bare-fisted" or "bare- knuckles" fighting, without many rules. He read stories in the newspaper about a man by the name of John L. Sullivan from Boston. Sullivan had been considered the best fighter, until he was finally beaten. Sullivan had a terrible temper and could break an opponent's jaw with one punch. It sounded awfully brutal to Emma. Mama just rolled her eyes and grumbled when Papa talked about boxing and leprechauns.

Emma wasn't inclined to read the sports pages; she preferred the newspaper articles about the library that was going to open nearby, in the West End. Mr. Andrew Carnegie, who was a wealthy Pittsburgh industrialist and philanthropist, had given the city money as a charter fund to construct several new libraries. Emma wouldn't mind not going to school if she could get books from the new library.

Another exciting newspaper story provided welcome details about all the trolleys, or "streetcars," that were currently operating in the city. Streetcars had run for years from downtown Pittsburgh across a bridge to Allegheny, and from downtown to Oakland. Now there would be streetcars traveling across a new bridge, from downtown to the South Side, West End, and Elliott.

Emma was eager to read aloud a description of the grand Museum of Natural History in Oakland. Andrew Carnegie had also paid for it to be built, along with a beautiful music hall next to the museum. Her siblings, especially her brothers, clamored to hear more about the trolleys.

The trolley tracks were being laid on Steuben Street, which was where Lorenz Avenue started in Elliott. The Moreau family now lived a block down the hill from there, and over one block, on Greenside Avenue. The tavern was a stone's throw from the bakery in the middle section of Lorenz, where the ground was flat. Then Lorenz ran up the hill for three or four blocks.

All the way at the end of Lorenz Avenue, on the left side, a street went up to St. Martin's Cemetery. Emma always thought that was a strange location, since the church and school were off Steuben Street. Opposite the cemetery, on the right side of Lorenz and at the top of the hill, was Emma's favorite spot: a long grassy stretch on top of a cliff that dropped straight down to a road along the river. She guessed the cliff was a good seventy feet from top to bottom. Luckily the city had constructed a wooden rail fence to keep careless people from falling over the hillside. The area was called the Overlook. Emma knew some fellows from the neighborhood who liked to show how brave they were by climbing up and down the cliff. She was always warning her younger brother, Fred, "Do *not* try to keep up with those older boys. All it would take is one slip of the foot for a catastrophe to strike."

Sometimes she wondered how boys could be so stupid, with so little common sense. Even the nuns at school complained. "Boys need to show more caution, or their tomfoolery will be the death of them!" they warned. Emma was glad her older brother Albert was studious and quiet, not inclined to be an adventurer. Emma worried more about Fred, who was daring and not afraid of physical challenges and horseplay with his pals.

Standing at the Overlook, Emma loved the spectacular view of the city of Pittsburgh and the Point, the spot where the Allegheny and Monongahela Rivers met to form the Ohio River. Unfortunately, most of the time smoke clouded the scenery. The black smoke was constantly billowing from the smokestacks that towered above the mills along the rivers. Emma was glad she didn't live in any of those dirty mill towns. Emma and her sister Estelle often walked up to the Overlook in the summer when the weather wasn't too hot. They especially liked the view in the autumn, when the leaves on the maple and oak trees were turning shades of orange, red, and yellow. Estelle loved to collect different types of leaves so she could draw them in her sketchbook.

Although Estelle was two years younger than Emma, they were both tall with dark brown hair and grayish-blue eyes. The girls had similar interests and were best friends. They were excited about the library, and Papa had promised to take them to Oakland in the summer to visit the museum. He also said they would have a picnic soon at Kenny's Grove along the Monongahela, on up past the South Side. Emma had read an article in the paper about the Monongahela Street Railway Company; the company had leased Kenny's Grove from the Kenny family. It had been a popular picnic area for years. At least once or twice every summer, Emma and her entire family, along with many of their neighbors, ventured out to Kenny's Grove for a Sunday picnic. They would load up several horse-drawn wagons with people and baskets of food: fried chicken, fresh berries, bread, and pies. The outing was always a merry time. The children played on the swings that hung from tree branches, the older boys played ball or tried to fly kites on the grassy field, and the young adults strolled about the tranquil grounds.

Emma found the article and informed her sister that the railway company planned on opening a "trolley park" to encourage people to use the trolley cars. The railway's biggest shareholder, Andrew Mellon, wants to name the park "Kennywood" in honor of the Kenny family and their picnic area. Emma was hardly able to contain her excitement. She continued reading the article to herself even as she related its details to her sister. "And listen to this, Estelle. They're making a small lake where you can go for a boat ride, and there will be a merry-go-round…also called a carousel. And best of all, they're constructing a dance pavilion, where music will be played by bands or small orchestras! I'll be able to write stories about all of these places and send them to the Young Writer's section of the newspaper." Emma loved both reading and writing stories; she couldn't decide which was her favorite. "We can both draw some pictures to send in too," Estelle chimed in. She had a good eye for drawing; it was her favorite pastime.

Mama saw to it that there was little idle time for her children, assigning chores around the house, making sure that both girls practiced playing the piano in the parlor. Simple sewing projects also kept them busy. Estelle was more efficient with the sewing machine than her older sister, but Emma was never jealous, and realized that not everyone possessed the same talents.

"That reminds me," said Emma. "We need to ask Mama for more paper and pencils. Next time we walk to the Overlook we have to draw the city buildings, with the rivers on each side. Or maybe just some trees and birds if it's too cloudy and smoky to see the buildings."

CHAPTER 6

August 1899—Jack

Working as an apprentice plumber in the summer of 1899, eighteen-year old Jack Quinn had already been employed by Mr. Pat McGee, who owned a union plumbing company, for several months. Mr. McGee and his crew had a big job installing the indoor pipes for water and drainage in one of the buildings under construction at the University of Pittsburgh in Oakland, within walking distance of downtown Pittsburgh.

There was much to learn. Different kinds of pipes, valves, fittings. But Jack was good with his hands and paid attention to instructions. He was happy to have escaped the mill, with its poor working conditions and tedious jobs. He was determined to never return to the blazing furnaces.

As a semi-skilled worker in the mill, Jack had been earning twenty cents an hour and putting in twelve-hour shifts. Dad was considered a skilled worker, making thirty cents an hour; he had been there for almost thirty years. As a plumber apprentice and then a journeyman, Jack would be making more than he had in the mill. He had heard that older, experienced plumbers were earning forty cents, even fifty cents an hour in some cases.

The plumbers in major cities, including Pittsburgh, were being organized into a national union called the United Association of Plumbers, Gas Fitters, and Steam Fitters. Jack learned that the union would enable workers to travel to other localities for work rather than being confined to one town or city. Wages would be consistent, as would the number of hours per day. Currently, McGee's employees were working ten-hour days, six days per week.

One morning when he was in the middle of fitting two pipes together, Jack felt someone standing behind him. He kept his eyes on the pipes, however, using his wrench to get them fitted properly. Then he turned around to find Mr. McGee watching him. "Jack," Mr. McGee said, "you're a hard worker and a fast learner. But it will still take you several years to be a full-fledged card-carrying union plumber." That was fine by Jack. He was satisfied to be out of the damn mill.

To get to the job at the college, Jack rode the streetcar that ran from Hazelwood to Oakland. His sisters were always excited when he brought home a newspaper, usually the *Pittsburg Telegraph* but occasionally the *Pittsburg Press*. One day he saw an advertisement in the newspaper for the new Kennywood Park across the river from Hazelwood. He had been to Kenny's Grove picnic area several times with his sisters, and with Clare, Johnny, and Alice. The walk across the bridge had been tiring, then they had followed the road that paralleled the river.

Apparently, according to the advertisement, the railway company had built a trolley park to encourage people to ride the trolleys. The name for the park, Kennywood, was in honor of the Kenny family, who owned the land. Now a streetcar ran across the bridge from Hazelwood and carried passengers directly to the new Kennywood Park. Jack thought about Clare and the two of them riding the streetcar together. "Clare really needs to see more than just Hazelwood," Jack had remarked to his sister Margaret. "She won't even walk up by the gardens unless I'm with her." He quietly reflected how Clare had no sense of adventure, and how his sisters were the same way.

The following Sunday, dressed in their cleanest clothes, the whole group from Hazelwood set off on the streetcar to Kennywood Park. Jack, his sisters, Clare, Johnny, and Alice. Jack always loved how the streetcars swayed and clanged. The rhythm of the rocking trolley was calming and soothing, while the noises kept him alert. Unfortunately, once they arrived at Kennywood Park, the skies darkened, even more than usual, and then rain pelted the side of the streetcars. After waiting for an hour in one of the Park shelters and realizing that the rain was not going to let up, they decided to head back home, disappointed. But just the streetcar ride was an enjoyable outing for the group, gazing out the windows. This was especially true for Clare and Alice. Even Florence and Margaret seemed to appreciate the experience. Looking out at the city as they sat side by side on the smooth bench of the rumbling car, the girls chattered about their sewing projects and church activities. Jack was bored with the conversation and started thinking about Mum and Dad....

He had labored in the mill at the insistence of his father, but now he was working with Mr. McGee's plumbing crew and would soon be able to leave the smokestacks of Hazelwood for good. The only way Mum could leave the smoke and grime was to die. Jack had always felt she was watching out for him, just like the guardian angels. He bitterly thought about all those prayers he had prayed, and how they didn't keep her here, alive on Earth, in Hazelwood. He had concluded that prayers were useless. He didn't pray anymore. He had given up on prayer years ago, after Mum died.

Jack would stop going to church on Sundays altogether if he could. But he would never hear the end of it from Mary and Dad. He had to admit that he cared about their opinions on most matters. However, he never paid any mind to much of what Florence and Margaret said; in fact, he ignored them as much as possible. One of Dad's rules stated: *If you live in my house, you do as I say—and that means you go to Mass on Sunday.* Jack knew there was no point in arguing.

As the streetcar rumbled along, Clare looked at Jack and squeezed his hand. "A penny for your thoughts." He leaned over and kissed her cheek then replied, "Oh, I'm just listening to the conversation." Clare and his sisters had been talking on and on about the new church being built. "The new St. Stephen's is going to be grand," Clare said. "Stone walls, stained glass windows—and a steeple with a cross at the very top. Even the Presbyterians will be green with envy. Father Donnelly says it should be finished in two years. How exciting!" Many of the mill workers and railroad workers helped with the church construction when they could spare a few hours. They contributed their sweat, muscle, and time, since they didn't have much money to donate to the cause. Usually, on any given Sunday, the men were toiling and sweating for the church. Sunday was supposedly the day of rest. *Not me,* thought Jack. *Even the church tries to take every damn penny and every ounce of strength that the workers have. Is there fairness and justice anywhere in the world?*

The priests seemed to hold the faithful hostage with their sermons about sin and eternal damnation. Even girls like Clare, Alice, Florence, and Margaret felt guilt. Guilt for what? They were obliged to polish the benches and clean the corners of the church…to wash and iron the altar cloths and even Father's robes and vestments. Why? So, they can go to Heaven? Or because a priest made them feel guilty for having sin on their souls? Maybe the girls needed to realize they could think for themselves and not be led like sheep.

Jack had debated the topic with his coworkers. "No," he had argued, "don't anyone, not even a priest, tell me I'm going to burn in Hell for speaking my mind. I don't care if they say that I'm being sacrilegious. How can it be a sin to say what I think?" Nobody could argue that point.

He knew that Clare, Alice, and his sisters would be shocked if he voiced these opinions to them. So, for now he kept his irreverent thoughts to himself, even though they were sprouting like weeds within him. Let Father Donnelly shine his own damn shoes. Or hire a housekeeper and pay her a wage. How much of St. Stephen's collection basket money was sent to the bishop in Pittsburgh? The bishop probably changed his clothes three times a day, so he didn't look dirty from all the soot in the air. He, no doubt, sat at a mahogany dining table covered with imported linens and ate fine meals served to him by faithful followers. Then he drank wine or brandy with his dessert. The bishop was no better than the greedy mill and railroad owners. Cake eaters! All of them thinking they were better than everyone else... intimidating all the poor folks.

Jack often said, "If I ever work in any of the 'big houses' I'll bet a day's wages that those people have shit just as brown as mine!" That statement always brought a laugh from his buddies at work. Even Dad and Johnny Finnegan chuckled at his sense of humor.

CHAPTER 7

May 1904—Jack

From the time Jack was twenty-one he developed a taste for whiskey. The seed had been planted years earlier, when Dad would reward him with a shot from his bottle in the kitchen. He figured he was like Dad and Uncle Mike: the whiskey helped him relax and let his mind wander and dream about what he wanted from life. He began keeping a small metal flask inside his coat pocket. Even on Sundays he would sneak an occasional swig.

Jack was now twenty-three and had been with Mr. McGee's crew for five years. He was an experienced plumber who McGee trusted enough to leave in charge on certain jobs. Jack was a perfectionist and always made the effort to do his best. He never attempted to cut corners by not following proper procedures. McGee had warned him and the others. "Do things the right way, or down the line it will come back to bite you in the ass!" He crowed loudly, "One time a young fellow didn't hook up a toilet properly, taking a few shortcuts. Then he sat down to take a shit and when he flushed, all the water shot back over his back and his ass, soaking his shirt with brown shit water. That guy smelled the rest of the day and was the butt of our jokes forever! His mistakes actually did bite him in the ass!" McGee had walked away laughing, patting his large belly, quite pleased with himself and his witty anecdote.

Jack got along well with the other men and always showed respect to the older employees. He tried to learn the tricks of the trade from those who had more experience than he did; in turn the gray-haired coworkers made an effort to be patient and were willing to teach him, training him in the best methods and the tried-and-true procedures. As he had learned years ago from Dad and his sister Mary, *Listen and learn, and keep your mouth shut.* That's how he survived the mill. Dad had reminded him often, "And know who to stay away from. Especially men who are troublemakers and eejits, like Joe Murphy, Clare's no-good brother."

Mary always said, "You're judged by the company you keep." Jack could never understand how Clare and Alice could be sisters to that low-life drunk. At least Joe Murphy was never drunk while he was working in the mill. He'd probably be dead if he had ever gone to work intoxicated. The mill was a dangerous place; accidents happened fast by the flames of the furnaces and the molten iron. Especially if you weren't paying attention.

In the bars and taverns, Jack knew to never sit by Joe Murphy or even have a conversation with him. Joe was missing a few teeth and had his nose broken at least once or twice as a result of his so-called "conversations" and erratic behavior.

Clare stated many times: "Joe will never get married, since no woman in her right mind would want him. I don't think he would be a kind husband or father."

Jack wondered what had happened to Joe to make him so mean and miserable. One day Clare finally explained it. "Well, when Joe was a young boy and Alice and I were babies," Clare began, "we lived with my grandparents in Johnstown. My grandfather was a nasty old tyrant who got drunk every day. My mum said that the old man had no patience and was always yelling at Joe and used to hit him with a stick when my dad was at work. This went on for years."

She continued: "One time, Joe spilled a bowl of hot soup on a kitchen chair, and my grandfather sat on it. His trousers were soaked. He got so mad at Joe that he beat him until Joe was bleeding. When Dad came home and heard what happened, he warned the old man that we would move out. We ended up moving down the street, which wasn't far enough. A few years later, when Joe was about sixteen, the old man came looking for Joe one night when he was drunk and wanted to fight him. You know, bare-fisted fighting. Well, Joe hated him and didn't care that he was his grandfather, so they started hitting each other. Joe pushed him and the old man fell and hit his head. He died two days later."

"After that, my mum and dad packed up the family, and that's when we moved to Hazelwood. My parents felt guilty about what happened to Joe, but I think there was damage that must've stayed with Joe and ended up making him act just like my grandfather."

Jack asked her if Joe ever bothered her or Alice when he came home drunk and mean. "No," she replied, "he knows not to bite the hands that feed him. And besides," she added, "he won't say much around Mother and Dad. They would knock him out the door—and then they both would drag him by his ears straight to Father Donnelly. Joe would never raise a hand to them."

"One time he hollered at Alice," she acknowledged, "and dear sweet Alice, who never raises her voice to anyone, held the point of a sharp carving knife right to his chin. She told him she'd take that knife and cut his throat when he was asleep. Imagine that! And then she went right back to cutting up a chicken! Joe stood watching her slicing and dicing, wide-eyed and speechless!"

"Calm as could be, that Alice," continued Clare. "I was shaking in my boots and had to go and pray the rosary after seeing that. Joe never hollered at Alice again," she noted, shaking her head and grinning.

Jack had often heard some of the neighborhood men in Hazelwood shouting at their wives and children. The yelling and swearing would end with a few slaps…or worse. Then the crying. The next day, the bruises were visible to all.

He had felt grateful that Mum and Dad didn't argue when he was young, and that Dad was never mean to his family. Even if Dad had too much to drink, he was never a "mean drunk." Those were the worst. They said things and did things that couldn't be taken back. Words and deeds remembered forever. Scars left within the mind and heart, not just on the body. He had overheard Mum telling Dad, "Sean, I'm so thankful that you're not like my father. Things were so bad back home in Ireland when I was a lass, that dad used to hit Mum, and I knew enough to hide, or I would have been next. Then one day he just up and left the family. There was no money and little to eat after the potatoes went bad. He just disappeared." After Mum's mother died from hunger and a broken heart, Mum, her brother Uncle Mike, and Dad, who was their neighbor, all decided to come to America. Mum and Dad got married before they stepped onto the boat: the village priest wished them blessings and luck. She always said, "Annie and Sean Quinn came to America with no money, but they had each other. Aye, love in the heart is more important than all the gold in the land."

Now, years later, Jack tried to remember her stories. Eventually it made him smile to reminisce. He hoped that she was watching him, his sisters, and Dad.

～·ecXo·～

For the last few years Jack had been working with Mr. McGee's plumbing crew in Allegheny over on the North Side of Pittsburgh. He rode the streetcar there and back every day except Sundays.

Allegheny had a population that numbered well over a hundred thousand people; it was almost a city unto itself, a crowded market town with factories and industry along the Allegheny and Ohio Rivers. Most of the population seemed to be German and Irish immigrants, or Germans who had been in residence for several generations.

Jack had heard that the best factory to work in was at the Heinz plant where the company bottled pickles, vinegar, and ketchup. The plant probably was one of the few places that valued cleanliness, providing showers and clean clothes for their workers. Many women were employed there, content even though they were paid lower wages than the male employees.

The worst factory jobs and the work in the slaughterhouses went to the newest immigrants. The streets were filled with shanties inhabited by the poorest of the poor…many Irish were included in this group. Some of these workers were recent immigrants from Ireland, willing to work in any of the factories that were hiring.

Jack had no desire to even walk down those miserable streets, they were full of mud and filthy people. Hazelwood was dirty and full of smoke, but Allegheny was worse.

McGee's crew had a job at the hospital that seemed to never end. Every addition added on to the already large hospital required more installations of pipes and toilets and sinks. The hospital was seven stories tall, with four hundred beds. Years ago, McGee had told them, the original building had only about fifty beds.

Not far from the hospital spread the huge town square that at one time had been grassy pastures and was now the town park. After leaving work, Jack sometimes walked along the sidewalks, which were bordered with flowers, and stared at the fountains. He thought he might have to bring Clare here some Sunday afternoon. Clare and Jack would occasionally take the street-car into downtown Pittsburgh on Sunday afternoons. They would stroll the streets of the business section and look in store windows and admire the tall office buildings. Clare was in awe of everything she saw but was always eager to return home. She would observe the modern styles of women's clothing and then incorporate the latest trends into her own sewing. She would make skirts and simple dresses for herself, her mother, and for Alice. Sometimes Johnny and Alice would accompany them on their Sunday excursions. Those two seemed so content with each other's company, always chatting, laughing, and holding hands.

One evening as they sat in O'Shea's, which by then had become their favorite Hazelwood bar, Johnny and Jack were sipping on glasses of whiskey, and Johnny mentioned that he had been saving as much money as possible. "Well, Jack," he continued, "I'm going to ask Alice to marry me. I'm twenty-four years old and not getting any younger. I found a house that we can rent up on Chatsworth Avenue that will be available next month."

Jack wasn't surprised. He had always figured Alice and Johnny were a good match. He knew they would be content living in Hazelwood forever. Johnny would eventually be a foreman in the mill, just like his father. Jack bought him another glass of whiskey and wished him the best. "You know that I want you to have a good life, and I know you'll be happy with Alice. I'm certain that she'll say yes." Johnny and Alice were both ready for marriage.

Clare was probably ready too.

Jack knew that he, himself, was not.

CHAPTER 8

July 1905—Jack

Jack had developed a camaraderie with the younger men at the job in the Allegheny Hospital. For the past two years he had worked every day with two other young Irish men who, like himself, had been born in Pittsburgh to Irish immigrants. Jimmy Kennedy and Joe Sullivan lived in the South Side and had wanted to become plumbers so they would not have to work in the steel mills. Just like Jack. Their fathers had also worked in the mills for many years, just like Sean Quinn.

During the past year, the three men had brought a change of clothes to work with them every Friday. After their workday ended, they washed up at the hospital and locked up their belongings with the tools in the gang box in the hospital basement. Then off they went for a night on the town.

Mr. McGee, who sometimes acted like a father figure to the young men as well as being their boss, usually hollered after them as they headed out the door: "Have a good time, fellas. But, not too good." Or, "Don't do anything I wouldn't do!" And then they would hear him laughing as he finished working on his time sheets. They still worked on Saturdays, so McGee also reminded them, "I expect to see all three of you bright and early."

Jack would reply, "Yes, sir, Mr. McGee, we'll be here, unless the devil decides to keep us!" That made McGee chortle even louder, probably wishing he was young again. So off they headed to a nearby tavern, one of many where they had become good customers. And this is how the trio became familiar with the after-dark side of Allegheny: the bawdy houses and the brothels that were part of the city's underworld. They were run by women of the night who could show a fellow a good time and give a young man all the education he could imagine. Everything had a price. And the women loved the young working men—they were always full of whiskey and had dollars in their pockets.

Over time, Jack and his friends each found a favorite lady with whom they liked to spend a few hours. After several shots of whiskey and a couple of beers, Jack would have an arm around a lady named Nellie. She was about five years older than Jack but enjoyed the company of younger men. Nel would laugh as loudly as the men whenever Joe told his jokes. By then Jimmy would already be kissing the neck of a pretty dark-haired girl he called Maggie.

Nellie had eyes only for Jack. She called him Charmin' Jack. Some of the others named him Jack of Hearts since he made all their hearts flutter with his sapphire eyes, his dark hair, his handsome features, and especially his shy smile. Nel laughed and told the other girls, "That Jack is the best thing that has come through the door since butter, and I can climb up one side of him and slide down the other! And don't get me started on telling you all how he is the best student that I ever tutored. So, hands off, girls, he's all mine!"

She drank shots with Jack at a table in a dark corner…her face would light up when he whispered in her ear. Nel was flashy and loud and would laugh at the nasty jokes the other men told. She wasn't beautiful; but she was attractive. Her skin was fair. She had curly raven black hair and brown eyes. Her small nose crinkled when she laughed. She had rosy cheeks and red lips, and she was the first woman Jack knew who wore makeup and perfume. Jack had grown up around hot flames, and this woman was fire in human form. Hot to touch but inviting and forbidden. Dare he touch? Yes, every time!

Even though she had small facial features and was small boned, Nel was endowed with quite an ample bosom: it spilled over the tightly laced corsets and low-cut short-sleeved silk blouses she wore. Her arms always sported a colorful assortment of bangles and sparkling bracelets.

After drinking whiskey and telling lies in the shadows of their corner table, Nel would show Jack how to properly hold a lady while slow dancing to the music playing on the phonograph. Jack listened, practiced, and learned.

Eventually, she invited Jack to her room upstairs. They would inevitably stumble and trip up the wooden staircase; then, once behind closed doors, they started things going by kicking off their shoes. Nel skillfully unbuttoned Jack's vest, shirt and pants, and then pulled his suspenders off his shoulders and slid them and his trousers to the floor. Together they rolled onto the soft bed and Nel flung off her stockings, skirt, and petticoat, followed by her corset and silkie knickers. Jack's underclothes followed his shirt to the floor. In the soft light from the oil lamp, Nel taught Jack the secrets of lovemaking and how to satisfy both his and Nel's physical desires in a variety of ways. Nel seemed to have an insatiable appetite for his body, and he was willing and able to please. After several hours, exhaustion would finally set in and they would sleep. Jack would slip out of bed in the early hours of dawn.

He always left the money on the dresser then walked through the park, back toward the hospital. He smiled, thinking about Nel and pausing to watch the fountains squirt water into the air. He quietly observed the water streaming back down to the waiting basins. Time spent with Nel was exciting and satisfying; the sound of flowing water was calming and relaxing. At that moment Jack always realized that he didn't mind flirting with temptation and the devil.

Occasionally he thought, *I wonder what Clare would think...* It had been a long time since they had talked about temptation, and he wasn't willing to give up Nel, or his good times.

Devil be damned, he told himself. *I'm just starting to live!*

CHAPTER 9

June 1906—Emma

"Hurry, Estelle. We want to catch the streetcar to the library, or we'll be walking and sweating like horses in this heat." Emma was fanning her face on the front porch, waiting for her sister. Summer apparently had decided to come early this year. Her long-sleeved, high-neck white blouse was already sticking to her skin.

Their Wednesday afternoon weekly meetings centered on discussions of current events. Today's group was focusing on the topic of women in journalism. Emma was enthralled by the investigative reporting done by a famous writer, Ida Tarbell, who had written a series of reports about the Standard Oil Company. Tarbell's newspaper articles had highlighted many of the company's questionable business practices. Emma had discussed this topic with Papa several times when they sat together in the evening, reading in the parlor.

Emma enjoyed reading the newspapers at the library and the copy of the *Pittsburg Press* that Papa always brought home. She had a keen understanding of the current news and had always found history an interesting subject. When she stopped attending school, the Carnegie Library in the West End had been her favorite destination at least twice a week. The librarian had asked Emma to lead some of the adult discussion groups. She had even read stories on Saturday afternoons to groups of children in the library's children's corner.

For years Emma had read books to her younger brothers and her sister Monnie. When they were small, she read nursery rhymes; they all could recite their favorites... from "The Muffin Man" to "Humpty Dumpty." There were so many to choose from.

In the evening Emma liked to read aloud the poems from *A Child's Garden of Verses* by Robert Louis Stevenson. The bedtime poems were a favorite, soothing and predictable, with a touch of fantasy. Monnie, even at eleven years old, still asked for the "The Land of Nod." She would recite the verses along with Emma: *"All by myself I have to go, up the mountain-sides of dreams..."* And Harry, now seven, still chuckled at the funny images in "My Shadow" and "My Bed Is A Boat." Harry was such a sweet boy, with dimples, soft gray eyes, and curly brown hair. Emma enjoyed watching the expressions on his face as she read.

In the afternoons, when Monnie was in the garden in the back yard, she would often climb onto the wooden seat of the swing that hung by two ropes from the lowest branch of the oak tree. Emma and Mama, while they prepared dinner in the kitchen, could hear Monnie singing lyrics from Stevenson's poem "The Swing":

"*How do you like to go up in a swing, up in the air so blue...*

Oh, I do think it is the pleasantest thing, that ever a child can do."

When Fred and Eddie were younger, they had always asked Emma to read from *Treasure Island* by Stevenson. They couldn't get enough of buccaneers and buried treasure. When they played in the backyard, she could hear them pretending to be Long John Silver, Jim Hawkins, or Billy Bones. Emma told Mama, "Thank goodness little Harry still enjoys hearing the pirate stories, since he has such an active imagination. He says when he grows up, he's going to be a soldier and a pirate. He wants to sail across the ocean and hunt for treasure and shoot the bad men that try to stop him."

Mama would just shake her head and laugh, not aware that the future would not be so entertaining.

Fred, at seventeen, was more interested in playing baseball. The men at the tavern said he had a real talent for the game. With a lean build and muscular arms, Fred could throw and hit the ball farther than any of the other young men. He was also a fast runner. The local teams around Pittsburgh were always asking him to play. Every evening, and on Saturdays as well, he was on a baseball diamond somewhere around the city playing ball. Fred's dream was to play for one of the professional teams: the Pittsburgh Pirates, or the Naps over in Cleveland. Maybe even the Cincinnati Reds. During the day he helped Papa at the tavern and enjoyed discussing baseball with the patrons. Eddie still attended school and said he wanted to follow in Albert's footsteps. He was never physically strong like Fred; he tended to tire easily. Albert, the firstborn, excelled in school, especially mathematics. After he had graduated from high school, he obtained a job in one of the accounting offices in downtown Pittsburgh. Papa had taught Albert how to help with the bookkeeping at the tavern when Albert was only ten years old. Papa proudly observed, "He took to it like a fish to water."

Now, at the age of twenty-four, Albert worked with numbers all day, using his ability to tally sums in his head and write columns of legible figures and all manner of reports for various companies. At dinner yesterday he had announced he was learning how to operate a new mechanical adding machine that kept a running total. Mama and Papa were quite proud of their eldest child: he always looked so very professional heading to work in the morning, sporting his gray suit and his white shirt.

In the mornings Emma and Estelle walked four blocks to the Becker family bakery where they stayed for several hours to help Aunt Sophia and

Aunt Louisa with the early morning baking of bread and pies. The aunts had never married. They ran the business now, as their parents, Emma's grandparents, both had passed away and were buried side by side up in St. Martin's Cemetery.

Estelle liked to tease Emma. She pointed out that if they, too, never married, they would be old maids running the bakery together, just like Aunt Sophia and Aunt Louisa. Emma enjoyed baking but her passion was for writing. She didn't see herself working at the bakery forever.

Four years ago, when she turned eighteen, Emma could no longer submit stories to the Young Writers section of the *Pittsburg Press*. The editor had always complimented her on her writing technique and had suggested that she could contribute to the paper as a freelance community reporter. He told her to write reports on church and neighborhood happenings. So occasionally she wrote stories on events at the library, the church, and community meetings. She tried to keep her facts accurate, and she *always* made sure she spelled names correctly. Albert delivered her articles to the editor at the paper's downtown office on his way to work. She was always excited when Albert returned home from his accounting office and delivered an envelope to her waiting hand—an envelope with her pay. "Honest money for honest work!" she crowed proudly.

One night after handing over Emma's pay, Albert told Emma, "Mr. Harrison, the editor, said to tell you to come into his office sometime if you would like to discuss taking on more assignments." Emma smiled with delight. She felt a sense of pride at being recognized for her work.

One Tuesday evening at dinner Papa announced: "This Sunday would be a good day to load up the wagon and go to Kennywood for a picnic. Albert, Emma, Estelle, Fred, and Edmund," he said, nodding at his children, "you five can take the streetcar and meet us there. Mama and I will take Monnie and Harry with us in the wagon, along with the baskets of food. Mama can ask Aunt Louisa and Aunt Sophie if they would like to come along."

So, the rest of the week the family made plans for the Sunday outing. Estelle said, "I think I'll mention to Frank Miller that we're going to Kennywood Park." She had known Frank since they had attended school together at St. Martin's, and he always smiled and chatted with her after church on Sundays. Emma knew that Estelle was sweet on Frank. And that Frank had eyes only for Estelle. He was quiet and worked at the hardware store near the bakery; Estelle was always looking for him when they walked past.

On Friday evening Albert came into the kitchen as Emma was washing the dishes. "Emma," he casually said, "you know I've talked about some of the fellows that work in my office. Two of them, Philip and Bert, are going to meet us at Kennywood on Sunday. Neither one has a steady girlfriend. You might enjoy talking to them. I always tell them how pretty and intelligent my sisters are." Emma rolled her eyes. "Well, I hope they can talk about something other than adding numbers," she replied. "Maybe Fred can show them how to hit a baseball. Unless they would be afraid of getting their suits rumpled and their hands dirty." Always serious, Albert didn't find Emma's words humorous.

~⸎~

Over the past few years, Emma had been courted by several suitors. Together they had enjoyed Sunday afternoon carriage rides and strolling through the park. However, none of the young men had held her interest for long; either they were boring, clumsy, or not the least bit intelligent. One young man *had* caught her fancy for a while *and* was especially handsome, but she found out quickly that he was conceited and self-centered. His favorite topic of discussion was himself. "I had to finally give Peter the gate," Emma told Estelle one night when they were sitting together on the front porch. "He thought he could have all the kisses he wanted just because he was so handsome. And then the next week I saw him with his arm around another girl. I've dubbed him Peter the Peacock." Estelle laughed. She thought that name was hilarious—and appropriate.

Sunday couldn't come soon enough for Emma and Estelle. Having anticipated their outing the past few days, they were eager to help load the wagon immediately after they got home from church. Papa gave the horse some water, and Emma waved to Monnie, Harry, Mama, Papa, and her aunts as they headed down the hill to the West End. Then Emma and her brothers and Estelle boarded the streetcar. The girls looked elegant, brandishing their new hats adorned with feather plumes and ribbons. The hats perched high on their heads so as not to disturb their hair. Emma was now twenty-two. She had been wearing her thick brown hair in a bun at the top of her neck since she had turned eighteen. Her brothers wore suits, as did all the men, with a jacket, white shirt, vest, and tie. And a hat, of course. Emma often thought that most men were vain about their appearance. Just like the women.

That day at Kennywood would be etched in Emma's mind forever. When they arrived, they found the rest of the family in the shelter set among a cluster of shade trees. Her aunts were covering one of the wooden tables with a tablecloth and setting out the plates and boxes filled with fried chicken, potato salad, bread, fresh berries, and two apple pies. Mama was adding water to several pitchers partially filled with sliced lemons and sugar.

An hour later, after they had finished lunch, Monnie and Harry ran over to the swings while the ladies sat on benches under the shade of the trees. Papa, Eddie, Estelle, and Emma watched Fred and Albert play catch, tossing a baseball back and forth: they had both brought their leather baseball mitts with them. After a while Emma caught sight of a large man with a big smile walking toward them. "Well, hello, Henry!" the man bellowed, coming near. He had bushy gray eyebrows, with a moustache to match. He shook Papa's hand and continued: "I bet you've missed me coming by the tavern the last few years." Papa laughed and replied, "Of course, Mr. McGee. How have you been, and where have you been keeping yourself?"

Papa introduced Mr. McGee to the rest of his family then offered him a glass of lemonade, which he knew would be hard to pass up on such a warm day. He explained that Mr. McGee had been an old friend of Mr. O'Leary's, the Irishman who had lived up on Steuben Street until he had passed away. Mr. McGee and Mr. O'Leary used to come in the tavern when McGee had plumbing jobs in Elliott and the West End.

Emma always liked to listen to stories Papa and his friends told. She learned much about the world simply by listening to conversations about politics and labor issues.

"I'm slowing down a little," Mr. McGee said. "I've got some back and knee problems; but the union keeps me and my crew busy, what with so much construction in the city. I've been stuck over in Allegheny the last few years working at the hospital. I'm training new young lads, and that takes up most of my time."

Papa and the others continued talking to Mr. McGee. Later that afternoon, Estelle took to strolling with Frank Miller. From where she sat in the shade of the shelter, Emma could see her sister giggling and making eyes at Frank. They were both obviously smitten with each other. Emma couldn't wait to tease Estelle later.

As the afternoon progressed, Albert and Emma decided to walk to the dance pavilion. They ran into Albert's friends, Philip and Bert. The four of them sat down by the fountains. Emma tried to keep the conversation going, but Philip and Bert were both very shy…and socially inept. The young men kept smiling and staring at her, but Emma felt as though she was the only one talking. She could tell Philip and Bert weren't used to speaking with a young woman who could converse about a wide range of topics. She tried to be gracious, but she glared at Albert, wanting to scream, *"Help! Why did you stick me with Pious Philip and Bashful Bert?"* Fortunately, Albert and Emma soon both spotted Papa and Mr. McGee, who now were speaking with a tall, attractive, young man. Emma waved at Papa, and the three of them approached the group. Mr. McGee and Papa, both being talkative and gregarious, each proceeded to introduce the handsome young man to them. "This here is Jack Quinn," Mr. McGee proudly said, politely cutting Papa off. "He's one of my best workers, and smart as a whip…since I've taught him everything I know." He nodded to the young man and said, "Now, Jack, Miss Emma here looks like she might enjoy some of that ice cream they're selling over there." Papa nodded at Emma and said, "Go ahead, Emma. Any friend of Mr. McGee's is a friend of ours. Besides, Mr. McGee needs to speak on a private financial matter with Albert and his associates." Emma hardly uttered a word as Jack led her across to the ice cream stand. He asked what flavor Emma wanted then offered to pay; but Emma would have none of it. She lied, telling Jack that Papa had given her spending money for the family's afternoon outing. After they had each paid for their purchase, they found a bench and sat together, side by side, enjoying their bowls of strawberry ice cream. But Emma found she was almost tongue-tied. She thought perhaps the ice cream was so cold it had frozen her tongue and left her speechless. Or maybe, she thought…perhaps she needed a break from talking after having to deal with Pious Philip and Bashful Bert.

She silently admonished herself. Now she felt like *she* was the one who was socially inept. She was truly rattled as those deep blue eyes of Jack's gazed at her. She thought she was being silly, but it was as if his eyes were staring right into her soul. He unbalanced her… in a good way. She had never experienced such feelings around any other young men who had tried to win her affection. Usually she had the upper hand and controlled the situation.

Now, she found herself mesmerized by this man's eyes, his quiet smile, and his easy manner. He was simply charming, as if it was effortless and natural.

Jack smiled. She noticed his large strong hands as he pointed out different flowers in the adjacent flower bed. Not very many of the young men Emma knew ever talked about flowers, let alone recited their names. Her cheeks grew warm and flushed. She told herself it was just from the heat of the afternoon.

Soon the conversation flowed easily between them. They sat and shared stories about their families, Jack's plumbing work with Mr. McGee, and the progress in building construction within the city. Emma felt comfortable, as if they had been friends for ages. She told Jack about her love of books and her weekly visits to the library in the West End. "My sisters like to read too," Jack replied. "The highlight of their day is when I bring home the daily newspaper. We read articles to each other in the evening."

Smiling, Emma started to relax. She thanked him for rescuing her from Albert's dull friends. Jack winked at her and said, "Well, of course, Miss Emma, I'm happy to be of service."

They heard music playing, and Jack asked Emma if she wanted to walk over by the pavilion. As they approached the wooden structure where the band was playing, he took her hand and asked if she would dance with him; they joined the other couples on the dance floor. Emma soon felt the pressure of Jack's strong hand on the small of her back, which made her tingle all over from head to toe. He was the most captivating young man she had ever encountered.

The band began playing "Beautiful Dreamer…"

Beautiful dreamer, wake unto me,

Starlight and dewdrops are waiting for thee.

Sounds of the rude world, heard in the day,

Lulled by the moonlight have all passed away…

Jack led Emma slowly and gracefully as they swayed to the music. Emma hesitated, then allowed her body to be pulled close to his, feeling his breath on her face. She closed her eyes and listened to the sound of her own breathing. "Beautiful Dreamer" was one of her favorite songs.

CHAPTER 10

May 1907—Emma

"Emma, wake up, sleepy head!" Estelle called from across their shared bedroom. She and Monnie were making their beds, fluffing the pillows and smoothing the blankets. "With that smile on your face you must be dreaming about Jack," she teased. "Was he kissing you and holding you tight in his strong arms?" She laughed as she exaggerated her actions like an actress: "Oh, Jack, fan me with your hat. Oh, darling Jack, I'm so warm I must unbutton my collar!" Terribly overdramatic, Estelle waved one arm and continued: "Oh, my charming Jack, I feel faint…you *must* kiss my lips to revive me. Dance with me, my love. You hold my heart in your hands and it only beats for you!" Estelle let herself drop slowly onto the bed, her arms hugging a pillow, pretending to kiss it. Finally, Emma sat up and threw a rolled-up stocking at Estelle as she rose from her bed. "Estelle, what about you and Frank? I saw you two kissing behind the lilac bush last night!" Young Monnie's attention, which had shifted back and forth between her two sisters, now turned to Estelle. Monnie was wide-eyed and didn't want to miss a word of the stimulating conversation.

"We were merely smelling the lilacs," Estelle replied quickly, "and then he said goodbye." After a few moments, the two sisters looked at twelve-year-old Monnie. She was in hysterics, her hands over her mouth, trying to stifle her laughter. Later that morning Emma and Estelle left the house to walk down the street to the bakery. They relished the cool air of the springtime morning as they walked. "Seriously, Emma," Estelle began, "if you and I both get married how are Aunt Sophia and Aunt Louisa going to manage without us? I guess we had better start training Monnie."

Emma stopped in her tracks and looked in her sister's eyes. "My goodness, do we have to have this discussion about the rights of women again? Haven't I taught you anything?" She smiled, but there was sarcasm in her voice. "Estelle, SO WHAT if you get married? Marriage doesn't make you a prisoner in your home. You can still work and think for yourself. And make sure to let your dear Frank know where you stand before you ever say any wedding vows." Emma continued, she was on a rant: "You are a strong, capable woman with your own thoughts and ideas. I don't care what the laws say—the laws need to be changed. Women need to have a voice in their own lives. Mama and Papa always worked together as a team and respected each other's ideas. You know as well as I do that not all men are as open minded as Papa."

She then added thoughtfully, "All throughout history, there have been men who are tyrants and women who put up with it. No man will ever be my master and expect me to obey."

"I hope your precious Jack is forewarned about your progressive ideas!" Estelle laughed as they stepped through the back entrance of the bakery and greeted their aunts, who were covered up to their elbows in flour. All that morning and into the evening Jack was in Emma's thoughts as she rolled dough at the bakery, helped Mama around the house, and rode the streetcar to the library. Ever since their first day together at Kennywood Park, Emma and Jack had always made plans for the following weekend. Sometimes she saw him on Sunday afternoons, and he would stay for dinner with the family. On those occasions Jack and Papa talked for hours, although Papa was friendly and sociable by nature. "Your Papa could talk the ears off a deaf horse," Mama claimed.

Emma noticed how extraordinarily gracious Mama was toward Jack. Margaret Moreau appreciated his good manners and was quick to give Jack an extra piece of pie after he complimented her fine cooking. Mama was overheard telling Aunt Louisa, "That young man has good looks, good manners, and good taste. That makes him a keeper in my book!"

Some weekends Emma saw Jack only on Saturday evenings. He would leave work early, change clothes, and come directly to Elliott on the streetcar. He explained that he had to occasionally spend time on Sundays with his family and visit with his friend Johnny. Emma thought it was an admirable quality in a man if he spoke highly of his own family. She noticed that Jack spoke negatively about only one person who he found revolting and vulgar; somebody named Joe Murphy, a man from his neighborhood in Hazelwood. Jack had worked with Joe in the mill for several years and never had a good word to say about him.

Lying in bed at night Emma imagined a home of her own, with Jack beside her in bed. She indulged her fantasies and pictured a life with him but knew she would never sacrifice her own interests and dreams. Most young men eventually started to bore her, but not Jack. Still dreaming of being a newspaper reporter, Emma attended meetings at the library and at the church. She was always careful climbing aboard the streetcar, holding up her skirt with one hand. If the streetcar had ears it would have heard her whisper, *"Fashion be damned, these long skirts were probably designed by men as another means of encumbering females. Long skirts and corsets!"* She never tightened her corset…when she wore one. She figured it was more practical to be able to breathe.

She carried a pad of paper and pencils in the fabric bag she brought to the meetings, always ready to record the facts. She had an air of confidence about her, bred by having a purpose and rewarded by a sense of accomplishment.

At the meetings Emma took careful notes, making sure she had correct dates, numbers, and names. The next day she wrote up a factual report and typed it on her typewriter at home. She had saved her wages from the newspaper and the bakery for two years to buy the typewriter. Papa and Albert had accompanied her to the office supply store on Liberty Avenue in downtown Pittsburg to purchase it. She was so proud to be the first person in Elliott to have a typewriter in their home, and she became quite skilled at using it, not even having to look at the keys as she typed.

Mr. Harrison, the editor at the newspaper office, would send her notes reminding her to stick to the facts. He edited out her personal remarks and told her that if she wanted to give her own opinions that was a different kind of column.

She enjoyed discussing her ideas and opinions with Papa and Estelle. Jack listened too. He was always impressed by Emma's knowledge, although she found his eyes gazing at her distracting. Then she would lose her train of thought. The meetings she attended were often boring affairs: women discussing church activities like bake sales and raising money for the school. It was more interesting when the conversations centered on politics, both local and national.

Papa would accompany her to evening meetings at the library, where the group consisted mostly of men. Her pencil couldn't move fast enough when they started arguing about corruption in politics and labor issues. Not every comment was suitable for print in the newspaper. And not every person with an opinion would even give her their name.

Most of the men were supporters of President Theodore Roosevelt, as he was a popular Republican who fought against the industrial monopolies. Emma remembered that Roosevelt had easily won his battle for re-election in 1904. She would have voted for him—if it had been possible for women to vote. Another reality that discontented her.

She had read an interesting story about President Roosevelt's life, and told Jack about it on a warm Sunday evening when they sat side-by-side on her front porch swing. She began, "In 1884, the year that I was born, Roosevelt's mother and his first wife both died. To overcome his grief Mr. Roosevelt lived in the Dakota Territory for two years, learning to ride horses and herd cattle. He even became skilled at big game hunting. He later was in the Rough Rider Regiment in the Spanish-American War, and was declared a war hero." She paused then stated, "My little brother Harry is fascinated by Roosevelt and his adventures out west and in the war." Jack seemed to find her stories interesting. He listened with attentive ears—and admiring eyes that twinkled when he smiled.

Emma was keenly aware that Jack found everything else about her interesting as well. When he said goodbye and had to return home, there would always be a long kiss by the door. A kiss that left her warm and breathless, instinctively wanting more. She was filled with a sense of anticipation of things to come and smiled with a quiet joy.

Jack had confided in Emma about his feelings of loss and sorrow when his mother had died. She could only imagine how awful that experience must have been for a nine-year-old child, to lose his mother's love at such a young age. And then it tore at her heart as she pictured him slaving in the steel mill when he was only ten. He had told her those experiences had made him strong and self-reliant, claiming, "I'm a survivor." He added: "My Dad looked out for me as much as he could and kept telling me the Quinn men are tough."

Emma agreed, well-aware that people generally live up to the expectations that their parents have for them. She looked into his deep blue eyes and whispered, "Yes, strong as steel, tough as iron." There were so many layers to this man that fascinated her. She squeezed his arm and leaned over and kissed his cheek, wanting to take away any pain that he felt, now and always.

She knew that her heart was melting…and if she had to put a name to her feelings then it must be love. Emma Moreau was falling in love. There was a satisfaction deep within her when Jack opened-up to her and talked about his childhood and his dreams. His touch and his kisses made her tingle all over.

Sometimes he would get quiet and have a far-off look in his eyes, almost like a curtain being drawn between them. Emma would wonder what was hiding behind the curtain. Or who?

CHAPTER 11

August 1907—Jack

Johnny Finnegan and Alice Murphy were married in 1906 during a small ceremony at St. Stephen's in Hazelwood. Jack attended but sat with his sisters, while Clare felt obligated to help Alice with the details. It was a short service, officiated by young Father Walsh, who talked about the joys of marriage, pointing out the importance of commitment and honesty in Johnny and Alice's relationship. A reception with cake and tea was held in the meeting hall located in the basement of the church.

The new church building was beautiful, and Jack knew how much Clare, Alice, and his sisters loved it. They had monitored and discussed every milestone of the construction process, from the baptismal font to the stained-glass windows and the statues of the Blessed Mother and St. Stephen. He had told his sisters, "Mum would have loved this place." He sensed the communal pride when he sat in those sturdy wooden pews surrounded by church-members he had known his entire life. Jack realized, but would never admit, that he might even feel a bit of remorse when he no longer was a part of this congregation. Which would be soon.

Father Donnelly was getting up in years, so the diocese had sent a young priest to be his assistant. The youthful vigor of Father Walsh complemented the wisdom and experience of the elderly priest.

Under the direction of the Diocese of Pittsburgh, the parishioners of St. Stephen's also helped build a school building behind the church. The diocese arranged for several nuns to serve as teachers for grades one through eight. They resided in a house next to the school, built with the same dull orange brick as the school, the church, and the rectory where the priests lived. Alice and Johnny told Jack that someday their children would attend the parish school and that the nuns would provide a wonderful education. "Certainly, better than what we had. Right, Jack?" said Johnny. He added: "And it will be nice and close." They were living in a house in the same block as Clare's family over on Chatsworth Avenue. They had originally rented the small two-story brick house but were now in the process of buying it. Jack's people were still living in their company-owned wooden house beyond Second Avenue and the railroad tracks. The cheaper rent enabled Dad to save up some money over the years; in addition, Jack had always given Dad a portion of his pay for his room and board. One evening Dad said, "Well, Jack, I like to plan ahead. I'm fifty-nine years old and can't keep working in the mill forever. My knees are starting to give out on me. I have pain in my hands, back, knees. If it's not one thing aching then it's the other," he claimed as he rubbed his right knee with one hand. "It sure is tough getting old," he continued. "I've been saving up, a little here and a little there. Next year when I'm sixty I can finally quit the mill. Now with the union helping us, there's even going to be a small bit of a pension."

Dad was moving a little slower these days, walking with a hint of a limp. His hair, which had always been so thick, was thinning and totally gray now, and his bushy moustache was gray, streaked with white. Jack saw how the years of hard labor had taken a toll on the man. He deserved a rest. Jack poured them each a glass of whiskey. "That will be a day to celebrate, for sure, Dad," he said. "Did you get to see Mary this week?" His oldest sister had married a railroad worker named Daniel two years ago. Daniel's first wife had died and left him with two young children. Mary knew Daniel's children from church and had been helping the family out with their meals and minding the little boy and girl. After a few months Daniel asked her to marry him. Mary was thirty-three years old at the time and said, "I'm not getting any younger. There's no point in having a long engagement." Father Walsh married them in another small wedding service at St. Stephen's, and Mary moved to Daniel's house up on Gertrude Street. "She found herself another family to raise," said Jack to Dad after the ceremony as they ate cake together. Jack smiled. He always knew Mary would be a wonderful mother. Just like Mum.

Florence and Margaret didn't clean at the big houses anymore. They both, along with Clare Murphy, had jobs sewing for one of the clothing shops on Second Avenue. One evening after dinner while Jack and Dad read the newspaper, Florence said proudly, "Jackie, look at this, I'm sewing a man's suit jacket. I brought it home to sew the buttons by hand. The shopkeeper showed us how to use the big industrial sewing machines that he has in the back room." Jack was glad to see Florence excited about something. "That's wonderful," he said. "I might have to stop by the shop to look at the suits. I thought that place only sold women's clothing."

"The shop owner, Mr. Hoffman, takes special orders for suits for men," Margaret replied. "He tells customers that he hires the best seamstresses in the area. Of course, he's referring to me, Florence, and Clare."

"And does he tell the customers that he won't hire tailors because he knows he can pay you girls a whole lot less money?" Jack inquired quickly. "Just like the textile factories over in Allegheny. Although those sweatshops hire hundreds of young immigrant women and pay them as little as possible."

Margaret shook her head. "Well, Jackie, what can we do about it? He won't pay us more. I asked once and he got mad and told me I can find another job if I don't like it. And, besides, I can walk to work, which is better than some people have it."

His sisters took good care of Dad and that made Jack happy, and grateful. He never said it, but Jack figured Florence and Margaret would probably end up being old maids. They were both shy and afraid to be sociable. They attended church and occasionally would walk with Clare to the new Carnegie Library in Hazelwood.

They all seemed content…satisfied with their limited existence, as Jack called it; even Margaret didn't complain much anymore, although her frowning had begun to etch lines on her forehead. Clare was a good friend to his sisters and often walked down to visit with them, even though she worked side by side with them, sewing in the backroom of the clothing shop. Jack still occasionally saw Clare on Sunday afternoons, but he knew Clare sensed something had changed between them. They were friends who had grown apart. There was now a distance between them he assumed probably worried her, evidenced by a gradual loss of passion when they kissed, as if it had leaked away. The passion had been slowly eroded by their different views of the future, unspoken now, but looming above them…clouds harboring an upcoming storm. His passionate kisses were now on Emma's lips, and occasionally Nel's.

In his mind, he sometimes pictured Clare stuck in a ravine, looking down and around at the way before and behind her, but refusing to look up, not wanting to escape. Jack had always been searching for a way out. He had managed to climb up and find a path leading out of Hazelwood, and Clare would not grab his outstretched hand. He had to leave Clare behind. The situation saddened him since he had always loved her. But now, his thoughts were elsewhere. He was thinking about Emma and the enjoyable times he spent with her in Elliott. She was waiting for him with open arms, saying, "Hurry Jack, don't look back. Cross the river!" Clare and Jack saw how happy Alice and Johnny were, and Jack realized that everyone had expectations that Jack would soon ask Clare to marry him. They could be neighbors with Alice and Johnny. Their children could grow up together. He knew that was Clare's only dream.

Jack had taught Clare to dream about the future. He knew that in her imagination, she pictured herself with Jack in his brick house. There was just one problem…one big insurmountable problem. Her dreams never involved leaving Hazelwood. Clare had grown accustomed to the smoke and black soot, never demanding anything better. She had become like Dad and his sisters, accustomed to a limited existence.

Jack had always talked about leaving Hazelwood, but Clare had told him many times that she couldn't move away from her family. And now that her mother and dad were aging, sick and bedridden, she felt it was her responsibility to take care of her parents. Jack knew Clare was grateful her brother Joe was able to provide for the family. Clare certainly couldn't make enough money with her sewing to support them.

He still had no use for Joe Murphy. Dad and Johnny told him Joe was worse than ever. "Once an idiot, always an idiot," Johnny remarked. Jack had no intention of having Joe be a permanent fixture in his life. Marriage was finally on Jack's mind, now that he was twenty-six years old and earning a good wage as a plumber. Sadly, he knew he couldn't marry Clare. He had known for years that she would never leave Hazelwood…and he couldn't keep living there. Some things never changed. He had dreamed of leaving the smoky, grimy town since he was nine years old.

Now things were starting to fall in place. The beginning of his dream was so close… finally within his reach. And Clare was not part of it. He still loved her…but he foresaw a better life with Emma. His heart was torn between two women, possibly three, if he included Nel; but he understood that Nel was not the marrying type of woman. With Nel, Jack knew, it was more lust than love.

Jack felt his future rested on the other side of the Monongahela River, down past where it met and helped form the Ohio. In Elliott, where the hills rose above that second river, he imagined a life with Emma Moreau.

He knew Emma adored him and her family accepted him. Jack got along well with Emma's father and brothers. Emma's mother, Estelle, and Monnie, all seemed to like him. After living his entire life with three sisters Jack felt that he understood women…better than most men, at least. One might even say he had a good rapport with the ladies, a certain charm that was appealing…or so he had been told.

Emma was the most captivating, confident, capable woman he had ever met. Her beauty was more than just physical. It encompassed her whole being. She had a spirit that energized him and made him feel confident. Her soft blue-gray eyes were alive with intelligence and insight. She had opinions on every subject and could hold her own in any discussion. Jack admired her and envisioned making a life with her. He asked himself, *is it possible to love two women? Would it be a sin to love two women?*

Jack rode the streetcars daily and pondered these questions. He knew what he had to do.

He decided to ask Emma to marry him. He was committed to following his dream.

It had become his custom lately to spend most Sunday afternoons with Emma. Usually they would stroll through the park or walk up to the Overlook. Jack enjoyed spending this time with Emma and was aware of other men's eyes following her as they strolled together. "What a handsome couple!" he heard people say as they gazed at Emma and Jack. Of course, that only made Jack want her even more. She was tall, possessed of a slender build and an ample bosom. She naturally looked quite stylish even when she wore just a plain white blouse and dark skirt. Her brown hair was always wound neatly, coiled and pinned at the nape of her lovely neck.

Emma would confidently take Jack's arm…they seemed to move in sync. There existed a rhythm between them when they walked. They moved well together, without any effort, and Jack was proud to be seen with her.

He fantasized about being in bed with her…being naked…showing her how much he loved her. He convinced himself he had outgrown his fascination with Clare, and that he didn't need her anymore. The selfishness of his plans was embarrassing, so of course he never discussed his situation with anyone. Men just didn't talk about such intensely personal dilemmas. He still occasionally visited Nel; but that was always a strictly physical encounter meant to satisfy his basic cravings. Nel made him realize that a man has needs, and she had shown him that women also have needs. He wanted to have *that* experience and closeness with Emma.

With Emma it would be even more satisfying, Jack thought, since they would be committed only to each other. When he kissed her, he naturally wanted more than just her lips. He knew she did too. He cared so deeply for her and wanted to share his life with her. She would help make his dreams of a better life come true.

～✥～

One warm Sunday afternoon when they were out together, Emma looked particularly fetching in her wide-brimmed hat, the one with feathers tucked in the band on one side. Jack complimented her on how stylish she looked, thinking again that she was elegant but not extravagant in her tastes. Practical, not flashy. He knew she could be trusted not to spend money on trinkets and baubles. They had taken the streetcar to downtown and then on to Allegheny. Jack wanted to show her the fountains and flowers in the center park, and the small lake, where they decided to rent a boat for an hour.

Ever the gentleman, Jack steadied the boat and held Emma's arm tightly as she carefully climbed in. Emma was not afraid of boats, or water, or…anything. The couple sat on the wooden seats facing each other. Emma put a hand on each side of the rowboat and watched Jack's every movement as the boat rocked gently on the calm water.

Jack took off his jacket, rolled up his sleeves, then rowed easily to the center of the lake. There were so many trees surrounding the shore that he couldn't even see the smokestacks. It was a sunny day, and light reflected off the water. Having rained that morning, the air was cleaner than it had been in days. He noticed how Emma's eyes watched his arms and his hands as he rowed…she laughed merrily, obviously enjoying their adventure. There were other boaters, but none in proximity. As they reached the middle of the lake, Jack let the oars rest. Then he leaned forward and took one of Emma's hands, holding it gently in both of his. With a serious expression on his face, he looked into her eyes and said, "Emma, remember the day we met at Kennywood Park? I knew then that you were special. I want to be with you every day and every night. I want to share my life with you." Jack smiled shyly as he asked, "Emma, will you marry me?" He took her face in his hands, feeling her warmth as he caressed her cheeks with his thumbs then leaned in and kissed her lips. Emma whispered, "Yes, Jack Quinn. I would love to marry you." She kissed him back and squeezed his hands. He kissed her harder and pulled her to him, but the boat was swaying back and forth. "My dear Emma, be careful not to rock the boat," Jack warned with a laugh. "We wouldn't want to upset."

"I think we can keep it afloat together…forever," Emma mused wistfully.

CHAPTER 12

September 1907—Jack

As Jack rode the streetcar back to Hazelwood, he played different scenarios in his head. First, he thought about how excited Emma had become when he proposed to her in the rowboat on the lake.

She was unaware of his discussion with her father earlier in the day. He had asked Henry Moreau for his daughter's hand in marriage. He knew from listening to his sister Mary that it was proper form—and good manners—to ask a father for permission to marry his daughter.

"That's what respectable people do," Mary said. "Daniel had apparently talked to Dad before he asked me to be his wife. Of course, Dad approved."

Henry Moreau gave Jack his blessing, as well as his encouragement. Henry was a friend and well on the way to becoming a second father to Jack. Henry had said, "My daughter has a strong mind and will voice her opinions, Jack. But with love and mutual respect, you two will get along just fine." He gave his permission readily, especially when Jack added, "We'll be living in Elliott, so let me know if you hear of a house for rent. The sooner the better. I make good wages as a plumber, so preferably a nice house with a decent bathroom would be perfect. I want Emma to be happy." Henry was pleased. He shook Jack's hand and patted his back. Then Jack had went out onto the front porch to wait for Emma to come downstairs. He thought about their boat ride later that day and his proposal. It had been such a perfect afternoon.

Now he had to break the news to his family. As the streetcar rattled and rumbled across the bridge to Hazelwood, Jack gazed at the smokestacks, black plumes of smoke billowing upward. He was satisfied with the thought of finally leaving the grime and soot. He *had* to leave. Soon. But first he must tell Clare.

Jack had wrestled with this problem for several months. It was such an impossible situation. He often questioned his own motives and tactics. *How can I love two women?* he asked himself. *I feel like I've been lying to both. I don't want to hurt Clare, but it's the only way. What we once had is long gone.*

He compared the two women to each other and tried to rationalize his reasoning. Emma was strong in mind and body, whereas Clare was fragile and sensitive. If he likened them to flowers, Jack thought Emma was like a lilac. The lilac bush is sturdy and can weather any storm…it grows back year after year. It doesn't need much tending but is beautiful and hardy. It can stand alone or with others and can be protective of other smaller plants. On the other hand, Clare was like a rose. Beautiful but delicate, with soft petals… easily damaged. A rose needs constant tending and care. Even Clare knew she couldn't be transplanted…she had to remain with her own kind.

It would be better for Clare to stay with her family, Jack finally concluded. They needed her, and she needed them, he reasoned. He tried to convince himself that this was for the best. Now…he must tell her. It had to be right away. Jack was determined to announce the news to his family first. Then he would find Clare. Today. He couldn't risk her hearing it from someone else, like his sisters. He could handle Mary, Florence, and Margaret, even though he knew they wouldn't be happy about him leaving Hazelwood.

Jack and Clare had been best friends since they were fourteen. People grow and change and sometimes grow apart, he rationalized. He couldn't help that everyone, including his sisters and Clare's family, simply assumed that he and Clare would someday get married. They probably *would* have married—if he had been willing to live in Hazelwood.

He had wanted more for so long, and Clare knew that. Hopefully, he thought, she wouldn't be too angry. She had always thought he would change his mind about leaving Hazelwood. But Jack's dream and his mind had never wavered.

Jack took a long drink from his flask, slipped it back into his pocket, and stepped off the streetcar. He was not looking forward to the rest of this day.

Mary and her family were eating dinner in the kitchen with Florence and Margaret. Dad was also sitting at the table. Mary's stepchildren, Jane and Mark, were carrying dirty dishes to the sink under Mary's watchful eye. Jack's sisters, as usual, had saved him some stew and biscuits. He ate hungrily, carried his plate to the sink, then said, "I have some news." He waved his arms for them all to come closer. Everyone gathered around the table, including Dad and Daniel, Mary's husband. Jane and Mark stared at Jack, their eyes wide with curiosity and anticipation.

Jack cleared his throat. Then he stood tall and began. "I've been spending a lot of time with my friend Emma in Elliott over the past year. She's a fine Catholic woman, intelligent, and industrious. She helps her family, works at her aunts' bakery, and even writes for the newspaper." He hesitated, then said, "Well, after a lot of thought, I have finally decided to ask her to marry me. Emma and I are going to be married as soon as we find a house in Elliott."

The room was quiet as Jack took a deep breath then continued: "I know you're close to Clare, but this is the way it has to be. I've told everyone for years, including Clare, that I will not live in Hazelwood. I plan on speaking to Clare as soon as we finish here." He paused, watching their expressions of shock and disbelief.

As he expected, Mary spoke first. "Jackie, how could you? You know this will break Clare's heart. She was hoping that the two of you would get married at St. Stephen's, just like Alice and Johnny." Mary continued, saying what everyone was thinking: "What's happened to you? An Irish girl isn't good enough for you anymore?" Mary was more disappointed than angry. She put a protective arm around Jane and Mark, who looked confused. Her husband Daniel kept his face impassive, not caring to be involved in this discussion, knowing that his opinion didn't matter.

Florence fumbled in her apron pocket for her rosary beads. "Oh, my Mother of God…sweet Jesus," she whispered. She quickly made the sign of the cross with the crucifix in her right hand, whispering, "I can't believe this. Poor Clare." Margaret started to sob and couldn't utter a word.

Dad walked over to Jack and looked him in the eye. "Is she a good woman, Jack?" Jack did not hesitate. "Yes, she is. And she will be a good wife. I've been around good women my entire life and know what one looks like," said Jack, as he gazed at each of his sisters, trying to soften the blow with a compliment.

Dad patted Jack's arm. "Your sisters here might not like your decision," he said, "but we all want what's best for you. Elliott is not that far away, so I hope you'll still come visit us. Aye, indeed, don't forget your roots."

After years of dealing with his sisters, Jack knew they couldn't stay angry at their Jackie for long. He had developed his charming ways as a child…trying to get what he wanted from them. Whether it be an extra cookie or their approval, they always gave in. He knew they loved him even though they were disappointed. Their Jackie could do no wrong.

Dad looked at him and nodded toward the door. "Now, go do what you need to do." Jack steeled himself for the next tirade as he walked to Clare's house. He took a sip from his flask before he knocked on the front door of the Murphy household.

When Clare answered the door, he was relieved that her brother Joe was nowhere in sight. Jack quickly said, "Clare, we need to talk. Can we walk over towards the park?" Clare wrapped her shawl around her shoulders as a cool breeze swept fallen leaves around their shoes. They sat on a bench at the far end of the park where there was some privacy.

Clare looked at Jack expectantly, as if he had a surprise for her. Then she noticed how troubled he looked as he lowered his head and stared at his hands.

He finally found his voice. "Clare, I have to keep moving forward with my life and I can't live in the past. We have been best friends for so long, and I've shared my hopes and dreams with you since we were fourteen. You've known for years that I can't live forever in Hazelwood. Even if that means leaving you behind. You've told me over and over that you can't, or won't, move from here. Well…I can't stay."

Stoic yet tender, moving closer to lowering the painful blow and delivering the unexpected news, Jack paused then continued: "I want you to know…I'm going to marry a woman from Elliott, and I will be moving there soon."

Silence. Even the air didn't move. Time stood still.

Clare looked dumbfounded, as if she couldn't process what her ears had just heard. She appeared to have been struck by an invisible hand. She whispered, "What did you just say?"

"I'm going to marry a woman from across the river, from Elliott," Jack repeated hoarsely. His fingers nervously touched the silver flask in his pocket.

Tears started to well in Clare's eyes as she cried out, "Jack, I thought you loved me? *Me! Me!*" She curled her hands into fists and pointed both thumbs at her heart. "Is this a joke? I don't understand," she whispered, shaking her head, her green eyes searching his face. She kept repeating, "I don't understand, I don't understand...you love me. You always told me that you loved me. I thought you loved *us* and what we meant to each other. We were going to be together forever…I can't believe this!"

Jack held both of her hands in his and pressed them to his heart. He was breaking her heart, even as he tried to harden his own. "Please try to understand. Please listen."

He continued whispering softly, his face close to hers. "I do love you, Clare, and I always will. But sometimes love isn't enough. I need more. And that won't change. I need to leave this town. I need a life away from here. I've told you that. My future is not *here*…I'm sorry."

He brushed a loose curl from her forehead then used his thumb to wipe away a tear running down her cheek. "Mr. McGee is talking about me running a job in Youngstown. There's a whole world out there. I need to marry someone who isn't afraid of life and opportunities. Someone not consumed with fears. You won't ever move away from this godforsaken town! Clare," he warned, "this place will be the death of you. And I want out of here." His voice and his hands were trembling.

Suddenly Clare's eyes flashed with anger as her face reddened. She yanked her hands away from him. Again, she cried, "I can't believe this! And, don't tell me, Jack Quinn, what I WILL or WILL NOT do!" She stood up, quickly raised her right hand and slapped him across his cheek. "There! I bet you didn't think I'd do *that*!" she shouted.

Jack could see that his cruel news was sinking in. He had never seen Clare so upset. The anger was taking over: she was practically spitting fire at him. "Go! Just go!" she cried. "You'll regret what you've done! Maybe not today, or tomorrow. But someday!" Her whole body trembled, and her hands were curled tightly into fists at either side of her waist. She turned and stormed off, muttering, "I never want to see your face again!" But after three steps she spun around and stared back into his eyes. "Jack Quinn, I hope you suffer until the day you die, and after that I hope you burn in Hell."

Then Clare was gone.

Jack sat on the park bench for several minutes. He felt bruised and exhausted. Then he pulled out his flask and emptied it into his dry mouth. He touched his cheek where Clare had slapped him. Then he stood next to the bench and stared at the trees dropping their leaves. Finally, he meandered slowly back to his house, kicking dry leaves, whispering over and over, "What's done is done…what's done is done."

He walked through the backyard, opened the kitchen door, and quietly removed his shoes. He was relieved that nobody spoke to him. He had heard enough words for one day, and now he felt empty after riding the whole gamut of emotions. The love and excitement with Emma, the disappointment and sorrow with his family, the ultimate desolation of anger, pain, and suffering with Clare.

He quietly climbed the stairs, shed his clothes, and crawled into bed, feeling like a rotten slimy snake. But this was the way it had to be.

~·exelo·~

Jack tossed and turned all night, replaying events in his head. He had brought such joy to Emma's face…and such sorrow to Clare's. When he closed his eyes, all he could see was Clare and her green eyes full of anger and betrayal. His heart ached and a sadness engulfed him. Letting out a long sigh, Jack rolled to his side and pulled a blanket up over his ears.

The next morning Jack was up before the sun. He boarded the streetcar to go to work at the hospital over in Allegheny. He told Mr. McGee and his friends about his engagement to Emma. Joe Sullivan and Jimmy Kennedy promised to buy him a couple of shots after work.

Mr. McGee was pleased with Jack's announcement. He had introduced Jack and Emma to each other. He shook Jack's hand and said, "Congratulations, Jack. The Moreau family is a step up in the world for you. Play your cards right, my boy, and you'll have a good life. Like my dear wife, bless her soul, always said: life is what you make of it, so don't screw it up and land yourself in the crapper! But for now, you best get to work." He walked away chuckling. Jack knew that Mr. McGee was always quite pleased with himself. He wondered why some men seemed to find life so easy. McGee probably never loved anybody other than his wife; probably never had to choose whom to marry....

After stopping in the closest bar with Jimmy and Joe after work, Jack began feeling better. Better, at least, than he felt yesterday. It was seven o'clock. He hadn't bothered changing from his work clothes, and he was hungry for dinner as he stepped off the streetcar onto Second Avenue in Hazelwood.

Fortunately, he had immediately spotted Joe Murphy sitting on the bench outside of O'Shea's Bar. Jack suspected Murphy had been waiting there for him. Slowly Jack started walking in the direction of his house, but out of the corner of his eye he saw that Murphy was following about ten feet behind him. "Okay, Joe, let's get this over with," Jack said calmly as he turned to face Murphy. Joe walked up to him, yelling, "Quinn, you're nothing but a lying, cheating piece of shit. My sister and I both hate your guts. In fact, my whole family hates your guts!" And with that Murphy proceeded to spit on Jack's shirt. Jack narrowed his eyes then started to smile at Joe. That enraged Joe even more. His face turned so red that Jack thought Murphy's eyes might pop out of his head. Jack laughed—and that did it. All hell was about to break loose. It was as if Jack had lit the fuse on a keg of gunpowder. Murphy exploded with anger.

Joe Murphy swung at Jack's face. Jack saw it coming and stepped back then danced to the right. Murphy swung again. Jack, being younger and quicker than Murphy, figured he could play this game for a while...weaving back and forth as Murphy kept swinging. Jack held his clenched fists up, leading with his right, just as Dad had always taught him. He kept his head down and remembered to always protect his face. Then Jack decided to take a few quick jabs at his opponent, such a pathetic excuse for a man.

By this time a crowd of spectators was gathering in the street, cheering and placing bets. Jack's adversary was finally going to get what he deserved. He had imagined this scenario for years but had always restrained himself because of Clare.

"Hey, Murphy," Jack taunted, "you're finally going to get what you've been asking for."

All those practice sessions with Dad when Jack was younger were now going to pay off. He poked at Murphy and jabbed at his face. Jack moved constantly, side to side, back and forth. None of Murphy's punches ever made contact.

Jack looked like the professional boxers he had seen photographs of in the newspapers. Murphy kept calling him a cheating scumbag. Then he started shouting, "Quinn, you shithead! I hate your bloody guts!"

"Come on, Murph, you swine. You're just a walking piece of shit. Come and get me...or are you scared?" Jack kept laughing at Murphy as he poked him.

Murphy was so enraged by this point that he lowered his head and charged at Jack like a mad bull. Jack lowered his right shoulder and brought his left fist up like a hook. He caught Murphy under the chin then brought his right forearm down on his back.

As Murphy fell to the ground, Jack kicked him hard in the stomach. The crowd cheered as Jack rubbed his fighting hand with the palm of his other hand. Then, bending over, with one swift movement, Jack picked up his hat and brushed the dust off it. He smiled at Murphy's moaning, crumpled body. Then Jack straightened the hat's brim and gave a nod and a wave to the crowd. Not one to boast or gloat, he relished the silent satisfaction that he felt.

A moment later Jack continued walking home, not even looking back.

When he described the incident for Dad, he knew his father was proud to know his son could stand up for himself and fight like a man.

Old Sean Quinn wanted to hear every detail, blow by blow. He enjoyed listening to his son and then asked Jack to repeat it again, painting the picture in his mind. "Thanks, Dad, for everything you taught me," Jack whispered into his father's ear as he patted his father's shoulder. Dad nodded with a satisfaction born of masculine parental pride, as he smiled and poured them both a glass of whiskey. And then another one.

CHAPTER 13

January 1908—Emma

The new year arrived with a blast of frigid winds and cold air from the north; the bitter weather was followed by a soft blanket of snow. Emma Moreau Quinn nestled in bed, trying to keep warm under the blankets. Jack had just left to catch the streetcar for work, and Emma did not have to go to the bakery for another hour. She scooted over in the bed and felt the warmth where her husband had been sleeping next to her.

Emma smiled as she thought about the events of the last few months. Back in October, Papa had heard about a house on Lakewood Avenue that would come up for rent by the beginning of November. The house was located close to Lorenz Avenue, not far from the tavern and the bakery, and was only a block from Mama and Papa's house. Emma and Jack both agreed it would be perfect.

A week after Jack had proposed, Emma asked the parish priest, Father Ryan, if she could speak to him privately after Sunday Mass. "Father," she began simply, "I need to talk to you about having my wedding ceremony at St. Martin's." Father Ryan smiled and said, "Well, certainly, Emma. Who is the lucky man?" The elderly priest had known Emma for twenty-three years: he had baptized her when she was just a week old, way back in 1884. Emma proceeded to tell Father Ryan all about Jack Quinn. "Yes, Father," she said, reassuring him, "he comes from a good Catholic family. They attend St. Stephen's church over in Hazelwood." Father Ryan nodded. "Emma, bring a paper that states the date Jack was baptized," he instructed her, "and tell your young man that it must have the signature of his parish priest. I've known Father Donnelly for years, and there is a new young priest assisting him now, Father Walsh."

After Father Ryan checked his calendar, he and Emma decided that the second Saturday in November would be a good date to hold the ceremony. Emma didn't want to risk the chance of snow showers on her wedding day, and by November their house would be ready for them to move into.

For years Mama had been putting extra blankets, sheets, dishes, and pots and pans in two wooden chests. She had told Emma and Estelle that someday they would need those items—and by *someday* she meant when they got married. The girls had never given their mother's gesture much thought, but now Emma was grateful Mama had been so practical. Mama had also saved some old furniture, which she gave to Emma and Jack to furnish their house with.

Papa arranged for a photographer friend to stop over at the house after the wedding. "You should have a proper portrait of you and your husband on your wedding day," Papa told Emma. Aunt Louisa and Aunt Sophie baked them a beautiful layered cake, stating, simply, "You have to have something sweet on your special day."

Emma was happy that she was able to purchase a new dress for the occasion. She went downtown, accompanied by Mama and Estelle, to one of the women's clothing stores on Fifth Avenue. Soon after entering the store and looking carefully through the collection, she pointed to a simple beige satin dress with a high neck. "Mama, look," she said. "This one will be perfect!" The dress had long sleeves with pearl buttons on the cuff and ruffle trim at the hemline. Mama and Estelle agreed that it was lovely. Mama offered to sew some lace trim on the waist and on the bodice and insisted on making a veil. She loved lace. She had crafted the delicate material since she was a young girl, using a tatting needle and thread.

"That would be nice, Mama," Emma agreed, "but nothing too fancy. I only want a simple ceremony with just our family. I hope Jack's family can come, but they may not since those people rarely venture out of Hazelwood."

Jack had told Emma about his friendship with a woman named Clare. They had been best friends since they were fourteen, and their families were close. He had said everyone assumed that he would someday marry Clare. Emma understood that people in Hazelwood would never welcome her. That was fine with Emma, since she had no desire to ever visit Hazelwood. From what Jack had told her it was a dirty, grimy, sooty place. And besides, she thought, Jack always said, "I prefer to spend my time in Elliott." As it turned out, most of Jack's family did not come to the wedding. His father had been sick and was not able to get out of bed for several days. And his sisters wouldn't attend without him, except for the oldest one, Mary. She came with her husband and two stepchildren, whom Emma chatted with briefly at the small party at Mama and Papa's house after the ceremony. Emma was impressed with the children's good manners and asked how old they were. The young boy, named Mark, answered, "I'm seven, and my sister Jane is six. We go to St. Stephen's School." Jane shyly smiled at Emma. "Your dress is so pretty!" she commented politely. "I'm glad Mummy and Daddy brought us." Emma smiled. "Well, I'm glad that you came. I'll make sure that you both get a big piece of cake. My youngest brother Harry is eight years old. He can show you the backyard and the swing." Emma asked Harry to take their guests outside after they all ate cake. She recalled Jack telling her that the children's mother had died when they were very young, and that his sister Mary had stepped in to help care for them—then ended up marrying their father shortly afterward. Some children were not so fortunate. Emma had heard stories of young children being sent to live in orphanages after the death of one of their parents, if there were no relatives to take them in. She was glad the situation had worked out well for Jane and Mark. After the wedding celebration, once

Jack and Emma were alone, Jack said, "In the spring, I'll take you to meet my other sisters and my father." He had always spoken so highly of them, and he was obviously close to them. Emma was sure his family would miss him after seeing him nearly every day for twenty-six years. As the first several weeks of their marriage progressed, Emma thought about Jack's old girlfriend, the woman named Clare. Suspicions nagged at her. She tried to picture what Jack's old flame looked like. She couldn't help but worry a little when Jack would go to Hazelwood to visit his family. Since their wedding two months ago, he had only gone three times, and each time he had stayed for only an hour. She tried to convince herself she had no reason to be concerned.... Hopefully, Jack would never run into Clare during his trips to Hazelwood, and if he did, Emma hoped that Clare had the good sense to be angry with him...and never want to see him again. The poor girl must have a broken heart. Although Emma knew that Jack's blue eyes and handsome features would be hard to forget. She couldn't imagine anyone being able to stay angry with him forever, as she contentedly rubbed the gold marriage band on her left hand.

Still nestled in her bed, she closed her eyes, picturing Jack looking at her and leaning over to kiss her then pulling her to him. Oh, those shoulders, those hands...! Then she smiled and thought about how he unbuttoned her nightgown and slid a hand up her thigh. Oh my, those hands and that mouth...that tongue! The things that man did under the covers! She giggled to herself and felt her cheeks grow warm.

Their first time, making love, was on their wedding night. Jack had been gentle, trying not to hurt her. Two months later she had grown to relish every moment of their lovemaking and looked forward to their private times together. She had never imagined that having relations with a man could be so...*pleasurable*. Emma wondered if all married couples enjoyed each other in bed the way she and Jack did.

"I love him so much," she whispered to herself. "I can't get enough of him! He is my weakness…." And then she thought about that other woman, Clare, wondering if he was Clare's weakness also.

Every day when Emma was working side by side with Estelle at the bakery, she would tell her sister how happy she was. Estelle was starting to think seriously about marriage. She wondered if she and Frank Miller would be next. Estelle enjoyed teasing Emma but in truth she was thrilled her sister was so full of joy and happiness. She discussed with Aunt Louisa how fiercely Emma would blush whenever they talked about Jack. Her aunt would always chime in, saying, "I haven't seen such giddiness since your mother married your Papa. Before you girls can blink an eye, Emma here will be popping out babies just like your Mama did."

Emma pulled the blanket under her chin, wondering if she and Jack would have a baby right away or a year or two would pass before that happened. She had heard of several couples who had to wait years before conceiving. Looking at the clock, Emma jumped out of bed, dressed quickly, and fixed her hair. She softly sang the words of the song they had danced to on the day they had met…. *Beautiful dreamer, wake unto me, Starlight and dewdrops are waiting for thee…*

CHAPTER 14

March 1908—Jack

S pring came early, and Jack had so many plans he wanted to share with Emma. He had told her several times about the gardens that were his refuge in Hazelwood. "I'd like to till up a small patch in the backyard and plant some flowers and maybe some green beans." Emma commented, "Jack, your face lights up like a boy opening a present at Christmas whenever you talk about your plans for starting a garden." Jack leaned over and kissed her cheek.

First, he figured he better discuss his plans with Emma's father, who possessed a wealth of knowledge about the subject; he had years of experience growing vegetables. "I have to get some gardening tools," Jack announced. "Then I need to follow Henry's directions on how to plant seeds and when to water. My Dad always told me if something is worth doing…it's worth doing right."

Henry and Jack visited the small hardware store next to the tavern. Frank Miller, Estelle's beau, was employed there. He quickly helped Jack pick out some basic tools. Henry told him to get a certain type of digging shovel called a spade. Frank showed Jack a hoe and a rake and advised, "Just start getting your soil ready. Turn over the dirt and keep chopping at it so you have it nice and loose. And get rid of any weeds. You won't need seeds yet since you can't plant until there's no chance of frost. You have to wait at least another month."

Jack also bought some wood to replace rotting boards on the front steps. Henry and Frank told him that he'd need a saw, a hammer, and nails. Frank said, "Any man who has a house needs basic tools…just like the women have pots, pans, and cooking utensils in their kitchens." Frank Miller wasn't much older than Jack but seemed to have quite a bit of expertise in the hardware business. Jack had knowledge of plumbing tools, and tools that he had used for specific jobs in the steel mill. He recalled seeing his father fix minor issues around the house when he was growing up, but he had never paid much attention.

Having never watched Frank in his work environment, Jack admired how he chatted easily with the customers and how well he knew the merchandise. Frank was usually so quiet: the type of person who just blended into his surroundings. Jack knew Frank didn't drink much. Henry usually had to twist his arm to have a beer or a shot of whiskey.

Jack understood that some men just didn't require alcohol to boost their confidence and help them relax; sometimes he wished he was one of those types, but then he quickly realized how boring that would be. He truly enjoyed a noisy saloon and the easy conversations and camaraderie that existed in such places…probably one reason he got along so well with his father-in-law, the tavern owner.

As Frank finished ringing up a sale, Jack found it interesting to observe his rapport with customers who needed his help and clearly respected his knowledge of everything from roofing tar and paint to nails and chicken wire. Emma had always spoken highly of him and was sure he was perfect for her sister Estelle. In retrospect, Jack realized he didn't really know Frank that well. He made a mental note to speak to Frank more often at family gatherings, especially now that Jack had a house that always needed something repaired.

Jack and Henry thanked him for his help. They stopped in the tavern on the way home.

Fred, Jack's brother-in-law, was behind the bar, pouring two glasses of whiskey for a couple of neighborhood men who had stopped by after work. Henry was grateful Fred could take over for a short time so Henry could help Jack. Henry was pleased Jack had asked for his assistance, and Jack knew that Emma was glad her new husband got along so well with her father.

Of course, Jack accepted a shot of whiskey, and Henry refused his money. "We're family," Henry said. "Let's have one more; then you better get on home to my daughter. I hear she's cooking some beef stew for you tonight." Jack looked at Henry. "I'm a lucky man," he said, "and I thank you for raising such a wonderful woman." This warmed Henry's heart. He patted Jack on the back. "You just take good care of her is all I ask. She's always looking out for everyone else. That girl has a heart of gold."

Jack then hurried home to show Emma his purchases and explain everything he planned on doing. They talked over dinner, and Jack complimented her on the stew. He was delighted when Emma served him a big piece of apple pie for dessert. "Emma," he said, "I don't know what I did to deserve you." As Emma finished washing the dishes, he came up behind her and untied her apron. Then he leaned over and started kissing her neck, his hand unpinning her hair. "Jack, my darling," Emma said casually, "you must be exhausted after your long day at work, and then your shopping excursion at the hardware store...." Nothing like a little playful sarcasm. She turned and began to unbutton his shirt, then blushed as he started unbuttoning her blouse. He faked a yawn and said, "Yes, I thought we could go to bed early." She laughed, pointing at the window. "It's not even dark yet." Jack kissed her long and hard. "My dear Mrs. Quinn," he whispered, "it doesn't matter what time it is...." Their passion wasn't ruled by the sun rising or setting.

Later that evening, they lay sweaty and naked under the covers. Emma observed the moon through the window, rising in the night sky. She wasn't tired enough to sleep, and she found herself wondering if their lives were governed by the stars and the moon, more so than the sun. "The stars are always there," she commented, "though they seem to move in the heavens and are sometimes hidden by clouds. The moon can be full and bright or wane down to a sliver. You know it's there but it's not always the same…."

In the moonlight shining through the window Jack playfully started tracing circles and stars with his index finger: first on her stomach and then on each breast. "Here's a star," he whispered, "and this circle is the moon." He brought his head down until his lips met his fingers. Emma was aroused again. Although it wasn't ladylike, Emma confessed to him that she enjoyed their lovemaking. Jack assured her he understood, and he had known it for a while. "Emma," he said, "it's nothing to be ashamed of, we're married…and it's a wonderful thing. Not all couples are so lucky."

Sometimes Jack would have her undressed before they even reached the bedroom. One evening she even encouraged him to chase her around the parlor; they made love right there on a blanket on the floor. Mostly they relished snuggling under the warm covers in their bed, in their own little world, discovering each other's secret desires. Jack awakened sensations in her she never imagined existed. He would kiss her neck, her breasts, her stomach… His tongue would venture to those spots where she was already moist and yearning for him. Emma wanted all of him. And he wanted her. He was like a musician—and she was his instrument. He would play her…knowing what chords to touch and when and how long. She wanted him inside of her and pulled him down on top of her. They would move together, their rhythms becoming more intense, the sweat from Jack's forehead starting to drip on her. Sometimes they would manage to release together….

Jack had mastered his skills, thanks to being tutored by Nel. She had taught him well and made him believe that practice makes perfect. Emma mentioned once that she imagined he had some prior experience in the art of lovemaking, but never asked who he had been with before their wedding day. He never wanted to mention Nel…and never would. He figured a man was entitled to certain secrets.

Jack knew his wife probably wondered about him and the woman named Clare, his old girlfriend. Although Emma knew Clare came from a religious family, and she probably correctly assumed Clare had been raised to believe sexual relations were sinful when they took place outside of marriage.

Jack allowed Emma to believe it was natural for a man to know what to do, and he didn't object when she called him her "boudoir" teacher, explaining that was a French word for *bedroom*. She also called him "my beautiful dreamer…."

"Sleep now, my love," she sometimes whispered; and he would hear her hum softly: *"Beautiful dreamer, wake unto me…"*

He appreciated her honesty and that she was confident enough in their relationship to confide in him. One night she commented, "You seem more content than I've ever seen you, Jack. The last five months have been like a dream come true. I hope you don't feel guilty about your old girlfriend, about breaking her heart; I'm glad you're away from the smoke and soot of Hazelwood." The guilt Jack felt about Clare still saddened him, but he wasn't about to admit that to his bride. He was content, and he agreed with Emma: he was happy with their life together. And he was happy, too, that he had finally managed to get away from Hazelwood.

Mr. McGee and the plumbing crew finished up at the hospital in Allegheny and began working in an office building in downtown Pittsburgh. After work Jack usually had a drink or two with Jimmy Kennedy and Joe Sullivan. Sometimes he rode the streetcar with them to the South Side, and they would go to a bar not far from their neighborhood. On Fridays, Jimmy and Joe would say to Jack, "We're heading over to Allegheny tonight…Nel has been asking where you've been. She says she doesn't care if you're married, and don't forget about her!" Then they would laugh; but Jack told them, "No, I have everything I want and need right in my own house in Elliott." And he meant it, not realizing that the winds of contentment and satisfaction are fickle. They can change direction without warning.

CHAPTER 15

May 1908—Jack

Jack finally took Emma to meet his family on an unseasonably warm Sunday after they attended Mass in Elliott. Emma tried not to be nervous, but she told Jack she didn't feel well as they rode the streetcar across the bridge from the South Side. Jack noticed that the rocking and jerking as they entered Hazelwood certainly made Emma look pale. She clutched his hand tightly.

"It won't be that bad, dear," Jack said. "I know they will like you. My family wants me to be happy, and I've told them how great you are. You'll see." He was surprised she wasn't her normal confident self.

Emma had dressed carefully that morning, donning her favorite hat with the feather, one of her finer Sunday dresses—it was the same shade of blue as Jack's eyes—and a pair of new boots. She regretted her choice of footwear when she noticed her boots were covered with ash and soot soon after she and Jack stepped down from the streetcar, before they even reached the small porch of the Quinn's house.

They arrived at noon and entered the house through the front door just in time for lunch. Jack had told Florence and Dad last Sunday that he would bring Emma with him today. Florence had prepared a nice meal in honor of their visit—beef stew and biscuits. Dad was sitting at the table. He stood and smiled when they entered the kitchen.

"This must be Miss Emma, who we've heard so much about." He turned to his son. "My, oh, my, Jack. She's even prettier than I thought." He nodded in approval then turned back to Emma. "Have a seat, Emma," he said, as he pulled out a chair for her.

"Thank you, Mr. Quinn," Emma replied. "It's so nice to finally meet you."

Dad smiled and said, "Everyone calls me Sean. We're not fancy over here in Hazelwood." Jack motioned to his two sisters. "Emma, meet Florence and Margaret." The women nodded then merely stared at Emma. Frankly, Jack was embarrassed they weren't more welcoming. Although Jack knew the reason for the chill in the air. On his last visit he had asked Margaret how Clare was doing. "She's still angry and hurt," Margaret had told him. "She cries whenever I mention anything about you, Jackie. Now I know what a broken heart looks like. Poor Clare…you really hurt her, Jack!"

While Jack and Emma sat at the table with Jack's family, Jack sensed that Emma was feeling uncomfortable. His sisters talked to Jack and practically ignored his wife. Emma, who prided herself on being diplomatic, complimented Florence on the stew. "I just can never make it this good," she commented, "even though Jack has tried to remember everything you put in it." Florence's demeanor softened a bit. "Well, I just do what our mum used to do. A little of this and a little of that. Stir some flour with the broth in a separate bowl, and then add it slowly. That will thicken it without making it lumpy." Jack noticed Florence smile a little. Finally. And she grinned and blushed when Emma said, "Well, that's it! I have to gradually mix the flour into a bowl of broth, then add it to the stew." She nodded quietly to Jack's sister. "Well, thank you, Florence, for the tip."

They finished up with apple pie, served by Margaret. "Jackie," she noted, "this has been your favorite dessert since you were a little boy." She put a gigantic piece of pie in front of him, but she served Emma last.

Jack could see the effort Emma was making and noticed that she was not eating much. He figured she must still have been nervous. It was hard for anyone to eat, he knew, when their stomach was tied in knots….

After they finished the meal, Emma helped clear the table. Florence brought over a pot of tea. Emma seemed a little calmer, stirring sugar in her cup. She smiled at Jack. Dad poured some whiskey into two glasses. Then he and Jack pushed their chairs back from the table and talked about the mill and the fellas that worked there.

Emma asked Florence about the library in Hazelwood. She told the sisters that Jack had pointed out St. Stephen's church to her. "It's beautiful. Our church is nowhere near as nice."

"*Everyone* misses seeing Jackie at Mass and around town," Margaret replied. Emma smiled. "I'm sure they do." Jack had told Emma that Margaret was a close friend of the woman named Clare.

Jack thanked his sisters for the meal and told them they had to get back to Elliott so he could finish planting his garden. Then he whispered to Dad, "I have to rescue Emma from my sisters. Don't want them pecking her eyes out!" Dad stood and walked Emma and Jack to the door, where he told them to come back soon, and added that next time Mary and her family would stop by to see them. Emma had told him she thought little Jane and Mark were delightful children, and that she looked forward to getting better acquainted with them. Jack was grateful that at least Dad was being friendly to Emma.

When Jack and Emma were finally back on the streetcar, Jack leaned over and kissed his wife on the cheek. "Thank you. I know that was hard for you. My sisters can be awful stubborn, but eventually they'll warm up to you." He didn't realize that Emma could be stubborn too. She had already made up her mind that it would be a long time before she returned to Hazelwood. "Where are we going?" Emma said, looking out the window of the streetcar. "It doesn't look like we're headed for the bridge." Jack replied, "I wanted to surprise you, so you wouldn't think our trip today was totally awful. I made sure we got on the streetcar that goes to Oakland, where the college is. I want to show you something. I confess," he continued, "I don't really need to work on the garden today. That was just a good excuse to get you away from Florence and Margaret." He cleared his throat then resumed his explanation. "Emma, when you commented on how beautiful St. Stephen's is, I had an idea. I want you to see the new cathedral, St. Paul's, over in Oakland. It's supposed to be the most spectacular church in western Pennsylvania. Mr. McGee was telling us that the old St. Paul's church used to be on Grant Street downtown. Well, Henry Clay Frick, a partner of Andrew Carnegie's, decided that he wanted the land. So, I guess he convinced the bishop to sell it to him. He then sold them property in Oakland to build a new church."

He paused. "The bishop must have a ton of money," he remarked. "Or maybe Frick and Carnegie made a large donation to the Church and the diocese said, 'Here, Bishop, build yourself the church of your dreams.' And the bishop replied, 'Mr. Carnegie showed me a picture of this cathedral in Germany that looks like a castle. It doesn't matter if the poor people in my city are living in shanties and barely have enough to eat. I want to say Mass in a castle.' So of course, the bishop gets his damn castle."

Jack quietly continued his rant: "You know, Emma, people with bags of money think they can buy their way into Heaven. Hefty donations ease their consciences and lighten their penance when they go to confession. They say, 'Here, Father, let's make a deal. I'll give you fifty thousand dollars and you can kindly erase this long list of the sins I committed against my fellow man…Yes, Father? Oh, my penance? Sure, I can say an Our Father and a Hail Mary on my way to the office, where I go to count my money. Thank you, Father. And yes, Father, I won't give my workers a raise or better working conditions…but I will give you money for some beautiful stained glass windows, wood carvings, and marble floors for your castle—oh, excuse me, I mean your church. Enjoy yourself, Father.' And then off they go without a care in the world. Then the bishop tells all his priests, 'Keep telling that poor old lady she's a sinner, and that she'd better give you some nickels to help save her soul.' *And* make her kneel on the hard floor and ask God for mercy!"

"And the priests fall in line," Jack continued, "and tell the children and their hardworking parents to put lots of pennies, nickels, and dimes in that collection basket so the priests can have cake and the bishop can drink brandy and enjoy roast beef for supper. It doesn't matter if the poor family down the street can't buy milk or new shoes for the children." Jack wasn't done yet. Leaning close to Emma's ear, Jack whispered: "And then there's the priest who trots off to visit the local convent, where he warms a few beds on chilly nights."

Emma was blushing as she listened to Jack's stories. Still, he quietly continued: "An old man in O'Shea's bar told me about the cemetery in Ireland that sits behind a convent where they buried babies that had been fathered by priests. Lies and sins carried to the grave! Those priests should burn in Hell, especially the ones who forced themselves on children—not just innocent girls but even young boys too. They trick them, lie to them, bribe them. In the name of Jesus! All for their own pleasure. Sick bastards."

"Late at night in the bars, some of those stories come out. The guilt and shame destroy the people who have been preyed upon…they need to tell what happened to them. Now I understand why Mum and Dad said my sisters and I should never be alone with a priest. Better to be safe than sorry."

"Every Sunday we hear the same rules," he went on. "No meat on Fridays. Do your penance. Examine your conscience. It's been pounded into the heads of children since they could talk. Say prayers, be good, go to church. Then maybe, just maybe…you can go to Heaven."

"Who knows? Maybe Saint Peter has his hand out, asking for a bag of money. Admission through Heaven's golden gates isn't free, he tells the poor beggar man. Sorry, but too bad. Saint Peter says your name isn't on the list of donations. Off you go! Maybe to purgatory, if you're lucky. And, of course, there's no charge to enter Hell."

"If you sin and don't ask for forgiveness and mercy, guess where you're going? Yes, of course you know. You're meeting the devil…*and* your soul is banished to the fires of Hell. You can shovel coal, have your skin melted right off your bones, and breathe soot for eternity. Burn with all the other miserable, bloody souls!"

Having a couple of drinks with Dad was all Jack needed to start a tirade against the mill owners, the factory owners, the railroad magnates, the bishop, priests, and anyone else with power. Every day Jack stood witness to the social injustices across the city, and he blamed the people in positions of authority; people he did not trust. He didn't care if he was being irreverent. He pulled out his silver flask and took a big sip, wondering why his mouth was so dry. But he was satisfied that Emma had let him ramble on so long, and that she didn't try to correct him or argue with him. Luckily there was no one sitting close to them, as he would not have wanted to embarrass his wife. After Jack had finished, they both stared out the window and savored the silence. Then, following a few minutes of quiet reflection, Jack glanced at Emma. He smiled then caressed her hand and brought it to his lips. "Thanks for listening," he said.

Finally, as they neared their stop, Jack grew excited. "I want to see the expression on your face when you see this new church."

Emma was naturally curious. She was filled with anticipation. "That would be wonderful," she replied. "I read an article in the newspaper about St. Paul's Cathedral when it was completed last year. It's supposed to be a perfect example of Gothic Revival architecture, which is probably why it looks like a castle. And I read that Andrew Carnegie paid for the pipe organ. Probably with quite a few bags of money, just like you said," she added with a giggle.

Jack winked at Emma and patted her knee in appreciation. He was glad she did not chastise him for his disrespectful, sacrilegious sense of humor.

The streetcar stopped, letting them off right in front of the huge church. They both stood and stared at the stone walls, the high sloping roofs, and the sharp spires that pointed up to the heavens. Then Jack took Emma's hand and they entered through one of the heavy wooden doors. Jack removed his hat, as was the custom for men, whether they were religious or not.

Jack could see that Emma was in awe as she gazed wide-eyed at the inside of the massive structure. They each dipped two fingers in the holy water font and made the sign of the cross. Then they genuflected on their right knee before sitting on a pew near the back of the grand church. There had to be at least fifty rows of pews on each side of the main aisle. They sat there speechless, trying to absorb the enormous scale of the building.

The couple admired the marble flooring, the wood paneling, the statues, the arches and carvings. They both pointed at the stained-glass windows, admiring the multitude of colors and the skills and talent needed to produce works of art so beautiful. Jack spotted the massive pipe organ. He whispered to Emma, "There's Carnegie's 'penance' organ. The man was forgiven a multitude of sins with that donation." They could only imagine the sounds such a grand organ might produce. Right then the church was so quiet they could hear a pin drop.

"Jack," Emma whispered, "this is the most beautiful place I have ever seen."

She squeezed Jack's hand and thanked him for bringing her to see the grand cathedral. On their way out, Jack saw a paper tacked on the wooden door. They stopped to read the handwritten message some poor soul had copied from the Bible. Emma read aloud:

"The GOD who made the world and everything in it, being LORD of heaven and earth, DOES NOT LIVE IN TEMPLES MADE BY MAN. Acts 17:24"

Jack slyly remarked, "Well, well, it looks like there are other disgruntled worshippers among us!"

On their way back to Elliott Jack noticed that Emma's cheeks had a little more color than earlier in the day. She said she felt better, and she kept telling him that she loved his surprise. "I can't wait to go to the library and look for a book on Gothic Revival architecture," she remarked. Jack knew she would do it too. He loved her curiosity and her thirst for knowledge. She inspired him to want to learn about everything too....

The next day when Jack returned home, he entered a quiet house. Usually Emma was in the kitchen at that time, preparing supper. But no pots and pans were on the stove, and no plates on the table. *That's odd,* he thought. "Emma...Mrs. Quinn!" he called out. No answer. Jack ate a piece of bread— he was famished—then poured a bit of whiskey, wondering where his wife was. He figured she'd be there soon as he went out to check his garden. He stood admiring the six-foot-square piece of ground he had managed to turn into the beginnings of a garden. *Well,* he thought, *it's a start.*

After several minutes he had drained his glass. Then he returned to the kitchen just as Emma was coming in through the front door. As soon as she saw her husband she went over and slid her arms around him then laid her head on his shoulder.

He kissed the top of her head and asked where she had been. "It's a long story," she replied. "You better have a seat." He could see Emma was trembling. Nonetheless she had a slight grin on her face. So, he sat, as instructed, and waited attentively.

Emma proceeded to tell him that she had felt ill all morning...she had even had to vomit before she went to the bakery. She said the same thing had been happening every day for a while now; but she had always felt better by the afternoon, so she hadn't said anything to anyone. Finally, this morning Aunt Louisa told her to stop working and to go see her mother. Then Aunt Louisa told Estelle, "Go with her, Estelle, and tell your mama to take her to see that old doctor." Emma continued, "Mama and Dr. Meyers kept asking me questions, and Dr. Meyers was listening to my heartbeat with his stethoscope…and then he was listening to my stomach. Finally, Jack, guess what he told me?" She took a deep breath and paused.

Jack noticed Emma's face was flushed and that she had a huge smile on her face. "Well, go on," he said. "What did he tell you?"

"I'm going to have a baby. Jack, you're going to be a father!" She put both hands on her stomach and started to laugh. "I can't believe it. I'm going to be a mother!"

Jack was stunned. When he thought about it later, he realized he shouldn't have been surprised. As much time as they had been spending in the bedroom—and on a blanket in the parlor—he supposed it was bound to happen sooner or later.

He walked over to Emma and embraced her, his mouth searching for her lips. They kissed then kissed some more, even as she pulled his hand and led him up the stairs. They ended up shedding their clothes and falling onto the bed. Jack kept kissing her stomach…along with the rest of her body. "Mrs. Quinn," he remarked, "I certainly like how you celebrate!"

Eventually they came back downstairs, realizing they needed to eat dinner. Jack felt a contented happiness, but they had both worked up an appetite and were starving.

They knew their life was about to change. Emma said she had helped care for Monnie and Harry when they were babies. Jack admitted that he knew nothing about babies and children—but he was willing to learn. Jack poured a whiskey after they ate chicken and noodles that Emma had brought with her from Mama's house. He thought about Dad and his father-in-law, Henry. He figured they were both good fathers, he could learn from their example. He knew he had learned how to be a good husband by watching Mum and Dad, and more recently by observing the relationship between Henry and Margaret.

Then Jack thought about Mum, and how she would be pleased with him. Mum would have liked Emma…even though she wasn't Irish. And she would have been excited to be a grandmother. His poor mother had been denied so much. Jack always knew that life wasn't fair.

He still dreamed about his big brick house surrounded by gardens. It was a vision he kept in his sights. Someday it would happen, he thought, as he pictured himself and Emma—and now a child—standing among the fruit trees. He wondered if the baby would be a boy or a girl. Would he have a son…or a daughter?

He smiled contentedly. As usual, he pushed away any thoughts of Clare, still feeling guilty. He hoped one day Clare would forgive him, and maybe even be happy for him.

CHAPTER 16

October 1908—Emma

After enduring a sweltering summer, Emma was glad the air was growing cooler. Carrying a baby within her had caused her to gain weight: she was tiring easily. On hot days her feet and ankles swelled. At night she liked to sleep with the window wide open, allowing a refreshing breeze to blow through the bedroom. Dr. Meyers had warned her to rest as much as possible. "You don't want that baby coming early. Infants are always healthier if they're full-term," he told her.

For several months Emma had felt the baby moving inside her, but for the last week or so there hadn't been much movement. This worried her. But Dr. Meyers said, "Nothing to be concerned about. The little one is running out of room to grow. Just getting too big to move around."

And she replied, "And I'm getting too big to move around too." She was starting to get impatient and wanted it all to be over. She knew a little about what to expect, remembering when her youngest brother Harry was born. Mama had recovered quickly. But the whole process still unnerved Emma.

She sensed that Jack was getting nervous also, not really knowing much about childbirth. He seemed to be drinking more whiskey than usual. She knew he missed their lovemaking. One evening when Jack had turned amorous, snuggling against her when they were together in bed, Emma had moved quietly away from him. "I guess this is what they mean when someone says the honeymoon is over," she commented jokingly. Jack saw no humor in that statement, probably because she and Jack had not had relations for two months; they had decided to forgo physical intimacy for the safety of the baby.

Emma couldn't help but think how men have it easy compared to what a woman had to endure. She tried not to be bossy or impatient with Jack, but sometimes just couldn't help it. After all, this was his fault…at least partially.

"Dr. Meyers says that when I start having labor pains, Jack, you'll need to go get Mama, Estelle, and Aunt Louisa. He said they should stay with me while I'm in labor. Then he'll come over here for the birth." She was glad Dr. Meyers' office was in his house, and that he lived only two streets away.

Emma knew there was nothing to do but wait. Nature couldn't be hurried, or so they said.

The following week Emma still was walking to the bakery every morning, always wanting to keep busy for a couple of hours. Plus, she enjoyed the company of her aunts and her sister. When she had finished helping at the bakery, she would walk to Mama's to eat lunch, since Mama was alone most of the day, given that Monnie, Eddie, and Harry were in school. Emma had told Jack that she couldn't sit around the house all day, and he knew better than to argue with her. Emma was frustrated that she had not been able to go to the library or attend any community meetings for the past several months. Dr. Meyers had warned her to stay off the streetcars and not even to ride in a carriage or wagon. She missed writing her articles for the newspaper. But Mr. Harrison, the editor, was quite understanding. "After all," he had told her, "a married woman expecting a child needs to stay home." Emma was annoyed by Mr. Harrison's attitude. She thought he wasn't so progressive after all.

One dreary morning as they walked to the bakery, she asked Estelle, "Why do men always think they know what's best for women?" Not waiting for her sister's answer, she continued: "I told Jack when we got married that he had better never think he can boss me around or tell me what I can and cannot do. I won't stand for it!" Even Estelle didn't want to make Emma more irritable than she already was. She just listened and nodded.

The following morning Emma was rolling out dough for pie crusts after pounding the balls of dough with her fists. She found the process quite relaxing. Suddenly she felt a sharp pain that seemed to encircle her, arcing across her stomach then curving around her back. She took a deep breath then gripped the edge of the worktable with both hands. The pain lasted for only a minute, but it made her double over as she squeezed her eyes shut. She knew this was the beginning.

Emma called for Aunt Louisa, who took one look at her niece's face. "Sweet Jesus, Emma," she said, "you look like a mule just kicked you!" She turned to Estelle. "Get her home to bed, and then run up to fetch your Mama. I'll stop by Dr. Meyers' office to tell him."

Within an hour Mama was at Emma's bedside, propping pillows behind her daughter's back and helping Emma sit up every time another episode of pain swept over her. The pains were coming every twenty minutes or so and were becoming more and more excruciating.

The doctor had stopped by and needed to examine her. The examination was embarrassing, but the kindly doctor reminded her, "I've been doing this for a long time, Emma; I've delivered hundreds of babies. You don't need to feel ashamed. Try to relax." He said it would be hours before the baby would arrive, and that he would return in the evening.

When Jack came home from work, he was greeted by a house full of activity. Estelle was scurrying about, washing sheets and clothes, hanging everything on the clothesline in the backyard. Mama was sitting in the bedroom with Emma. Aunt Louisa was cooking and washing dishes in the kitchen. Monnie had come down after school and was drying dishes for her aunt. Jack gave Emma a quick kiss before being shooed out of the house by the women. He said he'd be with Henry and Fred at the tavern as they waved him away.

The long day turned into night. Dr. Meyers came to the house at nine that evening. After examining Emma, he declared that it would still be a few more hours; he suggested that the three women try to get some rest. He sat in the bedroom with a book and the newspaper, trying to read in between her contractions. With his pocket watch in his hand, he timed the duration of each contraction and the amount of time between them. Estelle stretched out on the sofa in the parlor while Mama and Aunt Louisa rested in the other bedroom.

Emma was exhausted and sweating; but the pains were relentless and gaining in intensity. She alternated between moaning and screaming in agony. She just wanted to give up.

She was beyond the point of being embarrassed or even caring about how she looked or sounded. She realized that there was no dignity in childbirth. She just wanted it to be over.

Finally, around two in the morning, she was gripping Mama's hand and Aunt Louisa's also. Estelle brought in more hot water and towels. Dr. Meyers began urging Emma to push.

She felt as if she didn't have an ounce of strength left, and the old doctor kept telling her to breathe and push. "Come on, Emma, you're almost there. You want to meet your beautiful baby. Come on now. One more big push. Give it all you have!" And with that, Emma finally pushed that baby out into the world. Dr. Meyers smiled wearily. "You have a healthy little girl," he announced. "Congratulations, Emma." He gently wrapped the screaming infant in a towel then placed her in Emma's arms. Mama, Estelle, and Aunt Louisa were all crying tears of joy, relief, and exhaustion. Estelle was white as a sheet. She began shaking and grinning, practically giddy. "Emma, you did it, you did it!" she cried.

Emma was trembling and crying too, tired and joyous after the trauma to her body and twenty hours of labor. The doctor washed the baby in a basin of warm water then wrapped her in a small clean blanket and handed her to Mama to hold while he finished tending to Emma. He told her she would experience some bleeding for several days, maybe a week, and to stay in bed. At this point, Emma was just happy that the birth was over.

Dr. Meyers then took the baby from Mama and placed her on Emma's chest. "Now Emma," he said, "this baby is going to be hungry soon. It might be uncomfortable for a few days, trying to get her to latch on and eat. Just be patient and keep urging her to nurse. I'm sure you'll do fine. Your mother here will no doubt be able to give you more advice. She has some experience, what with having gone through this seven times." He chuckled quietly to himself. "I'll stop by tomorrow afternoon to check on you." With that said, the elderly doctor gathered his jacket, his bag, his book, and his hat. Then he said good-bye to the ladies and headed home in the darkness. Emma kept smiling and gazing at her baby daughter, gently stroking her cheek. She wished Jack was there, but knew he was spending the night at Papa's house. An hour later, as the first rays of morning sunshine filtered into the room, Estelle ran to fetch Jack and Papa and tell them the news. Jack had slept on the Moreau's sofa in their parlor. He was anxious to see Emma and raced home. Breathless, Jack appeared in the doorway of their bedroom and Emma greeted him with a beaming smile. He quietly walked over and sat on the edge of the bed. "Thank God, you're all right." He gently pushed some stray hairs from her forehead then leaned over and kissed her cheek. "I was worried. But your father kept assuring me everything would be fine." He smiled at her then looked down at the baby. He leaned over and kissed the top of his daughter's head. "What are we going to name her?" he asked. He liked the name Ann, after his mother; but Emma preferred something a little more modern: *Dorothy*, a name that had been popular ever since the publication of *The Wonderful Wizard of*

Oz a few years earlier. It was one of Emma's favorite books, a fanciful story about a girl named Dorothy Gale. Ever since reading it, Emma had just loved the name Dorothy. She told Jack their daughter's middle name should be Margaret, after Mama.

"After all, Jack," she explained, "this child has your last name…so I should get to pick the other names." So, there it was. Emma and Jack Quinn's baby girl was named Dorothy Margaret Quinn.

CHAPTER 17

October 1908—Jack

After Jack met his newborn daughter, he had to catch the streetcar to get to his job at the college in Oakland. He told Emma he was excited to tell Mr. McGee and his friends, Joe Sullivan and Jimmy Kennedy, the news.

Jack was grateful that Emma had her mother, aunts, and sister to take care of her. Even Monnie would be a big help, although she was only twelve, almost thirteen. After work, he rode the streetcar with Joe and Jimmy to the South Side, where the three friends drank shots at three different bars. His friends assured him that it was perfectly all right to celebrate the birth of his daughter. "In fact, it's more than all right, it's expected," Joe told him.

Jimmy kept buying rounds of whiskey for the three men and toasting the happy occasion. "Here's to Jack Quinn, to him becoming a father. A special day for every Irishman! May your child have as many blessings as there are shamrocks in Ireland. Now, drink up tonight, boys, for no one is promised a tomorrow!"

And then Joe Sullivan patted Jack's shoulder and said, "We have a surprise for you. You'll never guess who works here now." Startled, Jack looked up as a hand started to massage the back of his neck.

Nel leaned over and kissed Jack right on the mouth. "Well, if it isn't my Charmin' Jack!" she said. She pulled a chair close to Jack. "I have to get reacquainted with my old heartthrob here. It just might be a lucky day for both of us!"

Jimmy bought more whiskey for everyone. Nel drank one with her boys. She laughed at the jokes and rubbed Jack's leg under the table, just like old times.

It had been well over a year since Jack had enjoyed himself this much… celebrating with his friends. It had been even longer since he had consumed this much whiskey. Two more women joined the group, and the whiskey and laughter continued flowing easily. Jimmy and Joe were led away to dance; later Jack spied them heading up the stairs of the tavern, their two ladies leading the way.

Jack asked Nel how she had ended up on the South Side. "Well, I didn't want to get arrested," she told Jack, "and the cops kept raiding our establishment in Allegheny. So now I get a change of scenery. It keeps things interesting. I like the Irish—and there seems to be plenty of them on this side of town!"

Then she moved closer and whispered in his ear, "Jack, you were always my favorite. I've missed you!" She slowly kissed his neck and rubbed his leg. Heat rose within him. He knew it would be wrong, but the more he drank, the more he felt that maybe some female attention that night would be nice. He loved Emma but missed the good times that they used to enjoy in the bedroom. Their relationship had become so strained…these days he always felt so tense. Maybe some time with Nel might help him relax. Just what the doctor ordered, he thought to himself.

Nel said, "You know it doesn't matter to me if you're married. We're old friends…I just want to put a smile back on that handsome face."

Jack could smell Nel's perfume as those red lips came near and brushed against his. Teasing him, tempting him. Her brown eyes danced with merriment as his fingers lightly traced the top of her bodice and touched her warm skin. He leaned in and kissed her mouth hungrily, tasting her tongue and wanting more. They rose from the table; she steadied him as he stumbled, then she pulled him toward the stairs. "Come on, Jack," she said, "we have some catching up to do."

～ello～

Jack boarded the streetcar for home at midnight. Fifteen minutes later he was back in Elliott, walking into a quiet house. He peeked in the bedroom and saw Emma sleeping. The newborn was snuggled against her. Emma's mother was snoring softly in the other bedroom.

Jack quietly went back downstairs, drank a glass of water and reclined on the sofa. He was exhausted and fell asleep instantly. In the early morning light Jack washed quickly and found a change of clothes in a pile of clean folded laundry. He spotted some cinnamon buns from the bakery on the counter that smelled heavenly. He ate one of the buns then put a second bun on a plate for Emma. He poured a glass of milk for Emma and made tea for himself. He drank his tea quickly as he stared out the window at his small scraggly garden. He noticed that the weeds were invading, multiplying daily. Gardens needed constant attention. Henry had warned him. A few yellow marigolds were still in bloom as there had not yet been a frost. He went outside and cut six marigolds across the stems; then he brought them inside and placed them in a glass of water.

Carrying a tray on which he had placed the marigolds, the plate with the cinnamon bun, and Emma's glass of milk, Jack climbed the stairs. He saw Emma's eyes opening as he quietly entered the room. He placed her breakfast on the table next to the bed. "How are you feeling?" he asked, sitting down on the edge of the bed. "Totally and completely exhausted," Emma said. She smiled down at the infant, who was starting to stir. "Our baby Dorothy thankfully let me sleep some during the night." She took a bite of the cinnamon bun and washed it down with some milk. "Thank you, dear—and the flowers are pretty."

Jack said, "I'm looking forward to Sunday. I'll get to spend the entire day with both of you. I'm so glad your family can help take care of you and our daughter." He leaned over and kissed Emma's cheek. "Well, I'm off to work. I'll see you tonight." He smiled and turned, looking forward to a day at a job he enjoyed, making money to take care of his family.

On the streetcar his mind wandered as he thought about Nel. How he had loved the excitement of last night! He certainly didn't love Nel, but he loved the things she did, and the way she made him feel. He figured nobody got hurt…and Emma didn't need to know. He wrestled with his conscience. He had learned long ago to rationalize his behavior and compartmentalize the different aspects of his life. There were thoughts of Clare, Nel, and of course, Emma and the baby. He chuckled as he placed them according to location. Hazelwood, South Side, and Elliott. Different parts of the city, different parts of his heart. *A divided heart.* The phrase came to him suddenly.

He felt guilty; but this was his reality. How does a man give himself entirely to one woman? He knew his dad and Emma's father had done just that, but he didn't know if he was capable of such limited devotion. Or, rather, such *limited existence*, as he had called it. Emma and Jack had recited marriage vows on their wedding day. Vows Jack had already broken. He did honor Emma and cherish her; but he couldn't be faithful. He loved her and would provide for her; but he couldn't be loyal physically. He never even wanted to speak of his dishonesty. Trying to explain it to himself, he often thought that he was afraid of not being loved, of being abandoned, of being totally alone. In case one woman pushed him away or left him, there would always be another one who wanted him.

He remembered how it felt to be abandoned when Mum died. He had to protect himself. Knowing that it sounded selfish made him uneasy, but he couldn't help it.

Jack didn't go to confession anymore, reasoning that no priest could possibly understand his dilemma. Old Father Donnelly would chastise him and talk about the sins of the flesh and the evils that lie in a whiskey bottle. "Do your penance, young man," he would have said, "and go home to your wife. If you don't and want to dance with the devil, then you surely will suffer the flames of Hell." Jack *knew* that's what he would say.

Not being sure what he believed in anymore, he had stopped going to Mass when Emma could no longer attend, and now he didn't want to ever go back. If he confessed his sins to Father Ryan who had married them at St. Martin's, he knew the priest would always look at him with judgmental eyes. Damning eyes.

Even a priest doesn't forget what he hears in the confessional. Jack didn't want anyone knowing his business and his sins. *They all speak of forgiveness,* he thought. *But priests are men.* Men with ears that listened and remembered. All men were flawed, he believed. Flawed and imperfect.

And they say God forgives!

So, Jack decided he would just have to talk to God, and in the end maybe God would understand. Only God would know Jack Quinn's secrets… his sins of the heart.

Maybe God would understand why his heart was divided.

He never intended to hurt anyone. Nel didn't care, and what Emma didn't know wouldn't hurt her. Emma knew Clare was part of his past…but Emma didn't need to know anything about Nel, he reasoned.

The day after his daughter was born, Jack rode the streetcar to Hazelwood after leaving the job. He had to tell Dad and his sisters the news about the baby. He still didn't care for the name Dorothy, but there wasn't anything he could do about it. He didn't want to argue with Emma, so he kept his mouth shut.

Emma had shown him how to hold the infant, and he could hold her if she was wrapped securely in a blanket. It seemed as if she was always hungry, and Jack marveled at what the female body was capable of. He knew it would probably be months before Emma would want to have intimate relations with him. This saddened him, but he admired his wife's strength and her devotion to their child.

He went to the South Side at least once a week, drinking with Jimmy and Joe, and visiting with Nel. Jack hungered for her—and she was willing and able to satisfy his desires. He always made sure Emma got most of his paycheck, and Emma didn't ask questions when he came home late. She respected the fact that he liked to socialize with his friends, not knowing that one of those friends was a lady named Nel.

Jack stepped off the streetcar in Hazelwood, looking forward to a meal with Dad and his sisters. It was such a pleasant fall afternoon that he wanted to walk up the hill to the gardens.

He crossed Second Avenue and then Chatsworth Avenue, looking down the street toward Clare's house. He was glad Clare's brother Joe was nowhere to be seen. He thought he'd hate to have to waste energy dealing with that damn loud-mouthed fool again. It had been over a year since Jack had left him crumpled in the street. He figured that pathetic excuse for a man probably held a grudge.

Walking up the hill, he breathed in the sooty air that lingered over the entire area. Black puffs of smoke spewed from the smokestacks even on Sundays now. He was happy he lived over in Elliott, where the air was a little better than next to the mills and that dirty river.

As Jack reached the outer row of hedges that surrounded the gardens, he noticed that the bushes and flower beds were looking neglected and overgrown. As he gazed at the weeds, he mused that perhaps the old caretaker was slowing down and not able to keep up with his duties.

There had not yet been a frost at night, so quite a few hydrangea plants were still in bloom. He liked the full white blossoms on the taller hydrangea bushes and the rows of smaller plants with blue flowers. He knew he had a lot to learn about plants, flowers, and gardening. Someday he would ask Emma to bring him a book from the library that would explain how to create a garden like this.

He spotted an area covered with daisies and remembered how much Clare had loved the pure white flowers. Memories. Every time he had picked one and handed it to her, she would laugh as she pulled the petals off one be one, saying, "He loves me, he loves me not…."

Somehow, she always made the last petal end with *he loves me*. They would both laugh as she threw the stem at him. Then he would chase her to the willow tree. They would settle on the ground under the branches, where he would kiss her until they couldn't breathe.

The weeping willow still stood as majestic as ever. Its long sweeping branches whispered to him as he stared at it: *Don't forget, don't forget….*

So many memories surrounded him, no matter which direction he looked. He stopped at the edge of the garden that bordered the woods, where clumps of purple violets still grew wild beneath the tall trees. Nobody ever had to tend to them, yet they still thrived.

He strolled past a bed of chrysanthemums: reds, oranges, and yellows, colors he had associated with the bright flames in the steel mills. The hues brought warmth to the cool autumn days as the gardens prepared for the annual winter slumber.

Some of the towering shade trees were already starting to shed their leaves…they floated down and settled around his shoes. He turned and walked down the hill, past the small park where he had sat on the bench with

Clare, the last time he saw her. He remembered how angry she had been. Her red face. The tears. The slap. He couldn't blame her.

There was a slight chill in the air as he headed for Dad's house.

Dad and his sisters were always happy to see him. Jack shared the good news about baby Dorothy with them. "Aye, now for sure…this calls for a celebration," said Dad as he pulled out the whiskey bottle and set it on the table. "And I've been saving these cigars just for this day," he added, pulling two from the cupboard.

So, Jack and his father lit the cigars and smoked as they sipped from their glasses. Florence glanced at them both. "Look at you two," she commented. "You must have changed your last name to *Mellon* or *Carnegie*, puffing away like millionaires do." Margaret didn't bother saying anything to Jack about the baby, which didn't surprise him, since she was such good friends with Clare.

Florence handed Jack a package wrapped with paper and string. "This is from Mary, for the baby. She worked on it for the last two months since we knew the baby was expected in October. She knitted a blanket and a little hat and told me she used white yarn for when you have the baby baptized."

"Tell Mary thank you," Jack replied. "We're having her baptized next Sunday. Emma wanted to wait until she felt stronger so she could be there too. Not like the old days, Dad, when fathers took their babies to church shortly after birth." Dad nodded, remembering.

Much to Jack's surprise, Florence said she liked the name Dorothy. Margaret actually looked up from her sewing when Jack said, "Her full name is Dorothy Margaret Quinn. Margaret is Emma's mother's name. If we ever have another baby girl, I'll insist we name her Ann, after Mum." Then Jack added: "Sometimes it's best to let Emma have her way. It's easier than arguing about it."

Dad agreed. "There's not a woman anywhere that is going to go along with everything her husband wants. Marriage can be wonderful, but it isn't for everybody. I was a lucky man to find your mother. Aye, lucky, indeed."

CHAPTER 18

January 1915—Emma

Emma held the framed photograph in her hand, staring at the happy young couple on their wedding day. She sighed. It was hard to believe seven years had passed. She looked in the mirror in their bedroom, trying to smile like she had smiled in the photograph, back when she had been full of hopes and dreams.

Now that smile was gone.

Sadness, disappointment, frustration, and grief…Emma felt closed off from the world by her emotions. She had always been confident, perhaps even ambitious. Now she could barely get through the day without a tear streaming down her cheek.

She was tired. Tired of having to be strong for everyone around her. The last six months had been so very difficult.

Her only joy these days was seeing the smiles on her children's faces. Dorothy was now six: a darling, sweet little girl, always wanting to help with Nan, age three, and Johnny, almost a year old. Dorothy was Emma's little helper, always willing to entertain Nan and Johnny. Nan was headstrong and stubborn—and prone to temper tantrums. She was a more difficult child than Dorothy had been. Emma hoped she would soon grow out of this stage. Johnny was sweet and even-tempered and a good sleeper, as Dorothy had been.

Emma was grateful all three children were bright-eyed, strong, and healthy.

Mama had told her to nurse each child for as long as possible so as not to get pregnant again so soon after giving birth. Emma thought that advice obviously wasn't infallible. Jack was always so charming when he wanted to get close under the covers. Kissing her neck, gently rubbing her back, caressing her thighs. Emma couldn't resist the temptation. He was still her weakness. He knew how to make her relax and forget her troubles.

Having to care for three small children was tiring, and Emma soon realized she needed to get out of the house every day for at least an hour. A little fresh air and sunshine always improved her spirits. Often, she would bundle up the little ones and walk to the bakery to see her aunts. She smiled, watching Dorothy and Nan play in the snow. Johnny was a happy baby and would squeal with laughter, watching his sisters. Aunt Louisa always had cookies waiting for the girls. Emma's sister Monnie worked at the bakery in the mornings, having replaced Emma when Dorothy was born. Monnie was almost twenty years old now, a hard worker who everyone seemed to depend on. After her shift at the bakery, Monnie usually stopped at Emma's house in the afternoon to help Emma with the washing, or just to sit and talk.

Emma missed the days of working with Estelle and her aunts, the adult conversation, laughing, sharing stories. Frank Miller had finally proposed to Estelle; that was three years ago. Even after she married Frank, Estelle continued visiting with Emma, Dorothy, and Nan in the afternoons…until last year, when Estelle had a baby. Ever since then Emma had missed her sister, her best friend. Estelle rarely left her house, content to be a doting wife and mother consumed by her domestic duties. After Estelle gave birth she suffered from extreme sadness and had a hard time adjusting to caring for her fussy baby. The past few months had been a little easier for her since little Frankie has grown bigger and had adjusted to a regular eating and sleeping schedule.

Emma was glad Estelle and Frank were happy; they seemed to have a good marriage. Estelle never complained. Frank wasn't a drinker, nor was he a regular customer at the tavern, as he was always anxious to get home from the hardware store to his little son and his wife.

Since they were children, Estelle had always been Emma's best friend. But now they were both so busy with houses, husbands, and children. Endless cooking, cleaning, washing, and sewing. The carefree days of their youth were far behind them. Emma reminisced about all the walks to the Overlook and the long hours reading books from the library. *"You don't miss things until they're gone,"* people had always told her. Now she often thought that was true.

Emma gazed at herself in the bedroom mirror. She was thirty years old. She looked a little heavier than she had been in the wedding photograph. She wondered whether she would ever shed some of the weight she had put on when she had been pregnant with Johnny. Going through childbirth three times in seven years had taken a toll on her body.

Then her eyes glanced over at her typewriter, where it sat on a wooden table in the corner of the bedroom, covered with a cloth to keep dust off the keys. She remembered how she had saved for two years…she had been so proud to purchase an actual typewriter. She missed writing articles for the *Pittsburgh Press* and hoped to one day start attending meetings and typing reports again. She mused aloud, "I can't take three children with me to town meetings, or to talks on politics and women's rights at the library…."

Emma had not visited the library in almost a year, since before Johnny was born. She still read every article in the daily paper Papa dropped off on his way home from the tavern. That was her lifeline to the outside world.

Papa would always stop by and chat for a few minutes. Dorothy and Nan would both run to him, hugging him tightly as he knelt to their level wrapping his arms around them. Johnny would clap and giggle when Papa sat with him on the living room sofa and bounced him on his knee. Then Papa would have to hurry home, since he didn't like leaving Mama alone for too long. Emma missed the long talks with Papa she had enjoyed in the evenings before she married. He had encouraged her to be curious, to debate any topic. "Emma," he would tell her, "don't ever be afraid to speak your mind." She missed the intellectual stimulation their conversations had provided. Her brother Albert had moved to Massachusetts two years ago. The company he worked for had opened an office in Boston and had asked Albert to manage the accounting department. He found that being selected as a manager was an honor and would help advance his career. She had to agree with him, even though his move to New England saddened Mama and Papa. Emma was proud of his courage and accomplishments.

The truth was, Mama couldn't forbid Albert to go, especially after she hadn't let Fred follow his dream. Five years earlier, after Fred had turned twenty-one, his baseball skills had improved so much that he started gaining a reputation around the city's sandlots. Scouts from several professional ballclubs around the country had come out to Pittsburgh to watch Fred put his skills on display. Finally, a team from St. Louis, the Cardinals, had offered Fred a position in their organization. It didn't pay much, but Fred didn't care. He was over the moon at the opportunity to play ball for a professional club.

Mama had made an awful fuss about the prospect of Fred leaving Elliott. "St. Louis is in Missouri—hundreds of miles away. You won't know a single soul! And Fred," she added, "who's going to help Papa run the tavern? Your life is here; you just can't leave your family. You just can't. I forbid it!"

Margaret Moreau had put her foot down. She wouldn't speak to Fred until he changed his mind. She had guilted him into complying, and Fred had always been obedient. Too obedient, thought Emma.

Fred hated to see Mama so upset and he felt terribly guilty. He didn't ever want Mama or Papa disappointed. He knew Mama was right. Papa needed him to help run the business. So, Emma's brother let his dream of making a career out of playing baseball die. And when that dream was gone, it was like a piece of his heart had withered and died too. Fred had devoted himself to the business of running the tavern. He talked to the customers about baseball as he poured their drinks. He could spin a tale with the best of them, but every day he drank as he worked. He had whiskey for breakfast, lunch, and dinner. He rarely left the tavern…eventually he began telling Papa he was going to start sleeping in the backroom. At that point he saw Mama only when he went to the house for Sunday dinner. Emma glanced at the typewriter again. She missed the opportunity to write articles. She missed her older brother Albert, who was so far away. And now the old Fred was gone, too; in his place, the present-day Fred found joy only in a bottle of whiskey. Her Mama was saddened by her family's recent developments too. She missed the daily interactions she was used to having with both of her oldest sons. Sharing meals with them, talking about their days. Mama might have been able to recover from this sadness—but then came the tragedy of Edmond, dear sweet Eddie. Eddie turned twenty-three last year; for several years he had been working at the same company that employed Albert. He loved his job: he was almost as proficient with numbers as Albert, and he was grateful for the opportunity to use his math skills. He caught the streetcar with Albert every day—until Albert moved to Massachusetts, that is—both dressed in their suits, hats, shined shoes. He wasn't as tall or as handsome as Albert, or as strong and muscular as Fred; but Eddie was known as the sweetest, most kind young man in all of Elliott. He was soft-spoken and shy; but, after the tragedy, his supervisor commented to Albert: "Edmond was a responsible and diligent employee. He would have gone far with the company." Albert had told Emma, "I heard a young typist in the office had her eye on Eddie. Whenever she smiled at him Eddie's face would get beet red. Eddie had finally worked up enough nerve to ask her to go see a picture show with him at the Nickelodeon." That was six months ago. Then, on a hot day in July, Eddie started to experience mild pains in his stomach. When he came home that evening, he told Mama he didn't feel well. He went straight to bed, not wanting any dinner. He went to work as usual the next day, still not wanting to eat. The pain in his stomach grew worse and quickly spread to his whole abdominal area. He came home immediately and fell into bed. Then he started vomiting. Greenish putrid vomit. The following morning, he couldn't get out of bed and was running a fever. Mama sent Harry to get Dr. Meyers, who came to the house and examined Eddie. He gave Eddie medicine to lower the fever, and then he told Mama Eddie might need surgery to remove his appendix, or to unblock a bowel obstruction. That night Eddie cried continuously from the pain. He was confused. He could hardly walk. Papa went to summon Dr. Meyers again.

This time, when Dr. Meyers stepped out of Eddie's bedroom, he gently closed the door behind him; then he slowly descended the stairs. His eyes looked sadly at Mama and Papa, who were sitting anxiously in the parlor. The elderly physician softly said, "I'm so sorry, but it's too late. The appendix must have burst, and the infection spread…Once the bacteria gets in the bloodstream, there's nothing that can be done. He's gone."

Mama gasped in shock. A moment later, she fainted, crumpling onto the floor. The doctor got out the smelling salts, holding the bottle under Mama's nose. When she had revived and was breathing normally Papa helped her to bed. She was sobbing. "Why…why?" she kept asking her husband, searching his face for answers. "I didn't realize he was that sick. Dear God, why…?"

When Emma heard knocking on her front door that evening it was after dark. She knew something was wrong. She saw Papa's face through the glass and opened it quickly. He was sweating and stuttering as he pulled out his handkerchief and wiped his face. "Papa…what's wrong?" Emma said. She grabbed his arm and pulled him into the house. She made him sit down on a chair in the hallway. "Papa, what is it, what's happened?" Her father took a deep breath then proceeded to relay the story. Emma knew Eddie had been ill but never suspected how serious it was. After learning of Eddie's passing, she embraced Papa for a long still interval. Finally, Papa said, "I have to get back to the house. Harry and Monnie are sitting with Mama. Everyone is just in shock. I have to tell Fred and then"—his throat made a choking noise as he tried to hold back his tears— "I have to wait for the undertaker to take Eddie's body."

Moments later Emma sobbed as she closed the door behind Papa. Then she sat at the kitchen table, alone, processing all that Papa had told her, thinking about her little brother. She couldn't believe he was dead. Dear, sweet Eddie.

That night the house was quiet. All three children were sleeping. Emma was worried; not only about Mama, but also about Monnie, Fred, and especially Harry. Emma's youngest brother had shared a bedroom with Eddie his entire life. She looked at the clock on the wall. Where was Jack at ten o'clock on a Wednesday night? Probably another union meeting. Lately it seemed to Emma there was a union meeting two or three times a week. Or at least that's what Jack said. These days, when Jack would fall into bed, she always smelled the whiskey and smoke on him. She knew he often went to the bars in the South Side with those fellows from work. He had been friends with Joe Sullivan and Jimmy Kennedy for over ten years. Once she commented, "Well, they don't have wives and children at home waiting for them." Jack had gazed at her in silence; then he turned and slammed the door.

For the last few years, in fact, he seemed to be short on patience, acting as though he was annoyed, displaying a lack of understanding for her and the children. She often thought it wasn't fair that men got to go wherever they wanted to go, whenever they wanted to go there. That their wives weren't supposed to question anything their husbands did. That women had to put up with the hand that was dealt them. What a bunch of nonsense!

Maybe in a happy marriage a husband's late-night whereabouts were never cause for concern, but what if a woman was trapped in an abusive situation? Then what? Suffer in silence? She thought it didn't make sense that a woman had no right to property if she was married. Even the laws of divorce, written by men, put all the power in the hands of the husband. No surprise there! And concerning the guardianship of the children: if a woman wanted to leave her husband, she most likely would also lose her children. She didn't know anyone who had gotten divorced.

Emma was determined to find out more about the women's rights movement. She agreed with their stance on education and freedom of speech; that these rights were among the many things in life that matter. A woman should have the same rights as even the most ignorant man. Those were the thoughts that had rolled around in her head every day for the last several years as she washed clothes and cleaned the house. *It isn't fair!* Several times when she was washing her husband's clothing, she had noticed that his shirt collar was smudged with red lipstick and smelled of perfume. This only increased her suspicions. Her anger stewed inside of her. Jack worked hard and drank hard. Now, if he was perturbed or angry, he simply left the house without explanation. No telling what bar he was in, or even what part of the city. The streetcars could take him to Hazelwood, the South Side, Oakland, or over to Allegheny.

Allegheny was now called the North Side, since it had become part of the city of Pittsburgh. She was glad the politicians had finally put the *h* back on *Pittsburgh*…even though after spelling the city's name without the *h* for twenty years, it had taken Emma a while to get used to the original spelling. Politicians sometimes didn't make sense; Emma had always said they should be women. Men made much ado about nothing! Emma's thoughts were whirling in her head. She was tired but knew she wouldn't be able to sleep while thinking about Eddie. She wondered where Jack was as she glanced at the clock on the wall. Again. She wanted to forget being angry at him. At least for the moment.

He was a good provider. On payday he always brought money home and left it on the counter. There was enough money for food, rent, kerosene and coal, and clothes. Emma always managed to save a few dollars from each pay. She knew that they were more fortunate than many other families. It could have been worse. *A philandering husband isn't the worst thing in the world,* she kept telling herself. *Especially when dealing with a loved one dying unexpectedly.*

Emma often wondered if maybe she wasn't being realistic and should just accept Jack the way he was. *Be grateful for what he gives you,* she would tell herself. *Nobody's perfect.* She was disappointed that Jack wasn't content to come straight home from work. He was not the husband and father she had hoped for. Did she expect too much? He had three beautiful children. One would think he would want to spend more time with them. Show them more love. Teach them.

She needed to be able to talk and laugh with him. Like the old days. He seemed interested only in his whiskey and his life away from her and the children. Emma finished drinking her cup of tea. It was eleven o'clock when she heard Jack open the front door. She stood and started to cry as he walked into the kitchen. The tears fell. Her mouth quivered as she tried to speak. Finally, she told him what happened, and he wrapped his arms around her. "Eddie was a good man," Jack told her. "This shouldn't have happened…Oh, Emma. I'm so sorry; your poor mother must be devastated." He held her tight and rubbed her back, and then he sat her in a chair at the kitchen table. He got out two glasses and the bottle of whiskey from the cupboard. He poured them each a serving of whiskey. "Here, this will help," he said, handing her a glass. The whiskey burned her throat but warmed her. She just wanted it to numb her pain. She sipped the liquor slowly then took a deep breath. "The next few days are going to be so difficult," she said. She admitted to herself that maybe that night even strong Emma needed some liquid courage. She drained the glass then set it on the table. Jack poured them each some more.

Her husband put a finger under her chin and looked into her eyes. Then he said, "I'm here for you."

They both stood as Jack embraced her again. She found it enormously comforting. For so long she had craved those strong arms around her. He rubbed her back and kissed her hair and her neck as he started to unpin her hair. She kissed his warm lips and pulled him close. Then she whispered, "Let's go to bed."

Not wanting to admit it, Emma knew she needed him, that she had to have him. Now. Tonight. They had not been intimate since before Johnny was born. Her anger about his drinking always ended in an argument…and then stubborn silence. Jack was not going to change. Her expectations were not going to change. Her disappointment and discontent were not going to disappear. Tonight, none of that seemed to matter. Emma wanted Jack to hold her close. Neither of them wanted to talk about death anymore. She yearned for Jack to make her feel alive. She hungered for his touch. For her husband. If nothing else, maybe it would help dull the pain.

CHAPTER 19

December 1915—Jack

Jack had not been to a funeral since Mum had died when he was nine years old. That was way back in 1890. Jack still hated cemeteries and all the sorrow and grief he associated with them.

A year and a half ago, on that awful morning of Eddie Moreau's funeral, Jack had a quick drink of whiskey before leaving the house. He dreaded the long, sorrowful day ahead: the Moreau family was burying Eddie at St. Martin's Cemetery in Elliott, on the hill overlooking the Ohio River.

A neighbor came over to watch the children, who were happily playing with their toys on the parlor floor. Sometimes on payday Jack would stop in one of the stores in downtown Pittsburgh and buy a ball or wooden train for Johnny. He even brought home dolls for the girls. He enjoyed seeing their faces light up, and then their hugs. Maybe some of it was guilt for the times he felt impatient with their behavior and all the noise. And for the times he wasn't there.

As Jack and Emma rode in a covered carriage with Emma's parents, he thought about how he preferred the other side of Lorenz Avenue, where the Overlook loomed above the river. During the last few years, he sometimes walked there to be alone. He would gaze at the city and the smokestacks down beyond the Point, where the rivers met. He could almost see Hazelwood hidden behind a veil of smoke....

On the day Eddie was laid to rest the weather was hot and the air was stifling. Jack's mouth was dry, and he was sweating in the July heat. He kept touching the metal flask in his suit coat pocket.

The hole in the ground had been dug at dawn, before the family arrived in a procession of carriages and wagons. During the service Jack stared at the deep hole, aware of the two somber gravediggers waiting with shovels by the carriages. The pallbearers, six strong young men, Eddie's friends, stood nearby ready to lower the heavy wooden box into the ground.

The burial site was located next to the graves of Emma's grandparents, all of whom had passed away more than twenty years ago. Every spring and summer Henry would pull weeds from around their graves; then he would plant flowers. Henry softly said, "I never would have guessed one of my children would be buried here before me...."

Old Father Ryan said the prayers and sprinkled the holy water. Emma, Estelle, Fred, Monnie, and Harry laid flowers on the lid of the wooden casket. Henry tried his best to hold up his wife, who still seemed to be in a state of shock. Her sisters, Aunt Louisa and Aunt Sophie, cried softly while comforting each other. Jack, Frank Miller and Estelle, a somber assortment of neighbors, and a few of Eddie's co-workers stood close by in silence holding their hats quietly in their hands. Albert had not been able to come all the way from Boston. Without Albert, Emma was the oldest sibling in the group. She carried that weight with courage, looking out for everyone else, one hand on Harry's arm while holding onto Monnie with her other hand. The Moreau family was devastated to the core, and Jack Quinn felt their grief. He was painfully aware that life would go on, that there were some things humans have no control over. He was confident his wife would find the strength to guide herself and her family through the crisis: Emma was a pillar of strength and grace. He observed her at the cemetery and, later, at her mother's house as she tended to each member of her family, trying to infuse them with her own courage. She served them food for the body, and comforting words for their hearts.

Later that day, as they walked back to their home, Emma told him: "Jack, I'm worried about Mama and Fred. Mama blames herself for what happened to Eddie, and what's happening to Fred. She feels like she is slowly losing Fred too."

She continued: "Fred only finds comfort in drinking, and the alcohol will probably kill him eventually. He was already struggling with his depression—and now he has lost his brother. They had been close. He misses Eddie…and he's announced that he won't sleep at the house anymore. He had been sleeping in the backroom at the tavern for a while, but now he can't bear to ever go in the bedroom that they had shared since they were children. Especially since that's the room where Eddie died."

The family was resigned to the fact that Fred lived at the tavern now.

After all this time, Emma had to keep reminding her mother that even if her father had been able to get Eddie to the hospital when he was ill, surgery probably would not have saved him. She kept telling Mama, "Dr. Meyers told me that once that infection is in the bloodstream it's almost impossible to cure. The burst appendix led to peritonitis, and the bacteria traveled through his entire body. He's seen it happen to even the strongest men." Emma took after her father, who seemed to draw comfort from being with others. It was no wonder that Henry's tavern was successful. Henry could talk to anyone about anything, and his customers considered him to be a friend. He had a way of bringing out the best in people. Jack had admired Henry since the day he met him. No one ever had a bad word to say about Henry Moreau. He was a perfect family man, a perfect, businessman, and a respected member of his community. Jack knew that Henry and Emma were both still concerned about her mother. Now as it neared the end of 1916, it had been eighteen months since Eddie's passing, and Margaret Moreau's emotions had never completely recovered. She was still mourning the loss of her son. Jack thought it must be devastating for a mother to lose a child…just as it was for a child to lose his mother. That pain he understood.

He knew Emma missed her brother; but Emma was not consumed with grief. She had too much to live for and always tried to be happy around the children. He was glad that Emma enjoyed her role as a mother. She was teaching Dorothy to help in the kitchen. She always read books to the children before kissing them goodnight and turning out the light. Emma was a much better parent than he would ever be.

But—Emma was not happy with Jack. And he knew it. Jack's wife never missed an opportunity to tell him she didn't approve of his excessive drinking…and she did not like it when he failed to come home quickly after work. "Jack," she said, "you're avoiding your responsibilities. Your children need to see you!"

Jack remembered when he had first met Emma years earlier, how impressed he had been with her confidence. She wasn't afraid to voice her opinion on any subject imaginable. Politics, women's rights, unions. He admired it then, but now found it annoying. Especially when her criticism was aimed at him.

He often stayed out until ten or eleven o'clock at night. Sometimes he stayed out until midnight. The last few months had seen several nights when he had not come home at all. He would stay at Joe's or Jimmy's house if he had been drinking more than usual, sleeping on their sofas. Or, occasionally, he would spend the entire night with Nel. Emma would glare at him, asking, "Where have you been?" And Jack would reply, "It's none of your business! I can go wherever I want and come home when I want. I don't need your approval or permission, for God's sake! I go to work every day and leave money for you to pay the rent and buy food. You shouldn't complain!"

"You have it better than some wives," he would claim. "Maybe show a little appreciation for how hard I work. And when I go to union meetings, that's part of my job. And I go to the bars to relax. God knows I can't relax around here with Nan throwing fits and Johnny screaming—and you complaining...Damn it, Emma, it's enough to drive any man crazy!" Then he would storm out of the house. One day Emma had been so angry at him as he left, she had thrown a plate across the kitchen as he slammed the door behind him. Jack had heard the plate shatter against the wooden door. He had been tempted to go back in and slap her, but he knew he would regret resorting to violence. That wasn't his way.

He had never intended to be a husband who hit his wife. *Never.* He had vowed to himself to never cross that line.

Jack loved Emma but couldn't be everything she wanted him to be. Perhaps her expectations had been too lofty for an Irishman from Hazelwood. He liked to drink, and that wasn't going to change. He usually tried to avoid shouting at her. Instead he would just walk away—but that enraged her even more. Why was she always looking for a fight? He often accused her of trying to make him angry. Jack reprimanded himself. Even his Dad told him, "Jackie, put yourself in her shoes. Your wife is home all day taking care of three small children, probably missing the things she used to enjoy doing before she was a mother. Maybe she needs a shot of whiskey and an understanding husband. You can do better."

Four years ago, Jack had won the battle of what to name Nan. He had insisted that she be christened *Anna,* after his mother. Emma had finally agreed to the name *Anna Nancy.* Then Emma proceeded to always call her "Nan" or "Nancy." She refused to use the name Anna.

Jack was convinced Emma was just being spiteful to aggravate him. To avoid confusing the child, Jack gave in and started calling her Nan. *It's no wonder she's such an obstinate little girl,* he thought. He had never supposed children could be so exasperating. Jack figured Nan got her stubbornness from Emma. More recently they had been arguing about Jack's refusal to attend Mass. Emma said, "You're setting a poor example for the children, especially since Dorothy will soon be receiving her First Communion." She had even called Jack a heathen. "It's hard to believe you come from a religious family, even though they never acted in a Christian manner toward me! Are you sure you're really a Catholic?" Sarcasm was dripping off her every word. It made Jack's blood boil.

"I don't care what you say to me or about me, but NEVER talk about my family!" he said. "They may not be as perfect as your people. Although my mother, bless her soul, was a damn saint. My sisters don't pretend to be uppity, and my dad doesn't always use correct grammar, but they are good honest people! And if you have something against the Irish then you shouldn't have married me!" Emma's disrespect for Jack's family was the straw that broke the camel's back. He was genuinely angry. He could feel his face getting hot. Words began spilling from his mouth faster than he could think. "I can't help it that I didn't have a mother to raise me the way your mother raised you, Miss High-and-Mighty, Miss Prim-and-Proper! And I can't help that I was born in Hazelwood and grew up by the mills and the shit-filled river. And I can't help that I had to go to work in that God-forsaken mill when I was ten years old. Damn it…*ten years old*! If that had happened to you, you'd be drowning your sorrows in a bloody bottle of whiskey too! You wouldn't be so high and mighty. If it wasn't for my sisters, I would've been dead by the time I was fourteen. I owe them—and I don't have to explain anything to you. If I want to sleep at their house or stay with my friends in the South Side, then that's what I'm going to do. I don't have to ask permission from you or anyone else! You got what you wanted from me. In fact, I think you always *liked* what you got from me!" Jack winked at her then smiled and started to laugh; but his bemused expression wasn't intended to be kind or pleasant. It was meant to cut like a knife. Even he heard a bit of meanness in his own laugh…and he knew that Emma heard it too. That was when Emma walked over, raised her hand, and smacked him hard across his face. He was stunned. The next moment he watched her turn and storm up the steps. "Jack Quinn, I don't care what you do or where you do it. You can go to hell." Jack rubbed his cheek. He watched his wife ascend the stairs then heard her slam their bedroom door. He always had admired her courage. But not tonight. Who does she think she is? Damn it. She'll be sorry.

He looked at a pile of folded laundry that was sitting in a basket in the kitchen. He stuffed some clean clothes in a canvas bag. Then he put on his heavy coat and hat and stepped out into the cold night air, quietly shutting the door behind him.

"She'll miss me!" he whispered as he stopped to take a drink from his silver flask. He breathed deeply and placed a hand on his chest, trying to calm his racing heart. It was beating wildly.

He looked up. The skies were darker than usual. No stars and no moon tonight. It would soon be winter he thought as he buttoned his coat and waited on Steuben Street for the next streetcar.

~⸙~

Jack rode the streetcar to his favorite South Side bar, where he spotted Nel dancing with a young man who didn't look a day over twenty. Jack ordered a drink. Then he walked to a table in the back of the room. Nel had noticed Jack the minute he came through the door. She sent her dancing partner on his way then sauntered over and pulled up a chair next to Jack.

Jack pointed in the direction of the young man. "Isn't he a little wet behind the ears?" He wasn't jealous, just slightly amused. Nel patted his hand. "Don't you worry, my handsome Jack," she whispered, "I always save my best for you." She raised her free hand and pointed to her heart.

Jack was now thirty-four years old. He had known Nel for ten or eleven years, he figured, since the old days in Allegheny. Long before he married Emma. Nel had to be close to forty but looked as attractive as ever. She could always make Jack smile, he mused—and then he playfully ran two fingers up her milky white arm and touched her bare shoulder. She leaned toward him, as voluptuous and enticing as on their first night together, kissing his open mouth, teasing him with her tongue.

Nel looked into his tired eyes and said, "You look like you've had a long day, fighting the battles of the cruel world. Yes? Would you like to come upstairs?" She winked at him, ran the tip of her tongue around her parted lips, and smiled. "I might have something to make you feel better." Nel was willing and able, as usual, with no questions asked…and no complaints.

He spent the night with her…and didn't even feel guilty. "You—" he said, whispering into Nel's ear "—are just what the doctor ordered." At dawn he put money on the bureau by her bottles of perfume then quietly left her room.

The following day, after work, he took the streetcar from Oakland to Hazelwood. He asked his sisters if they minded if he stayed for a couple of days. Margaret snickered at him. "Oh Jackie, is there trouble in paradise?" He ignored Margaret, as Florence assured Jack that he could stay with them for as long as he liked. "You know you're always welcome here," she said. "This is still your home. I'll sleep in Margaret's room and you can have my bed."

Of course, his sisters proceeded to fuss over him like mother hens. The next several evenings they served all his favorite meals, from chicken and biscuits to beef stew with potatoes and carrots. Jack thanked them both as he drank a cup of tea.

Dad hadn't said much but pulled out his bottle of whiskey after dinner and poured some of the dark liquor into two glasses. Jack nodded to him. *Just like old times,* he thought.

Later, Jack watched his father go up the stairs to bed. He looked at his sisters and said, "Dad sure is slowing down." Florence glanced over from her knitting. "He has so many aches and pains. And the knees are getting worse. After all, the man is sixty-seven years old and deserves some time to just rest. I'm happy he's no longer going to the mill. Margaret and I both bring wages home from the sewing we do at the clothing store, so we manage. And Dad saved some money over the years; he even gets a small pension. I guess the union was at least good for that."

Florence paused then said: "Jackie, I'm glad you do well with your plumbing job. The best thing you did was to get away from the mill. You probably make more money than your old pal Johnny Finnegan, and he's a supervisor now."

"How's Johnny doing?" asked Jack. "And Alice?"

Florence replied, "They're both fine, although Alice is disappointed that they haven't had any luck starting a family. Alice would be such a good mother. They've been married for over nine years now." Jack poured himself some more whiskey. "Now there's a problem that I know nothing about," he noted, "as easy as Emma has gotten with child." His sisters did not say anything.

Finally, Margaret broke the silence. "Well, aren't you going to ask about Clare?"

Jack chuckled. "Go ahead, Margaret, tell me about the Murphy family and Clare's lovely brother Joe, too."

So, Margaret proceeded to report all the Murphy family news. She said that Clare was still working with them at the clothing store, but recently had to quit.

"I'm sure you remember, Jackie, how well she sewed. She taught me things I never knew how to do, like how to do buttonholes on the machines. And how to get collars just perfect. The shop owner really misses her."

She continued: "Clare does some hand-sewing from home but can't come in to work on the machines because her parents took ill. They are both bedridden, and Clare can't leave them alone for more than an hour or so. She manages to get out and shop at the market and the meat shop but then has to hurry home." Margaret stopped for a minute to take a drink of tea. She then continued to prattle on with her story. No one seemed to notice how attentively Jack was listening as he swirled the whiskey in his glass and stared at it.

"And of course, Clare goes to Mass every Sunday, and sometimes during the week too. Alice and Clare still wash and iron the altar cloths. Last year Clare sewed some beautiful vestments for both priests. She used to spend a lot of time talking to the younger priest, Father Walsh. Poor Clare takes such good care of her parents, on top of all the cooking and housework. And then she must put up with that brother of hers. She tells me he's as filthy as a pig and comes home drunk almost every evening. But the family needs his pay, so what can she do? She says that's her cross to bear. I guess Father Walsh told her that."

Margaret sighed. "Clare is stuck between a rock and a hard place." Jack listened and thought about the last time he had seen Clare Murphy, wondering if she was still angry at him. It was hard to believe he had destroyed her dreams more than eight years ago. The day he broke her heart by telling her his plans to marry the woman from Elliott.

He poured another shot of whiskey into his glass and filled the metal flask he always kept in his coat pocket. He tried reading the newspaper, the *Pittsburgh Press*, but found it difficult to concentrate. His mind kept wandering. He pictured Clare…all the good times they had enjoyed together. He could see her sitting with him under the willow tree, making bouquets from violets and plucking petals from a daisy….

The following day, Jack washed at work and changed his clothes like he always did. He shaved and combed his dark hair, then he put on a new suit he had bought in one of the men's clothing stores on Fifth Avenue in downtown Pittsburgh. He tied and straightened his necktie and smiled at his reflection in the small mirror that hung next to his locker.

Jack's locker was in a room in the basement of a building that housed classrooms at the University of Pittsburgh. The plumbers used the room to store their equipment and tools. McGee's crew had been working on this job for the past six months, upgrading the plumbing fixtures and installing new boilers. There was talk that in the spring the crew would move into an office building on Grant Street in the downtown area. The building was being constructed and financed by Henry Clay Frick, who had made his fortune in the coke and steel industry. Frick was constantly competing with Andrew Carnegie. They were rivals in every aspect of business, and their buildings reflected their rivalry. Frick wanted his buildings to be grander than Carnegie's headquarters on Fifth Avenue. Jack no longer admired Carnegie as naively as he had when he was a child. In his eyes that man had fallen off his pedestal years ago; nowadays Jack viewed him through the eyes of a cynical adult. He regarded all the industrialists as greedy, pompous men who didn't care a lick about any of the workers who had helped the men amass great fortunes. Although…at least Carnegie was trying to right some wrongs by establishing the library system and building the museum for the people. And at least Carnegie had a conscience—which was more than he could say about Frick.

These days, Jack was happy that the men with deep pockets just wanted to keep constructing buildings: places that would provide work for plumbers as well as many of the other tradesmen. Jack looked confident and handsome in his new clothes. He walked outside and noticed a few snowflakes floating down. The air was smoky, as usual, causing a gray tinge to appear on even the lightest accumulation of snow. He had hoped the snow would hold off until after Christmas, but he knew that the weather was always hard to predict. *Just take it as it comes*, he thought.

He quickly boarded a waiting streetcar. At this hour of the day it was crowded with people rushing to get home. This part of the city, in the heart of the university, was always bustling with office workers and students. Jack had gotten into the habit of wearing a suit to and from work. Most of the men who rode the streetcars wore suits, white shirts, neckties, and hats: the standard uniform for the average man, even if he was attending a Pirates baseball game or venturing out to Kennywood on a Sunday afternoon. If a woman was riding, every well-mannered gentleman knew to offer her assistance as she boarded or disembarked. With the high step and women's long skirts, even the most agile ladies had difficulty. But Jack had noticed that some of the women who worked in the offices were starting to wear their skirts a few inches shorter. That made good sense to him. Sometimes, he thought, practicality should win out over fashion. Those were his wife's words of wisdom echoing in his head.

The men who worked in the mills and factories generally lived close to their place of employment and didn't need to ride the streetcars, because they could walk to work. He remembered that Dad rarely needed to take a streetcar anywhere. For years Dad's world had revolved primarily around walking to the mill, O'Shea's bar, and St. Stephen's church. Jack considered that a prime example of his limited existence theory.

Jack felt confident in his new suit as he noticed a woman sitting across from him smiling in his direction. He sat straighter and gazed out the window as the streetcar made several stops along the familiar route. Since he was fourteen Jack had always taken pride in his appearance. He still remembered his sister Mary telling him: "Jackie, it's important to be neat and clean. Use good grammar and look a person in the eye when you speak." Jack's friends Joe and Jimmy had also benefited from Mary's advice. They liked to dress in clean suits, since they all rode the streetcars with office workers. Sometimes they would smile at the attractive young women as they boarded the streetcar and offered their seats if the trolley was crowded; but they had trouble initiating conversation. They seemed to be comfortable only around the ladies in the bar, emboldened by alcohol.

Jack often teased them, saying they were both hopeless and would never find a wife. Lately, however, Jack was thinking that might be the right course to take....

He would muse to himself, wondering if marriage created unrealistic expectations. Maybe men weren't designed to be faithful to one woman for a lifetime, always contemplating an escape, devising various routes to freedom. Or maybe that was just him.

Jack and his friends were proud of the work they did in all the new buildings in Oakland and the downtown area. Being members of the Plumbers Union enabled them to work in different locations and earn a good wage. He had become active in the union, always attending meetings and recruiting new members. The men, coworkers and bosses, all knew and respected Jack Quinn. He was now a bit of a legend among the members and bosses of the Plumbers Union for his negotiating skills, always bargaining in a calm determined manner. Jack was quiet by nature but had a commanding presence. Never having any tolerance for politics and long-winded speeches, Jack preferred to speak in a direct manner...He did not talk long, and he got right to the point. He found satisfaction in helping to obtain wage increases and other benefits, such as shorter hours and pension benefits, for his colleagues. He certainly enjoyed the socializing aspect of the union, meeting up with former coworkers and new recruits at bars all over the city. Sometimes he felt a bit of guilt because his nightly activities took away from his time at home with his wife and children.

Or was it just an excuse to avoid his responsibilities? After a couple of drinks, he would forget about the inner turmoil he felt…the conflicts, the psychological and emotional battles. After all, he knew that Jack Quinn was the master of rationalization and compartmentalizing his duties…his life. He liked to keep some issues wrapped in boxes and other matters hidden behind closed doors, having an explanation or excuse for everything.

Jack had stayed in Hazelwood for three nights when he figured he should probably go back to Elliott tomorrow since it was payday. Emma would be expecting the money.

As he stepped off the streetcar and onto the brick street, the wind began blowing briskly. He turned up his collar to deflect the chilly December air. It would be Christmas in a week, and he decided to walk down Second Avenue and look in some of the shop windows.

Before going to Dad's house, he thought about stopping for a drink in O'Shea's; but then he changed his mind. It was already late afternoon, and he didn't want to risk running into that loudmouth asshole, Joe Murphy.

Coming down the street toward him, Jack saw a woman he immediately recognized as Clare Murphy. There was no doubt about it, it was Clare. Jack thought about crossing the street before she saw him. She stopped to look in a shop window, pulling her cloak tight against her petite body. He couldn't help but walk toward her.

Clare was carrying several packages. Auburn curls along her forehead peeked out from under her dark wool hat. She turned just as he drew near and bumped right into him, almost dropping her parcels as their eyes met. It had been over eight years since he had gazed into those green eyes. Time seemed to freeze for several moments. He felt her eyes boring a hole right through him. Right into his heart. He didn't say anything as they both stared at each other, speechless. Finally, Jack managed to smile. "Hello, Clare," he said. "How are you?" Not knowing what else to say, he had figured he could at least be polite. He touched a finger to the brim of his hat.

Ignoring his query, Clare shot back her own question: "Well, if it isn't Jack Quinn. What are you doing in Hazelwood? I thought you were too good to socialize in this part of the city!"

Jack avoided the subject. "Here, let me help you carry these packages. I guess you still have to do all the fetching and carrying for your family." Clare looked tired. She probably wanted to say, "No thanks—and go to Hell!" Instead she handed over the two largest packages.

They walked to the next street in silence. When they reached the steps in front of Clare's house, she said, "It's cold out here, and Joe isn't home. Would you like a cup of tea?"

She pushed open the wooden door and switched on a lamp that sat on a small table in the front room. Jack was pleased to see the Murphy family now had electricity, just like at Dad's house. All the main streets in Hazelwood had electric lines running over to the houses.

Clare said, "Joe won't be home until after seven and my parents now sleep in a room off the kitchen, which makes caring for them a little easier. They couldn't get up and down the stairs anymore." She went in the kitchen to heat some water for tea and returned quickly.

Jack smiled at her. "I guess I'm the last person your brother Joe would want to see in his house." "Well, he's had eight years to calm down," Clare replied. "He was determined to throw you into the river for quite a long while."

When the kettle started to whistle, she quickly poured the tea, added some sugar, and returned with two steaming cups. He noticed her hands were trembling and averted his gaze, so as not to make her even more nervous. They sat quietly for a moment. Then she asked about his work.

Jack told her about his plumbing jobs and his union activities. Then Clare said, "Tell me about your children." Jack described Dorothy, Nan, and Johnny, which made him smile proudly.

At last, he mentioned that he was having problems with his wife and was staying at Dad's house occasionally. He didn't give details and preferred not to discuss his marital problems with Clare. She did not ask questions about Emma.

As they talked, he studied her face, noticing tiny lines around her mouth and eyes. Her green eyes still sparkled when she smiled, and that made him relax. She hadn't changed much…She was still so pretty, he thought to himself.

He looked at the clock. Then he finished his tea and stood to go.

"Jack, are you happy?" Clare suddenly asked. "Is it what you wanted?"

Jack gazed into her eyes, swallowing the lump in his throat. "I don't know, Clare. I really don't know." He felt an emptiness and the familiar turmoil that was always right beneath the surface of his chest. The pain in his heart. His damn divided heart.

He took a deep breath. "I've always felt guilty about leaving you, but I just couldn't stay in Hazelwood. No sense in rehashing old issues." Wanting to change the subject, he said, "I better go. Florence will have supper ready, and Dad always has a fork in his hand by six o'clock."

As Jack put on his coat and hat, Clare said: "Well, any time you visit them, you can stop by here for friendly conversation…as long as it's between four o'clock and six o'clock, so you don't have to run into Joe."

"I just might do that," Jack replied. He smiled to her and nodded. "Thanks for the tea. I hope you have a good Christmas."

Walking to Dad's house, Jack felt a weight had been lifted from his heart. He was grateful that Clare didn't hate him, that she possessed the grace to forgive.

CHAPTER 20

December 1916—Jack

By the summer of 1916, Jack was stopping at Clare's house at least twice a month. He never stayed long. The visits were merely pleasant conversations between old friends. Of course, he tried to avoid Clare's brother Joe. Not looking for a confrontation, Jack always left before that drunken loudmouth came home.

Clare's parents had passed away within weeks of each other in the spring. Mr. Murphy had a heart attack in March, and his wife died of pneumonia in April. Clare was heartbroken but knew their suffering was over and that they were together in Heaven. She was grateful that she had been able to care for them and had never complained.

Jack had told Clare his relationship with his wife Emma was still difficult, and that they hardly spoke to each other. He came and went as he pleased. He said he would never desert his children, and that he knew it was his responsibility to always leave Emma money to pay their bills. Sundays in Elliott were devoted to his family, when he tried to enjoy his limited time with the children. He still did not attend Mass on Sunday mornings. He didn't care what Emma had to say about it. In the afternoons on Sunday Jack, Emma, and the children walked up to Emma's parents' house. Jack liked to sit on the front porch and chat with Henry or visit in the parlor if the weather was inclement.

Henry always had a couple of cigars ready and greeted his son-in-law with a handshake. He never mentioned anything about Jack being absent from his family so much. Jack reasoned that Emma probably had not complained to her father about their marital troubles. At least he could be grateful to Emma for that; he valued Henry's friendship.

He spent several nights a week at Dad's and looked forward to his occasional visits with Clare and their conversations over tea. They talked about old times, his love of the gardens, old friends, his sisters, and Clare's sister Alice and her husband Johnny, Jack's old pal. Clare told Jack she had more time to sew now and was contemplating returning to the clothing shop to work with Margaret and Florence. He was surprised to see she was so excited about it. She said she wanted to start saving up some money, so she might as well get paid for doing what she enjoyed. One Friday evening when Jack was getting ready to leave at six o'clock, he and Clare were still laughing about how shy he had been the day they met when they were fourteen. Clare recalled: "You were sweating and couldn't even talk until you finally offered me some of your candy."

"You were just the prettiest girl I had ever seen," Jack replied. "I don't know what I liked better, those green eyes or your beautiful hair. I always thought you were prettier than Alice."

Before he opened the door to go, Clare said, "Jack, you won't be able to stop here in the afternoon anymore. Starting in October, Joe is going to be working the night shift. There's been some changes at the mill, and he'll be working from six in the evening until six in the morning. If you're in Hazelwood on Friday evenings, you could come by around eight o'clock. I'll put on a light by the window."

The first Friday in October, Jack finished eating supper with Florence, Margaret, and Dad. He had a drink of whiskey with Dad then told the three of them that he was going to O'Shea's for a few drinks. "I'll use my key in case I'm out late," he told them.

It was a little after eight o'clock and already dark when Jack headed up a block to Chatsworth Avenue and knocked quietly on Clare's door. She opened it and invited him in. He noticed she had a candle lit on the table; the light from the candle flame gave the room a soft glow. The evening air outside had been chilly, but in this small sitting room an abundance of heat radiated from the pot-bellied stove.

Jack took off his jacket and said, "Are you cold?" He then loosened his tie and unbuttoned his collar before he started to sweat. "I keep it warm in the evening," Clare replied, "because the house gets cold by morning, especially upstairs."

They stood looking at each other. Finally, after all these months of talking, he wanted to kiss those rosy lips and hold Clare Murphy close. Jack pulled her to him and put his arms around her.

It had been nine years since he had last kissed her, but now he felt a rush to make up for all the time they had been apart. He had longed for her and dreamed of those eyes. Her sweetness, her laugh, her beautiful auburn hair. He had truly missed her. He leaned down and kissed her soft lips, and she kissed him back. She then laid her head on his chest. He kept his arms around her as he gently kissed the top of her head. Clare was petite, several inches shorter than Emma. Jack was tall, standing at over six feet in height. For the sake of comfort, he sat down on a soft upholstered chair and pulled her onto his lap.

Jack lifted Clare's chin with his fingers and started to kiss her again. All the memories came flooding back. "Remember the many hours we spent under the willow tree...?" Clare said. He had replayed it in his head many times. When they were younger, they had never been completely intimate. There was never a chance for privacy. They had kissed and embraced...she had let his hands wander all over her body—even under her clothes. They had been passionate but felt the frustrations of young love and the conflicting emotions that forced them to keep their desires, their curiosity, their passion under control.

Jack wanted to catch up on all the years they had been apart. He wanted to have what they had been denied when they were young. When they couldn't give in to their passion. When they couldn't have what they desired. He wanted her now. They finally had the privacy they needed.

They were older and wiser—and Jack was no longer inexperienced and clumsy. He suspected Clare had little experience with being with a man, but he would be patient and gentle. He had been educated well by Nel: he knew how to please a woman. Emma had been a willing and enthusiastic partner when they were first married. Having babies and caring for the children had dampened her spirit, which he understood. Jack had not had intimate relations with his wife Emma in over a year. Jack kissed Clare's neck and started to unpin her hair. Her soft auburn hair cascaded about her shoulders. When he started to unbutton her white blouse, she suddenly stood up and took him by the hand. She pulled him toward the stairs. Then she looked into his eyes and said, "We're here all alone…Come upstairs with me." She walked back across the room, blew out the candle and then they went up to her room. To her bed. Jack knew to go slow and be patient. He was right about her being completely inexperienced; but he had been a good teacher with Emma and could be with Clare. He insisted she drink a few sips from his metal flask to help her relax. He made a quick mental note to bring a bottle of brandy next time, then kept reassuring her that everything would be all right. And it was. It was more than all right.

Jack stayed until midnight, watching the night sky out of Clare's small bedroom window. They both gazed at the full moon surrounded by stars, trying to make the minutes last longer. "Moonbeams and stardust…" Clare mused. "Finally, after all these years, just my Jack and me…I'll remember this night forever." The moonlight fell across her white shoulders and her bare legs. Jack didn't want to leave but knew he must. She slipped on her white cotton nightgown and followed him down the stairs, whispering, "I'll be counting the days until next Friday."

He heard her lock the door behind him. He pictured her returning to bed alone, like a ghost in the night. He knew she would be exhausted and hoped that she was happy. He could still hear her whispering, *"My Jack has finally returned to me…my one and only true love."* Jack missed her touch already.

～◦◈◦～

As he walked back to Dad's house, he contemplated the round silver moon again. It seemed to be smiling at him. He didn't know what the future would bring, but at least now Clare was no longer angry with him. He never wanted to hurt her again. Every Friday evening Jack found his way to Clare's door. Warming the sheets while enjoying Jack's heavenly body, Clare gave in to years of pent-up passion. The week before Christmas Jack brought Clare a green velvet box tied with a red ribbon. She opened it carefully, her slender fingers lifting the lid. Her face lit up and she gasped as she touched the gold oval-shaped locket inside. Two hearts were engraved on the front of the locket, which hung from a gold chain. "This is so beautiful," Clare said. "I love you, Jack Quinn!" The locket had cost Jack a full day's pay, but he figured Clare Murphy was worth every penny. He also gave her a box of chocolates and a bag of peppermint sticks. "Sweets for my sweetheart," he explained. "I remember how you liked to stir your tea with peppermint sticks." Holding Jack tightly, Clare whispered, "These are the best gifts I ever got in my whole life!"

Jack's love for her was deepening, and he didn't know what to do. So, they lived in the moment and didn't speak of the future. They savored every minute they had with each other. Later that night as Jack held her close to him in her bed, the moonlight fell across their bare arms. Clare softly remarked,

"I always believed in moonbeams and stardust, even though you can't touch them. Sometimes the best things can only be felt in our hearts. Like the magic of the willow tree in the gardens." They always searched for the moon in the night sky, sometimes seeing it, sometimes not. The weekly visits never seemed to be enough. Soon Jack planned to start stopping by twice a week. They were completely in love…they wanted to spend more time together. Jack's heart was still being torn in two directions. Being at cross purposes with himself hurt; but rationalizing what he was doing and trying to justify his mixed emotions was exhausting. He hated to think about it.

Jack usually went home to Elliott two nights during the week as well as on Saturdays and Sundays. He slept on the parlor sofa. He had not spent time with Nel for several months; although he made his rounds to his favorite bars, he now avoided the place where Nel worked. Emma still was hardly speaking to him. Most of the time her silence did not bother him; at least she wasn't complaining about his drinking. It was the holiday season, so on pay day he bought a box of chocolates for Emma: one for her family and one for his family. He also brought home presents for the children. A china tea set for Dorothy, a Raggedy Ann doll for Nan, and a stuffed Teddy Bear for Johnny. Emma said they had to hide the gifts until Christmas morning. Frank, Estelle's husband, had chopped down small pine trees in the woods behind his house. He was selling the trees at the hardware store. He gave one to Emma, with a wooden stand that had screws to tighten against the trunk. He told her to put water in the stand: the tree would last for a week or two before it started dropping needles. Jack dragged the tree into the house and set it up. On Christmas Eve he watched Emma decorate the tree with strings of popcorn and cranberries that she and Dorothy had made. Emma had cut out snowflakes from folded pieces of paper, which they hung from the tips of the branches. She also hung several small wooden ornaments her grandfather had hand carved and painted many years ago. Emma had helped Dorothy make a paper star for the top of their tree. "Daddy, can you lift me up so I can hang the star way up high?" "Of course, my sweet angel," he replied warmly as he held her up in the air.

"You know, Dorothy, some people put candles on their trees," Emma commented to her daughter, ignoring her husband.

"No, no," Jack cheerfully chimed in. "We are not going to burn down the house."

The children were up early on Christmas morning. Jack was pleased to see them excited about the tree and their presents. Emma had hung stockings for them from the mantel and had filled each one with an apple and an orange. Jack had added some peppermint sticks and small pieces of wrapped chocolate.

As Nan cuddled her Raggedy Ann doll, Jack reminded her that her real name was also Ann—Anna Nancy, after her grandmother Annie Quinn. He glanced at his wife as Emma tightened her mouth and rolled her eyes. She looked annoyed but didn't comment. Nonetheless Emma thanked him for his help. In turn, he was grateful to have two hours of peace and quiet when Emma left with the children for church in the morning. Jack knew that Emma had to accept the fact that he would not be going to Mass with them on Christmas —or any other morning. He had looked forward to spending the afternoon at the Moreau house with Henry and the rest of Emma's family. The day went well and did not disappoint. Emma's mother, Margaret, was finally cooking big meals for the family again. Her grief over Eddie's death had diminished, replaced with acceptance of God's will. "Mama spends more time reading the Bible now," Emma told Jack and her father. "She tells Bible stories to Dorothy and Nan. Johnny gets bored easily and can't sit too long, except for the tale about Noah and the Ark. He loves to hear about all the different kinds of animals. When Mama told them about Daniel and the lion, Johnny spent the rest of the day walking around roaring." Jack enjoyed listening to

Emma talk about the children. Her descriptions of their accomplishments and behaviors made him proud of his handsome children and thankful that his wife was such a wonderful mother.

Estelle, Frank, and their son, little Frankie, also celebrated the holiday at Henry's house. Aunt Louisa and Aunt Sophia came too, bearing baked goods and gifts for the children. Little Johnny and Frankie Miller were destined to be lifelong friends as well as cousins. They liked to sit together on the floor playing with wooden building blocks and rolling balls of yarn to each other.

Jack had always wished he had cousins when he was a young boy. Holidays would have been more bearable with cousins sitting alongside him at the dinner table, especially because he had grown up with three older sisters and no brothers. It dawned on him that Johnny needed a brother. He quickly realized Emma would probably not like that idea. The tavern was closed for the day, so Fred joined the family for dinner. Jack anticipated sharing a few drinks with Henry and Fred. Jack couldn't believe how grown up Monnie and young Harry were now. "Before you know it," he commented to Henry, "Monnie will be getting married, and Harry will be having a drink with the men." Henry laughed. He quietly replied, "That boy is eighteen now. He's almost as tall as you, Jack. Harry keeps telling me if America joins the war over in Europe, he's going to enlist in the army. He's talked about being a soldier ever since he wore short pants, marching around the yard with a stick on his shoulder." Then Henry added, "Hopefully President Wilson will keep us out of that mess, and let those countries solve their own problems."

CHAPTER 21

October 1917—Clare

It had been a long hot muggy summer and Clare was elated that autumn was here with the cooler breezes. She might finally start sleeping better and stop sweating constantly. She kept telling herself she needed to stop worrying so much. She was always tired, and her constant coughing was keeping her awake at night. Even her friends Margaret and Florence Quinn were starting to complain about it. They worked beside Clare every day.

The clothing store now had eight industrial sewing machines jammed in their back warehouse, and the owner had hired more women in the past year. He was selling some of their nicer creations to clothing stores on Fifth Avenue in the downtown section of Pittsburgh. Among the new workers was a young girl named Beth Ann who sat next to Clare. She was a pale dainty little thing who told Clare she was only seventeen. Beth Ann was constantly coughing; she didn't have a handkerchief to cover her mouth. Clare brought an extra handkerchief from home to give her. Occasionally Clare and Beth Ann shared the same cup when they stood from their sewing machines to get a drink of water. One day back in August, Mr. Hoffman, the owner, announced that Beth Ann had moved away and wouldn't be coming back. So, when Clare started coughing, she just figured she had caught a cold from Beth Ann. She was much more concerned about her relationship with Jack… she loved the time they spent together. Their arrangement was working well.

Her brother Joe was still on the night shift at the mill, enabling their visits to continue. Jack usually stopped by twice a week. Over the last year they had become so familiar with each other's desires, they could almost read each other's thoughts. They both knew that their affair was an impossible situation, but neither of them could put a stop to it. Sitting at her sewing machine, or drifting off to sleep in her bed, Clare would think of moonbeams and stardust. Things that just happen, things you can't explain. They just exist, she thought, and you enjoy them in the moment. The hopes and dreams from long ago were starting to fill her heart again, but she had to stop being a dreamer and become a realist…even though she didn't know what to make of this new reality.

Wearing Jack's gold locket close to her heart, hidden under her dress, served as a constant reminder of their love for each other. She couldn't wear it openly; there would be too many questions from Alice, Margaret, and Florence—and even from her brother Joe.

She saw Jack's sisters almost every day at the sewing machines at the clothing store. She couldn't tell them Jack had been in her bed making love with her for the last year. And if Joe ever found out he would kill her and Jack. She pushed those thoughts out of her head.

Clare couldn't even confess her sins in the confessional. Father Donnelly and young Father Walsh would both recognize her voice. She hated being a sinner, but she loved Jack too much to give him up. A good, devout Catholic woman should not be sleeping with a married man. A married man with three children.

Adulterous. That was the word used in the biblical story about the woman who was going to be stoned to death. Jesus saved her from dying at the hands of the angry crowd. Jesus showed her kindness, and most of all, forgiveness. Her mind admitted that her illicit affair was wrong, but her heart didn't care.

In church for the past year, when she knelt to receive holy Communion, she felt guilty. When she sat in the wooden church pews before Mass, staring at the giant crucifix, she felt as if she couldn't breathe. Her guilt was consuming her.

Clare knew Jack felt a sense of duty and responsibility to his wife. And maybe there was some love there, between Jack and Emma. She wasn't sure. Maybe it was loyalty. She was certain, though, that he loved his children. He felt obligated to provide for them and be a presence in their lives. Wanting Jack for herself…was that selfish? There must be a way, she thought. But then she would chastise herself, realizing it wasn't possible. It was selfish to desire what she couldn't have. Jack belonged to someone else…He belonged to his wife!

Clare wanted to be with Jack in the daylight so they could walk to the gardens. She wanted to be his in the sunshine, not just in the moonlight. Maybe someday, somehow. She could only hope and pray.

"Wake up, Clare," she whispered to herself, "you're chasing what you can't have. Think with your head, not your heart!" She realized perhaps she was just hoping and dreaming. She was so confused, but facts were reality, not dreams. She wished she could talk to somebody about it. The only person who might understand would be Alice. If she ever had enough nerve to confess her sin of adultery, she could imagine what Father Donnelly would say: "You must stop seeing this man and never sin again. Sins of the flesh will land you in Hell."

But Clare knew in her heart that she couldn't give Jack up. She had waited so long for him to come back to her. She would rather die. When she thought about Jack, she saw those blue eyes beneath the dark brows, and that handsome face. Those strong hands, and how they made her feel. She loved how he held her, and how he excited her. She had waited so long. Now there was no turning back. She refused to lose him a second time.

Clare prayed silently every day: "Please, dear God, let me have him. He was supposed to be mine. Please, please forgive me for this awful sin, but I am weak and a victim of my heart's desires. Help me, sweet Jesus."

Lately, walking two blocks to the clothing shop or even one block to St. Stephen's had become so very tiring. She no longer could blame the hot weather and didn't understand why she kept coughing.

Jack had mentioned how thin she had become. Clare explained that she just didn't feel like eating; but Jack was mostly concerned about the coughing. "Clare, you need to go see a doctor," he told her. "That Dr. Moore is still around, isn't he? He can give you some medicine or a tonic. Please promise me you'll go." One evening after another of Clare's coughing spells, Jack noticed a spot of blood on Clare's bed pillow. Clare was sitting up in the bed, throwing off the sheets from around her. "Oh Jack, my chest hurts— and look at me, I'm sweating. What's wrong with me?" He kissed her warm damp forehead and held her close. Worried, he insisted she tell Alice and made her promise she would go to the doctor's office the following day.

Weeks earlier, when Alice had noticed that Clare was losing weight, she started bringing stews and soups to her house. "I know you don't feel like cooking, but Joe expects some supper before he goes to work in the evening." Alice did not want Joe getting angry with Clare. She was also concerned about Clare's constant coughing, especially after hearing rumors about outbreaks of tuberculosis in the Pittsburgh area. She had read articles in the newspaper about tuberculosis… how the disease was becoming common in the mill towns along the river. Clare had only recently told her about Beth Ann, the poor girl at work who had sat next to her for weeks…coughing. And that Beth Ann was no longer there. Alice was alarmed. She did not mutter the words *tuberculosis* or *consumption*, as it was commonly called, to Clare, but she had read that anyone in a weakened condition could contract tuberculosis, especially someone who was in close contact with another person who had contracted the disease, and who didn't eat properly. Some people afflicted with the disease even died if their symptoms were not treated in time. Alice had good reason to worry.

The day Clare told her that she was coughing up blood and having trouble breathing, Alice became so alarmed she ran to fetch Dr. Moore. She found him at his office. He agreed to stop by to see Clare that afternoon.

The elderly doctor confirmed Alice's suspicions and gave Clare some medicine to ease the coughing spells. Alice had told him how exhausted Clare frequently was, and that she had stopped going to work a week ago. Dr. Moore said he would come back the next day to check on Clare, and he cautioned her. "You must start eating," he said, "and rest as much as you can… Clare, this is serious."

That evening when Jack stopped by, he was glad to hear that Clare had been seen by Dr. Moore. She told him the doctor had told her to rest, and that he had given her some medicine. Jack was still concerned. He sat next to her, holding her hand. Later, he made her some tea and tried to get her to eat some soup, telling her he wouldn't stay long since she needed to sleep. He was relieved that Alice was bringing food to the house and checking on Clare. He knew her brother Joe wouldn't do anything to help her. Even Clare admitted, "That man doesn't have a caring bone in his body." As he sat close to her, Jack finally said, "Clare, I have some news that you probably won't be happy about. My boss, Mr. McGee, wants me to take charge on an out-of-town job. He thinks I'm ready to be a supervisor and told me how much he trusts me, and that he's confident I can handle the responsibility.

"I have to go to Youngstown, Ohio…tomorrow," Jack continued. "We're leaving on a train in the morning. McGee is going with me and staying for the first couple of days. We'll be hiring a local union crew; the work will be in a new addition to the hospital there. McGee will pay for my lodgings in a nearby hotel. He says I'll probably have to stay there for around two months. The good news is that it pays a lot more than I've have been making." He stopped, caressing her hand. Then he kissed it gently.

Clare tried to smile, but her eyes were sad. She whispered, "I'll miss you. But when you return, I should be better. Don't worry, my dearest Jack, I'll soon be good as new." Jack kissed her forehead. Clare thought he looked worried. "Please take good care of yourself," Jack told her. "Let Alice do the housework for you, and the cooking too. You need to rest and get your strength back. I love you…and will miss you so much. Every night I'll look up at the moon and think of you. And us." He kissed her again.

"Goodbye, my love, my sweet Jack," she whispered as she let go of his hand. She didn't want to let go but knew she must. She was afraid. Then he was gone.

Two weeks later Dr. Moore told Clare and Alice he saw no improvement in her condition. In fact, Clare had begun coughing up small amounts of blood daily. Dr. Moore suggested Clare go to a special hospital for tuberculosis patients, where she could get more care.

Removing his spectacles, the white-haired doctor sat and explained the details. "A newer hospital, a sanatorium, as they are referred to, was opened two years ago in Armstrong County, about thirty miles from Pittsburgh. The sanatorium is staffed with doctors and nurses who are specially trained in the treatment of patients with tuberculosis. You'll have good food and a lot of fresh air." He looked at Clare and Alice sternly. "Tuberculosis is very serious—and if you want to get better, Clare, this is the best option. I'll take care of all the arrangements."

Alice, trying to hold back her emotions, asked, "How long will she be gone?"

Dr. Moore replied, "Well, to be honest, every case is different. Some patients only stay for six months, sometimes a year. In Clare's case, it all depends on how advanced her illness is, and how well she responds to treatment. We try to be optimistic. You may correspond with her by writing letters; no visitors are permitted until she shows improvement."

Concerned about the cost, Alice was told that the government wanted tuberculosis patients isolated from the general population. Everything was paid for by the government in order to contain the disease. Alice figured that was one small silver lining to a very dark cloud.

~e&e~

Dr. Moore arranged for a special hospital motor car to transport Clare to the sanatorium. She was only allowed to take one small bag containing her bare necessities. He assured both Clare and Alice that everything would be provided for her.

During the week that Dr. Moore was making the arrangements, Alice kept asking Clare about the gold locket on the gold chain, since Clare stubbornly refused to remove it. But Alice repeatedly questioned her about it—where had it come from? Who gave it to her? Her eyes welling up with tears, Clare finally blurted out the story…how she had been seeing Jack for the past year. She swore Alice to secrecy. "No one can ever know," she told her. "Please, Alice, swear that you won't tell a soul!"

Ever since they were children, Alice had protected her sister; so of course, Alice promised: her lips were sealed. Still, she wondered if Margaret or Florence had any idea their brother had been visiting Clare….

The day for Clare to move to the sanatorium finally came. Alice helped her sister get ready and carried Clare's bag to the waiting automobile. Clare was too weak to protest. She just wanted to sleep. Sleep…and dream about Jack. She waved goodbye to Alice and kept her other hand on the locket over her heart.

CHAPTER 22

December 1917—Emma

The first Sunday in December the air was chilly, but the sun was trying to peek out from behind a gray cloud. After Johnny had his nap Emma bundled him up in his knitted hat and wool coat, brushed his hair back from his eyes, and reminded herself to give him a haircut tomorrow.

"Nan, Dorothy," she called, "get your coats on. We're walking up to see your grandparents." Dorothy jumped up and grabbed her wool coat along with her sister's. Then she stood patiently by the door, watching as Nan dawdled as usual. Dorothy had been such a big help to Emma during the past two months. She was always trying to be so grown-up, as nine-year-old girls tend to do. She helped with the cleaning and cooking, and she liked to play with Johnny. She was hoping Emma would tell her Daddy what a good girl she had been when he came back from his job in Youngstown. Secretly, Dorothy hoped he would bring her a present.

Jack had told Emma that the job would last about two months. His crew was working six days a week, ten hours a day. Everything was going according to schedule; Jack would be home before Christmas. He occasionally sent a letter in the mail for Emma to read to the girls. Jack wrote that he missed them, and Johnny...and their mother. He always told them to work hard in school and to be very, very good, reminding them to listen to their Mama.

As Emma and the children walked up to her parents' house, she was looking forward to spending the rest of the day with Papa, Fred, and Harry, and joining in their discussions about the war. Back in April, after the United States had remained neutral for as long as possible, the U.S. Congress had voted to declare war on Germany. America was joining Great Britain, France, and Russia against the Central Powers of Germany and Austria-Hungary.

For months Emma had been reading articles in the newspapers detailing the events that had finally led to the declaration of war. Although one of the reasons the United States had tried to remain neutral was the many immigrants in America , who had ties to both sides, recently Mama had stated: "*Moreau* is a French name, and we must support our country and our French allies." That was fine with Papa: he had always said the only good things that had ever come out of Germany were beer and sauerkraut.

Anxious to keep informed of all the facts, Emma had read about German U-boats sinking several American merchant ships in the North Atlantic. Up until that point the United States felt it was in the national interest to continue trade with both sides.

Public opinion was starting to change. Naturally the United States had strong ties with Britain based on history and the English language. And now the British strategy involved blocking trade with Germany. America was predominantly trading with England and France and had cut most of its trade with Germany.

Dorothy and Nan played with their dolls on the rug in Mama's parlor, as the adults discussed the news. Even young Dorothy asked her mother, "What's a U-boat?" Emma explained, "It comes from the German word *unterseeboot*, which means 'undersea boat.' Sometimes they are called submarines." Little Nan thought the German term was the funniest word she had ever heard. She repeated it slowly: *"Unter-see-boat."* Then she laughed hysterically.

That afternoon, while Mama and Monnie were preparing dinner in the kitchen, Emma went in the parlor to check on Johnny, who always liked to sit in the upholstered chair with his grandfather. Emma also wanted to join the conversation about the latest news about the war. The men were speaking in hushed tones, and Emma knew that they didn't want Mama to hear them discussing the topic of conscription. Mama didn't want to talk about the possibility of Fred and Harry being drafted into service.

Back in May, Congress had passed the Selective Service Act, which required all men, ages twenty-one to thirty, to register. Apparently, there were not enough volunteers for the military, so the government would have to start drafting men into service. By September, the law was updated: now it was mandatory for all men between the ages of eighteen and forty-five to register for the draft. Emma had seen the army recruiting posters with the white-haired man in a red, white, and blue hat and jacket pointing his finger at potential recruits: "I WANT YOU for U.S. ARMY!" the posters had read. Many young men were full of enthusiasm, volunteering even though they had never seen any military action. The men being drafted also wanted to show their patriotism and support their country by fighting for peace and justice. Emma's brother Harry, who was eighteen, had always wanted to be a soldier. Theodore Roosevelt was still his hero, and Harry had always been impressed with the fact that his own grandfather had served in the Civil War. Filled with a sense of adventure, he immediately wanted to volunteer for service. Mama had cried and made a fuss. "Absolutely not!" she told him.

After losing Eddie, Mama didn't want her remaining sons Fred and Harry going off to war. Hopefully, her oldest son, Albert, wouldn't have to go. Although Papa thought if he did, maybe the army would allow him to work in one of their offices. Surely, they needed intelligent men like Albert for jobs other than crawling around in ditches with a rifle. Albert was thirty-six, the same age as Jack.

By summer the first troops had been sent to Europe, and by October they were fighting the Germans in France. Mama had good reason to be worried: more and more young men were being drafted, and there had been several reports of heavy casualties.

Emma was afraid that Jack might have to go. Papa tried to calm her fears. "Emma," he told her, "I wouldn't worry too much. Men with children are being deferred. The government is also granting deferments to men with medical problems or who are considered unfit."

"I'm ready, willing, and able to enlist," Harry said, "when I get a notice." Papa replied quietly: "We won't talk about it in front of your mother, until the day comes." Emma looked at Harry, thinking how tall, handsome, and strong he had become. Her baby brother would make for a proud and courageous soldier.

Then she glanced at Fred, who had just poured himself another glass of whiskey. He did not say anything as he stood looking out the window. Emma thought to herself, *the army would be crazy to take Fred. He wouldn't be able to march in a straight line or, God forbid, shoot a rifle.* Fred was only twenty-eight, five years younger than Emma, but the alcohol and his depression were slowly destroying him, physically and mentally. Anyone with two eyes could see it.

Papa said, "I still think America should have remained neutral. Our country should have stayed out of it. Let England fight its own battles." Harry argued, "They were sinking our ships, Papa. So of course, we have to defend what is ours. Americans were on board those ships. We have to fight for freedom on the high seas as well as freedom on land." Harry was passionate about the cause and eager to fight.

Emma chimed in. "President Wilson gave it a lot of thought. He said this will be a war to end all wars. And it will make the world safe for democracy. I want to believe that." A moment later she thoughtfully repeated, *"A war to end all wars...."*

Monnie had set the dining room table for dinner, using Mama's good Sunday china. "I hope everybody is hungry," she called out. "It's time to eat."

Before they filled their plates, Papa recited the prayer "Grace before Meals." The many members of the extended Moreau family bowed their heads and folded their hands. "Bless us, O Lord, for these thy gifts, which we are about to receive," Papa recited. "From thy bounty, through Christ our Lord. Amen."

Johnny echoed, "A-a-men!" which made Nan giggle. Mama had prepared baked chicken with noodles and gravy, which was everyone's favorite meal. She had also cooked green beans grown in Papa's garden. Monnie had baked rolls and an apple pie. The adults drank tea, and the children sipped their milk. Emma noticed that young eighteen-year-old Harry preferred milk. Her little brother was still a boy at heart. After the women washed and dried the dishes, Emma gathered the children around her. She told them to thank their grandma for dinner. Then she instructed them to give their grandparents each a hug and a kiss on the cheek. They also hugged their Uncle Harry and Uncle Fred. Harry knelt and gave each child a tight embrace.

They especially loved Uncle Harry. He would sit on the floor with them to play. In the summer he would chase them in the yard and give Johnny piggyback rides. Johnny would laugh until he couldn't breathe. "More, more!" he always insisted.

Emma missed Jack. *Maybe absence does make the heart grow fonder,* she thought. She had always been independent. During the past year she had started attending meetings of several organizations she belonged to. She was grateful Monnie was occasionally able to come to the house in the afternoon to watch Johnny while the girls were in school. Monnie's visits enabled Emma to attend church meetings and meetings at the local Carnegie Library. She now belonged to the Confraternity of Christian Mothers, a church group that performed charitable works for parish members. The ladies visited the sick, cooked food for bereaved families, and knitted blankets for newborns and the elderly. Emma also belonged to the local auxiliary of the Ladies of the Grand Army of the Republic. She had begun going to meetings with Mama about twelve years earlier and now wanted to become more active. To be a member, one had to be a descendent of a veteran of the Civil War. Mama's father, Emma's grandfather, had fought in the war, even though he was an immigrant from Germany. He had been proud to wear the army uniform and fight for the Union. "He was only gone for a few months and was shot in the leg," Mama said. Emma remembered that her grandfather, Grandpa Becker, had always walked with a limp from his battlefield injury. She wished now that she had asked him more questions about the Civil War. She knew only that he had been at the Battle at Gettysburg. Mama had no recollections of that time, since she had been a small child when her father had served in the military.

She understood that the mandate of the LGAR was to teach patriotism. The organizers strove to preserve the history of the Civil War and worked toward the preservation of historical battlefields, like Gettysburg. They also worked to support the Grand Army of the Republic, which was the corresponding group of men's veterans and their male descendants.

Emma had also resumed attending meetings and lectures at her favorite venue, the local Carnegie Library. She had been to several interesting discussions concerning women's rights during the last few months. In truth, the women's suffrage movement had been active for years; women were finally realizing that to achieve reform in laws and attitudes, they needed to be able to legally vote. *Yes!* thought Emma, as she smiled. She had been saying as much for a long time. She was excited to see the pictures in the newspapers of picket lines in New York City and Washington, D.C.: women marching, carrying signs reminding politicians that they wanted equality and the right to vote. Emma knew President Wilson was in favor of supporting the cause. She knew it would happen soon.

Right now, though, the nation's politicians were concerned with the war over in Europe, and the government was sending more troops there every day.

Emma was aware Jack didn't approve of her attending all the meetings she went to, but she wasn't going to give them up. Jack got to go wherever he wanted, especially in the evenings, with all his union meetings, and going to bars all over the city. And what about the nights when he slept at his father's house in Hazelwood? She had told Jack many times, "You can't tell me what to do or where to go, since you do whatever you damn well please!"

Emma was determined to become even more involved with her club activities, maybe join some committees or run for a club office. She was already thinking of ways she could use her typewriter again...typing up minutes of meetings or corresponding with officers at other club locations.

"Dear husband of mine," she mused aloud, and to herself, "you haven't seen anything yet."

CHAPTER 23

May 1918—Clare

The two-story red brick hospital had been Clare's home for the past seven months, ever since she had arrived at the sanatorium situated in the green rolling hills of Armstrong County in western Pennsylvania, about thirty miles northeast of Pittsburgh. The thirty miles might as well have been three hundred. Everything looked so different from Hazelwood. No steel mills or smokestacks spewing soot into the air. No dark, smelly river.

Clare had gone for a walk that morning, enjoying the beautiful landscaping as she strolled along the cement sidewalks that ran through the grounds. She had spotted some lilac bushes that were in bloom and wanted to get close enough to smell them. They reminded her of the times she had walked in the gardens with Jack when they were young. Those were the days of innocence and young love. Days of her past. Memories she treasured.

She did not remember much from when she had first arrived at the sanatorium, back in the fall. Her chest had hurt so badly, especially when she had those coughing fits that almost made her pass out, when she could not catch her breath. She had been certain she was dying. She was consumed by exhaustion. The only thing she wanted to do was sleep. Never seeing a familiar face, she had been so lonely and sad, missing Alice, Margaret, and even her brother Joe. But most of all she missed Jack.

The doctors had explained everything that they knew about her illness. Tuberculosis was a serious disease of the lungs, sometimes fatal. Clare was glad the doctors were truthful with her and did not give their patients false hope. They said most patients eventually return home after their condition improved. They stressed how important it was to get lots of rest and eat good, nutritious food. She had seen other patients come for a while then leave when they were better. She had also seen the ones who didn't improve and eventually disappeared. The doctors and nurses were efficient and kind; but they were always busy, having so many sick people to care for. Clare figured there were twenty beds in her ward—and one of the nurses had told her there were five wards. Men and women resided in separate wards. Each member of the staff wore white clothing; even the orderlies, who kept everything so clean, wore white. Female patients were furnished with white nightgowns, male patients were dressed in pajamas. Everyone had been given a robe to wear for when they walked in the hallways.

Finally, when Clare was feeling better and well enough to walk outside on warm spring mornings, she was permitted to dress in a simple blouse and skirt.

Most days, when Clare sat on the edge of her bed, she admired how clean everything looked. All the beds had white sheets and blankets. The sheets were changed daily. Clare kept thinking, *That's a lot of washing!* Her favorite nurse was a woman named Helen, who appeared to be a little older than Clare. Helen told her that the hospital employed people in the big laundry room. All they did all day was wash and iron sheets, blankets, and the nightclothes of the patients.

Helen had become a friend, and she helped brighten the monotony of Clare's days. She always greeted Clare with a smile and liked to talk, though she never could chat more than a few minutes as she made her rounds. She had told Clare that her father had been a doctor, and that she had grown up helping him and learning. He had arranged for her to go to a nursing school in Pittsburgh; the school was run by Catholic nuns at one of the city hospitals. She loved her work and said she had never married. She had even considered becoming a nun at one point, when she was younger. "But no," Helen said, "that wasn't for me. A little too much time spent praying, when all I wanted to do was help patients get better. And you can't do that when you're on your knees with your hands folded. I figured that I'd never have time for a husband, children, and taking care of a house. You know how it is, everyone has to make choices." Clare was happy that all the nurses and doctors were so dedicated. She felt fortunate to be in such a new modern hospital and was grateful old Dr. Moore had been able to make the arrangements. If she had refused to go, she realized now, she probably would have died.

Back in December, Dr. Jones, one of the older physicians, a kindly gentleman, was examining her. He began by listening with his stethoscope to her heart and lungs. He had Clare lean forward, then he listened to her back… then her chest…then he was pressing on her stomach area and listening there too. He then moved the stethoscope lower to her abdomen, listening, and then pressed gently with an open hand and two fingers. Finally, he sat down in a chair next to her bed, took off his spectacles, and rubbed his forehead with his thumb and forefinger. He cleared his throat and looked at her chart, saying, "I see that you are thirty-six years old, Miss Murphy, and that you have never been married. I think we need to discuss what I have suspicions about."

Clare studied Dr. Jones' face with a worried expression, thinking he was going to tell her she would be dead soon. She took a deep breath and braced herself. Dr. Jones rubbed his trim white beard, and Clare stared at his blue eyes and bushy eyebrows, waiting for him to give her the bad news. But then he completely shocked her. "I believe you are pregnant," he said. "In other words, you are with child."

Clare's eyes widened. Her cheeks grew warm and red. She couldn't believe what she had just heard, thinking her ears were playing tricks on her. The physician asked her if she remembered when she had her last monthly period of bleeding. She thought for a moment. "Last summer, maybe August," she said. "I figured I wasn't having it because I was sick." Dr. Jones then told her, "I can hear a heartbeat, so you most likely are in your fifth month. You'll start feeling the baby's movement within the next month," he explained kindly, as though he was uncertain how much Clare might know of these matters.

Clare was confused. Tears started to fill her eyes. Her hands began trembling, and she was suddenly at a loss for words. The walls were closing in, perhaps they would collapse, crushing her, hiding her secret life. She had no idea what would happen. "Dear Jesus," she whispered, "what am I going to do?"

Dr. Jones looked at her with kind eyes. "Now, I know you aren't married, so I'm not going to ask you a lot of questions; but this situation does complicate matters. Your health has improved, but you still will be a patient here for some time, most likely until summer."

"In the next three or four months," he continued, "we'll have to decide what happens after the child is born, which would be in the spring, probably in April. You will give birth here in the hospital, but the child will obviously not be able to remain in this environment. However, there is plenty of time to make decisions about the future."

"When will I be allowed to have visitors?" Clare asked, finally grasping the seriousness of her predicament. Dr. Jones reflected for a moment then answered: "If your lungs continue to improve and you get stronger, I will permit a visitor or two by the first of March."

During the next few weeks, Clare spent every waking moment pondering her dilemma and praying. What would Jack think? She needed to talk to Alice, and soon. Especially since Alice was the only person who knew about her seeing Jack.

Soon she started feeling little flutters of movement which made her smile. Clare touched her gold locket, missing her Jack. The doctors told her it was a good sign that she was getting her appetite back. She was finally able to eat three meals a day. She still was experiencing some pain in her chest, but it was much better than it had been, and she wasn't coughing as much.

By the beginning of March, she had begun writing letters to Alice every week. She had also written several times to Margaret. She was sadly aware there was no way she could write to Jack, although she was sure Margaret had told him of her diagnosis, and that she would be gone for quite a while. She tried to sound cheerful in her letters, saying she should be able to return home by summer.

Hoping that Alice would be able to visit her soon, Clare realized that her sister would be in for a surprise when she saw her. She was now very much with child and had quite a big round bulge under her loose dress. Clare needed to talk to Alice and get her opinion about what should happen with the baby. Dr. Jones had mentioned several foundling homes in Pittsburgh that arranged adoptions. She obviously would not be able to keep the child. Nurse Helen continued to be kind and compassionate. She brought Clare some knitting needles and yarn, which helped keep her mind occupied. Clare enjoyed talking to some of the other patients in the activity room where they played checkers, or a board game called Parcheesi. She tried to learn how to play chess, but it was too difficult, and she couldn't concentrate.

One older lady, Catherine, had been friendly. Clare enjoyed chatting with her, playing board games, or walking in the hallways side by side. Sometimes they would just sit by the window in the sunshine, talking about the weather and the flowers that would be blooming in the spring. Their conversations reminded Clare of the days when Jack would point out the lilacs, hydrangeas, daffodils, roses, and daisies in the gardens above Hazelwood…. She remembered how Jack had always admired the tall purple irises and even the tiny violets that grew wild by the fence surrounding the gardens. Closing her eyes, she pictured Jack holding her hand as he explained: "Clare, all of the flowers in the gardens have been planted with purpose and high hopes, except for those purple violets, which grow everywhere in the woods and hillsides." Jack had even pointed out some wild roses, which were not as plentiful as the violets.

Clare thought wildflowers such as violets must be special…planted by God. That's when she decided if her baby was a little girl, she would name her Violet. Her child was not planned but had been planted by God. She hoped whoever raised her baby would not change the name. Violet Rose. She also liked the name Rose Mary. Finally, she decided that either name would be fine. Her head started to hurt when she thought about it too much.

Her friend Catherine was a widow with two adult sons in their twenties. Her husband had been killed two years earlier in a factory accident. She was from the North Side of Pittsburgh and was hoping to go home soon, so she could help care for her baby grandson. Catherine was almost like an older sister to Clare, and Clare liked talking with her. She could tell Catherine had been a very pretty woman when she was younger, though her face had some wrinkles, and gray streaks were starting to come out in her dark hair.

Clare encouraged Catherine to talk about herself and her family, and she was glad Catherine didn't ask questions about Clare's situation, and what would happen to her baby. Clare, herself, was wondering about the future of her baby. Decisions had to be made. Soon.

During the long nights lying in her bed, Clare dreamed about living in a house with Jack and their baby. Jack would have a beautiful garden, and he would go for evening walks with Clare and their child. They could enjoy each other in the daytime, not just by moonlight. Maybe seek sunshine, not just stardust. They would be so happy, being together every day. She imagined cooking in their kitchen and sewing clothes on her sewing machine. She pictured her and Jack in a big warm bed, every night, all night. Dreams weren't real and never last…She always woke up and felt the baby moving within her, she heard other patients coughing as she stared at the cold white ward of beds…her cold world…her reality. The tears welled up and spilled out from the corners of her eyes. No matter how she tried to stop them, they rolled down her cheeks, dripping on the gold locket that sat guarding her heart.

One morning back in February she had stood looking out the windows in the activity room, touching the cold glass where her breath was causing a hint of frost to form. She kept thinking that perhaps her illness was a blessing in disguise. Since she had to be quarantined with tuberculosis, she had been forced to go away…and no one in Hazelwood would ever know that she had been pregnant, and that she had given birth. It would be her secret, and Alice's. Nobody else would ever know. She struggled with what she would tell Jack when, eventually, she saw him again. She would have to tell him, even though he would never get to hold their child. Then the darkness of the situation would cloud her thoughts. Clare wrestled with the idea that her illness was God's punishment for her sins. After all, God sees all and knows all. Every action and every deed. Sinful deeds, sinful desires. Clare's baby was a mark on her soul forever, a reminder of her sins. Would God ever forgive her? She could never confess this to Father Donnelly or Father Walsh. Maybe she could find another priest to talk to, one who did not know her family or Jack's family.

Jack's father, old Sean Quinn, and Jack's sisters must never ever find out. Margaret and Florence were her friends, but they would never know the secret. And then there was her brother Joe, who had hated Jack Quinn ever since the day Jack had humiliated him in front of all his drinking buddies. Joe despised Jack—and he made sure everyone in Hazelwood knew it. He had sworn up and down for the past ten years that Jack had cracked his ribs and caused him to lose two teeth that day they had fought in the street.

Joe would threaten and berate Clare: "That Jack Quinn acts like he's Jesus Christ, walking around in his fine suits, pretending he's better than us, thinking he's too good for Hazelwood. I bet *you* even think he can walk on water. Someday I'll see if he can swim in that damn river. If I ever see you even looking in his direction, Clare, I'll stick my knife in his gut. Maybe in yours too." Then Joe had showed her a knife he kept hidden in his boot, underneath his pant leg. Her brother's craziness, his drunken rants and lack of good judgement worried Clare. She had felt sorry for him because of the abuse Joe had endured as a child at the hands of their grandfather. But his behavior had gotten worse the older he had become; this was especially true after their parents had died. With most people, age brought wisdom and tolerance, but not in Joe's case. She had heard the government had started a military draft: men up to the age of forty-five were required to register. Joe was almost forty; if the army was really getting desperate, maybe he would be drafted. She hoped it wasn't a sin to wish her own brother would be forced to march off to war. Even the Germans would be sorry if they ran into Joe Murphy on the battlefield!

Clare had always recognized that Joe had a hot temper and drank too much, but when he threatened her as well as Jack, she knew her brother could cause a lot of trouble if he ever found out what had been going on right under his nose. She sometimes imagined what would have taken place if he had unexpectedly come home from the mill and found Jack in his house. She shuddered at the thought.

~ ⁍ ~

By the second week in March, Clare was finally allowed to have visitors. She wrote to Alice, informing her that she would be the only person allowed to see Clare. This was a lie, but Clare couldn't risk anyone else seeing her in her condition. What if Alice brought Margaret with her? Even the most loose, ill-fitting dress could not mask the fact that she would soon be giving birth. She told Alice that she needed to discuss a very private matter with her, and that it was urgent.

The last Sunday in March, Alice and her husband rode the train from Pittsburgh. Johnny refused to let Alice travel by herself, and Alice was relieved to have his company. She had informed him he would have to remain in the waiting room while she visited with Clare.

"No problem, dear," Johnny Finnegan had said. He had always been good-natured. "I'll read the latest on the war in the papers. And the train ride will be a nice adventure away from Hazelwood and the mill."

When Alice was brought into the activity room where Clare was waiting, she was stunned when she saw Clare's huge stomach. "Dear Lord!" she exclaimed. "I can see we have a lot to talk about." They hugged each other. Clare couldn't stop the tears from rolling down her blushing cheeks. She kept repeating, "I'm so glad you're here. Finally." And Alice said: "My dear sister, you look so much better than the last time I saw you. I was afraid I would never see you again!" As they sat in a private corner of the room, Clare held tightly to her sister's hands. She proceeded to tell Alice that finding out she was pregnant had been a great surprise. She told Alice what Dr. Jones had said about the foundling homes, how the institutions could arrange to put Clare's baby up for adoption. "I wanted to talk to you and get your opinion before I make any decisions," Clare said. "It's important no one in Hazelwood ever know anything about me having a child. Can you imagine if Joe found out, or Jack's sisters?" Alice looked lovingly at her sister and said: "Clare, you know that I have always protected you, so I don't want you to worry about that. I wish I could be with you when the baby comes, but I'll come back here as soon as possible. I'm looking forward to you being healthy again and coming home." Clare assured her sister that all the doctors agreed she should be able to return home in the summer if she has a good recovery from childbirth.

The sisters were able to visit with one another for an hour; then Alice was informed she would have to leave. She hugged Clare, telling her, "Don't worry, and I'll be back as soon as I can." She gently patted Clare's stomach. "I'll say twice as many prayers as I have been."

On the train ride back to Pittsburgh, Johnny sensed that something was wrong. Alice kept squeezing his hand, and she seemed lost in thought. They had always confided in each other. Finally, Alice looked him in the eye, and said, "I have to tell you something, but you have to swear to me you can keep a secret." Johnny was a trustworthy man and had always told Alice he would do anything for her. He was the finest man she had ever known. Kind, honest, hard-working, with an Irish sense of humor she loved. She felt lucky to be married to John Finnegan; he was her rock. Johnny smiled. "Of course, I can keep a secret. I swear on my mother's grave, on my father's grave, and on the bones of dear Saint Patrick!"

There were no other passengers sitting close to them, so Alice told Johnny everything. All about Clare and Jack seeing each other secretly, and about the baby, which had been an unanticipated, overwhelming surprise. Actually…a shock!

It was a lot to absorb. Johnny was speechless for the next twenty minutes as the train headed toward the station in downtown Pittsburgh. They were both lost in thought, gazing out the window of the train as it rumbled noisily along the tracks. It was after six o'clock in the evening when they hurried to catch the next streetcar to Hazelwood. By seven it was almost dark. They walked in silence up to their house; but now for some reason, Johnny looked like he was ready to burst. Once they were inside their home Alice saw he was glowing—even more than usual, given his ruddy complexion. "Johnny, what is it?" she asked. "Is something wrong?"

Johnny tried to appear serious, but Alice noticed his eyes twinkling. "Alice, dear," he said, "would you please sit down for a minute. I have an idea we need to discuss."

Alice and her husband sat at their kitchen table. Johnny reached for her hand. "We've been married for a long time and have never been blessed with a child," he began. "I was thinking perhaps we could adopt Clare's baby. I mean, well…Clare is your sister and Jack used to be my best friend. *That child is already one of us!* And we could give it a good home. We would keep Clare's secret. No one would ever know it was her baby."

They both stared at each other. "Well, what do you think of my idea?" Johnny finally said, then he inhaled deeply and waited.

Alice couldn't speak. There was such a lump in her throat, she stood up and wrapped her arms around her husband; tears of joy rolled down her face. She couldn't believe it. She grabbed Johnny's shoulders, kissed his cheeks and then his full lips "Johnny Finnegan, I love your idea, and I love you!" she exclaimed. She kissed him again.

Johnny was quite pleased with himself. He couldn't stop grinning. His entire face was glowing. Even his eyes were smiling.

The following Sunday, much to Clare's surprise, Alice and Johnny returned to the hospital to visit her. Alice proceeded to tell Clare about their plans to adopt Clare's baby. Clare trusted Alice and Johnny more than anyone else she knew. She was quickly persuaded. And Clare's doctors agreed with her when she told them of her plans: placing the infant with a family member was the best and easiest solution. Two weeks later, on the third Friday in April, Clare started to experience mild back pains as she walked the grounds of the hospital. It was a fine spring day, the warmest so far. Clare and her friend Catherine were strolling near the one willow tree that was, of course, Clare's favorite tree on the hospital property. But Catherine was not recovering as well as Clare. She tired easily and wanted to stop to rest on every bench they passed. Clare gazed at the light reflecting off the leaves of the willow tree.

Suddenly, Clare felt an intense pain across her abdomen and lower back. Watching the long willow branches gently swaying in the breeze, Clare waited until the pain passed. Then, as she stood again, she felt water running down her legs. It gathered in a small puddle around her shoes. Clare gasped. "What is happening?" she asked, slightly embarrassed. Catherine took her hand and smiled. "Your water just broke," she said. "Don't worry, dear, this is all part of childbirth. I've been through it twice in my life. We better get you back inside, and let nature take its course. By this time tomorrow you'll be holding that little baby." The two women headed back to their ward. Clare was happy to see Nurse Helen standing by the door. The nurse quickly ushered Clare to her bed then went to find Dr. Jones. The doctor examined her and told her that Helen would escort her to another area in the hospital where she would be in a private room and would not disturb the other patients. He also told her she was fortunate to be in a hospital environment where she would have the best care, benefitting from the latest methods of childbirth. Clare had no idea what that meant. Seeing that Clare had little knowledge of such matters, Dr. Jones smiled. "These days hospitals administer pain medicine and a little morphine to women in labor; it has started to become standard practice. You'll have a much more pleasant experience than women who deliver at home. So, don't worry," he said, "everything will be fine."

Clare was taken by wheelchair to another white room at the far end of the hospital. The room was much smaller than the ward she was used to. As her pain became more intense, she welcomed the relief offered by the pain medications. She heard the staff mention the words *ether* and *morphine*; after what seemed like an eternity, she gradually drifted off to sleep. When Clare awoke, she was so groggy and confused it took her several minutes to focus her eyes and remember where she was. Her head hurt, and she could barely move it. Then she realized that her whole body was trembling and cold. *Everything* hurt. She couldn't find her voice as she started to cry. She felt alone. A nurse she didn't recognize was standing by her bed. The nurse looked at Clare with kind eyes. "Everything is over," she said. "You are fine, and your baby is fine." The nurse covered Clare with another white blanket. "You probably have a lot of questions. The nurse smiled. "Dr. Jones will be in soon. He'll be glad to see that you're awake." And then she left the room. Clare was thirsty but could barely lift her head off the pillow. She drifted back to sleep—for just a few minutes, she thought. When Clare opened her eyes again, she could see Dr. Jones and hear him saying her name. She managed to raise her hand in a small wave. "Come on, Clare, open those eyes. Somebody wants to meet you…." She managed a smile and saw nurse Helen standing next to him. Helen was holding a little bundle wrapped in a white blanket. She leaned forward, pulled down the edge of the blanket, and Clare could see a tiny red face with dark hair. She saw a little fist and then managed to gently touch the top of the tiny hand. She heard a little gurgle and then a whimper. "I just fed her with a bottle," Helen said. "She's ready to sleep."

Clare blinked back tears and whispered, "It's a girl?" "Yes," said Dr. Jones. "A healthy baby girl." Helen left the room, carrying the infant. Clare noticed the doctor pull up a chair next to her bed. "She was born yesterday, Clare," Dr. Jones told her. "The medicines we used allowed you to sleep through it, although that makes for a more difficult delivery, since you weren't able to assist by using your muscles to push the baby out."

"Using these medicines is not an exact science," he continued. "Every patient is different. There should be no lasting effects to mother or child. However, I did have to use an instrument called forceps to help pull out the infant. So, you'll notice that the baby has several red marks on her forehead and sides and back of her head. These will fade in time. Your pain will diminish, and eventually, as your body heals, you shouldn't experience any lasting damage from the birth experience."

As the information started to sink into her foggy brain, Clare thought it sounded barbaric. She was glad she had not been awake. Dr. Jones said. "We need to start getting some water and food into you; then, in a couple days, you'll feel strong enough to walk a little. The most important thing now is to get your strength back. Recovery takes time. I've contacted your sister Alice, so I would venture to guess that next Sunday she will be here to visit. You're fortunate to have such a caring sister. Some of our patients have no one."

The thought of seeing Alice made Clare smile. Dr. Jones continued: "We, and I mean this hospital, will only be able to care for the infant for a limited time. She must remain completely isolated from other patients, for obvious reasons. So, the sooner arrangements can be made for your sister and her husband to take the baby home the better for all involved. We'll keep you in isolation also, until the infant is removed from the premises. Do you have any questions?"

"When can I go home?" Clare asked.

Dr. Jones smiled quietly again. "Hopefully by June or July. We want to make sure that you're not coughing at all and that your lungs are healed. You must be eating well and have a good appetite. The stronger you are, the less chance of a relapse. So, time will tell."

Time will tell… The words kept floating around her. *A baby girl…Home.* "I have to tell them her name…" Clare muttered to herself. "Her name is Violet, or Rose…Rose Mary…" Her eyelids grew heavy; she was overcome again by the need to sleep.

CHAPTER 24

July 1918—Jack

In December of 1917, Mr. McGee informed Jack that he was pleased with his supervisory skills on the job in Youngstown. Jack got along well with the men in his crew, and there hadn't been any labor disputes or problems. So of course, McGee was content. The job had made a lot of money for McGee's company. Jack had put forth a conscious effort to stay away from the bars in Youngstown. He didn't want to let Mr. McGee down by having a hangover at work or getting mixed up with unsavory characters. Jack kept a bottle of whiskey in his hotel room and did not socialize with any of the men who worked on his job. After working long hours every day, he ate dinner in one of the local family-run eateries. Then he returned to his hotel room, had a drink of whiskey, and went to sleep.

He was proud of himself when he mailed letters to Emma, asking her to read the letters to the children. He told them how much he missed them. He promised them he would be home a few days before Christmas. Jack had shopped for some gifts for them, buying a dress for each of the girls and a wool cap for Johnny, just like the big boys wore. He also bought a small bag of marbles for Johnny and a set of paper dolls for Dorothy and Nan.

Jack also wanted to find something special for Emma, perhaps as a peace offering. He finally spotted a gold brooch in a jewelry store window in downtown Youngstown. The brooch had a sunburst in the center and three small diamonds. Emma could pin it to a coat or dress. He hoped that she would like it, especially if he told her that the diamonds represented their three children. Sometimes Jack would stare out the window of his hotel room at night, gazing at the moon, and wonder if Clare was looking at the moon too. Moonlight and stardust…memories that tore at his heart. He hoped her health had improved and figured he'd find out soon enough, when he visited Dad and his sisters next month.

In January after Jack returned from Youngstown, McGee sent Jack to work in one of the office buildings under construction on Grant Street in downtown Pittsburgh. Jack enjoyed being back with his old friends Jimmy Kennedy and Joe Sullivan; he was surprised to find out they were both courting women who were sisters they had met on the South Side streetcar. The ladies worked in an office, performing clerical duties. Jimmy hinted that he and Joe were thinking about marriage…. Over lunch one day as they all put their feet up on wooden crates filled with tools and plumbing supplies, Jimmy said: "Well, like my mother keeps telling me, it's high time I grow up and become respectable. She reminds me that most men are married by the time they're thirty-five. I suppose I'll have to finally move out of my parents' house."

Joe added, "My mum says she's sick of washing my dirty clothes and having to worry about where I am at night. She told me I need to find a nice girl and settle down. She warns me constantly that those women in the bars aren't respectable girls, and no decent man ever marries one of those tramps." The three men laughed at the comment. "Mum even says the bar tramps are known to not want babies," Jimmy remarked. "So, they have back alley 'solutions' to any unwanted problems. She says it's a wonder more of them don't end up dead from botched operations performed by people that aren't even doctors."

There was no laughter now. The trio sat eating, each lost in his own private thoughts. The conversation made Jack think about Nel. He had once asked Nel if any of her girls ever got pregnant, and Nel had replied, "Yes, it happens. But we know a doctor that fixes the situation." She disclosed, "It happened to me once, when I was sixteen—and that operation left me scarred for life, so badly I could never get pregnant again. Almost died. So maybe that ended up being a good thing…only had to go through it once. I never wanted babies anyways."

After a couple of minutes, as he took a bite of an apple from his lunch, Joe continued: "Mum says to me just yesterday that I need to be more like that Jack Quinn who has a wife and children and his own house."

Jack teased them. "Geez, I go out of town for a couple of months and you two forget how to have a good time! Well, I guess it's time you both started listening to your mothers. I'll even give you my blessing…we can drink to that after your weddings!"

Jimmy and Joe were also concerned about being drafted into the army. They hoped all the younger guys would be called to serve before them. Jack was certain he was exempt from service since he had three children. He had been informed as much after he had registered, as required by law.

He told Jimmy and Joe that Emma's brothers had received draft notices last week, but Fred had been found medically unfit to serve—no surprise there. "Fred drinks more in one day than the three of us put together," Jack said. "I guess working and living in a bar makes it too easy to give in to the temptation to guzzle booze and smoke cigars constantly. And Fred doesn't have a wife to make him feel guilty."

Jack continued: "However, eighteen-year-old Harry is scheduled to leave for basic training on the first of February. Harry had wanted to enlist last summer, but his mother persuaded him to wait until he was drafted. The young fellow is full of enthusiasm—he's looking forward to going. It's as if he's embarking on a great adventure."

Jack, Jimmy, and Joe had all heard about the trench warfare in France and the British and American soldiers who were fighting to the death, many being killed by rifle fire, poison gas, flamethrowers, and machine gun fire. There was also a new form of explosives, hand grenades. Many of the soldiers were maimed and wounded, some dying from infections of their injuries. They had read the reports in the newspapers about the battles and the Germans' brutality. The war was the main topic of conversation among the men over lunch, on the streetcars, and in the bars and taverns.

"I try not to talk about it in front of Emma and her family," said Jack. "They are all concerned about Harry being drafted. And Emma's mother is going to have a rough time. She's already praying and worrying…and once he leaves it will be worse. Hopefully, the war will be over soon."

At home in Elliott, Jack was determined to be more patient with the children and with Emma. While he had been in Youngstown, he had time to think about his marriage. He was ready to acknowledge that most of the blame for their problems was his fault. He had reflected on how he treated Emma and realized he needed to be a better husband and father.

He finally admitted to himself that his relationship with Clare was wrong. It wasn't fair to either of the women. After much soul searching, Jack concluded that he was responsible for his own happiness. Not Emma. Not Clare. If he envisioned and desired a peaceful home life, then he needed to make it happen by showing his wife and children that they were important to him. They were the reason he worked hard, and he needed to enjoy the fruits of his labor with them.

If he showed Emma that he cared and that he loved her, then hopefully she would want to be happy with him. She would stop being angry…and maybe she would remember how to love him again. Her suspicions would diminish if he started coming home early and didn't stay in the bars until midnight….Perhaps he could regain Emma's trust if he visited Hazelwood only for an hour or two, just enough time to have a meal with Dad and his sisters…and then, he told himself, he would come straight home. These thoughts floated around in his head as Jack pulled the blankets around his shoulders at night. He had been pleasantly surprised when Emma suggested he would sleep better in their bed instead of on the sofa, but then he was overwhelmed by loneliness and guilt. His wife was so close yet so far away as she slept with her back to him. Jack would never have been a brute by forcing himself on his wife; but he dreamed about the possibility his wife would want him again and encourage his touch. He missed what they used to have. Emma's laughter. Their intimate moments….

Jack knew in his heart this was his last chance to be a decent family man. A man like Emma's father, Henry. Like his own dad. He had to vow to himself, and to Emma, to be a better man…a better husband and father.

If he wanted Emma to trust him again then he had to put some effort into making things better. He figured showing Emma he could be the husband she had hoped for would take time. But he was determined to make it happen.

He realized he had to make a sacrifice, he had to give up Clare. The thought of never holding her again saddened him. It made his heart ache… that familiar pain. Maybe God was giving them both a warning when she had become sick. *Wake up, sinners, it wasn't meant to be.* God will send down pain and suffering. God was punishing them. What would Mum think? She had always told him to do what's right, be honest, not hurt anyone. Even Mum would be disappointed in him. "There's all kinds of lies, Jackie," she had once told him, "but a lie is still a lie, no matter how you sugarcoat it, and God sees everything we do."

His life was meant to be lived with Emma and his children. His sunlight was in *their* eyes. His future was in *their* faces. They should be part of his dreams, his promises. Why had it taken him so long to figure that out? His life was in Elliott. Somehow, he had lost his way…for a while. His heart, his home, was with Emma. No more time with Clare, stealing kisses, sneaking into her bed. No more Clare Murphy. Ever. *Never again, damn it!* Sacrifice? Yes, it was hard to make sacrifices. But that was his penance—and he didn't need a priest to tell him he needed to do penance, or to point him in the right direction. He knew what needed to be done.

Moonlight and stardust. He had to sacrifice them both and deal with the reality of the situation. The consequences were too risky and dangerous. Awful things could continue to happen…Maybe Clare would never be healthy again. What if his wife and children and Emma's parents found out and could never forgive him?

And then there was always the possibility that Clare's brother, despicable Joe Murphy, might discover them and go on a rampage. He could hurt Clare and come after Jack. He had already threatened to kill Jack, and not just once. Clare had told him about the knife Joe kept in his boot….

Jack knew he was wrong to get involved with Clare again, after all those years. He was selfish to encourage her, to let her get swept up in his dreams. Again. They were doomed. It never should have gone as far as it did. Clare needed to forget about him. She needed to have his name erased from her mind and heart forever. He knew now: he must stay away from her. *It isn't meant to be,* he thought, *so let her go.*

The rest of his self-inflicted penance involved his relationship with Nel. He needed to put her in his past also. He needed to adjust to the fact that he wasn't a young man just out to have a good time. To be young and wild wasn't meant to last forever. Everything had a season. All men were supposed to grow up. Jack Quinn had responsibilities and a family to take care of. *Grow up, damn it!* he told himself. He hoped it wasn't too late.

If he was lucky it wouldn't be too little, too late. Maybe Emma would forgive him and love him again. Maybe she could forgive and forget. He most likely would have to settle for just forgiveness. Women never forget.

The last Sunday in January Jack told Emma he should visit his sisters and Dad but assured her he would come straight home after a short visit. He was sorry to have to leave early from the usual Sunday afternoon get-together at the Moreau house.

When he arrived in Hazelwood, he noticed how everything in the town looked the same: still smoky, dreary, and gray. The streetlamps were illuminated, uncertain if it was night or day.

When he arrived at his Dad's home his sisters were surprised to see him and insisted that he stay for supper. Dad poured him a small glass of whiskey and wanted to hear about the job in Youngstown. Florence and Margaret took turns reporting all the news about the neighbors, activities at church, and their work at the clothing shop. Finally, Margaret said, "Clare is still at that special hospital for her tuberculosis. Alice says the disease is awful bad, and Clare won't be back for quite a while. She's not even allowed to have visitors." Jack tried not to look overly concerned. He commented, "That doesn't sound good." Immediately, after supper, he left to return to Elliott, as he had promised his wife.

In February Harry left for basic training. He was told he would be shipped over to France by April. Emma, her mother and father, as well as Monnie and Fred all fussed over him and wished him well. They tried to hold back their tears as they hugged him and patted his back; but boyish and naive Harry was anxious to leave and go fight for his country. He insisted he would be fine, and that he would write to them as often as possible.

As Jack waited his turn to say goodbye, he thought Harry seemed young…totally unprepared for what he would encounter. He was starry eyed, merely wanting to fight for peace and justice. Jack remembered the young boy who used to play soldier in the yard. He thought how all children and young men think they are invincible, immune to suffering, death, and evil. Jack shook Harry's hand and said, "Godspeed, Harry. Stay safe and be careful."

Harry told everyone it was an honor to serve his country, that this was his duty as a physically fit young man. Even his brother Fred had such a sad look in his eyes, probably feeling pangs of guilt that he, himself, wasn't going off to war. Jack thought Fred felt sorry for himself as well as for Harry. When Harry left, Fred shuffled back to the tavern. Back to his life, back to his own personal sorrows…missing baseball, missing Eddie—and now missing Harry. Fred lived one day at a time, with no dreams and nothing to look forward to.

By the end of April, the Moreau family had been receiving a letter from Harry every week. He was doing well, learning how to shoot a rifle, march, climb walls, and a host of other things all soldiers learn. He never went into detail, writing only that the army kept the recruits busy most of the time. Although he did mention that some of the fellows had taught him to play cards. He almost sounded like he was enjoying being a soldier, unaware of the dangers still awaiting him….

He encouraged his family to plant vegetable and herb gardens; the army called them Victory Gardens. The war effort was straining the nation's food supplies. Harry commented that the soldiers never seemed to have enough food to eat. Even that news was upsetting to Emma's mother.

I am leaving for France next week, Harry wrote, *so I most likely won't be able to write as often. Just know, my dearest family, that I miss you all and please keep praying for me.* He signed the letter, *Your loving son and brother, Harry.*

⁓⟨✦⟩⁓

On the first Sunday in May, Jack turned over the dirt in his garden in the backyard. He had bought Johnny a small shovel so he could help. Johnny was four years old; he enjoyed following his father around the yard. Jack had showed him how to pull weeds out of the ground. Today he had him make a pile of the small rocks they had dug out of the dirt. Johnny also stacked up small sticks and twigs at the far corner of the yard.

Johnny, Dorothy, and Nan had all liked the idea of planting a garden to help the soldiers. They missed their Uncle Harry, who had always taken time to play with them. Harry had spent hours pushing them on the swing, finding insects in the yard for them to examine, and telling them stories about pirates and buried treasure. Emma's father, Henry, had brought a basket of apples to the house for Emma earlier that day. She was in the kitchen, boiling the apples to make applesauce with Dorothy and Nan. The girls enjoyed cooking with their mother, practicing how to measure ingredients, stir the pot, and carefully follow the instructions given in the recipe. Now that Dorothy was almost ten and Nan was seven years of age, they could be counted on to help around the house. When Nan whined and complained, crying that she wanted to do more, she sometimes pinched Dorothy as hard as she could. Dorothy would retaliate with a slap to Nan's arm. Seven-year-old Nan would then scream and pull Dorothy's curls. That's when Emma picked up her wooden spoon and gave them each a quick smack on the hand. They both had to apologize, and Emma threatened to ban them from the kitchen, telling them: "You girls can go outside and dig in the dirt with your father and brother, or learn to be polite to each other."

Jack admired Emma's patience. He had started complimenting Emma on her cooking, how she managed the children, even her housekeeping. "Emma," he had told her one day, "I don't know how you do it. Listening to Nan's whining and complaining is enough to make anyone insane. I heard her call Dorothy a piece of horse shit—and then she spit at her. I couldn't believe it. I hollered at her, loud enough to scare her, and she ran out of the house. I told her I was going to wash her mouth out with soap."

Emma agreed: Nan was a handful, not as kind or easygoing as Dorothy and Johnny. She told Jack even the nuns at school had to occasionally sit her by herself in the corner, her punishment for disrupting the class. Apparently, this had happened several times during May and June. Dorothy always made a point of tattling on Nan when her little sister got in trouble. Of course, that just added fuel to the fire, as far as Nan was concerned. "Perhaps," said Emma, as she stirred a pot of beef stew that was simmering on the stove, "I was thinking that Nan is upset because she misses Harry so much. Maybe she's worried about him and is afraid to talk about it. She might be acting up and misbehaving because she's angry and scared."

Jack replied: "You could be right. I remember when my mother died. I was only nine…I was confused and angry. That's when I refused to go to school. Dad punished and threatened me, he even hit me with a belt; but I was stubborn and wouldn't go." Emma looked at him with tears in her eyes. "I hope and pray that Harry comes home," she said. Jack pulled her to him and wrapped his arms around her. He held her until the girls walked into the kitchen. Jack had begun making a conscious effort to let Emma know how much he appreciated her. He had seen it work on the job: how his men responded when he commended them on how well they were doing. He remembered Dad telling him, "You can catch more flies with honey than with vinegar."

Emma tolerated the messes made in the kitchen but insisted that the children help clean up afterward. Jack and Emma both agreed on the importance of chores. "Chores are important in bringing up responsible children," Emma declared. Then she added: "Idle hands are the devil's workshop."

By the end of June, Jack had decided that Sunday was his favorite day of the week. He still refused to attend Mass, but Emma didn't complain. She would leave Johnny home with Jack. In the afternoon he would walk with Emma and the children to her parents' house. Emma's mother always prepared chicken and noodles. Henry Moreau kept a chicken coop in the backyard. The chickens supplied the family with eggs and meat for their Sunday dinners. Next to the chicken coop was a garden where Henry had planted cabbage, cucumbers, green beans, and beets. His Victory Garden.

All the neighbors also had Victory Gardens. Everyone in the town felt it was their patriotic duty to support the war effort, even if that simply meant growing their own vegetables. Emma said the women from her church club were knitting socks for the soldiers.

Jack mentioned to his father-in-law that his vegetables were not looking as good as Henry's. Still a novice at gardening, Jack seemed to have better luck with his flowers. His peonies and lilies of the valley were doing better this year than last. Henry had told him, "Be patient, Jack, gardens take a few years to get everything right. Patience, effort, and a lot of trial and error." *Just like marriages,* Jack thought to himself.

~ex&e~

On Sundays Monnie always baked two kinds of pie for the family. Jack preferred the apple and the cherry, instead of blueberry. Monnie was still working at the bakery with Aunt Louisa and Aunt Sophie, taking on more and more duties and expanding their line of cakes and pies. After dinner, Emma played her mother's piano in the parlor while Estelle and Monnie entertained the children. The men – Jack, his father-in-law Henry, Frank, and Fred escaped to the front porch with a glass of whiskey in one hand and a cigar in the other. Their conversation centered on the latest news from the war in Europe. The family had received only two letters from Harry since he was shipped overseas. He had been in France for almost two months. In his letters he never said much about the fighting, probably since he didn't want his parents to worry. He wrote that he missed his mother's cooking, and that he had made several good friends among his fellow soldiers.

Jack and Emma never mentioned that Emma had also received a letter from Harry; a letter that she kept hidden in a drawer.

My Dearest Sister,

This place is Hell on earth. War is a dreadful, awful thing, and I am hoping that we can defeat the Germans soon, as we push eastward here in France.…I have seen my comrades sickened from poison gas, shot, and killed by bullets and machine gun fire. The worst was when my best friend had his face burned by a flamethrower. And another fellow had an arm and a leg blown off by a hand grenade that blew up next to him. Our men sometimes die from infections after they have been wounded. Even at night I must be prepared for attacks and ambushes by the Germans. Emma, I hope we can defeat them. Time will tell! Some days we are bored, with no action to speak of. And other times the battles go on for days. The enemy is well equipped; they are outfitted with all the weapons of modern warfare. Our soldiers are brave and courageous, even when they must fight to the death. Pray that the war ends soon, and I can return home. Give my love to the children. Sending love to you and Jack. I miss all of you so much. Pray for me. Your loving brother,

Harry

P.S. Please keep this letter hidden so Mama doesn't read it.

P.P.S. If anything happens to me, my commanding officer is Captain Howell of

the 320th Infantry. He will provide you with details, just in case, if I do not survive.

Emma cried as she showed Jack the letter. After he read it, a lump formed in his throat, he could barely swallow, let alone speak. He held his wife, feeling her fear, rubbing her back in comfort, attempting to calm her. He didn't know what to tell her. Finally, he whispered, "Hopefully he'll be home soon. All you can do is pray. Be proud he is so brave and doing his best to survive."

~ ⨫ ~

Jack felt he and Emma were getting along better than they had in years. She often smiled at him when he sat with Johnny on the back porch. Johnny loved to look at the marbles Jack had bought him. Jack showed his son how to aim them and make them roll swiftly by flicking one at a time with his thumb or index finger. The little boy carefully lined them up in rows, touched each one, and admired the brightly colored ones the most. Jack was also teaching him how to count as Johnny dropped them one by one into the little leather bag with the drawstring.

Recently, Jack thought he saw that familiar twinkle in Emma's eyes. The sparkle she used to have when she looked at him. Maybe. Perhaps there was a flicker of hope; perhaps the flame had not been totally extinguished.

Or…maybe Emma was smiling more simply because Jack was paying attention and noticing her love of their children.

Or…Emma was happier because the chill in her heart was thawing.

One Saturday evening after the children were asleep Jack asked Emma if she would like a little glass of brandy. He poured one for each of them, and they sat on the back porch, looking at the fireflies flitting about, blinking their lights. The night was clear as they gazed up at the stars and the moon. A bright full moon smiled at them, which seemed to encourage Jack.

He reached for Emma's hand and softly said, "Emma, I hope you can forgive me for not being a good husband, but I'm truly trying to be better. I want to make you happy. I want to find our way back to where we used to be, when we were both content.

"Emma," he continued, "I remember one night when we were first married, you were talking about the moon. You said the moon is always there, sometimes full and sometimes just a sliver. There are times when it is hidden by clouds. But it is always there, you said, we just can't always see it. I think about that at night…about how our love and our marriage are like that. Our love is always there, even though sometimes we can't see it."

Still holding her hand, he caressed it tenderly. "We had a couple of bad years, but I hope we can get back what we used to have together. I really want to try, and I hope you feel the same way. I will do anything to convince you."

As the fireflies blinked their encouragement, Jack leaned over and tenderly kissed his wife. Emma finished her brandy, stood up, and turned toward her husband. "Let's go to bed…and get reacquainted."

And that is what they did. Twice.

The twinkle in Emma's eye had surely returned, a testament to the charms of Jack Quinn. Those charms could rekindle any dying fire where the embers still glowed ever so slightly. The last Friday in July was the hottest day of the summer. Jack had decided to stop after work to visit his sisters and Dad. He was eager to escape the sweltering streetcar loaded with sweaty riders. He hadn't been in Hazelwood since May, more than two months ago. As he stepped off the streetcar, he was pleasantly surprised to see his oldest sister, Mary, walking down Second Avenue with her two stepchildren, Mark and Jane, who were now as tall as Mary. Folding his suit jacket over his arm, Jack stood and waved, waiting for them to draw closer.

"My goodness, Jackie, how are you?" his sister said as he bent over to kiss her cheek. "And how are Emma and the children? We were just coming to pay a short visit. Daniel is in Cleveland working and won't be back until tomorrow. His job on the railroad keeps him busy riding back and forth between Pittsburgh and Cleveland."

Jack replied that his family was fine and that he had worked for several months in Youngstown, riding the train there; he told her his boss said he would be going back again, probably by the end of August. He mentioned that Harry, Emma's brother, had been drafted and was fighting in France. Mark and Jane both said they remembered playing with Harry in Elliott over ten years ago, on the day Jack and Emma were married. Young Harry had made quite an impression with his friendly personality.

Chatting and walking slowly in the heat, they crossed the tracks. Jack spied Dad sitting in his rocking chair on the porch. When they reached the house, Dad led them inside to surprise Jack's sisters. Florence was overjoyed to see her entire family all in one place. Dad, and even Margaret, both had big smiles on their faces. Jack stayed for dinner—and then a drink with Dad—but informed them he wanted to get back to Elliott before his children went to bed. During dinner, Jack had asked, "How are Johnny and Alice doing?" Florence replied happily. "You'll never believe it, Jackie. You know they've been married for such a long time, and they always wanted to have children. Well, they decided to adopt a baby and chose a girl at one of those foundling homes in Pittsburgh, back in May. She is just the prettiest little thing. Her name is Rose Mary…Rose Mary Finnegan.

Jack remarked, "Well, that's great news. I guess that's the thing to do if you can't have your own. Tell them I'm happy for them."

"Not to change the subject," Margaret said, "but Clare is still away at that special hospital. Alice said she went to visit her, and Clare is doing much better. They might finally let her come home next month."

Jack couldn't resist. "What about Joe Murphy?" he asked. "How's he surviving without Clare cooking and cleaning up after him?"

At Jack's question Margaret grew excited: "Jackie, that's the best part. Joe got drafted and had to go into the army. Imagine that…Joe Murphy fighting the Germans!"

Even Dad chuckled at that thought. He said, "Aye, the Germans will run for the hills if Joe Murphy gets in one of his blind rages! That they will. Although the army probably won't give him any whiskey to get his motor running!"

"I'm surprised the army took him," Florence added, "since he's almost forty years old. They must be getting desperate!"

When Jack was riding the streetcar back to Elliott, he kept imagining Joe Murphy charging the Germans with a rifle aimed at their heads, firing away. *Yes*, he thought, *France is a dangerous place all right, with the likes of Joe Murphy running around armed to the hilt!* Jack would never say it out loud, but Joe was one soldier no one would ever care a whit about if he never came back. *Although with no alcohol to fuel his rages,* Jack realized, *that ass might have to act like a normal person.* Jack would bet ten dollars that Joe was still insulting people, calling them dickheads and bastards…and he probably still didn't know how to throw a punch.

CHAPTER 25

November 1918—Emma

The story in the Pittsburgh newspaper read: *WAR ENDS!--On Nov. 11, 1918, fighting in the war to end all wars came to a conclusion following the signing of an armistice between the Allies and Germany that called for a ceasefire effective at 11 a.m.— the 11th hour of the 11th day of the 11th month.* Bells rang, flags waved, the nation was rejoicing; but there was no reason to celebrate in the Moreau household in Elliott. The telegram still lay silently on the dining room table where Henry had placed it four weeks ago, one month before the official end of the war.

Their worst fears had come to pass. Every member of the family was still in shock. Perhaps there had been a mistake…perhaps Harry would come walking through his family's door any day now…. he had been in France for less than five months before he was killed in battle at the front. The telegram said he had died a hero, defending his country with courage and honor. No details.

The horrible telegram was thankfully delivered in the evening, right before bedtime, when both Papa and Monnie were sitting with Mama in the parlor. Mama had fainted immediately; Papa caught her before she hit the floor. Monnie had stood there wailing and shaking. Poor Papa and Monnie managed to get Mama to the sofa. Then the three of them sat for hours, crying, grief stricken....

Papa waited until early morning to tell Emma the awful news. Emma kept Dorothy and Nan home from school and told Papa to go inform Estelle and Frank before Frank left for work. She said, "Papa, tell Frank to bring Estelle and Frankie to my house. Then we'll all walk up to see Mama." Rubbing his forehead, Papa mumbled, "I'll go and get Fred and have him close the tavern for a few days. Then I'll go to the bakery and tell your aunts. Monnie won't be going to work today, she needs to stay with Mama. I'll have to send a telegram to Albert in Boston. Next, I want to go ask Father Ryan to stop at the house to talk to Mama. And then I'll have Dr. Meyers mix up some medicine to help Mama sleep. She was sobbing all night."

His clothing was disheveled, which was uncharacteristic for Papa, who looked so sad. He seemed to have aged overnight. Emma hugged him tight before he left with his agenda of things that needed to be taken care of. He hadn't slept either. His gray hair was sticking straight up and needed to be combed. He had even forgotten his hat.

The family mourned for weeks, not learning any more details. Harry had been killed in battle at the front. That was all they knew. After reading and rereading the last letter that she had received from Harry, Emma decided to write a letter to his commanding officer. She needed to know more about how her brother had died. Emma needed facts and details.

She carefully put a piece of writing paper in her typewriter, rolling and positioning it meticulously. Addressing the letter to Captain Howell with the last address she had for Harry in France, she hoped she might get some answers to her questions. She mailed the letter on November 4th, a week before the armistice agreement was signed that ended the war to end all wars.

Jack had been working in Youngstown; he returned the last week of October, after being in Ohio for two months. Emma needed his strong arms around her, feeling the need to lean on him after having to be the rock for everyone around her since they had gotten word of Harry's death.

There was no funeral, no burial. Father Ryan offered a special Mass for Harry's soul; but it did not seem real because there was no body to bury. Harry had most likely been buried in France with his fallen comrades. Mama had several framed photos of Harry she displayed in the parlor, next to pictures of Eddie, who they had buried four years before. Monnie had put a black fabric bow above each photo of Harry and tied black cotton bunting to the railings on the front porch. She had also fastened a black bow to the front door. Emma considered how devastating Harry's death must be for Mama and Papa. The natural order of life demands that children outlive their parents. War disrupts this order; along with accidents and disease…things that can't be predicted. She watched as Dorothy, Nan, and little Johnny played. She couldn't imagine losing one of them. She kept thinking, *God gives us blessings then takes them away, with no reason or explanation.* Father Ryan had said, "God likes to test us and never gives us a cross to bear that is too heavy. God has more faith in us than we know, and we must trust in His plan. We need to have faith."

One dismal gray afternoon the third week of November, Papa stopped by Emma's house before the girls had come home from school. Emma and Papa sat at her kitchen table having a cup of tea. Papa looked tired and said, "Emma, thank you for being so strong. Your strength has been so helpful and comforting for Mama. It was bad enough when Eddie died, but at least we were able to give him a proper burial. This is just so different. Mama needs us all to be understanding."

Emma appreciated her father's words. "Papa, I've always had to be the strong one. I always looked out for Estelle and Monnie, and the last few years I've gotten used to the idea even more, with Albert living in Boston and with Fred not being available, what with the way he has sunk into his depression. And Monnie is so busy with the bakery business. Papa, it's you and me…we must be there for the family. I'm glad Estelle is married to such a good stable man, but I wish we could somehow help Fred. I do worry about him."

"As far as Fred is concerned," Papa said, "there's really no helping him if he doesn't want to help himself. Although if the temperance movement has its way, he might have no choice, he'll be forced to cut down on his drinking. Once they start passing laws against alcohol consumption, my tavern business is bound to be hurt. It's a good thing I've been saving money, and that I own that building. Fred might have to find another job if we have to close."

Emma sighed. "Well…I'm glad Jack isn't drinking as much, and I'm happy that he's back from Youngstown. The girls and Johnny missed him so much."

Papa looked her in the eye. "And how about you? You two seem to be getting along much better nowadays. I was worried about you a lot…for a couple of years."

Emma smiled. "Yes, things have improved. Jack's been trying to be a better husband, and he admits he must work at it and be more understanding. He's gotten much better with the children too. And to answer your question, yes, I missed him too."

"He told me he'll probably be working in Pittsburgh until springtime," Papa said, "and then he might have to go back when the next building in Youngstown is ready for the plumbers. Mr. McGee is proud of Jack's performance."

Emma was glad Papa didn't want to discuss the crosses she had to bear, the several years when Jack was not a good husband; she referred to that period of her life as "the bad years." When they hardly spoke to each other. When Jack didn't come home for three or four days at a time. Emma figured he was staying in Hazelwood, but was he seeing someone besides his father and his sisters?

She had always been suspicious and wondered if he was meeting his old girlfriend, Clare? And what was he doing in the bars, and who was he with, especially when he came home with lipstick stains on his shirt collar? So, at least Papa didn't say, *"That's what you get for marrying that Irish rascal!"* She knew Papa always liked Jack, so she never complained to her father about him.

She felt that it was difficult to have to raise three children without much help from a philandering husband. A husband who happened to be as handsome as the day is long. Jack was her weakness, always was, and probably always would be.

Now, however, she was tired of punishing him…and he did seem to be trying to be a better husband, a better person. Emma changed the subject back to her mother. "I'll do anything to help you and Mama," she remarked. "You've both always been there for me and my children. I'm thankful Mama's sisters are healthy and live close by. And thank God for Monnie. I don't know what we'd do without her."

Just then the front door flew open, and Dorothy and Nan ran into the house, laughing and giggling. Johnny jumped up from the floor where he had been building with his wooden blocks. He was always excited to greet his sisters: they each hugged him and tickled him. He jumped up and down, waiting for the girls to hang their coats next to the door. "What was so amusing?" Emma asked. "You were both laughing up a storm."

Dorothy replied: "Oh, Mother, it was the funniest sight. Sister Martha went down to the basement to tend the coal furnace. There was a loud boom and she came running up the steps and into the classroom. My goodness… her face, the white bib on her dress, and her white headpiece were covered with black coal dust. She was black from head to toe! She was so angry…and she looked so funny! Sister Ann Mary came running in and she shrieked, and then the whole class was trying not to laugh. Sister Martha had to leave to go get washed up, and she never did come back. So, Sister Ann Mary took our class over to her room and we had to sit on the floor. There were sixty students smashed into one room." Dorothy paused to catch her breath.

"I saw Dorothy," Nan added, "and I was waving at her and Sister yelled at me." Then she added proudly, "So I tried to be good and did my work."

Dorothy exclaimed, "Sister Ann Mary was walking around with her wooden pointer and if anybody made a sound, they got their hand smacked with the pointer." Wide-eyed, Johnny was watching Dorothy as Nan rubbed her knuckles and knowingly said, "And that hurts!"

"Well, you're there to learn," Emma sternly replied, "not to have a good time. I'll listen to your spelling words while we get dinner ready. Tell your grandfather goodbye and then go wash your hands." The girls complied.

A week later, on the last day of November, Emma received a letter from Captain Howell concerning Harry Moreau of Company "H" of the 320th Infantry, A.E.F. It had been sent from Dijon (Côte d'Or) France. Her hands shook as she retrieved her letter opener and quickly slit the long envelope.

Dear Madam (the letter read),

I beg to acknowledge receipt of your letter of 4 November, regarding your brother Corporal Harry J. Moreau. I am very glad that you have written, as our army records containing his family address had been sent to the War Department, and I have been unable to communicate with you and the rest of Corporal Moreau's family until now. On the morning of the 4th of October, the Company was in the front line of a sector in the north Lorraine Area near the border of France and Germany. The attack was made in good shape, and we had progressed possibly three miles into German territory. At this stage we had considerable tall weeds to pass through; the various units of the Company became a little scattered on this account.

It so happened that about twenty men of the Company were with me, among them your brother, and we had gotten considerably in advance of the units on both flanks. Our mission was to neutralize German machine gun fire that was targeting us from a concealed position. We were maneuvering around this gun when your brother was killed by machine gun fire. His death must have been practically instantaneous: he was hit on the body by several bullets. The attack continued, and I was not able to get back to the locality where your brother had fallen for a few days, when I took a burial detail out, collecting the men of the Company who had fallen. Father Wallace, the Catholic chaplain of the regiment, and I buried your brother on the top of a small hill overlooking the field of battle, alongside other brave men from the Company.

Your brother's personal effects, what few there were, were sent to the Central Effects Depot, which will in due course of events forward them on to you. I know that it is very hard to lose those whom we love, but you will realize that your brother died facing the enemy, leading his men forward on the day of the critical attack, which marked the opening of America's greatest advance in this great war. I am sure that you will agree with me that if our loved ones must be taken away, we can derive great satisfaction knowing they died as heroes, men fighting for the Republic. I wish you would convey my sympathy to your brother's parents and forward this letter on to them.

Very truly yours,

R.O. Thomas Howell, Jr. (signed)

Commanding Capt. 320th Infantry

Emma read the letter three times, until she couldn't see through the tears. She dabbed at her eyes with the corner of her apron then attempted to put on a brave face in front of the children. She planned to show the letter to Jack that evening. They both sat quietly at the kitchen table and had a glass of brandy as they read it again together.

The following day she mustered her courage as she prepared to take the letter to Mama and Papa. When she entered their house, she took a deep breath and stared at the envelope. Finally, with the unfolded paper in her hands, she refused to look at her parents' faces as she softly read the words aloud, the words that were now etched in her memory.

She listened to her mother's quiet sobs and moaning cries; then Papa held the letter to his heart and asked if he could keep it for a few days so he could read it again…and again.

That night Jack and Emma shared several glasses of brandy as Emma described the day's events. Jack listened attentively and continued to comfort his wife, caressing her hands. She welcomed his attention and understanding, and his touch. From then on, she only cried in private, while praying for her brother's soul.

CHAPTER 26

August 1919—Clare

"Influenza is highly contagious," Dr. Jones explained, "and tuberculosis patients, in their weakened state of health, can easily become infected. You would surely develop pneumonia after contracting influenza and it would most likely cause your death. Even strong healthy people sometimes die from it." He looked at Clare with a stoic expression. "I'm sorry, Clare, but it is in your best interest to stay here."

Having become accustomed to her surroundings and the routines of institutional confinement, Clare accepted the decision with no argument. So many people in the Pittsburgh area were contracting influenza during the summer of 1918, Dr. Jones had explained, that the doctors at the sanatorium would not allow Clare to return home. She felt disappointment but didn't know what her life would be like once she returned home. There was nothing to be excited about or look forward to.

She knew it was over with Jack, a relationship she now acknowledged had been doomed from the start. Her emotions and feelings had been extinguished. That flame in her heart was a candle that finally had burned itself out. Sickness, childbirth, having to deny herself the joys of motherhood...they all had taken their toll. She felt like an empty shell. She wondered whether it was possible to be dead on the inside.

Clare and Alice continued writing letters to each other every week. Alice could not visit, since she wasn't permitted to bring an infant to the sanatorium, and she didn't want to leave baby Rose in her neighbor's care for an entire day.

In her letters, Alice described Rose as a beautiful child with dark brown curls and bright blue eyes. Clare was relieved the baby didn't have green eyes and auburn hair, like Clare. That might make neighbors suspicious…and Clare wanted to avoid any suspicions that might lead to wagging tongues. Even Margaret and Florence might start to wonder if the child looked like Clare. Alice had always had brown hair and blue eyes, so perhaps the child eventually might resemble Alice…. Hopefully, Clare mused, the little girl wouldn't look like Mary, Margaret, or Florence. She was almost positive Jack's family did not have any photographs of his sisters when they were children. She didn't want anyone noticing similarities between Rose and any Quinn.

In the month of May, Alice had written:

Rose is starting to walk and now has four teeth, which have been making her a little grumpy lately. The women at church told me to rub a bit of brandy or whiskey on her sore gums. Otherwise, she is generally pleasant and has full, rosy cheeks. She is finally sleeping all night and is still taking two naps during the day. And this child has quite the appetite. I baked a special cake for her birthday and gave her a small piece, and Johnny brought home some vanilla ice cream. Rose proceeded to rub her hand in the ice cream—and then the ice cream was all over her face and in her hair. Johnny and I laughed so hard there were tears running down my cheeks. Happy tears. Thank you, my dear sister, for the wonderful gift you have given us. I am looking forward to the day you can come home. Clare remembered that she, herself, preferred the name Violet, but Alice liked Rose better; she insisted that Rose Finnegan sounded prettier than Violet Finnegan. Clare finally had to agree that Alice was right, as usual. So, the baby was baptized Rose Mary Finnegan. Alice had told people in Hazelwood they had adopted the baby through one of the foundling homes in Pittsburgh. Alice and Johnny were so very grateful they finally had a child to raise. A very special child. Clare's child. No one ever needed to know she was Alice's niece.

∽⁓ℰℛℬ⁓∼

One warm afternoon in June of 1919, Clare was sitting on one of the rocking chairs on the porch of the hospital. Her friend Catherine sat next to her, both women knitting small blankets. Nurse Helen kept a steady supply of yarn available to them: the two women knitted the afghans used by the other patients in their ward. Clare closed her eyes. Then she took a deep breath and said, "Smell the lilacs, Catherine. I'm surprised these bushes are still filled with them. They are usually done blooming by June."

Catherine smiled at Clare. "I'll miss the flowers here, but the doctors told me this morning that I will be able to go home soon. I can't wait to see my sons and my little grandson." The news took Clare by surprise, even though she knew neither she nor Catherine could stay here forever. "Yes, that's wonderful. I probably will have to leave soon too."

In one of Alice's letters she told Clare their brother Joe had returned home from the war in France in March. The army had kept him hospitalized several months after the end of the war due to a bullet and shrapnel wound to his leg. Alice also reported that Joe had been told he had a mild case of shell shock, which caused him to have trouble sleeping. Sometimes he experienced nightmares as well.

Imagine this, dear Clare, Alice wrote. *Our brother Joe was given a medal for his extreme bravery on the battlefield. He saved two of his comrades from certain death by carrying them off the battlefield and hiding them in a trench until the battle was over. It's truly amazing—our crazy brother is a war hero! Mum and Dad would be so proud. So, Joe is finally back home and wants to know when you will be returning. I think he misses your cooking! He returned to his job at the mill, and so far, has not been drinking much. Thank God! He seems very jumpy and nervous since he's been back, which they say is normal for the returning soldiers who have been in the battlefield. He'll probably talk your ear off about the battles.*

Clare was finally released from the sanatorium in Armstrong County on the last day of June. She had been a patient there for twenty months. Alice had arranged with the hospital for Clare to ride the train to Pittsburgh—she would be traveling with Catherine and Catherine's son. Johnny Finnegan would be waiting at the train station, where they would board the streetcar to Hazelwood.

When the train arrived at the station, the trio was greeted by Johnny; his broad smile welcomed the ladies back to Pittsburgh. He was just as pleasant and cheerful as ever. Clare introduced her brother-in-law to Catherine and her son, and then Clare tightly hugged her good friend as they bid each other farewell. Of course, they promised to write to each other. As Catherine walked away with her son and boarded the streetcar to the Northside, Clare wondered if she would ever see her again. Probably not. That part of her life was over, best kept locked in a box labeled "The Past." She planned on burying those memories of sickness, pain, and loss, those long months spent in a sanatorium.

As the streetcar rumbled along, they passed Calvary Cemetery, where her parents were buried, then descended the long winding hill into Hazelwood. Clare began feeling nervous with anticipation. Probably sensing her anxiety, Johnny was not his usual talkative self, which was fine with Clare, as she just wanted to gaze out the window at familiar sights along the way. Perhaps her life could return to some semblance of normalcy. Finally. Her new normal…with no visits from Jack.

Johnny held her arm and carried her travel bag as they stepped off the Hazelwood streetcar at Chatsworth Avenue. She immediately noticed the same old smokiness, like a gray low-hanging cloud. She would miss the cleaner mountain air. Clare stood for a moment to take in the sight of the long street of small brick houses—mostly dull orange, some yellow—that lined either side of the street. She recalled always being happy her family had lived here instead of in the wooden row houses down by the railroad tracks beyond Second Avenue. Where the Quinn family lived. Where Jack had lived. She immediately pushed his name out of her mind. Clare and Joe still rented the house they had grown up in, three doors past where Alice and Johnny lived. They walked a half block; then she could see Alice standing on the porch, waving. Johnny watched the joyful scene as the sisters cried and embraced each other. Alice took her hand. "Come in and sit down," she said. "You're probably famished and tired. Rose is napping but should be awake soon, so we can have a bite to eat while we wait. You're not going to believe how big she is." Clare ate some of Alice's warm stew and bread. Then, with a wistful smile, she told Alice, "It was sad to say goodbye to Nurse Helen and Dr. Jones… and the other patients in my ward. I thought of Helen as a friend—and of course, Catherine too. I'll miss them. That place was my home for well over a year and a half. It seems like a long dream now, but I'm happy to be back. I missed you so much, and St. Stephen's, and the whole town."

Trying not to stare, Alice gazed at her sister as she poured their tea. She noticed a hint of color in her cheeks; Clare's face was no longer deathly pale, as it had been when she was gravely ill. Her hair lay neatly coiled at the top of her neck, some gray beginning to mix with the reddish strands. Clare looked thinner and older…the illness had taken a toll on her body, as had the pregnancy. More lines were etched in her forehead and around her eyes. The deep lines and dark shadows framed those green eyes that had lost their sparkle, their joy.

As they sipped the steaming tea, Alice couldn't help but smile; she was happy to have her sister back. She said: "I went over to Joe's and cleaned the entire house. Your bed is waiting for you. I put some food in the icebox and cupboards. I told Joe you would be home this evening. I'll cook extra and bring meals over. I've been doing that for Joe, the few months since he's been home."

Clare reached across the table and squeezed her sister's hand. "Thank you so much. I don't know what I'd do without you." Alice smiled and replied, "I'm glad you will be close by. Remember that you're only a few houses away now. I'm here if you need anything, or anytime you just want to visit."

They heard cooing and babbling coming from upstairs. Johnny came in from the porch. "You ladies just sit," he said. "I'll bring her down."

Clare was excited to see little Rose as Johnny carried her into the room. "Look, Rosie, my pretty girl, we have company," he said softly. The child reached out for Alice. Rose snuggled her face against Alice's shoulder and peaked shyly at Clare.

"Rose, sweetie, this is your Auntie Clare. You're going to get to see a lot of her now that she's home," Alice said. She kissed the little girl's dark curls.

Clare was speechless. She simply stared at this beautiful child. Those lovely blue eyes. She reached over and gently touched her daughter's chubby little hand.

"Hello, Rose," she whispered as a solitary tear escaped from her eye. She quickly swept it away then folded her hands in her lap, squeezing tightly, pressing her thumb as hard as she could into her palm, hoping some self-inflicted pain would distract her from the ache in her heart.

Just then there was a solitary knock on the door. A moment later Joe walked in. "Well now, there's a sight for sore eyes," he said. "How's our Clare doing?" He bent over and awkwardly gave Clare a quick kiss on the forehead. He was happy to see his sister, and she realized she had missed him, if only a little. Clare noticed Joe was thinner and walked with a limp. "Joe," she said, "we have a lot to catch up on. You'll have to tell me about your time in the army. I hear you were quite the hero."

Joe snorted, not wanting to talk about the war. He asked Alice what she had made for supper. "Got to deal with the here and now. And, right now, I'm feeling awful hungry."

That night, Clare was content to be back in her own bed, in her own room, not a hospital ward filled with other patients. She slept soundly, unaware of the moonlight streaming through the curtains. She rarely looked at the moon anymore.

~⊶⊷~

Over the next few weeks, Clare began feeling almost like her old self. She even started to cook again, simple meals, mainly stew and soups. Joe was working daytime hours ever since he had returned from the war; he came home at six o'clock for supper, saying he was too tired to go to the bars.

They would sit in rocking chairs on the porch in the evening as Clare worked on her knitting; two recovering souls calmed by peacefully rocking. Joe never had much to say as he stared at the sky. He seemed to be lost in another world, and he still didn't want to talk about his wartime experiences. Clare respected her brother's need for quiet, not knowing what burdens he carried in his mind.

Once she had heard Johnny comment: "Many of the men at the mill who were overseas during the war aren't their old selves. They were changed by the brutality of war, no one knowing what these men had seen on the battlefield. Most of them are like Joe and don't want to talk about it. One fella won't talk at all, does his job, goes home. Never utters a word."

Every day around lunchtime Clare walked to Alice's house and spent time playing with Rose. She marveled at what a good mother her sister was. "Alice, you're so patient with Rose, always seeming to know just what to do," she remarked. Alice would nod and smile, and the sisters never discussed their secret. Some things were better left unsaid. Rose always waved bye-bye to Auntie Clare when it was her nap time, and Clare was content to go home and take a nap also, realizing babies are exhausting work.

One sweltering night in the middle of August, after being overcast all day with the sky holding foreboding, dark clouds, it finally started to rain. Initially the raindrops were gentle, but soon they kept inviting more to join in, as if a ruckus was long overdue.

Standing in the kitchen, Clare wiped her face with her apron. "It looks like we're going to have some thunderstorms," she said to Joe. "I hate to even think about closing the windows, being it's so hot in here. I've been dripping with sweat all day!" They finally both retired to their bedrooms. Clare kept wondering if she would be able to get any sleep at all, what with the heat and the thick air that made breathing difficult; not to mention, the noise from the rain beating against the house and the distant rumbling of thunder. Sometime around midnight, the wind was howling, and the sky had opened with the most intense downpour of rain she could remember. The thunder was louder than earlier, and she whispered, "Well, I can't sleep so I might as well go downstairs and make some tea." Clare didn't bother to switch on a light, since flashes of lightning were continuously illuminating the stairway and the kitchen. She was attempting to light the burner on the stove when a lightning strike lit the room brilliantly, and a loud clap of thunder made her trembling hand drop the match before she could strike it. She stooped down to look for the match on the floor when she heard the most ungodly, bloodcurdling scream.

Startled, she jumped up. Her breath stopped, and she looked toward the stairs. Just then she heard Joe's bedroom door fly open as it banged against the wall. Instinctively, she crouched back down on the floor, partially hidden behind one of the kitchen chairs.

Another quick flash of lightning and a roar of thunder sent her brother barreling down the stairs, screaming and yelling, "You goddamn Germans, I HATE every one of you BASTARDS, I'm going to kill you all….You fucking murderers, dickheads…ASSHOLES!! I hate you!" Clare peaked around the leg of the chair and saw her brother Joe's furious, twisted face. He had a knife in his hand, the same eight-inch blade he had always kept hidden in his boot. The same blade that he had threatened her with years ago. She sat on the floor, hugging her knees to her chest, her back hard against the cupboard, eyes squeezed shut, trembling, too scared to move. Afraid even to breathe.

Realization of the severity of her situation was setting in. *Oh, dear God,* she thought. *If Joe catches sight of me, he might think I'm a German soldier! And he has a knife!* Clare had never been so terrified.

Several claps of thunder followed more lightning flashes, and Joe kept shrieking as he ran back up the stairs. Then she heard him throwing a chair in her bedroom.

"I'm going to kill every one of you filthy rotten shitheads! Fucking bastard Germans!"

He hit the glass in a window in his bedroom, probably with another wooden chair. As the window shattered, Joe was still screaming and hollering.

Clare knew she had to get out of the house, and quickly. She inched her way up quietly from the floor, holding the table with one hand to steady herself. Then she grabbed a butcher knife that was lying on the counter next to the stove.

With her eyes glued to the front door, she whispered below her breath: "Help me, dear God…sweet Jesus." She had to cross the kitchen and the small parlor to reach the door. She was determined to escape from the house without Joe seeing her or hearing her.

Her heart began pounding.

Clare prayed Joe wouldn't hear her. Thankfully the thunder continued outside, and any small noises she might make would be masked by the sound of rain pounding against the house. She tiptoed across the wooden floor.

She had on only a thin cotton nightgown, and she was not wearing shoes; but she didn't care. She could hear Joe upstairs, still yelling and throwing furniture. She reached out to grab the cool glass doorknob. She was shaking and could hardly breathe.

She tried to slide the lock as quietly as possible. When she heard Joe starting down the stairs again, she flung open the door and ran, still gripping the butcher knife in her hand. Across the front porch and down the steps, moving swiftly. *Go, go! Move! Faster, faster!* The wind hollered in her ears. Her arms flailed wildly in front of her, searching for the way.

Then she heard Joe screaming from the doorway, "You dirty German, I will kill you… fucking BASTARD!"

Running through the storm, down the sidewalk, as fast as she could. *Run, run, run. Go…go, go.* "Oh God, please help me!" she cried. The rain pelted every inch of her body, slashing at her nightgown.

She knew she had to get to Alice's, only three houses away. Then she finally heard her own screams, the sounds finding an exit from her head. Not wanting to look behind her, she ran through puddles, the rain beating against her face, her heart pounding, feet racing.

Another lightning flash as she turned toward Alice's porch, she could see the three wooden steps ahead, but her bare feet slipped on the second step. Her free hand clawed at the edge of the porch as her other hand still gripped the knife handle.

She screamed as she felt her hair being grabbed…and then her brother pulled her to the ground. "Joe, no, no! It's me, CLARE! *Noooo!*" she screeched as she saw him standing above her with his hand raised, clenching his knife, spitting and swearing, "Fucking German!! Now I have you!"

Lightning flashed, illuminating the sky and the ground. Joe's face glistened with rain and sweat. His eyes were wild, nostrils flared. Clare didn't even recognize this ugly, twisted, tortured creature. This wasn't her brother, this monster. *Before me stands the devil,* she thought, as she realized her butcher knife was still clutched in her hand.

She rolled quickly as Joe's hand came down. She slashed at his leg with her knife then rammed the tip of the blade into the top of his bare foot. He screamed in pain, becoming even more enraged as she crawled across the ground back toward the bottom wooden step.

Joe lunged at her. She slashed her knife at his arm then pushed herself along the ground with her feet, trying to get away from him. Joe turned and stood with his back facing the steps separating Clare from Alice's house. She was crying, ready to give in to exhaustion, raising one arm to cover her face.

Just then Johnny Finnegan burst through the front door. He charged across the porch, rushed down the first step, and leaped on Joe's back. Joe dropped his knife, bent forward, and hit Clare in the face with his fist. Then he wildly swung his arms, trying to shake Johnny from his back. Johnny's legs were wrapped around Joe's waist. He hung on to Joe, wrapping one hand around Joe's neck; his other fist kept punching Joe in the head. Joe stumbled. Johnny slid off his back. As Joe slowly turned to him, Johnny landed a solid punch to Joe's face.

Joe fell to the ground. He lay there in the mud, still as a stone. Clare was shaking and crying by the porch steps. Johnny helped her to her feet then led her up the steps, into Alice's waiting arms. The next-door neighbor had heard the commotion and rushed to Johnny's front yard. He told Johnny he would run down to the next block to summon the police. He said he'd tell them to notify a doctor. Ten minutes later, the police loaded Joe into the back of their police wagon; later that night at the station, the doctor cleaned and bandaged the knife wounds on Joe's arm, leg, and foot. The following morning the doctor stopped at Alice's to examine Clare. Her cheek was badly bruised, and her eye was cut where Joe had punched her. Several cuts slashed across her feet. The doctor commended Clare for having the good sense to escape the house. "Your quick thinking saved your life," he told her. "Your brother truly thought he was on the battlefield; he is most certainly suffering from combat stress. Last night's episode most likely was triggered by the lightning and thunder. You're lucky to be alive."

The doctor gave her some medicine to help calm her nerves. Clare was still shaking under the covers in the third bedroom of Alice and Johnny's house. Given her history of tuberculosis, the doctor suggested that she stay in bed for several days and not exert herself. Clare ended up staying at Alice's for the next few days. Joe was transferred from the local jail to a hospital in Pittsburgh. The doctors were going to evaluate his mental condition.

CHAPTER 27

May 1920—Jack

"You know I'll help you with anything you need, Henry," Jack agreed without a moment's hesitation. Henry Moreau, Emma's father, had asked Jack for a favor. Last October, on an unseasonably warm Sunday afternoon, Henry, Fred, and Jack had been sitting on Henry's front porch. They were enjoying afternoon drinks while casually watching Frank Miller, Estelle's husband, play ball with the children in the yard. Fred shook his head in disbelief as he observed Frank. "You would think every grown man would know the correct way to throw and catch," he said. Johnny and young Frankie were both six years old. In between gleeful moments of running and jumping in piles of fallen leaves, they had started playing toss and catch with a worn baseball, one of their Uncle Fred's old ones.

Leaning forward in his wooden rocking chair on the porch, his demeanor more serious than usual, Henry said: "Jack, Fred and I have been discussing the subject of Prohibition a lot lately. It looks like the politicians in Washington, D.C., are going to pass that blasted amendment in January, even though President Wilson vetoed it. We're not sure how they are going to enforce this ridiculous law, and how well local police will cooperate with the federal agents. The point is, I want to be prepared."

"Since I own my house," he continued, "and the building where the tavern is located, I need to change the ownership of the business. I want my name off the license...so I'm changing the name from Moore's Tavern to the French Club. The license is due for renewal, and I'm putting Fred's name as the owner of the business. He'll be listed as a tenant of the building. The French Club will also be considered a tenant."

"Now, this law apparently is going to state that consuming alcohol is legal, but it will be against the law to make it, transport it, or resell it. I have enough money set aside to start buying up some of what is now stored in warehouses around the city. Over the next couple of months, I plan on storing as much as possible in the basement of my house and the basement of the tavern. As many cases as I can get of whiskey, gin, and wine. Mostly whiskey. And cordials, mostly brandy. No beer." Henry paused for a minute to take a drink of his whiskey.

Jack and Fred were both listening carefully. "So, every morning Fred and I will take the horse and wagon into Pittsburgh and buy stock at different warehouses, in various locations, so as not to raise suspicions. When we return to Elliott by noon, we'll park the wagon behind my house, not unloading until it's dark."

"My question for you, Jack, is...when you come home in the evening, will you help Fred unload the cases and stack them in the basement of my house and the tavern?"

Jack immediately agreed. "Of course, Henry," he repeated, "I'll help you with anything." "Thank you, Jack," Henry replied. "You won't be doing anything illegal, since the laws won't be effective until January. It just involves time and muscle...and a bit of secrecy. After the official starting date of Prohibition in January, we won't be able to transport alcohol, even though it will still be legal to drink in your home or private establishment. No selling to the public. And Fred will be operating a private club, serving only those who are members. The door will be locked; no one will be able to enter unless

Fred knows them. We should be able to avoid being raided by the police, and I certainly don't want Fred to be arrested."

"We're making the first warehouse run tomorrow morning," Henry said, "right after we file the necessary paperwork in the city for the name change and the transfer of ownership. Can I count on your help in the evening, right after darkness sets in?" "Of course, I'm happy to help," Jack said. "It sounds like a good plan, that will work out well," he added, "since I wanted to be around more to help Emma, since she's expecting again. I'm glad McGee doesn't need me to go to Youngstown anymore. And there aren't as many union meetings around the city nowadays."

Henry nodded. "When is baby Number Four due? I think Emma said something about February or March? My wife is looking forward to another grandchild to hold. Rocking a baby will do her good. She still misses Harry so much…A baby to fuss over will be a good distraction."

Jack drained his glass then replied, "Emma said the doctor told her it will be around the middle to the end of February. Dorothy will be able to help with the baby. It's hard to believe she's eleven years old now! I think Monnie was around that age when Dorothy was born."

Henry suddenly looked at him with sad eyes, nodding. "Yes, time flies—and there's nothing we can do to stop it. We just need to make the most of it. You never know when the Good Lord will say, 'Your time's up!' Look at Harry and Eddie. Both gone too soon." Henry rocked in the wooden chair, watching his grandsons playing in the fallen leaves. Fred stood to refill his glass. He brought the bottle over to give his father and brother-in-law another shot. He always declared that discussions about life and death were so depressing. "Memories are best when buried," he claimed. "That's my philosophy. What's the point of living in the past?" Apparently, he was just trying to get through each day as best he could. "Would you like to know my motto?" Fred asked. "Better to be on top of the grass than below it." He raised his glass in a mock toast, exclaiming, "And I'll drink to that."

By January the snow was flying. The cold winter was setting in. The daily alcohol runs were finished: cases of liquor filled Henry's basement floor to ceiling. The basement at the French Club was also full—whiskey, gin, wine, and brandy sharing space with the cheeses and sausage Fred stored there. Emma's mother had shown Fred how to let cheese age for months in the coolness of the French Club's basement. Jack's favorite cheese was Limburger, which happened to be Emma's parents' specialty. They delighted in making sandwiches with mustard smeared on rye bread and slices of Limburger. Fred and Jack enjoyed the sandwiches at the table in Emma's kitchen, but Emma said, "Jack, you and Fred can eat those at the tavern, not in our home, please!" She could not stand the smell, especially now that she was with child. "That stuff has the most awful odor. It makes me want to vomit." She smiled and her eyes twinkled. "I refuse to kiss you if you've been eating that Limburger cheese!"

Jack would pretend to be offended then rinse his mouth with water, take a sip of whiskey—and kiss her anyways.

Lately Emma seemed to be obsessed with braunschweiger, a German form of pork liver sausage. She made sandwiches—and insisted on putting ketchup on the braunschweiger. The combination always made Jack laugh. "To each his own, I suppose," he would say. And then Emma's strange food predilections got worse. Jack couldn't watch when she put ketchup on her scrambled eggs and encouraged the children to try it. Still, at least once a month he would bring Emma a bottle of Heinz ketchup. "I have a present for my lovely wife!" he would announce. During the last week of January, Jack had brought her a jar of Heinz pickles. He told her, "Just please don't put ketchup on the pickles." Emma laughed. Even she thought that would be a disgusting combination.

By the middle of February, Fred had been serving liquor to his regular customers at the French Club for a month without a raid by authorities. Henry had a heavy door installed that had a six-inch sliding wooden panel at eye level so he or Fred could see who was knocking. They admitted only men who they knew. Men who paid "dues." Good club members paid their membership fees and had to abide by the rules, one of which was secrecy. Members were also encouraged to socialize quietly, or "speak easy," so as not to attract unwanted attention.

Occasionally Jack would stop by for a drink; but usually he just had a glass or two from his own bottle at home. He did not have any desire to go to the South Side bars, even though most of that neighborhood's saloons were run by Irishmen. Some of them were targeted for raids whenever they failed to pay off their suppliers…who just happened to be friends with certain city politicians. Even Jack's pals, Joe Sullivan and Jimmy Kennedy, were no longer frequenting the South Side bars. They were both married now to the sisters they had met on the streetcar, much to the joy of their mothers, who no longer had to worry their sons were keeping company with bar tramps.

Jack didn't get to Hazelwood very often. He explained to his sisters and Dad that Emma was expecting. He was needed at home to help with Johnny and the girls. Jack did not mention anything about his father-in-law's tavern business to Dad or his sisters, figuring they did not need to know any of that. But when he did visit, he brought Dad a well-concealed bottle of whiskey, in case he wasn't able to buy any in Hazelwood. Dad was quite pleased. He kept saying, "One of my few comforts…and the damn Feds are trying to take that away!"

Florence and Margaret kept Jack updated on the Murphy family saga. Back in the fall they had told him about Joe going crazy and attacking Clare; how the thunderstorms had triggered battlefield memories…and how Joe had thought he was fighting the Germans. They reported that Joe had been committed to a psychiatric hospital in Pittsburgh. He was still a patient there, and by February Clare found she could no longer pay the rent on their house. She moved in with Alice, Johnny, and their little girl Rose.

Jack wasn't surprised Joe Murphy had ended up in an asylum; but he found it unbelievable that the bloody idiot was a war hero! With a medal! "If that's not a kick in the ass, I don't know what is," Jack said to Dad. Old Sean Quinn shook his head in agreement.

Jack couldn't appear to be overly interested in the story but was silently outraged that Joe had attacked Clare. If he had been present, he would have put Joe Murphy out of his misery. Permanently. He was proud of Clare and her courage; proud that she had the presence of mind to run out of the house and fight back. And he was grateful Johnny Finnegan had saved her.

On the last Friday in February, Jack was anxious to get home after work. The doctor had said Emma's baby would be here any day now. Understanding from experience that it was hard to predict exactly when Emma might go into labor, Jack nonetheless knew his wife's labor pains would soon start. Emma was huge. She could hardly walk up and down the stairs, and she wasn't sleeping well.

Jack took his paycheck to the bank then rode the streetcar home. A couple inches of snow had fallen during the day, so when he stepped off the streetcar at Steuben and Lorenz Avenue he slid, almost playfully, down the hill to Lakewood Avenue. In the twilight he felt carefree as he hurried toward home, noticing lights shining from every window in his house. When he opened the door, he was greeted with squeals of excitement from his children. "Daddy, Daddy, the baby is here!" Nan and Dorothy announced the news together.

Johnny was almost breathless. "And guess what? It's a boy! I have my very own brother!" Jack knew Dorothy and Nan were hoping for a girl, but they were also old enough to know that babies are not returnable. Jack had told them, "You have to take whatever God sends."

He hung his hat and coat by the door then took off his snow-covered shoes. He looked up to see Henry and Monnie sitting at the kitchen table. Henry stood and shook Jack's hand. "Congratulations," he said, "you have another son!" Monnie was ready to relay the details. "The baby came fast; thank goodness you have a telephone now. Emma had just sent the children off to school when she started having pains. She rang up Papa's telephone and told him to send Mama down and to go find the doctor. I had already gone to the bakery, so Papa came and got me after the doctor got to the house." She took a deep breath before continuing: "You won't believe it, but by one o'clock, Emma was holding her new little boy. The doctor said he's big and strong. Go on up to see them. Emma's been waiting for you to get home." Jack took the steps two at a time. Henry watched him go then told the children to wash their hands and sit at the table. "Time to celebrate!" declared Henry as Monnie began cutting slices of an apple pie then poured them each a glass of milk.

Henry poured some whiskey for himself, and a glass for Jack.

~ ⚹ ~

By the first of May, Emma was feeling like her old self. She was completely recovered from the birth of Paul Henry. She had been in labor only three hours, so she wasn't as exhausted as she had been after the births of her first three children. The young doctor who had attended her had never seen a baby enter the world so quickly. In the evening after supper, Jack usually walked up to the French Club to see Fred and have a couple shots of whiskey. Then, after an hour, when he knew his house would be quiet and the children asleep, he headed home. He had gotten used to the routine of work and family life. Emma seemed content, and that made Jack happy.

On Sundays Jack tended to his garden and talked with Henry and Fred on the porch of the Moreau house. Fred said business was good. The police and politicians seemed to be turning a blind eye to the French Club, at least for the time being.

"The damn temperance people aren't getting much support in the big cities," Henry noted. "They think the new Prohibition laws are going to be a cure-all for immoral behavior. Well, the government can't regulate morality! And all the hard-working men in the mills and factories aren't about to give up their liquor. The smart politicians know that! And now that women are going to be able to vote, most will go along with whoever their husbands tell them to vote for."

Jack laughed. "Not all women, Henry. Your daughter Emma, for one, sure as hell won't let anybody tell her who to vote for." Henry nodded in agreement. "She'll be telling us who to support," he said. "That's for sure."

CHAPTER 28

September 1923—Emma

"Come on now, Paul Henry, Grammie is waiting to see you." Emma coaxed her three-year-old son as she watched him pick up stones and throw them into the street. The morning was lovely and cool as she pushed one-year old Michael in the stroller. He had grown too big for the baby carriage—and too heavy to carry on her hip. "Maybe Grandpa will be feeding the chickens," she added, trying to get Paul Henry to hurry. Paul loved to imitate the chickens. "Cluck, cluck, cluck!" he chanted. He folded his arms and flapped his hands like wings.

Emma's older children were at school. The afternoons were for napping, so Emma insisted that Paul and Michael get some fresh air in the mornings. Also, she felt it did Mama good to spend time with the little ones. They made Mama smile and laugh. *Laughter is music to the soul.* Emma had read that somewhere. And Papa always said, "There's nothing like a good belly laugh to cure what ails you!"

That morning when Mama greeted them, she said, "There's my boys." She tickled Michael under his chin then led Paul into the kitchen for a piece of cinnamon bun.

Emma couldn't help but think how Paul and Michael probably reminded Mama of Eddie and Harry when they were young. Those were good memories for Mama, back when all her children were together at home. Back before the world showed them how unsafe it could be, and how cruel.

After lunch Emma wanted to relax and think over a cup of tea in her own kitchen. Her afternoons were special, private times. Both boys were asleep, and the older children were still in school. She could read the newspaper and organize the paperwork for her club meetings. She was trying to keep informed about national and local politics, still finding all the stories about President Harding's strange death the month before quite intriguing. Calvin Coolidge became president when Harding died; Emma was predicting he would win next year's election. That's who she planned to vote for. She was excited to have the right to vote. Finally!

In local matters, the state of Pennsylvania had not strictly enforced the Prohibition laws. But when the new governor took office he promised to crack down on violators. Emma had not voted for him, seeing how it would affect her brother's business. Fred and Papa were constantly telling stories relating to the corruption in all levels of Pittsburgh's police force and political hierarchy. Certain federal agents were being bribed to look the other way. Fred had to pay money to one of the local police chiefs to ensure his establishment wouldn't be targeted for a raid. Papa kept warning Fred he might have to think about closing the French Club. Emma wondered... *what is Fred going to do then?*

During the week Emma was heavily involved in the activities of her clubs. She had been elected to the board of the Christian Mothers Society, one of her church groups, and she was on the board of the Ladies of the Grand

Army of the Republic. She served as secretary to both groups on a local level: she enjoyed recording the minutes of the meetings and could type her reports at home on her typewriter. She was also planning to attend the state conventions for both groups in Harrisburg, the state capital, next summer. She figured she would take Michael with her on the train since she would still be nursing him. All the other ladies fussed over him when she brought him to local meetings. He was a pleasant child, not prone to tantrums the way Nan had been, she thought. Nan was now twelve. She still threw fits of anger, still stubborn as the day was long.

Emma figured that Dorothy and Nan could be trusted to take care of their brothers; they were good at watching Johnny and Paul. By next summer, Dorothy would almost be sixteen. She was quite capable of taking care of the younger boys. Paul would be four. Already he was following his big brother Johnny around the house, trying to be just like him. Johnny would be ten and was a cooperative, helpful child.

Emma smiled, picturing Johnny's handsome face with that big, confident grin. *The girls will be chasing after him in a few years,* she thought. Johnny was going to be as charming and good-looking as his father....

Her thoughts turned to Jack. She planned not to mention anything about her trip until next spring. She would be gone only for five days, but she knew Jack would not be supportive of the idea.

She would explain to him that Monnie, Dorothy, and even Nan would help in her absence. And. frankly, she didn't care whether Jack got angry, she planned on going no matter what he said. He never was around that much anyways, at work all day and then always going to the club right after dinner. He knew to not tell her what to do—or what not to do. She had always been independent. Jack had been aware of that from even before they were married.

Sometimes when it was quiet in the house, she would think back on their bad years. She realized recently she still harbored some resentment born of those times. Especially when Jack blamed her for having more babies—as though it was all *her* fault. This last time, when she told him she was pregnant with Michael, Jack wasn't exactly thrilled. He hadn't talked to her for two weeks.

Fine, go make love to your bottle of whiskey, she thought. Emma decided she needed to talk to her doctor about ways to prevent pregnancy. Dr. Adams was young; he had delivered Paul and Michael. He seemed informed and quite knowledgeable. She had heard great strides were being made in the area of birth control, thanks to the women's rights movement. Another item on her mental list of tasks: discussion with Dr. Adams.

She was glad positive changes were being made in working conditions for women, and women's opportunities for education. Even child labor laws were being implemented in the factories and mills. She thought of her own daughters, how their lives would reflect these new changes.... Recently, Nan had begun making a fuss about school. "I hate the nuns! They're *mean*, and I *hate* school. I want to *quit* next year when I'm thirteen. I can't help it that I'm not as smart as Dorothy. Sister Martha just *loves* Dorothy...Miss Perfect Dorothy! I want to slap them both!" Then she would storm out of the house, slamming the door. The girl was dramatic!

Later, Emma had told her, in no uncertain terms, "You'll go to public high school, just like everybody else. And...you *will* graduate. At least at high school you can take typing classes and learn office skills so you can get a respectable job. You certainly don't want to end up working in a factory, sewing garments in a sweatshop or running machines filling bottles and cans at the Heinz plant."

She reminded both girls how important their education was. "Always try to better yourself," she would tell them. She reflected on how smart and pretty Dorothy was. She imagined her one day marrying a successful businessman or doctor, although she never wanted her girls to think marriage and having children was their only goal in life. Emma pointed out how successful Monnie had been improving the bakery. Monnie had goals and plans for the business that constantly surprised her aunts. Just last week, Monnie had said, "Aunt Louisa, with motor vehicles becoming popular, we can think about opening a second bakery, one with tables and chairs, and we could sell tea and coffee." Aunt Louisa marveled at her niece's creativity, while Emma recognized that spark of determination in her sister's eyes. "Your Aunt Monnie finished high school while also working at the bakery," she told Dorothy and Nan. "She did well in her business classes, taking courses in bookkeeping and typing. She's already taken over the bakery ledgers and will keep the business going now that Aunt Louisa and Aunt Sophie are getting up in years and can't be on their feet as much. They're getting the arthritis, just like my grandparents had."

Emma did not want her daughters to end up depending on a husband. She liked to encourage them to be independent women, not afraid to speak their minds. Her aunts never married, and she figured Monnie might follow in their footsteps—which served as a good example to Dorothy and Nan. Marriage should not be a woman's goal in life, Emma believed. Times were changing, she wanted her daughters to be well prepared. And Nan, with her nasty temper and bad attitude toward life in general, well…she might have a more difficult time, married or single. Emma never openly compared the girls to one another, but she thought Dorothy was sweet like honey while Nan had a lot of vinegar inside her. Emma was glad her own sisters had always been easygoing. She and Estelle were two years apart in age, but they had always gotten along like two peas in a pod. She didn't think Dorothy and Nan would ever be best friends. The best she hoped for was that they would tolerate each other and be supportive. *Oh, well…time will tell,* she thought. *Just like Papa says.*

Stirring her tea while daydreaming, Emma wondered how her life would have been different had she gone to high school. What if she had kept working for the newspaper? She could have become a regular reporter or even attended college. Maybe she would have worked for a magazine or written stories for the *New York Times*. But then she wouldn't have her five children and her handsome husband. Nobody could have it all. But…it just wasn't fair. Mama had always remarked: "Emma, life isn't supposed to be fair."

Back to reflecting on her husband….

Jack had recently suggested an idea she had not agreed to. Not yet. But she told him she would give it some thought. Just last week, he had said: "Emma, remember when I rode the train to Youngstown? The first stop the train always made going west was in the town of Woodbridge, which is just a couple of miles from Elliott. A nice, new, clean town." He meant there was no smoke, and lots of trees. "A lot of buildings have gone up in Woodbridge over the past twenty years. Houses and small businesses, no factories or anything industrial. Cleaner air, better than close to the city. There's a nice Catholic church…beautiful, in fact. St. Joseph's. And they have a Catholic school, and a new public high school. There's newly paved streets, new water, gas, sewer lines, and electricity." He looked at Emma with an expression she had never quite seen in him before. "Woodbridge is a fine place for a growing family, my dear," he told her. "A family like ours."

Emma had just stared at him, letting him talk. She could not believe how excited he was about the whole idea. Wide-eyed, gesturing with his hands, Jack continued: "I found out Woodbridge is still selling parcels of land for new houses." She listened attentively, enjoying making him campaign for his idea. "And you've been so good at saving money the last few years, we could buy a nice big lot. Then, with a bank loan, we could start building a brick house, with a yard with trees and a cement sidewalk."

"Close your eyes," he instructed. "Now picture Johnny playing ball in a big grassy yard with Paul and Michael. I could have my fruit trees and gardens...lilac bushes...hedges. I'll give you a garden of roses. Just think about that...a trellis with roses blooming all over it."

"We have five children now, Emma," Jack concluded, "and this old wooden house is just too small for us."

Emma was admiring Jack's presentation. She felt like applauding. She had never imagined he could be so eager and determined about anything. "Jack," she said, "you should have been a street vendor, selling snake oil." She started to laugh. "Or maybe cure-all tonics. You'd have all the women just throwing dollars at you!" Jack didn't see the humor, but that didn't stop him from putting his arms around her and whispering in her ear: "Come on, my dearest Emma, just say you'll think about it. You wouldn't be that far from your family. And Monnie, Estelle, and Fred are here in Elliott to keep an eye on your parents."

Emma never was good at refusing her husband whatever he wanted, he was just so damn persuasive. That Jack Quinn charm! Not wanting to agree right away, Emma did not immediately give him an answer. She thought she might be able to use Jack's dream of building a house in Woodbridge as a bargaining chip...soon.

Jack always got what he wanted, but this time Emma wanted something in return. He would have to agree to her terms. She thought she just might enjoy the whole process. When she told him about her plans to take a trip next year, he wouldn't make a fuss. In fact, he might be quite agreeable to anything she wanted.... She finally might have the upper hand with Jack Quinn, or at least an *equal* hand. Let the negotiations begin.

CHAPTER 29

July 1925—Clare

"I just love the smell of apple pies baking in the oven," announced Johnny Finnegan as he breathed in the heavenly scent. He quickly kissed Alice on the cheek, picked up his toolbox, and headed toward the back door. "And Rosie, my girl, I want one of those sugar cookies when I come back." He gave one of Rose's braids a gentle, playful tug. Rose Mary had white flour covering her nose and arms. Nonetheless, the cheerful girl replied, "I'll save two special cookies just for you, Daddy."

"Well, I can't wait to return, my ladies," Johnny said. "I'm off to the church yard…to help transform the place into a land of fun and games." The Finnegan household was busy with preparations for the annual church festival. Alice's husband was organizing the men who were constructing wooden booths, benches, and tables on the church grounds. Alice was baking pies and cookies with seven-year old Rose at her side. The child was pouring flour and sugar into mixing bowls while she stuck her tongue in the gap where her two front teeth used to be. Outside, on the front porch, Clare was finishing up her knitting and sewing projects; they would be for sale at one of the booths. She sat in her favorite porch chair, moving her knitting needles with such skill and efficiency she didn't even have to look at her hands.

Every summer St. Stephen's held a parish festival on the grounds of the church. The games and items for sale during the event helped raise money for the school. The nuns ran the school with the precision of a well-oiled machine. They lived in the yellow brick convent that stood between the church and school. Clare admired these women for their saintly patience with the children, as well as for their tolerance of the summertime heat: the nuns wore dark habits reaching down to their ankles. The habits' long sleeves covered their wrists, and short capes were wrapped across their shoulders. The ensemble was topped off with a black bonnet that fit close to the head. To Clare the entire wardrobe looked hot, especially during the summer months.

Young Rose had completed first grade; she would be entering second grade in September. She was a kind and gentle child, filled with compassion for those who suffered. After learning about St. Stephen, the patron saint of the church and the school, Rose announced, with tears in her eyes, "Saint Stephen was the first martyr and died because some people didn't like that he believed in Jesus. They threw rocks at him until he was dead. I said a prayer and told him that I was sorry that the mean people did that to him." At home Rose loved to read her beginning readers to her mother, her father, and her proud Aunt Clare. The nuns had only good things to say about Rose Finnegan, although Rose reported to her family that some of the boys occasionally got a smack with rulers and long wooden pointers. Clare and Alice told Rose that the teachers in the public school were just as demanding as the nuns—and just as quick to punish. Alice, Johnny, and Clare had all attended public school. Johnny agreed that the boys were always getting punished for their restlessness. "Yes," he said, "and if you got in trouble at school, you were sure to be in double trouble at home. That's how I learned to run fast!"

"I have a painful memory of getting my knuckles cracked with a ruler for talking too much!" admitted Clare. "I quickly learned to think first and speak second." Alice added: "And *then* you begged me not to tell Mum and Dad, since you didn't want to get hit again at home with the belt. They didn't believe in sparing the rod!"

Rose stared wide-eyed at the three adults, not able to imagine being in that much trouble. The child was an angel, never guilty of any wrongdoing, taking the Ten Commandments quite seriously. She didn't have any brothers or sisters to even get in an argument with, and she wouldn't dream of being disobedient. The child had never been the recipient of any form of corporal punishment. She calmly said, "I would die if I got smacked."

Clare wondered what Rose would say in the confessional when she had to make her first confession. Customarily, Catholics received the sacrament of penance—which involved going to confession—before they made their First Communion. Rose would receive both sacraments at the end of second grade, marking a special holy occasion in the life of any Catholic child. Clare was looking forward to designing a beautiful white dress and veil for Rose. She had already shopped for several yards of lace.

Of course, the first sacrament every Catholic received was the sacrament of baptism. Clare had not witnessed Rose's baptism, since that had taken place when Clare was still a patient in the tuberculosis sanatorium… the long ago, distant past, which sometimes seemed like a different lifetime. It pertained to another Clare, someone who today's Clare barely remembered… the sinful, deceptive Clare who now had to live with her mistakes, who now had to do penance for her sins.

"Auntie Clare, will you listen to me spell my words?"

"Auntie, will you tie my hair ribbons?"

"Will you please read me a story, Auntie?" Clare vowed to do anything for her lovely child, who provided her with a reason to get dressed every day. Clare existed as the ever-doting aunt, full of praise and love; she felt blessed to be allowed to witness the little girl grow. Clare had noticed that Rose's eyes were now an interesting shade of bluish green. Her hair had remained a very dark brown, almost black, just like Jack's. And the child was tall for her age, Self-aware, as opposed to self-conscious, she exhibited a healthy amount of self-confidence. She announced one day after school that she was the tallest girl in her class. "I'm even taller than some of the boys," she claimed. She wasn't upset about this, she just seemed to take it in stride, saying: "I can even win races, so I get picked first when we have to choose teams."

Johnny Finnegan had bought a new Singer sewing machine for Alice and Clare. Mostly though, Clare was the one who used it, practically daily. She was grateful Johnny had wanted to make such an expensive purchase: she had never regained enough strength to return to her former job sewing in the backroom of the clothing store.

Clare enjoyed designing and sewing dresses, critiquing the newer fashionable styles, saying, "I really like the dropped-waist look with the pleated skirts." When she sewed dresses and skirts for Alice and herself, she always commented, "I'm so glad hemlines are shorter now. At least we aren't cleaning the streets with our skirts and dragging all that dirt into the house like we used to." Alice agreed. "It's no wonder we only had two or three dresses. That was a lot of fabric. Yes, and they were hard to keep clean."

Every day Clare attended morning Mass, enjoying the short solitary walk to the church; then she kept busy with her sewing and knitting. She still made vestments for the parish priests and was highly regarded and respected by the congregation, which had continued to grow. Its numbers had doubled during the past ten years. Most of the people Clare was acquainted with now did not know her from when she was healthy, before her confinement in the sanatorium, back when she was young and in love with the good-looking Jack Quinn. She assumed not many even remembered him, since he had moved away eighteen years ago.

Alice was always cooking and baking. Clare helped her with the washing and housecleaning. The sisters enjoyed a cup of tea together in the morning and again in the afternoon. They both looked forward to Rose's arrival from school every afternoon. The living arrangement had worked out well for all members of the little family.

During the summer months Rose helped around the house and read picture books from the library. Clare made doll clothes for Rose's favorite doll. On Sundays Clare liked to curl Rose's hair with a hot curling iron before adding ribbons to her thick mane. Most of the time, Clare braided her hair and tied ribbons to the ends. Rose still ran to greet her daddy as soon as he walked in the door, and he called her "my sunshine."

<hr>

Every morning Clare looked at herself in the bedroom mirror while sitting at her small dressing table, brushing her hair then pinning it in a bun on the back of her head. She looked at her forty-four-year-old face, which was pale and beginning to show deep crease lines around her mouth and eyes. Even her forehead displayed a few lines. Her hair was still reddish, but there were now some gray and white strands mixing with the red. Alice, a year older than Clare, did not have any gray hair yet. She remembered her old friend Catherine from the sanatorium used to say, "Every line, every gray hair has a story to tell. Nothing to be ashamed of."

Clare no longer wore the gold locket on the chain that Jack had given her. She kept it wrapped in a handkerchief, hidden in a dresser drawer with her underclothes and stockings. She wanted to give it to Rose someday. Occasionally, she unwrapped it and caressed the two hearts engraved on it....

Her brother Joe never did return from the state mental hospital where he had been a patient for the last five years. Alice told Clare that the doctors had tried shock therapy on him, but he was still unresponsive to any treatment. His condition was labeled *catatonic depression.* He usually existed in a dazed, silent stupor. But his behavior sometimes became wildly erratic, triggered by thunderstorms; then he had to be confined, away from the other patients, while the doctors administered drugs to calm him down. Clare remembered the night Joe had almost killed her. She shuddered thinking about it.

The hospital informed Alice that given Joe's unpredictable behavior, allowing him to return home would always be dangerous. They said he would be institutionalized forever, most likely.

Clare felt sorrow and a trace of pity for her brother. She always prayed for him at church. She also prayed for Jack,,,and hoped that he was happy. She realized that she probably would never see Joe or Jack again. She had resigned herself years ago to the reality of the situation. Then, last Monday, Margaret had stopped to visit. She happened to start talking about Jack. As Clare made them each a cup of tea, she couldn't resist asking a few questions. "How many children does he have now?" she said.

Margaret replied, "The last time he came over, he said his wife was expecting again! So, let's see now, he has the two girls. The oldest is almost seventeen and the other one is fourteen. Then his oldest boy is eleven…it's amusing that his name is Johnny. I think Jack named him after his old best friend, although Jack won't admit it. Then the two little boys are Paul, who is five, and Michael, who is three. And soon there will be another one."

Clare couldn't help herself. "I wonder if Jack is a good father to his children. I hope so. It sounds like things must have improved with his wife… he doesn't come around Hazelwood much anymore."

She sighed. Margaret echoed the sigh, as they both took a sip of tea. After a silent pause, Margaret continued: "He brought his oldest son with him a few times, and that made Dad happy. Such a handsome boy, just the way Jack was. Although Jack is starting to get a few gray hairs, just like the rest of us." Margaret grimaced as she smoothed her hair with one hand.

"Clare," she said, "he was also telling us that he bought a building lot in the town of Woodbridge, which is a couple of miles from where they live in Elliott. A bit farther away from the city. He said he makes good wages as a supervisor of his plumbing crews, and they've been able to save up some money. Jack seemed excited about having a brick house built and having a nice yard. He said the house should be finished in about two years."

Margaret added, "I guess with all those children they need a bigger house." Clare merely nodded in agreement. She briefly pictured Jack with his brick house and his gardens. *His dream!* She sighed pensively as her stomach churned with emotion. Then she changed the subject to the church festival next week.

"Our Rose is looking forward to the games and seeing her friends from school. She's been helping Alice with the baking…a lot of pies and cookies are needed. I hope you and Florence will be coming. Johnny is even organizing some races for the children, which will be entertaining to watch."

Margaret smiled. "Absolutely. We'll see you there Sunday afternoon. Probably just me and Florence, and I hope Mary will come with her children, who are all grown up now. You know my Dad won't want to come, being he thinks picnics and festivals are silly."

After Margaret left, Clare couldn't stop thinking about Jack…and his family…and his new house. Alice and Rose had left to go to the market, and Clare was alone in the house. She went to her room and lay on the bed, sobbing. She thought about Jack. He would finally have his dream. His brick house and his gardens.

She opened her dresser drawer and took out the gold locket then held it to her heart. She kissed it and returned it to its hiding place.

She dried her face and blew her nose. *Enough of that,* she thought. *No feeling sorry for yourself.* Self-pity was a sin…another one to add to the list.

Clare slipped her rosary beads into her pocket then went out to the porch. She walked down the street to the church. She knew she had to ask God for forgiveness every day. Prayers and good works were her only salvation, her only hope. She entered the church through the side door and lit a votive candle in the transept. Standing alone she studied the late afternoon rays of light that filtered through the stained-glass windows. She made the sign of the cross, genuflected, and knelt in the coolness of the stone-and-brick building. Whispering to herself, she began: "Oh, my God, I am heartily sorry for having offended Thee, and I detest all my sins…"

~ex∞~

The following Sunday afternoon was hot and sunny. The usual low clouds of smoke had lifted; the mill was now idle on Sundays. Some men had been laid off, but Johnny's job was secure because he was a foreman. Clare and Rose walked behind Alice and Johnny as they headed to the church grounds. Rose was attempting to step on their shadows as they walked along the cracked sidewalks. Wanting to secure a seat in the shade, Clare searched for the best spot to watch the children play their games. The nuns were setting out pitchers of lemonade next to a table where they were selling slices of pie and cookies. A large booth situated prominently in the center of the church grounds sold items that Clare had donated. She had knitted hats, shawls, several afghans, and baby sweaters and booties. Even the priests had complimented her on her fine handiwork. Father Walsh exclaimed, "The Lord has blessed you with enormous talent, Miss Clare! Thank you for sharing it with us." She had also donated children's clothes she had designed and sewn. Several little cotton dresses and two little blue sailor outfits were lined up in an attractive display. Clare was sitting on a wooden bench under a tall maple tree fanning herself and sipping some lemonade when she spied Margaret and Florence walking toward her. Behind them she spotted a tall, familiar figure, trailing a gangly long-limbed young boy.

Oh no. She almost panicked, dropping her fan. She started to feel faint but remembered to take a few deep breaths. *Be brave.* "God help me," she whispered.

She had not seen Jack in almost eight years but recognized him immediately. She had never forgotten the way he walked, his broad shoulders, how handsome he looked in his suit and hat. As he approached, she saw him look straight at her. He touched his hat and nodded. Their eyes met, and she felt the color rise in her cheeks. There were those blue eyes she had loved…that pierced her heart. Looking away, she stared at Margaret, then at the boy.

Her heart was beating hard as she raised her hand to her chest. *Be as strong as steel. Stay calm,* she told herself. *Just breathe…*

Margaret gestured toward her brother and hastily said, "Well Clare, we were just leaving to come here, and look who showed up." Jack's lips parted as the corners of his mouth turned up. "Hello, Clare," he said. "How are you?" Then, not awaiting a reply, he put a hand on the boy's shoulder and said, "This is my son, Johnny."

Clare's eyes moved from Jack's face to the dark blue eyes of the boy. She observed how much he resembled his father; then she smiled and said, "Hello, Johnny. I'm pleased to meet you." Her hand gestured toward the brick courtyard. "The boys and girls are getting ready to play some games. You might want to join them."

Just then Rose skipped over to the group. Clare felt faint but managed to look at Jack. "This is Alice and Johnny's daughter," she calmly announced. She quickly turned back to Rose. "Rose, dear, this is an old friend of your parents, and his son. The boy's name is Johnny, just like your dad's name. You can take him over to play some games with your friends." Not the least bit shy, Rose grabbed Johnny's hand. "Come on," she said. "I bet I can run faster than you." And off they raced. Young Johnny had no choice but to follow the pretty girl with the dark curls.

Jack watched after them then looked back at Clare. "Well…Clare… how are you?" She nervously replied, "I'm good, now…finally, after surviving a few bad years. You know what they say about people that live in the steel city. We're strong as steel, we might bend but never break. Survivors. I guess you heard about everything with my health and the hospital…and then what happened with Joe." "I did. Yes, Margaret and Florence told me everything. I was sorry to hear about your troubles."

She looked down at her hands and thought, *Well, you certainly didn't hear* everything, *not the whole story.* She knew she could trust Alice and Johnny to never tell their secret.

He took off his hat and used a handkerchief to wipe the sweat on his forehead, then looked away from Clare and gazed at the children playing. As he stood under the shade of the tree, a slight breeze made shadows dance across his face. Clare glanced at his profile…She wanted to shout, "Look at her, Jack, our baby! Isn't she beautiful?" But she folded her arms across her stomach and unconsciously pinched the tender skin on the inside of her elbow crease, warning herself to beware of revealing her feelings. Jack leaned slightly toward her, whispering, "I was so worried when you went away, and wanted to talk to you, but it was impossible. I'm sorry…"

Just then Florence hurried over, interrupting their conversation. "Jack! Come and see all the things Clare made that are for sale!" Jack smiled at Clare, put his hat back on, and dutifully went with Florence. Clare watched him as he walked away. She felt a pain in her heart, but at the same moment she realized there was nothing else they needed to say to each other. She vowed never to be swayed by his charms again. What they had once shared should remain in the past, locked away. Over and done.

Jack ended up buying some baby clothes, which gave Clare some satisfaction, especially when he came back with Florence and complimented her. "Clare, I see you are still a wonderful seamstress!"

Florence noticed how Clare and her brother were looking at each other. She wanted to put a stop to whatever was going on, so she sharply said to Jack, "Your wife will be glad you bought something for the new baby…who will be here any day now." Florence had never been jovial or merry; in fact, she had a knack for putting a damper on any festivity. Or, perhaps, she was just suspicious, like an old prudish schoolmarm.

After talking for a few minutes longer, Florence saw an opportunity for Jack to speak to Alice and Johnny, who were talking to Rose and little Johnny. "Come on, let's say a quick hello," Florence suggested, taking his arm. Reluctantly, Jack set the package of clothes next to Clare and accompanied Florence as they walked across the church grounds.

Always good humored, Johnny Finnegan stood up with a big grin when he saw them approaching. "Hey Jack, this young man told me his name is Johnny Quinn and that his dad is Jack Quinn," Johnny said. "My, oh my, so you named your son after your old best friend! Well, I'll be…" Jack and Johnny Finnegan shook hands; then Jack smiled and replied, "Not exactly. As I told my Dad years ago when Johnny was born, *Sean* is the Irish form of the name John. So, Johnny is named after my Dad." The next moment he added, "It's good to see you, Johnny…and hello, Alice." He touched his hat and nodded, smiling at Alice, who he hoped did not still hold any animosity toward him. He had been well-aware the Murphy and Finnegan families were not happy with him when he broke Clare's heart and married Emma. Glancing at Rose, Jack commented, "I heard a while ago that you two had a daughter—and I see she is quite a little beauty." Alice replied, "Yes," gazing at Rose, "she is a gift from heaven…and such a blessing."

Watching Jack interact with Alice and Johnny, Clare was glad her sister and brother-in-law were gracious and not prone to holding grudges. Many years had passed since they had last seen Jack, even though he had been best friends with Johnny Finnegan, back when life was much simpler. As Jack shook hands with Johnny, Clare observed that Alice stood with her arms crossed in front of her, one arm bent, her hand raised, her fingers pinching at her lower lip. Then Alice smiled at both men. Clare found herself wondering whether it was awkward for Jack.

She couldn't help but imagine the scenario if her brother Joe had been present. He would have approached them from behind, poked Jack's back, and started a fight. Joe held onto grudges and *never* let them go. The priests and nuns would have been horrified! Nowadays, poor old Joe was locked away, wrestling with the demons in his head. Even Clare still suffered flashbacks, sending her back to the night Joe had almost killed her. She shivered at the memory.

Jack, Florence, and Margaret strolled back to where Clare was sitting in the shade. "Well, that was a little strange," admitted Jack. "Although it's good to see them again after all these years. And I'm happy they finally have a child to raise." Clare stared at her hands folded in her lap and did not reply. She glanced up, finding Rose and young Johnny walking toward the table where the nuns were selling lemonade. She noticed that Jack kept staring at Rose. Or was it her imagination…perhaps her mind playing tricks on her?

She wondered what Jack would say if he knew Clare's secret. Sometimes she debated silently whether there was any difference between a lie and a secret. How could protecting the people she loved most be a sinful lie? She had arranged for her baby to have the best life possible, given the circumstances at the time. She loved Alice and Johnny, she was happy to have given them a most wonderful gift, enabling them to be the parents they were meant to be….

Surely God would understand why she never told Jack.

What would he do if he realized Rose was his daughter? Would he be angry that she had never told him? Did he have the right to know? She knew that she had done what she thought was best for everyone.

Thank God Rose doesn't look like me, she kept thinking. If Rose had red hair and green eyes and freckles, Jack would have known right away. Thank goodness the girl had dark hair, that she was tall, not short and petite like Clare.

Finally, Jack said to Clare, Florence, and Margaret: "Johnny and I are going back to the house to visit with Dad for a bit before we get the streetcar."

Then, he looked at Clare. She could see the sadness in his blue eyes. She felt a strange sensation, a suspicion that he wanted to talk with her. Alone. Her intuition told her Jack had questions. Questions she didn't ever want to answer. Or, was her guilty conscience making her believe he had suspicions?

"Bye, Clare," Jack said. "It was nice seeing you again." He turned to his son, who had returned with Rose. "Come on, Johnny, we have to go. Say goodbye to your Aunt Florence and Aunt Margaret." Johnny finished his lemonade. "Bye Rose. Goodbye Aunt Florence. Aunt Margaret. And Miss Clare, it was nice to meet you." Clare couldn't help but think what a nice polite young boy Johnny was. She wondered what Jack's other children were like. Their personalities…their looks. She wished she could have seen a photograph of his family.

She glanced back as her sister and brother-in-law walked toward the pie booth. Clare noticed the two of them whispering to each other and turning back carefully watching Jack. She wondered if they had also noticed the way Jack kept studying Rose.

Her eyes followed Jack and his son as the pair headed down the hill and crossed Second Avenue. Jack's purchases had been wrapped in brown paper and tied with string. He had tucked the package under his arm. Clare thought he had better not tell his wife that those baby clothes were made by his old girlfriend. She wondered what Jack's wife looked like, and she realized that the woman must have a forgiving heart. Jack was fortunate to be loved by such a woman. Clare hoped Jack knew that.

CHAPTER 30

October 1926—Emma

"I'm just *so* angry," fifteen-year-old Nan grumbled, apparently hoping that her mother was listening. Nan loved to have an audience. Emma sighed as she held baby Charlie on her lap, rubbing his back and waiting to hear him burp. Then she finally answered, "My dear daughter, what is the matter now?" She felt obligated to try and diffuse every volatile situation that arose with Nan.

"Well, for starters, I have to wash all of these dishes while Dorothy is out shopping for new clothes for her fancy job where she'll be making loads of money. *And* she gets to dress up every day wearing silk stockings and shoes with straps and heels…*and* work at the front desk of *the* best hotel in Pittsburgh. *And* I still must go to school *and* wear scratchy, hot stockings!"

Emma tried to be patient with her disgruntled daughter. "Nan, you know how hard Dorothy worked to finish high school, and *you* will graduate too. Then, you'll be able to get a decent job in an office *and* wear pretty clothes.

"Nan," she continued, "I appreciate your help with the house chores, the baby, and your brothers. I truly do; and I don't know what I'd do without you. You're such a blessing." Emma tried to give the girl a hug with one free arm as she juggled Charlie with the other. But Nan merely shrugged as she scrubbed a pot in the sink.

Emma's perpetual challenge was to boost her daughter's confidence rather than add fuel to the fire of competition raging between Nan and Dorothy. She continually tried to encourage Nan, who consistently had to work hard to achieve all that came so easily to her older sister.

Blessed with the best of Jack and Emma, Dorothy possessed Emma's grace, her poise, her intelligence. She was tall, as were both her parents, but she had a beautiful face, clearly reflecting Jack's perfect straight nose and soft blue eyes. She had a lovely complexion, perfect teeth accenting a radiant smile that lit up the room, and thick, wavy dark hair worn in a modern style cut just above her shoulders. Emma had never considered herself beautiful or glamorous, but she knew she was attractive. She tried to impress on her daughters that beauty was only skin deep; that what lay inside was what counts. She reminded them, "Beauty fades. Young ladies need to be more concerned about their character, their intelligence, and their personality."

Nan was also tall. Her hair was black as coal, darker than Dorothy's. She was attractive, with a small nose and pretty, deep blue eyes; but she had a slightly protruding lower jaw. This was accentuated by her refusal to smile; consequently, she looked as though she was perpetually frowning, even when she was in a good mood. Nan also hated her crooked teeth. She claimed they were another reason not to smile.

Just recently, Jack had remarked to Emma, "Nan reminds me of my sister Margaret. She was always dissatisfied with *everything* and wore a constant frown on her face. I guess having two older sisters and a sick mother who ended up dying was the reason. I don't understand what Nan has to be unhappy about."

Jack's comment made Emma feel vindicated. He had practically admitted Nan took after his sister as opposed to anyone on Emma's side of the family. The thought made her smile.

Emma was genuinely thankful for Nan's help…but recently Nan had complained more than once about how large her family was getting. "Well,

I certainly hope there won't be any more babies, Mother. You're getting too old!"

Her daughter's comment stung, but Emma was accustomed to Nan's outspoken remarks. She felt slightly to blame. She had always encouraged her daughters to be open and honest. Emma mused to herself, *Well, leave it to Nan to be so blunt!*

Emma realized that, yes, being forty-two and having a baby was challenging for certain women; but she was strong and healthy, and her last three deliveries were easy. She found it hard to believe that Paul Henry was now six years old, Michael was four, and little Charlie had just turned a year old. *But this is it,* she told herself. *No more!*

Last year, after Charlie was born, she was fitted with a new birth control device. She was proud to have taken control of the situation. She wanted to be a true modern woman. Doing so meant getting on board with educating herself about contraception.

Jack had tried using condoms, which had become increasingly popular after the Great War. Many American soldiers had become infected with diseases contracted through sexual activity, so the army had finally started to distribute condoms for the sake of public safety. Jack had heard men where he worked discussing the topic of condoms. So, Jack tried them. They kept breaking, and he finally gave up. The result was Michael (*Oops!* Emma thought) and *then* Charlie.

Two summers ago, when Emma had attended the women's Grand Army of the Republic veterans' convention in Harrisburg, she wandered over to several booths set up by the women's rights groups. The women sitting at the booths passed out pamphlets describing birth control and contraception. She had brought Michael with her, since she was still nursing him at the time. With one hand on his stroller, Emma happily took every pamphlet she was offered. Later that night in her hotel room, she read the pamphlet titled "The Sex Side of Life." *Sex should be treated as a natural and enjoyable act*, she read. She chuckled to herself, thinking that both she and Jack would agree with that idea....

She tucked the pamphlets safely in her suitcase before leaving her hotel to catch the train back to Pittsburgh. She would show them to Jack in the privacy of their bedroom.

Looking back, Emma had been quite proud of herself: she had the courage and the confidence she needed to assert herself, and she had *told* Jack that she was going to Harrisburg, come hell or high water. When she finally agreed to move to Woodbridge, it had made Jack so happy he didn't even try to argue with her. He had accompanied her to the train station in Pittsburgh, kissed her and waved goodbye to little Michael. He had even told her to have a nice time at the convention.

That same summer Emma had also attended the Catholic Christian Mothers convention in Harrisburg. Of course, nobody was passing out birth control information at that event. The Catholic Church was very much opposed to any artificial form of contraception.

Now as she rocked and nursed little Charlie, Emma felt deeply satisfied. She had insisted that her family doctor in Elliott, young Dr. Adams, write her a prescription for the birth control device she wanted—and then she went to a clinic in downtown Pittsburgh to have it inserted. It took a lot of courage, but she did it. Her sister Estelle accompanied her to the clinic, while her other sister Monnie came to the house and watched Paul, Michael, and baby Charlie. Estelle marveled that Emma had six children and she had only one. Young Frankie was now twelve, the same age as Johnny. Estelle said: "I don't understand why I couldn't get pregnant again. Frank and I have tried. I guess I'll never have to worry about birth control. I would have loved to have another baby. I suppose it wasn't meant to be."

Emma never said as much to Estelle but remembered how Estelle had been so overwhelmed and sad after Frankie's difficult birth. "The baby blues" was what the doctor had called it. She secretly thought perhaps it was for the best that Estelle had only one child, suspecting more children would probably have been very difficult for her sister to handle.

After Frankie's birth, Estelle had been prone to weeping over every little thing. Her husband Frank had been worried when Estelle couldn't even cook dinner and provide basic care for the baby. Many nights poor Frank had sat rocking Frankie for hours because Estelle was in bed crying....

The man was a saint. He did what he had to do until Estelle finally was able to handle taking care of a fussy infant. Mama and Monnie had tried to pitch in and help Estelle during the daytime. Emma had wanted to do more to assist her sister, but that was around the same time she had given birth to Johnny. She also already had two other children. "Somehow everyone survived," she whispered to herself. She noticed Baby Charlie had fallen asleep. Emma cuddled him, rocking in her favorite chair as she rested her eyes, enjoying the few moments of quiet in the usually noisy household....

She had recently bought several books she had seen advertised in the newspaper. They were delivered to the house in a plain wrapper package: *Private Advice to Women* and *What Every Mother and Girl Should Know*... So much valuable information for only three dollars, according to the newspaper advertisement. With Dorothy being eighteen and venturing out into the working world, Emma wanted her to be prepared, to be armed with the most up-to-date knowledge that was available. Many girls ended up getting pregnant because they did not know even the most fundamental facts about how the human body functioned. Emma had always known knowledge was power, and that there was no excuse for ignorance.

One of the biggest opponents of birth control was the Catholic Church...a truth Emma was none too happy about. She had always been a good Catholic but didn't think the bishops and priests should have any say in how many children a family chooses to have. And she could not agree with the idea that the only purpose in having sex was to procreate. She didn't go around talking about the subject; but she knew she and her husband both enjoyed their bedroom activities, considering it one of the joys of marriage. And she didn't feel that she owed anyone an explanation…especially not a priest.

Emma was glad her sister Monnie was so independent and had never married, at least not yet. Apparently, there was no time for a steady beau in Monnie Moreau's busy life. Monnie had grown up watching her aunts and her father running their businesses and had learned from their experiences. She also had seen how husbands, babies, and children had tied down her mother and her sisters. That wasn't a path she wanted to travel. In fact, she had recently declared, "Emma, I enjoy your children, but I don't believe I want any of my own. I certainly don't have the time or the desire to raise a child."

The three Moreau sisters, Emma, Estelle, and Monnie, were all aware that many men were intimidated by a woman who was involved in running a profitable business. Monnie was immersed in the everyday affairs of the bakery and making the operation even more successful was her priority. She had hired several girls to bake pies, cakes, and breads. They worked early every morning, long before sunrise; then the delivery wagon shipped the bakery's items to grocery stores and markets in the area. With her aunts' blessings, she had even changed the bakery's name, from *Becker's Bakery* to *Monnie's Baked Goods*. She bought paint and half a dozen small brushes from Frank's hardware store; then she hand-painted the name on the side of the delivery wagon.

Aunt Louisa and Aunt Sophie still came into the bakery for a couple of hours every day, but they seemed content with letting Monnie run things. They spent their afternoons playing cards with their sister Margaret in the parlor at the Moreau house, delighting in leisure time after years of hard work. Emma was extremely proud of her sister. She had a shrewd head for business. It reminded Emma of how the Moreau boys had helped their father with the bookkeeping for the tavern: Albert, then Eddie, then Fred, tallying up the daily receipts and keeping track of business expenses. Emma had not realized Monnie was carefully watching and learning from her immediate family, as well as from her aunts. Monnie also possessed a kind heart, which was apparent in the manner she dealt with her employees and any problems that cropped up in the day-to-day operations.

Monnie looked out for her family. She had even recently hired her brother Fred to drive the baked goods to markets and grocery stores within a five-mile area of the bakery.

Papa and Fred finally had to close the tavern. Prohibition had slowly taken its toll on the business; obtaining high-quality whiskey had become too difficult. With a shift in political power after the last election, the new governor of Pennsylvania and the Pittsburgh mayor were now leaning on the federal agents to enforce the laws. Papa did not want the Feds to raid his establishment…but he also did not want to buy low-grade alcohol from bootleggers and moonshiners. Too risky. Some of them were peddling gin, which had become popular during Prohibition because it did not have to be aged like whiskey. But crude gin was dangerous, it could cause blindness if it had been made carelessly, say by using toxic methyl alcohol instead of ethyl alcohol. "Isn't worth the risk," Papa said, "and I'm getting too old to worry about such things."

Closing the French club was disappointing for Papa and Fred, but it was necessary. Papa admitted: "There's a time for everything…and the tavern's time is done."

Papa put the building up for sale: a sturdy, well-maintained two-story brick building on the main street of Elliott. He quickly found a buyer and closed on the sale shortly afterward, realizing a handsome profit. One benefit derived from the whole situation was Fred's health. He had slowly but surely stopped drinking so much. Papa and Fred had depleted their stored stock of bottles of whiskey, bourbons, and wine. And now that Fred was living back at the house with Mama and Papa he was eating better and much more resembled the old happy-go-lucky Fred everyone remembered from years ago. He had recently proclaimed how much he enjoyed riding around making deliveries every day, how much he appreciated talking to the store owners. He was starting to enjoy being outside in the sunshine again. Monnie was grateful that Fred took good care of the wagon and horse, although one of her goals was to buy a small truck for deliveries. "Fred better start learning how to drive a motor car," she announced. Emma was quite surprised one day in the summer when Monnie told her, "Fred is going to a Pirates baseball game at Forbes Field over in Oakland next Saturday. He's taking Frank, young Frankie, and Papa. Do you think Jack and Johnny would want to go with them?" "I'll ask Jack," Monnie replied, "but he probably will be going over to Woodbridge to see how the house is progressing, and Johnny usually goes with him." Johnny had been receiving quite the education simply by watching all the different trades performing their jobs at the Woodbridge house. It had widened his understanding of the entire building process. Last week Johnny and Jack were both excited when the builders finally finished the roof and the brick work on the house. But there was still so much to be done. "I was a little perturbed when Johnny told me Jack allowed him to climb up onto the roof to watch the workers nail shingles!" Emma said. "Thank God, my son is sensible and knows to be careful; he doesn't seem to have much fear of anything!"

"When do you think you'll be moving in?" Monnie asked. She was sitting at Emma's table, reviewing her day's receipts. "Not for another year, at least. The interior will keep the workers busy throughout the winter, running wires for electricity alongside the gas pipes. There will be some gas lighting and some electric lights. After the plastering, they'll be busy with painting, wallpapering, and installing wood trim and cabinets. Jack is planning on doing all the plumbing himself, including installing radiators in each room for hot water heat." Emma was beaming with pride. "He told me that the town of Woodbridge is paving our street with bricks, and that he's looking into buying a motor car by the time we get ready to move. That will make getting around town quite nice once we get situated." Her excitement was noticeable as she anticipated moving into a new house with four bedrooms and two bathrooms. She did not mind discussing details with Monnie, who was not jealous of her sister and was always anxious to hear about the construction progress.

When Papa had sold the building that housed the tavern, he had made a nice profit. One Sunday afternoon in September, he had asked his daughters, sons-in-law, and Fred to gather in the dining room. He cleared his throat then said, "I have an announcement to make, so ladies and gentlemen, have a seat." Once everyone was comfortably seated, he continued: "As you all know, I made a bit of money when I sold the tavern building. I'm seventy-one years old, and won't be around forever, and obviously I can't take my bank account with me when I meet old St. Peter at the pearly gates of heaven." He chuckled, probably trying to picture himself shaking hands with an elderly bearded man fumbling with a set of brass keys. Emma recalled how often Papa had made references to St. Peter over the years. She noticed how he smiled at Mama when he spoke, always including her in his plans, and how Mama nodded back, encouraging him to go on. Emma observed that her parents had both seemed to shrink in height the last few years, each being a few inches shorter than they had been earlier in life. She assumed that was what aging did to the body. *It must be nature's way of telling you to get your damn head out of the clouds because you'll ultimately end up in the ground, six feet under!*

Reminding herself to sit up straight in the wood-backed chair, Emma looked content as she felt Jack's presence behind her. His hand rested on the top slat of the chair, near her shoulder.

Papa continued his soliloquy. "Mama and I decided that you should all share in our good fortune now, instead of later. You may use the money to improve your own lives, considering how you have all brought such joy to our lives."

Emma knew her father enjoyed talking, so she wasn't surprised when he rambled on to his captive audience. "Your oldest brother, Albert, has been quite successful with his accounting job in Boston, and we all know that he never married and does not have a family. I called him and discussed my plan; he said that he doesn't need the money so I should divide his share among his sisters and brother." Emma thought how Albert was being true to form…independent, but still caring about his younger siblings. She wished he would come for a visit. The man was always working, married to his job.

"I'm sure Emma and Jack can use extra help to get their new house finished, and Monnie can invest in her bakery. Estelle and Frank will surely welcome some cash for home repairs, or for Frankie to go to college in a few short years."

"And Fred, since you live here with me and Mama, I'll talk to you privately about your share—although I think you and I need to go look at some automobiles. I've had my eye on one of those Model T's, and I want to pay cash, none of that buying on credit that you see in the advertisements. I was raised to only buy what I can afford. None of that 'buy now, pay later' nonsense! That's a quick way to end up in the poor house! Monnie, remember that, when dealing with your business affairs. Although, I do agree with you… your bakery would benefit from buying a delivery truck."

Papa looked tired as he stroked his balding head, probably missing the thicker, wavy hair he had possessed in his younger years. He kept his full moustache neatly trimmed, the way Emma preferred, compared to the old-fashioned handlebars he had sported in her childhood days. Nowadays, most younger men, Jack included, liked the clean-shaven look; but Emma was certain Papa would never shave his moustache. It was as much a part of his identity as his wire-rimmed glasses.

After pausing briefly, Papa added, "Fred, you might want to put your share of the funds in a bank account…in case you ever decide to get married. You never know. Anything could happen now that you're out in the world socializing. And especially when the women see you roaring around in an automobile one day and a delivery truck the next." That last remark made everyone laugh, especially Fred. He had mentioned to Monnie he liked chatting with one of the attractive lady clerks at a market in Woodbridge. Of course, Monnie had shared that information with her sisters.

Later that day Jack and Emma met privately with Emma's father. He handed Emma a check for five thousand dollars. "You have six children," he said, "so I want you two to have a little more than the others." Emma was stunned. She hugged her father. Jack shook his hand while simultaneously patting Henry's shoulder, telling him, "Henry, thank you so much for your generosity. We can put it to good use! We'll need a stove, one of those new refrigerators, a washing machine—and a better radio than the one we have now. And I know Emma has her eye on some of that fancy wallpaper." The previous day, Jack and Emma had listed all the items they would need to purchase for the new house. The gift from Papa was a godsend.

Quite pleased, Papa announced, "Well now, this calls for a celebration."

Given the traditions of the Moreau family, Emma knew a bottle of whiskey or brandy would soon appear from Pap's private supply. Sure enough, before everyone departed for the evening, the men had enjoyed a glass of Papa's finest Scotch whisky. Emma, Estelle, Monnie, and even Mama had a bit of brandy with their tea as they gathered in the kitchen. The men eventually went outside on the porch to watch Johnny, Paul Henry, and Frankie toss a football. The game was the boys' favorite sport in the fall. That day Johnny was showing Paul the correct way to hold the ball. Emma was happy Jack wasn't drinking as much anymore. Between his job and going to Woodbridge to oversee work on the house, Jack was too busy to socialize with his old friends in the South Side. *Thank you, God,* she mused. Everyone in her family had opposed Prohibition, so she hated to admit that her husband and her brother had been helped by the despised law. It was a shame that it forced the tavern, also known as the French Club, to close; but ultimately the shuttering of the club forced Fred to stop drinking overly much.

She found it hard to believe and somewhat amusing that Prohibition had improved her marriage. Jack was still able to bring home a bottle of whiskey or brandy occasionally, and Emma enjoyed having a little glass of brandy with Jack in the evening, when the house was quiet, and the children were all asleep.

～⚬✦⚬～

During the summer months, Jack had taken Johnny with him several times to visit his relatives in Hazelwood. Twice they had even let Paul Henry come along. Being a typical six-year-old, he of course was quite excited to ride the streetcar. Johnny and Paul later told Emma, "Mother, we had such a good time playing with all the boys and girls at the playground by the church. And then Aunt Florence and Aunt Margaret cooked lots of food, and gave us tea with milk and sugar, and *then* we had cake for dessert." "I hope you boys always remember your table manners, to say 'please' and 'thank you' and I trust that you don't chew with your mouth open. And no talking at the table unless you are asked a question by your aunts or your grandfather."

"Mother, you should come with us next time," said Paul Henry.

Emma patted his head, smoothed his dark hair, and looked into his sapphire eyes. "Well, we would have to bring Michael and Charlie, and it would be hard to take them on the streetcar. And your aunts don't have a big enough table for all of us. But I'm glad you both had a nice time."

She knew she never wanted to go to Hazelwood, and never would. Her children didn't need to know the reason.

Johnny looked over at them. "It sure is a smoky town! Dad told us he worked in the steel mill when he was my age, and he said he hated it. He says I better study and do good in school…so I don't have to work in a steel mill or a dirty factory." Emma nodded and said, "Yes, that's good advice. You need to listen to your teachers and do the best that you can. Your sister Dorothy is going to work in the finest hotel in downtown Pittsburgh because she always did her best with her schoolwork."

At the end of August before school started, the children were quite excited about a picnic at Kennywood Park. Many of the churches with schools were advertising a special Sunday at the park, with reduced price tickets. By coincidence the Plumbers Union was also having its annual picnic the same day. Jack was anticipating having a fine day, socializing with old friends and coworkers.

Plans were set, and Emma and Jack found themselves busy getting ready for the big day. Dorothy was in training for her job at the hotel, so Monnie had promised to take care of Charlie for the afternoon. At noon on the last Sunday in August, Emma and Jack boarded the streetcar with Nan, Johnny, Paul, and Michael. Jack had informed Emma that his union was supplying food for all members and their families. "That's wonderful… what a treat," Emma said. "A day with no cooking!" She smiled at Jack as she held tightly to Michael; the streetcar bounced along from Elliott through the South Side to West Mifflin, where Kennywood was located.

Emma soon found herself thinking about the day twenty years earlier when she met Jack at Kennywood. They had danced in the Pavilion and eaten ice cream. She glanced over to Jack and said, "Remember when we danced together after Mr. McGee introduced us?" Jack's eyes twinkled. "You were the most beautiful girl in the park. Of course, I remember," he replied. "You've reminded me many times over the years; your favorite song was being played that day...."

He closed his eyes and listened while Emma hummed softly, her cheek pressed to Michael's hair.

"Beautiful dreamer, wake unto me,

Starlight and dewdrops are waiting for thee.

Sounds of the rude world, heard in the day,

Lulled by the moonlight have all passed away.

Beautiful dreamer, queen of my song,

List while I woo thee with soft melody.

Gone are the cares of life's busy throng,

Beautiful dreamer, awake unto me!"

The streetcar slowly screeched to a halt. The bell clanged, the doors opened, and the passengers hurriedly stepped off, anxious to have a pleasant and memorable day. Even though they visited the park every summer, Emma found herself amazed at how much Kennywood had changed during the past twenty years. It wasn't even known as a Trolley Park anymore: so many customers now owned automobiles. Although streetcars were still the primary means of transportation to travel in and around the city, more and more people were purchasing autos for longer trips. The place was now called Kennywood Amusement Park, offering more than just a merry-go-round and the dance pavilion. Row boats still plied the lagoon, but now patrons found a wide variety of rides to choose from, and a gigantic cement swimming pool with a place where older children and young adults rented swimsuits, since most people did not own one.

Emma wanted to take Paul Henry and Michael to Kiddie Land, where small rides mostly went around in circles. She told Jack to stay with Johnny, but Nan was permitted to walk around with her friends from school. Everyone was instructed to meet at the merry-go-round at four o'clock, so they could go to the picnic pavilions together to eat dinner with the union members and their families.

It was a lovely warm day, with no threat of rain, and Johnny was looking forward to riding the Jack Rabbit, a wooden roller coaster. "It has a double-dip and two tunnels!" he exclaimed. He couldn't believe he was finally getting the chance to ride it.

Meanwhile, Emma enjoyed watching Paul and Michael ride the miniature train and waving to her. And every time they got off, they begged, "Again, Mama, again!" She was looking forward to the meal the Plumbers' Union was providing. She counted down the minutes for meeting her family at four o'clock at the carousel, never suspecting that this would be a day she and Jack would talk about for years to come.

CHAPTER 31

February 1927—Jack

When he was a boy, Jack remembered his Mum saying, "The only thing in life that doesn't change is God's love and mercy. Accept the things we cannot change and fix the rest, if you must." Changes were taking effect at his job and the company that employed him, and Jack wasn't looking forward to them. He realized he must be getting set in his ways. He didn't like change but knew it was a necessary evil...and a person must accept and adjust. He had been working in office buildings in downtown Pittsburgh for the past several years, and he was content with the work routine and managing various crews. His boss, Mr. McGee, was retiring. He was getting up in years and suffering from health problems. McGee had always favored Jack and trusted him. Therefore, he consistently gave Jack the most sought-after work assignments. He had recently asked Jack to prove himself to the company and the union one more time...by going to Youngstown for two months. They needed an experienced workman to supervise the plumbing installations in a new office building.

In January, Jack kissed Emma goodbye and promised telephone calls and letters. They were both disappointed he had to go, especially with the construction of their house getting closer to completion. Jack assured her the two months would go by quickly. He informed his wife, "The workers have a lot to finish inside the house before springtime, and they know what to do. I went over every aspect with the foreman and made sure he knows what we want."

"And, Emma," he added, "the two stained glass windows we ordered for the living room were finally delivered last week. We're lucky your father gave us that money, or we wouldn't have been able to afford them." Emma had her heart set on having stained glass windows, and French parlor doors with glass panels between the entrance hall and the parlor—or "living room," which was what Jack was supposed to call it nowadays, at least according to Emma. And then she wanted sliding pocket doors between the living room and dining room. The kitchen had a slew of built-in cabinets and a large pantry, even an ironing board cupboard. Jack had also ordered the wallpaper that Emma had picked out.

Jack and Emma were both excited about every aspect of the project, and Jack was elated he had been able to convince her to move from Elliott. They would have much more room in the new house, and Woodbridge was the perfect community for a young family with growing children. Although, Dorothy had already warned her parents she wouldn't be moving with them. She was nineteen now, with a good job in the city; she planned to rent a room in a boarding house for women. "It will be much more convenient for me," she told them. "One of my friends at the hotel is going to rent a room too."

Emma had told Jack how jealous Nan was of her older sister: Dorothy had begun buying pretty clothes, wearing makeup, going to movies, and eating at restaurants with businessmen. She had been teaching Nan some of the crazy movements to a new dance that was all the rage, something called the Charleston. And last Saturday, Dorothy was even nice enough to take Nan downtown to a beauty shop, where Nan had her hair cut in a "bob."

Jack listened carefully. "Well, Dorothy deserves everything she has," he replied. "She's all grown-up now. Maybe it will inspire Nan to work a little harder in school. Nan should be grateful Dorothy wants to spend time with her."

While Jack rode the train to Youngstown, he gazed out the window at the passing countryside, which was mostly covered with a thin layer of snow. His mind wandered, and he began thinking about the day last summer when the family went to Kennywood Park. The morning had started off with everyone looking forward to a fine day; the children and Emma were excited. He recalled riding the streetcar to the park that day, when he and Emma had talked about how they first met twenty years ago at Kennywood. As the train rumbled along, he sat back in the soft, cushioned seat and started to hum his wife's favorite song. He stopped soon enough, though, after receiving a few quizzical looks from his fellow train passengers.

He folded his arms across his chest and closed his eyes,...picturing Kennywood and the flowers, the fountains, the rides, and how the entire family was anticipating having a good time. Then he recalled the series of events that had occurred on that memorable August day....

After the Quinn family had entered the park, Emma took the two younger boys to Kiddie Land. Jack remembered how he had envied the young families in the enormous cement swimming pool, enjoying the cool waters as he sweated in his suit and hat. Johnny wanted to ride the roller coaster, so Jack had stood in line with him for an hour. He was starting to feel hungry and realized how much he was looking forward to the meal his union was providing. Johnny told him, "Dad, if I see one of my friends from school then you won't have to ride with me." Jack knew that Johnny realized his father didn't really want to ride a roller coaster, especially one named the Jack Rabbit; but Jack would do it if nobody else wanted to. Afterall, Jack was trying to be a good parent, and Johnny was a good boy and never asked for anything. Jack really didn't mind.

They had waited in line in the heat of the early afternoon. Jack was sweating and finally loosened his tie then removed his suit jacket and hat. When they were standing by the maintenance shed, Johnny wrinkled his nose and said, "What's that smell?" Jack sniffed and replied, "Hot tar. That's what they use to grease all the metal moving parts. The ride won't function correctly if there's any rust on the wheels or chains."

As the line inched along, Jack spied Alice and Johnny Finnegan, his boyhood pal, standing by the carousel. His son had also spotted them. "Hey, Dad," he said, "there's your friends from Hazelwood. I bet their daughter is on the merry-go-round." Jack nodded and replied, "I guess St. Stephen's is having their yearly picnic here today too." Before he had finished the sentence, his son was waving his cap, and Alice and Johnny were waving back. And sure enough, Jack watched as their daughter Rose climbed off the ride and ran toward her parents. Within a minute the trio was walking over to Jack and Johnny.

Rose spoke up right away, saying hello and smiling at Jack's son. Jack just stared at her. He tried to push thoughts of Clare out of his mind. The next moment, Rose said, "Johnny, you are so lucky. My mum and dad say I'm not old enough to ride the roller coaster yet, but maybe next year, after I've turned nine." Jack chatted with his old friends for several minutes. He was relieved when the line started to move and their turn to board the coaster finally arrived. He told Rose and her parents, "Enjoy the rest of your day." He had wanted to ask about Clare but decided against it: his son was listening to their conversation. A young Kennywood attendant buckled them into their seat as Johnny, lightheartedly, said, "It's so funny that the name of this ride is the Jack Rabbit. Did they name it after you, Dad?" Just then, the ride jerked forwards and the operator yelled out, "Hold on to your hats!"

As the coaster slowly crept along the track then ascended the first high hill, Jack and Johnny felt the car suddenly jolt. Then it stopped dead in its tracks, near the top of the wooden structure. Nothing moved. Jack and Johnny sat in their car and looked down over the park from at least fifty feet in the air.

Johnny pointed. "I can see the smokestacks at the steel mills, Dad. And the tall buildings in downtown, and the river." They took in the view, waiting patiently. Finally, Johnny grabbed Jack's arm and whispered, "What happened…why aren't we moving?" His eyes were wide. Jack noticed a slight tremor in his son's voice.

Two girls Johnny's age were sitting behind Jack and Johnny. The girls had started to cry. Jack turned around and tried to reassure them. "Everything will be all right," he said. "The operators will figure out what's wrong."

After ten minutes, Jack saw two park employees walking up the narrow wooden platform that bordered the tracks on either side. They appeared calm. As they approached the lodged cars, they told the riders the roller coaster had malfunctioned; they were going to ask all the riders to climb carefully out of the car and walk down the platform. "Come on, two at a time," the employee nearer Jack and Johnny said. "Don't worry…we'll help you." The girls behind them started to cry even louder, holding on to each other.

The employees helped the two boys in the seat in front of Jack and Johnny climb out first. The workers held their hands and firmly gripped their arms so they wouldn't lose their balance. The boys held on to a wooden railing that ran parallel to the tracks as they descended the hill. Although the platform had seemed steep when the car had climbed the hill, Jack now saw that the incline was shallow enough to walk down.

Once the two boys were safely back on the ground, the two employees climbed the wooden platform again and returned to the stuck car. Jack told the men to assist the two crying girls next. That proved to be a difficult task. The girls were screaming and shaking, practically hysterical. They followed the employee's encouraging directions and finally made it to the ground.

Then the men came back for Johnny and Jack. Johnny climbed out first and Jack followed him. They walked slowly down the inclined wooden platform, steadying themselves on the wooden railing. It was a nerve-wracking fifty-foot walk. Jack was extremely proud of Johnny for being so brave. "I'm not afraid of heights, Dad," Johnny explained later. "Not after all the years

I've been playing on the cliffs by the Overlook. I wasn't even nervous on the roof of our new house watching the workers nail on shingles!"

When they were safely back on the boarding platform, Jack saw a crowd of people gathered by the entrance to the ride. As Johnny and Jack approached, the crowd clapped and cheered so loudly Johnny and Jack felt like celebrities. The next moment Jack saw the two crying girls being cared for by a nurse who was trying to get them to calm down. Johnny spotted his mother; then he waved his cap at Emma, Paul, and Michael, who stood in the middle of the crowd of onlookers. Jack and Johnny exited down a ramp and headed directly over to the water fountains to get a drink and splash water on their faces. They heard a familiar voice calling, "Jack, Jack!"

Emma rushed towards them. She immediately began asking questions, anxious to hear the whole story. Jack grinned. "We're fine," he said. "Just hungry, right?" He looked at Johnny and patted him on the shoulder. Then he picked up Michael, who seemed tired from all the walking.

They did not see Nan anywhere but decided to go to the pavilions to eat dinner. It was after four o'clock. They figured their daughter was with friends and would find them when she got hungry; Nan knew where the pavilions were located. The food provided by the union was excellent and plentiful, and Jack spent time talking with coworkers and union leaders. Mr. McGee indulged himself with a second plateful from the buffet. He was delighted to see Emma and the children. He inquired how Emma's father was doing these days, now that he no longer had the tavern to keep him busy.

Before they knew it, Emma realized it was six o'clock—and they still had not seen any sign of Nan. After saying goodbye to Mr. McGee, Jack, carrying Michael, went in one direction to look for her, while Emma, Johnny, and Paul went off in another direction. Later, Emma told Jack she and the boys had searched for an hour before Emma finally saw one of her daughter's friends, a girl named Lizzie. "Last I saw her, Mrs. Quinn," Lizzie told her, "she was riding on the Old Mill with one of the older boys from school."

Emma was worried. She was well-aware of that ride's reputation: she and her friends had called it the Tunnel of Love when they were much younger. The ride featured individual small boats floating slowly through dark tunnels. It was a favorite attraction of young couples who desired a little privacy. She knew the Old Mill wasn't the kind of place where she wanted her impulsive fifteen-year-old daughter to be alone with a boy.

As they headed that way, Emma spotted Jack. He joined them, still carrying Michael. Together the family approached the entrance to the ride. They did not find Nan but described her features to the operator. He nodded and laughed. "That girl has been riding through the Old Mill all afternoon with her boyfriend."

Emma and Jack both seethed. They tried to contain their anger as one of the ride's boats emerged from the darkness…and there was Nan, sitting on the lap of a boy who was at least eighteen. The young man had draped one arm around Nan's shoulders. His other hand was slipped up under Nan's dress, clasping her thigh. Nan's hair was a mess. She laughed broadly as the fellow tickled the back of her knee. Then Nan saw her parents. She immediately scooted as far from the young man as possible. Then she quickly adjusted her stockings above her knees. She looked down at the floor of the boat, her face turning a bright shade of red.

Nan jumped out of the Old Mill boat as soon as it stopped, smoothing her skirt. Then she stumbled—and started to giggle. The young man followed behind her, a sheepish look on his face. He turned away and threw an empty bottle in a nearby trash can. He then swung himself over the railing that wrapped around the entrance platform and ran quickly in the opposite direction. Nan was attempting to speak. "Hel…looo, Mother…Mother, do you want to…perhaps…do you want to…um, go for a ride?" As soon as Jack heard his daughter slurring her words, he yelled, "*What* is going on here?" He recalled how Nan had stumbled after stepping out of the boat. "Nan! Have you been drinking?" Still carrying Michael, he grabbed Nan's arm and pulled her close enough to smell her breath. Nan started to sob. "I'm sorry, Daddy…But, but…he said it was okay, that a few sips weren't a big deal. And…we were just having fun." She tried to twist away. "Ouch!" she said. "You're hurting my arm!"

Jack let go. He turned and glared at the ride operator. "What kind of ride is this?" he shouted angrily. "You allow drinking? And you let no-good hoodlums ride with innocent young girls?"

The beady-eyed operator smirked and replied: "It's not my job to police the people that buy tickets. And besides, she doesn't look innocent to me… In fact, she was having a good old time."

Incensed, Jack turned Michael over to Emma, then took two steps and grabbed the man by the front of his shirt. "Slimy bastard," he hissed, "that's my *daughter*!" With a single, swift punch to the jaw, Jack knocked the man right on to the ground. "You'll never see me or my daughter again. And if I ever see your face again, I'll kick your ass into the river."

"Come on, Emma," he said, turning to his wife, "let's get out of here."

The operator sat rubbing his cheek and chin as he watched Jack and his family heading for the exit to the park. Jack took Michael back from Emma. They walked swiftly out of the park, toward the streetcar. Jack tried to calm down as he carried his four-year-old son. Johnny followed his father, holding Paul's hand. Close behind them, Emma was helping Nan stay upright as she held tightly to her arm. Nan kept sobbing. "I'm sorry, Mother!" she cried.

Before they boarded the waiting streetcar, Nan covered her mouth and turned by a bush. Then she leaned over and vomited. Emma pulled out a handkerchief to wipe Nan's face; Jack noticed how embarrassed his wife was. He hoped none of the people in the crowd passing by were anyone they knew. Nobody in the Quinn family spoke as they rode back to Elliott. The boys were exhausted; Nan had buried her face in her hands. Jack stared out the window, watching the sun creep below the tree line. He knew they had a problem…Nan's behavior had to be addressed. He felt frustrated, clueless as to what to say to his daughter, wanting to warn her of all the evil in the world. How does a father explain that alcohol affects judgement and common sense? How does a father protect his daughter from men who don't care about her... who would stomp on her heart and laugh about it later? Jack blamed himself for not being around more when his daughter was young.

Emma would know what to do.

He didn't even want to look at Nan. And who was that fellow she was with? Jack was certain that young man did not have good intentions. Jack's heart hurt for his naive daughter; and when he looked over at his wife, he could see sadness in her eyes too, even as she gently rubbed Nan's back as the girl rested her head in her mother's lap.

Tomorrow. No point in even trying to talk to Nan that night. *God help us,* Jack thought, *she's only fifteen.* Where did the years go? In a span of a mere six hours he had felt so much pride for the bravery of his son—and then so much anger and disappointment over his daughter's reckless behavior. That night, after all the Quinn children were asleep in their beds, Jack and Emma sat at the kitchen table with a bottle of brandy and two glasses. They rehashed the events of the day, both agreeing there had been too much excitement for one day.

Emma reached over and rubbed the knuckles on Jack's hand. "Does it hurt?" she said. "I don't encourage fighting, but I was so proud of you for defending Nan. I even wanted to slap that beady-eyed guy!"

Jack smiled at his wife. "I don't know what was more exciting...getting stuck on the roller coaster or slugging that asshole." Emma's eyes were tired; but Jack noticed a twinkle when she said: "Could you handle a little more excitement today? Although you might have to lie down to fully enjoy it...." They both laughed. Then they emptied their glasses, turned off the light, and quietly climbed the stairs, stepping over the loudest of the well-worn, squeaky boards.

Sometimes Jack was content to let Emma lead the way. He had learned to trust in his wife's ability to handle a crisis. He had always admired her strength and confidence, ever since the first day he met her. Being by her side brought him peace. *She'll know what to say to Nan tomorrow,* he thought. Tonight, she knew how to make Jack feel better. She made him feel loved, and he knew she would never leave him. After all these years he realized he did not have to be afraid of being left alone. He needed only *one* person—his wife, his Emma.

As the train pulled into the station in Youngstown, Jack was still thinking about Emma. He knew the new project would entail a long two months of six-day workweeks, but he and Emma could use the extra money. He was happy that he and his wife were sharing his dream, that their family would soon be moving to their new home. Feeling a sense of accomplishment, Jack realized his years of hard work were paying off. His daughters were older, but at least his sons would be able to have a normal childhood, something he himself had been denied.

CHAPTER 32

August 1927—Emma

Wooden boxes were packed with clothing and household items, sitting lined up from the front door into the kitchen. Johnny and Paul Henry had arranged the boxes to resemble a train, much to the delight of five-year-old Michael and little Charlie, who had just celebrated his second birthday. "*Woo, woo!*" squealed Charlie every time Paul hollered, "What's the train say?" Then Michael would pretend to be the engineer, yelling, "*Choo, choo...chugga, chugga, chugga, chugga, choo...choo!*"

Back in March, when he had returned from Youngstown, Jack had bought Michael and Charlie small metal toy trains. The two boys had been obsessed with trains ever since. Michael especially remembered riding the Kennywood train last August.

Jack had bought gifts for the rest of the family as well, surprising Paul with his very first leather baseball mitt. Johnny received a new football. "When we move to Woodbridge," Jack said, "the high school has a football team—and there's fields to play baseball in the summer. The Quinn boys will be ready!" The boys had all missed Jack, almost as much as Emma had. On the day Jack arrived home from Youngstown, the children had giggled when Jack kissed Emma, hugged her tightly, and lifted her right off the floor.

He told her how much he had missed her—and then he gave her a small box containing a pearl necklace with matching earrings.

Jack had bought Nan a very simple gold bracelet, even though he was still disappointed in her behavior at Kennywood the year before. Emma had assured Jack she was keeping a close eye on Nan, making sure she came directly home from school every day. On weekends Nan went into Pittsburgh only when she was accompanied by Dorothy or Monnie. On Sundays she attended Mass with Emma and the rest of the family. And, of course, she had a list of chores to perform every day.

However, Emma could sense a storm brewing inside her daughter. Nan was upset that Dorothy had moved into downtown Pittsburgh, where she was sharing a room in a boarding house with a coworker. And now with her own family moving to Woodbridge, Nan realized she would be living even farther from the city. According to Nan: "The city is the only place where there are fun things to do. Dorothy gets to go dancing and goes to restaurants and movies. And…she gets to shop at department stores. I can't wait to get a job in the city!"

Emma was not happy that Dorothy had bought makeup for Nan. Although, Dorothy had pointed out to her mother that Nan was now sixteen, and all the young girls were wearing a little lipstick and a touch of rouge on their cheeks….

Dorothy had even bought silk stockings for Emma and Nan at Christmas—some sheer, others dark in color. They were expensive, but women *loved* how they looked with the shorter skirts that were currently popular. Nan proclaimed, "Only children wear cotton and wool stockings nowadays!"

After Nan and Dorothy each had their hair cut into stylish bobs, Dorothy persuaded Emma and Monnie to come into the city on a Saturday to get their hair cut too. Dorothy told them, "Mother, you need a new hairstyle and an entire new wardrobe for your move to the new house. And Aunt

Monnie, you need a nice modern style that will be cooler in the summer when you're working in the bakery." Later, Emma commented to Jack: "Dorothy could probably sell snow in January! She bats her eyelashes, looks right at you with those big blue eyes, and has such a sweet smile. *That Quinn Charm!* Just like you! And you know I can't resist *your* powers of persuasion!"

On the first Saturday in June, Emma enlisted Estelle and Mama to watch Paul, Michael, and Charlie, while Jack and Johnny went to Woodbridge to work in the house. Then Emma, Monnie, and Nan met Dorothy in Pittsburgh and visited a beauty salon for haircuts. Afterward they had lunch at a restaurant in Jenkins Arcade.

After they spent two hours browsing through Horne's department store, Emma found herself hauling two shopping bags filled with three new dresses, a long string of pearls, and two new pairs of shoes. She had even bought lipstick and a bottle of perfume. Dorothy had suggested they sample the new Chanel perfume, telling them it was all the rage with the women she worked with at the hotel. "See, Mother, it doesn't hurt to treat yourself once in a while!" she exclaimed. "Wait until Daddy sees you in those dresses and smells that perfume. Just remember to wear a little dab behind your ears… not too much!"

Emma was amazed how worldly Dorothy had become as she showed them around the store. Her daughter was so beautiful that men were constantly turning to look at her as she walked by. Of course, her sister Nan noticed too. Not wanting Nan to dwell on how much more attractive her sister was than herself, Emma bought Nan a cotton short-sleeved summer dress. Nan tried it on and was excited when Emma agreed to buy it for her, along with a straw hat that complemented the dress nicely.

That evening Emma told Jack what a fine day she had enjoyed in the city with her daughters and her sister. Jack admired Emma's hairstyle. She showed him the dresses, and Jack asked her to put on the dark blue silky one. In the privacy of their bedroom, she modeled her new purchase by walking seductively around their bed. Jack draped the string of pearls over her head then pulled her to him. Nuzzling his nose by her ear, he said, "Are you wearing perfume, Madam?"

Emma was in such a good mood that she untied Jack's necktie then kissed him more passionately than she had in months. He carefully unzipped the back of her dress as he whispered, "You might have to go into the city more often, Mrs. Quinn…and I do like that perfume!"

By the first of July, Jack proudly informed Emma they would be able to move by the middle of August. Emma was relieved. She wanted the children to start their new schools in September. Michael would not be in first grade until the following year, but Paul would be entering second grade and Johnny was looking forward to eighth grade. He was going to miss his old friends at St. Martin's, but he was friendly, athletic, and handsome. Emma was sure he would adjust quickly. St. Joseph's School in Woodbridge was run by the Sisters of Charity, which Jack said was the same order of nuns that taught at St. Stephen's in Hazelwood. He had never attended Catholic school, as he had already begun working in the mill by the time St. Stephen's parish opened their school. However, his sisters had kept him updated on the church and school news, whether he was interested or not. He had informed Emma that Alice and Johnny Finnegan were sending their daughter to the parish school. Emma remembered her son, Johnny, had become acquainted with Jack's old friends at the St. Stephen's festival the past two summers, and had seen them at Kennywood last summer. Emma was hopeful that Nan would be able to make the transition to the high school in Woodbridge without any problems. She still had two years, but if she dedicated herself to working hard in her secretarial classes, she might be able to finish in one year. That, by itself, was incentive for Nan to perform well in school; she was looking forward to getting an office job in the city. "I can't wait to start living my life out in the world!" she commented. She was like a horse chomping on its bit, anxious to move things along. But her words shocked Jack when he heard her say them for the first time. "Emma," he told his wife, "I remember saying those exact words when I was her age."

One afternoon in August, a week before they were scheduled to start moving, Charlie was taking his nap and Emma sat at the kitchen table with a box of photographs. She had lined up approximately twenty photographs, arranging them in chronological order. She found some small photographs of Johnny, Nan, and Dorothy that had been taken at school, beginning when they had been in first and second grade. While Emma arranged the photographs, Michael, Paul, and Johnny were in the small backyard, throwing a ball around and making up games. Soon they came into the kitchen, dripping with sweat and asking for some lemonade. Emma glanced at them. "Wash your hands and then you can each have a cookie and a drink to take outside."

After Johnny washed his hands and poured drinks for his brothers, he looked over his mother's shoulder at the photographs lined up across the table. He spotted a couple of his school pictures and started to laugh. "Every year that photographer tells us not to smile or people will think we're crazy, and we wouldn't want to be shipped off to the asylum!" Emma replied, "I wonder if that's the same man with the camera who goes around the city neighborhoods with a pony for the children to sit on while he takes their photo. Your sisters were always afraid of him and his pony."

Johnny leaned over and picked up a photograph of Dorothy when she had been in second grade. She was wearing a big bow in her dark hair, which Emma had curled, as she had known Dorothy was getting her photograph taken that day. Johnny was examining the picture carefully.

"Mother, why do you have a picture of Rose Finnegan from Hazelwood?"

Emma looked at her son. "What are you talking about?" she said. "That's Dorothy. I've never even seen Rose Finnegan."

Johnny looked at another picture of Dorothy; this one was from third grade. This time he commented: "Well, Rose is around ten years old now, but she looks just like Dorothy did back then. She's the spitting image of her. Same color hair…and her face looks the same. Show it to Dad. I bet a quarter he'll agree with me."

"You're not betting quarters on anything. You know gambling is a sin!" Emma wanted to change the subject. She had never liked discussing Hazelwood or the people who lived there. And for good reason. She didn't like to think about the bad years of her marriage, when her husband had spent too much time in Hazelwood.

She slipped the photographs of Dorothy into the pocket of her apron then put the rest away in the small box. She set the box inside one of the wooden crates stacked by the door. The Quinn family would be moving to their new home in Woodbridge next week. Emma was looking forward to starting a new chapter in her life. The memories of her troubled marriage sometimes resurfaced and were unsettling…and Johnny's observations about Dorothy stirred up some old suspicions that Emma had been trying to bury for years. Jack might get angry, but she didn't care. She had some questions that needed answers, and he had better have some convincing explanations. She was feeling the long-buried emotions and pent-up anger beginning to brew within her…. That evening after Jack finished his dinner, he looked at Emma and said, "You've been mighty quiet since I got home. The stew was good…as usual. Is something wrong?" He walked over to the sink, where Emma was washing the dishes. Then he ran his hand slowly up and down her spine. She stiffened at his touch. She turned to dry her hands on a towel, not even wanting to look in Jack's eyes. She did not intend to weaken or get side-tracked, and she did not want to become distracted by his seductive charms.

"We need to talk about something, but not until the children are asleep. After I read to Michael and Charlie, and they are all in bed, we have to discuss an important matter." She figured it wouldn't hurt to make her husband worry.

Charlie fell asleep quickly in his crib. Then Emma kissed Michael and Paul on their foreheads and tucked them in. Johnny, thirteen, liked to sleep in the attic and tended to read a bit at night. Emma softly called up the steps, "Turn the light off soon, Johnny, we have a busy day tomorrow with more packing. Goodnight, dear." Nan was in her room with the door shut; she valued her privacy, what with four younger brothers. Emma knocked softly and opened the door to peek in, "Goodnight, my darling, sleep tight." Nan was brushing her hair, admiring her reflection in her dressing table mirror. "Goodnight, Mama, I love you," she replied.

When Emma came back downstairs, she walked past Jack as he sat at the kitchen table, reading the newspaper. She noticed he had set out a bottle of brandy; she knew she might need a little bit of liquid courage herself. She poured herself a drink and some for Jack as well, then carried both glasses to the table. She felt Jack watching her but still did not meet his eyes.

"What's going on? You have me worried," Jack said. "Is it something with the new house? It will be ready for the first of the week, and I'm taking two days off work to get us all moved. Fred is going to help, and Monnie is letting us use the bakery truck, which will make the move much faster."

"No, it's not about the house or moving," Emma replied. "It's about this." She reached into her apron pocket and pulled out the photographs of Dorothy as a child. She set them in front of Jack. He picked up a photograph in each hand, glancing at them. "Why are you showing me old photos of Dorothy?" he asked.

Emma took a gulp of brandy. "I had an interesting conversation with Johnny today," she began. "I was sorting through a pile of their old school photographs, and Johnny held these up. You'll never guess what he said." She did not wait for Jack's answer. "He asked why I had photographs of Rose Finnegan, the little girl he met in Hazelwood. The daughter of your old friends. He said he would bet a quarter that Rose Finnegan looks just like these pictures of Dorothy from years back…and that you would agree with him."

Jack examined the photographs again then shrugged. "Well, maybe there is a resemblance, but so what? A lot of people look like other people." Emma could see Jack was trying to act nonchalant about the resemblance between Dorothy and Rose Finnegan.

"Well, I have questions. First, how old is Rose Finnegan? And isn't her mother the sister of your old girlfriend? And…I seem to remember hearing that your old friends were married for years and couldn't have children. Isn't that true?" Emma paused and finished her brandy, her eyes turning steel-gray in the dim light of the kitchen. Her gaze met Jack's dark blue eyes head-on, blink for blink. Steel versus sapphire…which is stronger? After all these years, this was one confrontation Emma refused to back away from. She spoke quietly but directly, almost spitting her words. "What I really want to know is who are the real parents of this little girl your friends adopted? This little girl who just happens to look exactly like OUR oldest daughter!"

Emma could see that Jack was starting to get angry, his jaw set, and his teeth clenched. Finally, he said softly, "So what exactly are you suggesting… that Rose Finnegan might be my daughter?" He continued swiftly: "I have no idea who her parents are…all I ever heard was that they adopted her in Pittsburgh when she was a baby. From one of those foundling homes."

Emma hissed at him: "I can't believe you didn't have questions, especially after you saw her. And it seems to me, if she is around nine or ten years old, that it would fit right in with when we had our troubles…our *bad years*, when you were spending a good bit of time in Hazelwood. What was her name, Jack, the old girlfriend?" Emma continued. "I want a name! I know you mentioned her years ago, but I didn't think at the time that I needed to remember her name!"

"Her name was Clare. Clare Murphy. Alice is her sister. And Alice married my old pal, Johnny Finnegan. And, yes, they were married for a long time and couldn't have children. All I know is that Clare got very sick. She had tuberculosis and was sent to one of those sanatoriums for a long time. My sisters said she was gone for about two years. They had no contact with her. No letters. No nothing. And I had no contact with her either. That's the truth." Emma tried to stay calm. "It never occurred to you that she could have possibly been pregnant when she left?"

Jack shook his head. "No, the thought never crossed my mind. She had been very sick with a horrible cough. Margaret even said she almost died. And my sisters mentioned that she couldn't even have visitors; not that it mattered to me. You and I were getting along so good, and I was back in Elliott again. With you. And when they told me she came home, I never saw her, or spoke to her. Well…not until two years ago when Johnny and I went to the festival at the church. And I only spoke to her for a minute, just to be polite. I know Johnny played with that little girl Rose and her friends several times after that. He seems to like her quite a bit."

Emma leaned forward, bringing her face within inches of Jack's. She whispered: "And what happens if in ten years our Johnny decides he wants to go out with her, go dancing…and then maybe wants to marry her? Then what, Jack? Will you see there could be a problem, since she might be his SISTER? Yes, Jack, how sick is that? She could be his damn sister!"

Jack had rested his elbows on the table. He set his face in his hands, closing his eyes. He took a deep breath, remaining silent for a long while. Finally, he said, "Emma, I'm sorry…but what do you want me to do? That's all in the past now. Jesus! That was ten years ago! Do you want me to go and talk to Clare, and ask her? If it is true…then I will never take the boys to Hazelwood again. Never again!" After a long moment, Emma calmly replied, "We're moving to Woodbridge and will need to get settled. Then you'll have to talk to that woman, Clare, because we need to know! I would think you would want to have that information. And the girl, Rose, doesn't ever need to be told, but I think it's important that you should know. One way or the other."

CHAPTER 33

September 1927—Clare

The telephone in the hallway rang, and Clare answered on the third ring. "Hello."

A male voice replied: "Hello…is this Clare?"

She recognized the voice instantly. "Yes, it is," she said.

The caller continued: "This is Jack…I hate to bother you, but we need to discuss something privately, and it's important. I need to see you in person."

Clare was relieved that Alice, Johnny, and Rose were outside on the front porch. She spoke quietly into the phone: "If you are coming to Hazelwood on Sunday afternoon, I could meet you inside the church at two in the afternoon…I'll be sitting in one of the back pews. Alice and Johnny are taking Rose to the museum in Oakland on Sunday."

"I'll see you at the church," Jack said. "That will probably be better than at your house."

The remainder of the week passed slowly. Clare paced endlessly and wrung her hands. Alice had inquired several times, "Is everything all right? You're as skittish as a horse when a gun goes off." Clare tried to calm herself. "I'm fine, just feeling a little nervous lately," she explained. "Probably since I haven't been sleeping well."

On the following Sunday, after they attended Mass and ate cheese sandwiches for lunch, Clare waved as her family headed down to the corner to wait for a streetcar. She called after them, "Have a nice time. I can't wait to hear all about it." She went back inside, put on the dark green jacket that matched her skirt, grabbed her small handbag, and headed down the street toward the church. She walked briskly even though she had been feeling tired recently, knowing that she could rest in church, waiting for Jack. When she entered through the side door of the church, she lit a candle for her parents and one for Joe. She said a prayer silently then walked to a back pew, alone in the large church. Waiting…worrying about what Jack wanted to discuss. She had some idea, especially after she had observed him staring at Rose. Clare silently repeated one of her favorite Bible passages that had given her strength through the years: *The Lord is close to the brokenhearted and saves those who are crushed in spirit.* Psalm 34:18.

After waiting for fifteen minutes, she heard the heavy outer door open. She glanced out of the corner of her eye. Jack sat down on the wooden pew next to her, not too close. He looked around nervously, making sure there was no one else in the church, then placed his hat between them. With his gaze looking straight ahead, he whispered, "My wife Emma suggested that I come and talk to you." He then pulled the photographs of young Dorothy out of his jacket pocket, handing them to her. He told her about the comments his son Johnny had made. Then he repeated the conversation he and Emma had that night two weeks ago. Finally, he concluded, "Emma wants some answers, and so do I."

Clare had always feared this day would come. Her hands trembled as she spoke softly, her eyes looking at the photographs. "I'm amazed at the resemblance…I had no idea, since I obviously never met your oldest daughter. Yes, Jack," she said, nodding, "it's all true. Your suspicions are correct. Rose is actually my child…and yours too." She swallowed hard then took a deep breath. "I didn't know I was pregnant until I had been at the hospital for several months. She was born there, and I knew it would be best to give her up for adoption. I was prepared to never see her again…and then Alice and Johnny wanted to adopt her, and everything just fell into place. They told people in Hazelwood they had adopted her from a foundling home. It was the perfect solution…and they are such wonderful parents."

She stared at her hands, blinking back tears, afraid to look at him.

"Then when I finally came home, she was already over a year old, and I was, and still am, her Auntie Clare. I've been blessed to be able to watch her grow, even though I have had to lie and keep a secret; it's been the best way to handle it."

Jack leaned forward, his elbows on his knees, his face in his hands, not moving for several minutes. The silence was making Clare uneasy: she tried to imagine what Jack must be thinking. Tears started trickling down her cheeks, and she squeezed her hands together so hard that they began to hurt. She bowed her head lower, whispering, "I'm so sorry that I never told you, but it was such an impossible situation. I knew I couldn't be with you, and that we could never be together with our child…our beautiful little girl. I insisted that Alice name her Rose, since you always loved all the flowers in the gardens." Clare made a choking noise, trying to hold back more tears. She couldn't talk anymore, taking a handkerchief from her handbag. As she glanced over at Jack, he looked up. She saw that there was a solitary tear on his cheek. He wiped it away then looked down at his hands as he whispered, "I'm sorry you had to go through that by yourself. I wish I had known. It practically breaks my heart to know our love ended up causing you so much pain."

He moved closer to her as he reached one hand over and gently squeezed her hands. "Clare, my dear sweet Clare. I'm so sorry that I ruined your life. I'm sorry you live with so much guilt and need to keep this secret. And, for what it's worth…I think that you did the right thing. At least now I know, and you know that I know. We always did like to share secrets…and now we can take this secret to our graves with us. Clare, it would not do Rose any good to tell her." Jack continued caressing her hands, gently rubbing each of her fingers. Then she put a hand over his and pulled it to her lips, giving it a gentle kiss. "Jack, you didn't ruin my life…You made my life worth living." Then, after several minutes, she finally said, "You realize that this is goodbye for good. Forever." Jack's eyes glanced around the empty church. He slowly pulled his hand back and picked up his hat, nervously running his fingers along the brim. He cleared his throat. "I can't bring my boys to Hazelwood anymore," he whispered, staring down at the floor, "and I hope Rose forgets about ever playing with them. And you can assure Alice and Johnny that I would never make any trouble with them and Rose. They are wonderful parents, and if they ever want to tell her the truth, I hope they wait a long time, until she is grown-up, and you and I are dead and buried."

Clare smiled at him. "Thank you, Jack Quinn," she whispered. "I will always be grateful for the love we shared, even though every day I pray for forgiveness."

Jack stood. He tucked the photographs back into his pocket then leaned down and kissed Clare Murphy's cheek. "I know you will think of me when you look at our daughter…kind thoughts, hopefully. Remember that I loved you and always will. Goodbye, Clare."

Then he was gone. Clare knelt and made the sign of the cross. She thanked God for giving her the strength to finally tell Jack. It was as if a burden had been lifted from her heart.

⁓ↄ◈ↄ⁓

The following day, when Clare and Alice were alone in the house, Alice looked at her sister and commented, "Well, you seem happier today…not all jumpy like the last few days."

Clare smiled sadly. "I'll explain it all to you when we have our tea at the kitchen table," she said. "And yes, Alice, I do feel better." But Alice, being quite curious, announced, "Goodness, it's time for tea already." She immediately went to the kitchen and turned on the flame under the tea kettle.

Clare described every detail of her meeting with Jack. When she finished, Alice looked worried, as she held her warm teacup with both hands. "So, Rose looks like his oldest daughter?" she said. "My, oh my. I hope they never run in to each other when Rose is older. You said her name is Dorothy, and she works at the William Penn Hotel in downtown Pittsburgh? We'll have to remember to never go near there, although at least they are a good ten years apart in age." A moment later Clare added, "Oh, and he said he doesn't want his sons playing with Rose anymore. You can just tell her, if she asks, that they moved and won't be coming to Hazelwood anymore."

Unfortunately, two weeks later, Jack's father, Sean Quinn, died from a massive stroke while sleeping in his bed. He had lived to the ripe old age of seventy-nine, always crediting his longevity to the good food his daughters served him. "Good food and a shot of whiskey will cure what ails you," was one of his best-known sayings. One that Jack repeated often. Alice told Clare that Jack's father would be laid out for the viewing for one day at the funeral parlor on Second Avenue, across from the church. The Funeral Mass would be the following day. Clare expected Jack would be there with his sisters, so she encouraged Alice and Johnny to visit the funeral home to pay their respects, or go to the Mass, or both; she would stay home with Rose. Alice and Clare made potato soup and beef stew, along with several pies, for the Quinn family. Johnny and Alice delivered the food; then they visited the funeral parlor. Alice reported to Clare that Jack was there alone and did not bring his wife or any of the older children. Jack told Alice the children could not miss school, since they were just getting situated in their new home.

Clare, Alice, and Johnny thought it was sad that those children had barely known their grandfather, but all three nodded in agreement…It was best the Quinn children stayed far away from Hazelwood.

CHAPTER 34

June 1929—Jack

Jack leaned against the cool brick of the house as he stood on the back porch and contemplated the best locations for the small fruit trees that had been delivered to his property that morning. Johnny brought out two shovels from the basement. Father and son were going to spend the rest of the day digging the holes. The saplings were each around four feet in height, their root balls covered with burlap. Jack had purchased two apple tree saplings, one pear, and one cherry. He wanted to start a grape vine within a few weeks, and he planned on planting several small pine trees: two in the front yard and one in the back. He couldn't help but smile, his dreams realized...dreams that had been years in the making.

As for next year...He anticipated starting the placement of the hedges, which would surround the entire property, front and back. The grass had taken root nicely over the past year, and last month, in May, he had planted tomato seedlings and rhubarb plants in the vegetable garden located in the side yard, which paralleled the alley. Acres of woods lay beyond the alley.

Last Saturday, Johnny had helped Jack plant several two-foot-tall lilac bushes and the rhododendron plants. He imagined how they would look next spring, hopefully with the beginnings of their purple blooms. There would not be any rose bushes, and Emma never requested any. No roses, ever. She and Jack kept their reason private.

When it was lunchtime, Emma called them inside for ham-and-cheese sandwiches and lemonade. Johnny poured himself a glass of milk, and Emma asked him to pour some for his brothers. Paul, Michael, and Charlie were already sitting at the kitchen table. Hungry, as usual. When their father came to the table, they all knew to eat quietly since Jack did not tolerate misbehavior at mealtime. They all had learned that the hard way. Their outdoor playtime could be replaced immediately with a list of chores that included washing windows and scrubbing clothes in the laundry tubs in the basement. Sometimes if Jack was feeling impatient, he would simply reach over—and the perpetrator was immediately on the receiving end of a quick slap on the side of the head, not hard…but hard enough, so Jack made his point. Direct and no questions asked. Nobody wanted to be the recipient of a slap; the boys learned quickly to mind their manners.

Jack and Emma Quinn were determined to raise respectful, well-mannered young men. The older boys even reminded the two youngest: "Don't talk with food in your mouth and get your elbows off the table!" And of course, the cardinal rule was…don't be a slob, or a pig. Emma would remind them: "You don't live in a barn. Food should be on your plate or in your mouth, not dropped all over the table and floor, and not all over your face!"

Having just finished his first year at Woodbridge High School, Johnny was looking forward to exploring Woodbridge with his pals…maybe they could find a swimming hole. He was fifteen and enjoying the elation of being done with his classes. Paul had completed third grade, and Michael had struggled through first grade. Both boys had attended St. Joseph's Parochial School. Little Charlie was only four. He was excited to have his brothers around for the summer; he had missed their company during the school year.

Jack watched his wife as she bustled around her new kitchen. It boasted a modern gas stove with a large oven and the latest style of linoleum flooring. Jack had told her on several occasions, "Emma, I'm glad you like our house, and that you're happy in Woodbridge." Realizing he could not have done it without her, Jack vowed to be eternally grateful for his forgiving wife. He thought they made a good team, and that he finally had his dream…the brick house, the large grassy yard with trees, bushes, and flowers. Handsome children.

Everything was coming together at last. Jack had even purchased an automobile, paying cash, heeding the advice of his father-in-law, Henry, who opposed the use of credit to make purchases. Having a good income from a steady job, Jack would have been easily approved for a loan, but frugal Henry warned him: "No, Jack, you pay cash. Then, if for any reason, you can't make a payment, you never have to worry that the bank will be knocking on your door, demanding the keys to your vehicle."

Henry had persuaded the automobile dealer to give them a lower price if Jack and Henry each bought a 1927 Ford Model A sedan, and if Monnie purchased her delivery truck from the same Ford dealership. Not wanting to pass up on selling three vehicles, the salesman agreed to Henry's terms, succumbing to Henry's bargaining skills and the fact that they were paying cash. They each paid six hundred dollars for their vehicle. Monnie was excited to finally have a modern truck for her deliveries. She knew the truck was a symbol of her success, and she could hardly wait to have "Monnie's Baked Goods" painted on the side. The old horse that had pulled the delivery wagon could now spend its time resting. The beloved animal had earned the luxury of eating grass all day in Henry's backyard.

Fred also shared the spotlight with Monnie: he proudly drove the delivery truck around the local neighborhoods, even as far as Woodbridge, where he would pop in to say hello to Emma in her three-story red brick house.

Although they owned an automobile, Jack still preferred to walk down the hill and catch the streetcar into the city to get to work. He claimed riding the streetcar was easier than dealing with traffic congestion and finding a place to park, never wanting to admit that he found riding the streetcars calming, as opposed to driving a vehicle where one had to be constantly vigilant and make quick decisions. He preferred to leave the driving to others, most of the time.

He learned to drive their black Ford sedan, and he taught Emma, delighting her as well: the automobile gave her the freedom to drive to several markets in Woodbridge to shop for groceries. She also drove to church, and to her club meetings. She was confident enough behind the wheel to take Charlie with her, and she enjoyed driving to Elliott to visit her parents. Jack had never seen her so excited and content, thriving on the challenge of driving, and the freedom that accompanied it.

One of Jack's co-workers declared, "My rule for a good marriage is *happy wife, happy life.* Jack had laughed…but when he reflected on that statement, he realized how much truth there was in those four words.

His father, old Sean Quinn, may he rest in peace, had always told him, "Do your best, and the good Lord will take care of the rest." Jack agreed with those words of wisdom too. Jack had remained unsettled for a time last year over the sudden death of his father, and the revelation of the secret about Rose Finnegan…Now five people knew the truth instead of three. Emma had been supportive and understanding on both counts. Each night, after the children were asleep, she would encourage Jack to share stories about his father… but the couple had a silent agreement to not discuss Jack's illegitimate child.

Emma continued to act as if Hazelwood was miles and miles away, not just on the other side of Pittsburgh. Jack had promised to keep his distance from that area and had not returned to Hazelwood after his father's funeral. Occasionally, he called his sisters Florence and Margaret on the telephone, but that was his only contact, especially since Emma had handled the subject of Rose so well, for which he was grateful. But, just to be on the safe side, and not rock the boat, Jack had promised to never speak to Clare, Alice, or Johnny Finnegan again. When he attended Sean Quinn's funeral Mass at

St. Stephen's, that was the last time he had set foot in a church. Emma kept telling Jack how beautiful St. Joseph's in Woodbridge was, but he refused to go to any services, including Paul's First Communion last year. Emma had finally conceded defeat; she knew she had to pick her battles carefully. When Jack wasn't working at his plumbing job, he just wanted to dig in the yard and design his gardens.

Last winter, when the boys had grown tired of shoveling snow, Jack had roped off part of the basement. He had decided to teach Johnny how to box, just like his dad had taught him. Johnny was now almost six-feet tall and starting to develop some muscle. The younger boys enjoyed watching the training sessions, with Jack and Johnny jabbing and sparring; they perched on overturned wooden crates, cheering for Johnny. Emma didn't approve. But she figured Johnny's boxing lessons with Jack weren't worth arguing about, although she made one simple suggestion to Jack. "Why don't you buy some of those boxing gloves? It would keep Johnny's and your hands from getting bruised." But Jack had insisted, "Boys need to know how to fight bare-fisted… it's an Irish tradition, along with the swig of whiskey afterwards!"

The entire summer of 1929 Johnny stayed busy. Either he was digging and planting for Jack or riding in the truck with his Uncle Fred, delivering his Aunt Monnie's bakery products to the local markets. Emma had decided she did not want Johnny gallivanting all over Woodbridge with his friends, assuming that was a recipe for trouble. "Idle hands are the devil's workshop!" she reminded him.

Johnny's Uncle Fred drove him home when they finished their delivery route, and then Fred stayed and played baseball for an hour in the Quinn's backyard. He still loved the game and showed Johnny, Paul, and Michael some of the finer points: how to correctly throw the ball, how to catch it with two hands to make sure it did not pop out of your glove, and the proper placement of your feet and height of your arms when you took your stance in the batter's box, preparing to hit the ball.

Jack admitted to Emma he was proud of all their children, but especially Dorothy and Nan, who were both working in the city. Dorothy was still at the front desk of the William Penn Hotel. Emma had told him Dorothy liked living in the boarding house near her job, and that she was dating a wealthy businessman who was heavily invested in the stock market. Jack didn't know much about stocks and bonds, but he knew Emma was going to check out a book from the library near Elliott to learn a bit about buying stocks. She informed Jack that Dorothy might want them to meet her stockbroker boyfriend soon, and Emma wanted to at least be able to have an intelligent conversation with him. As most fathers would feel, Jack missed having Dorothy at home; but he realized that she was almost twenty-one, a bright young woman who had always made good decisions and acted responsibly. Jack still worried about his oldest daughter, though, and wanted to protect her, especially now that she was spending time with young men. He hoped they were men of good character, not wanting to visualize his daughter being offered drinks and cigarettes in a speakeasy, or frequenting the dance halls, dancing some of those crazy new dances and wearing a short flapper dress. He had seen pictures of those dresses in Nan's magazines...not a lot of fabric, and lots of leg and arm. They didn't leave much to the imagination!

At work, he had heard the younger men telling stories about the speakeasies and nightclubs, describing how wild some of the young women acted after a few drinks loosened their inhibitions. They would compete to see who could dance the longest and drink the most. It made him recall the bawdy houses and brothels of his youth; but those women, like his old friend Nel, made a career out of being loose and wild. Nowadays, apparently even the respectable young women wanted to be daring and uninhibited. This was cause for concern for any father who had a daughter.

Besides worrying about Dorothy, Jack was also concerned about Nan, who was so eager to start working in the city. She had been hired as a clerk in an office downtown the week after she graduated from high school. She was an expert typist and would soon be advanced to a secretarial position.

He hoped she acted professionally. "Pouting and snide remarks are not acceptable in the workplace," he had told her. And Emma reminded her, "Look people in the eye, speak clearly, and for Heaven's sake, try to smile." In reply, Nan smirked, grunted, and then rolled her eyes at both of her parents.

At least Nan was still living at home, where Emma and Jack could monitor her comings and goings. But she had started talking about moving out next year, after she saved some money. Jack thought, *we'll cross that bridge when we get to it.* Although, Jack had noticed that Nan came home every day carrying bags from her shopping adventures during her lunch hour and after work. He figured it might take Nan a while to save any money. He knew she was immature. He and Emma both worried about Nan's lack of self-control and self-discipline.

Jack did not realize at the time that Dorothy needed him more than Nan, and that they should have been paying more attention to her life in the city.

CHAPTER 35

May 1930—Emma

Emma gazed out at the yard from where she sat on the back porch. Her hands snapped green beans into a pot. She could see a few purple lilacs beginning to bloom, and the pinkish blush had begun to appear on the buds of the rhododendron bushes Jack had planted last year. He had mentioned that it would take a couple of years before the plants started issuing full blooms. At the end of the sidewalk, parked in the alley running behind the house, the sun's rays reflected off the shiny black paint of their Ford automobile. The sedan had brought her much joy, even though it had been a challenge to master shifting gears; but like most things she attempted, success had come to her eventually. Persistence, patience, practice. Jack kept reminding her, "Practice makes perfect!" Emma had never expected to enjoy driving so much; she was an extremely careful driver, now that she knew, in hindsight, that automobiles could have the potential to cause tragedies, impacting lives for years. A personal, unpleasant experience will have that effect!

Emma relished how much freedom she possessed now that she could drive to club meetings around the community. This past year she had joined the Woodbridge Women's Club and the Catholic Daughters organization at St. Joseph church. The clubs were more than happy to draft her into service as their secretary, as she was experienced in writing reports, typing them up on her typewriter, and submitting copies to the local newspaper, when necessary.

Since Woodbridge was a young thriving community, the Women's Club had developed a list of projects to focus on—and of course every project had a committee. Emma had her work cut out for her. She was already earning a name for herself as a person who could handle the intricacies of fundraising, the details of organizing events, and the management of teams of volunteers. It became common wisdom to enlist the aid of Emma Quinn whenever goals were to be met and projects accomplished.

Emma was proud of the fact that she was gaining a favorable reputation in her new community. One of her favorite projects was fundraising for a local library. All the Carnegie libraries were in the older neighborhoods of Pittsburgh; and since Andrew Carnegie was dead, there would be no chance of obtaining new funds from that source, especially since Woodbridge lay beyond the city boundaries. The town of Woodbridge was an independent borough, relying on local taxes to fund the growing list of operating expenses. A love of reading had always been dear to Emma's heart. As she continued to snap the ends off the green beans, she found herself thinking about the speech she had made when she had proposed the library project to the members of the Women's Club. Emma Quinn had been confident…pointing out why every community needed a library, a place not just for adults but for children too. Libraries provided access to newspapers and magazines, as well as to books. She had also pointed out that libraries provided a place to conduct meetings for a wide range of groups. As she sat feeling the warmth of the spring sun on her face and arms, she pulled her cotton dress and apron above her knees, letting the sun warm her legs as well. She smiled contentedly, counting her blessings, which far outnumbered her problems, reminiscing on the ups and downs of her forty-six years of living life the best way that she knew how. And then she reflected on the events of the past year—and not all of them were good memories. She was a firm believer in accepting the bad along with the good…

Emma wondered if God had been testing her…*again*, this past year. In her daily prayers, she thanked God for her family, her good health, their beautiful house, but most of all for Dorothy's recovery, and for helping Jack deal with his brush with tragedy. Back in September of last year, Dorothy and her gentleman friend, William Jones, visited the Quinn home in Woodbridge. Dorothy had wanted to introduce William to her family. She had told Emma, "Mother, William and I have been spending time together all summer, and he just treats me like a queen." Her daughter was obviously smitten.

Conversing with her daughter's beau, Emma discovered that Mr. Jones came from a wealthy family in Philadelphia and was employed by a local bank in Pittsburgh. He stated that he also dabbled in the stock market—and he appeared to be very successful, judging from his fine linen suit, expensive shoes, and his fancy automobile.

Dorothy privately showed her mother the diamond bracelet and earrings William had given her. The two women were alone in the kitchen, preparing sandwiches for lunch. "It looks like this is a serious relationship, Dorothy," Emma observed. "How much do you know about Mr. Jones' life in Philadelphia? His family?" Those were just two of the many questions Emma had about this man, who appeared to be about ten years older than her daughter. "He doesn't talk much about Philadelphia," Dorothy told her mother, "even though he travels there for business at least once a month."

"Where does he live in Pittsburgh?" asked Emma. "He lives in a suite in the hotel, on one of the top floors. It's convenient for him to be close to his bank, and besides, he does travel a lot, so it makes it easier in that respect too."

"And Mother," she added, "he takes me to the nicest restaurants in the city…and to nightclubs…." Emma had read in the paper about the illegal speakeasies that served alcohol, and the resulting wild behavior; but she figured this was not the time to lecture her daughter. She could see Dorothy was blushing. Anyone could tell Emma Quinn's daughter held her beau in high regard.

Lunch that day had consisted of ham salad sandwiches with cucumber slices, iced tea, and fresh apple pie. Mr. Jones suggested Emma and Jack call him William, and then he told them he had attended the Wharton School of the University of Pennsylvania, where he had studied banking. He seemed well-mannered and sophisticated, but Emma gathered that he liked to talk about himself…a lot. He never asked Jack or Emma about their new house, or about Woodbridge, or about Dorothy's brothers. He prattled on about his new automobile and the fanciest restaurants in Pittsburgh. "Dorothy, come here, sit next to me," he insisted as he patted the empty chair beside him, almost demanding instead of asking. Emma sensed that he enjoyed being in control and giving orders. He was handsome and charming, but Emma felt that he was too old for Dorothy. She wondered if he was sincere and trustworthy, and how he acted if he didn't get his way, as she abhorred boorish behavior.

Maybe it was her maternal instinct, but Emma started to feel uneasy, observing how William watched Dorothy closely…and how Dorothy seemed overly attentive to her beau, catering to his every wish, pouring his tea and serving his pie with a little ice cream, even as she whispered in his ear, "Just the way you like it, darling." Emma was slightly unnerved by Dorothy's doting behavior and her daughter's uncharacteristic nervousness; she looked forward to discussing it with Jack as soon as the couple left. After lunch William thanked Emma for her hospitality. He thanked Jack as well. He informed Dorothy that it was time for them to leave. Then they were gone, roaring off in his shiny new roadster.

When Emma was young, she remembered Mama instructing her, "Emma, find a man who likes you more than you like him, a man who shows you that he loves you just a bit more than you love him…and a good man won't be afraid of showing it." Now, she realized how smart her mother was, and probably why her parents had enjoyed such an enduring marriage. She regretted not impressing this wisdom on her own daughter, feeling embarrassed watching Dorothy trotting after William like a love-sick puppy. She desperately wanted to have a private conversation with Dorothy, hopefully soon. She had also noticed that Dorothy was thinner than she had been in years…During lunch her daughter had nibbled nervously on her sandwich and barely touched her apple pie, which had always been her favorite dessert. Dorothy had seemed quieter than usual, too. Emma wondered what was bothering her normally talkative daughter.

After the couple had departed, Emma and Jack sat in somber silence on their new wicker porch chairs. Finally, Emma commented, "Well, Dorothy's birthday is soon, and I sure hope Mr. Jones doesn't plan on giving her an engagement ring. I'm sorry, but I don't like that man, and I can't really put my finger on it, but I have the feeling that William shouldn't be trusted." Emma had always considered herself a good judge of character.

"I agree," Jack replied. "I think there's something shady about him. He seems a little too uppity for my tastes. I suppose we have to trust Dorothy's judgement; after all, she deals with businessmen every day at the hotel."

Rubbing his cheek with worry, Jack added, "He just seems too smooth, from his slicked back hair to his expensive shoes…and those damn cigarettes! In fact, I'm going to refer to him as Slick Willy—and let me tell you, I would never give him one dollar of my money to invest in his stocks! I wouldn't trust him any farther than I could throw him!"

Normally, Dorothy made a telephone call to her mother at least twice a week. When there were no calls for ten days, Emma became concerned. The beginning of October, she called the front desk at the hotel where Dorothy worked and asked to speak to Dorothy Quinn. After waiting for several minutes, Dorothy finally got on the line. "Oh Mother, everything is fine," she proclaimed. "I've just been very busy, working extra hours." When Emma asked about William, Dorothy said: "There's been a few problems at his bank…I guess some customers are nervous about their investments, which has put him in a bad mood. But he told me he's made special plans for my birthday." Much to her parents' dismay, Dorothy and William visited two weeks later to announce their engagement. Dorothy showed Emma and Jack a beautiful diamond ring. She was radiant with excitement. Jack and Emma congratulated them both and asked about their plans.

"Things are a little unstable right now at the bank," William stated. "We won't be planning a wedding yet." Dorothy lowered her eyes and stared at her ring.

And that was that. The couple did not stay long, as William said he and Dorothy had to get back to the city. Jack and Emma's concerned eyes met from across the room. They were thinking the same thoughts: they did not approve of their daughter's engagement to William and knew there was nothing they could do about it. "I plan on going downtown to the hotel next week," Emma said later. "I'll insist on having a conversation alone with Dorothy." She did not want her daughter to make a mistake she would eventually regret. However, Emma never got the chance.

~∽✢∼~

On Thursday October 24, 1929, the stock market crashed on Wall Street in New York City, and continued to spiral downward over the next several days. Emma heard the news on the radio and read about it in the newspaper. The crash devastated investors, many of whom lost huge sums of money. Emma wondered how Mr. William Jones, Dorothy's beau, was dealing with the news.

The following Tuesday when Jack came home from work, he said everyone at his job and on the streetcar was talking about the crash. Everyday brought more bad news for investors. Several Wall Street stockbrokers and bankers had committed suicide, he told Emma, jumping out of their office windows in New York. "Well, I hope Slick Willy didn't lose too much money," Jack commented. "I bet his bank is one of the ones that will have problems."

Emma was more worried about Dorothy. How would she handle William if his world was falling apart? He didn't seem like the kind of man who would calmly handle a crisis…. One evening the next week, while the boys were finishing their homework at the kitchen table, Nan was helping Emma wash and dry the dinner dishes. Jack was reading the newspaper. Just then the telephone rang. Johnny jumped up to answer it. A moment later he said, "Dad, they are asking for Jack or Emma Quinn." Jack stood and took the receiver from Johnny. Emma watched Jack's face, sensing that something was wrong. After listening to what the caller had to say, Jack looked grim. He turned to Emma as he spoke into the phone: "Yes…yes, we'll be there as soon as possible."

"Emma, get your coat," he said after hanging up the phone. "We have to go to Mercy Hospital. They said Dorothy was admitted two hours ago and she just had emergency surgery." He was already putting on his shoes. "Oh, my God," whispered Emma. She tried to stay calm. "Nan, please get Charlie ready for bed, and make sure Michael and Paul say their prayers and get to bed by eight. We'll be back as soon as possible. Thank you, dearest." She hurriedly kissed Nan, and each of the boys.

It was seven o'clock when they parked their Ford and rushed into the lobby of the hospital. The receptionist gave them Dorothy Quinn's room number, and they stopped at the nurse's desk in the hallway before going into the room. The nurse, a nun, since the hospital was a Catholic institution, told them to sit and wait while she fetched the doctor, who wanted to speak to them before they saw their daughter.

Emma and Jack sat patiently waiting on two wooden straight-backed chairs in the hallway outside of Dorothy's room. After ten minutes, a gray-haired doctor in a white coat approached them. He pulled up a chair to speak to them. Emma blurted out, "Please, doctor, what happened to our daughter?" "I'm sorry, but your daughter was assaulted at the hotel where she is employed," the doctor quietly replied. "Apparently, it is also a police matter. They arrested a Mr. William Jones." Emma shivered when she heard that name and tightened her grip on Jack's arm. The doctor paused as he referred to the pages on a clipboard he was holding. "She was in his hotel room…According to the guests next door, they heard arguing and objects thrown against the wall. They notified the front desk when they heard a woman crying and screaming. When the police arrived, Miss Quinn was unconscious; they took Mr. Jones into custody. Your daughter was brought here by ambulance. Now, this will be difficult for you to hear, and you need to be prepared before you see her." He paused for a long moment before describing Dorothy's injuries. "Miss Quinn has multiple facial injuries where there is bruising and swelling. She has five stitches on her head to close a gash where she was supposedly struck with an empty liquor bottle. She also has a broken wrist and two broken fingers on her left hand, two cracked ribs, and bruises on her back and abdomen where she was kicked."

Emma reached for her husband's hand, squeezing hard as she covered her mouth with her other hand. "Oh, dear God…" she whispered.

The doctor shook his head. "I'm sorry, but apparently, she was about three months pregnant. Her injuries caused a miscarriage…I am so sorry. She will need to stay here for several days before you can take her home. She should be awake from the anesthesia soon if you would like to sit with her in her room."

Jack and Emma were both speechless. They managed to thank the doctor then went into the dimly lit room where their daughter lay covered with blankets. She looked as if she was sleeping. Emma gasped when she saw Dorothy's face. "Oh…my baby girl, no …" She sobbed as Jack wrapped his arms around his wife. After several moments he said what had been on the tip of his tongue ever since the doctor read the list of Dorothy's injuries. "That bastard," Jack whispered. "I'm going to kill him."

Two days later a police detective interviewed Dorothy in the hospital. He brought a bag of Dorothy's jewelry the police had gathered at the scene of the assault in William's hotel room. The bag contained Dorothy's diamond earrings, several gold-and-diamond bracelets, and, of course, the diamond engagement ring. The detective assured Dorothy that Mr. Jones would be in jail for quite a while, since he was also facing criminal charges associated with his banking practices.

After a week in the hospital, Dorothy was discharged. Emma brought her daughter home, telling her that Nan wanted to share her room with Dorothy. Emma had visited her daughter in the hospital every day. Gradually, Dorothy had told her mother the whole story. She had endured months of William's moodiness, his irrational exuberance whenever the stock market rose so much as a single point, his manic depression and anger when the markets fell. Then he started drinking heavily…he began making unkind remarks, wanting to argue…The physical abuse started later. He had grabbed her arm one night, leaving bruises. Another night he had ripped her blouse. But he always apologized, he always kept telling her he loved her.

Dorothy had been embarrassed. She didn't want anyone to know about William's temper, especially how his demeanor changed when he was drinking, which had been happening more and more. He was also extremely jealous and began accusing Dorothy of flirting with other men. When she told William she was pregnant, he said the baby wasn't his, that she was having affairs with other businessmen in the hotel. That was when he called her a tramp and slapped her. But he apologized and promised it would never happen again. Then he bought her the engagement ring and proposed to her. Since she was pregnant, Dorothy felt trapped and tried to rationalize his behavior, hoping he was sincere.

When the banking and stock market crisis spiraled out of control, William started to completely unravel…drinking heavily, yelling at Dorothy, blaming everyone and everything for his problems. But he blamed her the most, he took out his anger on her…Nothing she said to calm him seemed to help. Dorothy realized now that he could have killed her.

Every day in the weeks that followed the attack, Emma and Dorothy sat at the kitchen table, drinking tea. Dorothy would tell her mother more details of her relationship with William. One day the week before Thanksgiving, she tearfully confessed, "Oh Mother, so many times I just wanted to get on a streetcar and come home. But I had my duties at the front desk, and since he lived in the hotel, he was always lurking around, watching me. At first, it seemed harmless and I thought it was part of being in love."

"But during the last month, he started getting mean and unpredictable. The night I ended up at the hospital, I had tried to break it off with him and was trying to give the jewelry back. He had been drinking, and his bank was having problems, and he just turned into a raging beast. I was scared and couldn't get away from him. When he punched me in the face, I hit him back…and then he went totally out of control." She hung her head and dropped her still-bruised face into her hands; then she wept and wept. Emma cried too as she hugged her darling Dorothy. Her beautiful, bruised and broken daughter.

Dorothy grieved her lost pregnancy and the loss of her relationship, and she sadly told her mother: "It will be a long time before I will want to get involved with a man again." She also missed her job at the hotel; but she couldn't see how she could ever return there…it would be too embarrassing and painful. Right now, she just needed to be surrounded by the love of her family. She slowly recovered from her injuries and was relieved that there would be no permanent scars on her body. Over the next few weeks, as fall turned into winter, she enjoyed her mother's cooking and spending time reconnecting with each of her brothers. She played cards with Johnny in the evening and board games with Paul and Michael and loved reading stories to five-year-old Charlie. She even spent time talking with Nan, as they both looked through magazines, discussing the latest fashions. Emma was thankful when she heard her two daughters laughing together, reminding her of the days long ago when she had spent pleasant hours with her own sister Estelle....

When the boys had a week's vacation from school at Christmas time, they listened to music on the radio. Dorothy showed them some of the popular dances. On the weekends Nan would join in the fun, especially the music and dancing, no longer feeling any bit of jealousy toward her sister. She had never wanted to see Dorothy hurt and damaged.

The Quinn boys, much to Emma's surprise, came up with an idea for a gift for their sister Dorothy. They had all felt sorry for her and wanted to help her feel better by giving her something special for Christmas.

One day after school about two weeks before Christmas, Johnny cornered his mother in the kitchen. Dorothy was resting upstairs, and the other boys were playing outside. Putting his hand on Emma's shoulder, he quietly said, "Mother, I need to talk to you about something. Paul, Michael, and I have come up with a plan for a present for Dorothy, something that she will love, but you and Dad have to agree."

After drying her hands on her apron, Emma put a lid on the simmering pot of vegetable soup then sat down at the table. "Johnny, you sound so serious, hurry and tell me what's on your mind."

"Do you remember about six or seven years ago, Dorothy found that little dog and took care of him? She was always brushing him, walking, and feeding him."

"I do," Emma replied. "She called him Georgie...carried him around and fussed over him. She loved that little dog. Yes, she had him for several years until he died right before she graduated from high school."

"Well," continued Johnny, in his deeper manly voice that Emma still wasn't used to hearing, "there's this dog that keeps following Paul and Michael home from school every day. They've been giving it some scraps of food from their lunch pails, and it keeps hanging around, walking to school with them and then coming home with them. They want to keep it. So, my point is… we thought we could clean up the pup and give him to Dorothy…maybe tie a big red ribbon around him for Christmas morning. It would help her feel better if she could take care of this little mutt. You know how she loves dogs. Well…Mother, what do you think?"

At Johnny's question Emma stood up and hugged her oldest son, who was now taller than she was. "I'm so proud of you boys for having such kind hearts and wanting to do something nice for your poor sister. I want to have a look at this dog, and then I'll see what your dad thinks, although I'm sure it will be fine with him since it might help Dorothy think about something besides her troubles."

That is how the Quinn family ended up with their mixed breed mutt. He looked to be part Scottish terrier and part cocker spaniel. He had black wavy fur and floppy ears. Dorothy loved him the moment she saw him. She named him Smokey.

Of course, Jack agreed to keeping the dog…anything to see Dorothy smile and laugh again. Anything to help her heart heal.

~ ✑✦✑ ~

After Smokey became part of the Quinn household, whenever Jack was at home in the evenings, he would sit and read the newspaper, sipping his whiskey, watching his family play with the dog, occasionally smiling at Emma. She would sit across the room, working on her knitting, and would look up and wink at him, anticipating keeping warm under the covers with her husband during the long winter nights.

Sometimes Dorothy, Emma, and Jack would hold long discussions about politics as they sat around the kitchen table, reading the newspapers. Prohibition was always a favorite topic of conversation. Even though Emma personally saw both sides of the Prohibition debate, she was still against it, claiming, "The government has no business legislating morality. Banning alcohol simply makes people want it more, and it encourages a disregard for the law."

"And what about all the men that lost their jobs in the breweries and saloons?" Jack remarked. "Yes," Emma replied. "And people like Papa and Fred that eventually had their businesses affected? Although, I'm glad Fred got out of that atmosphere." She didn't want to say it in front of Dorothy, but she was thankful Jack had quit going to the bars and taverns, and that he just had a drink or two at home now, instead of God-only-knew where. "So, Mother," Dorothy said, "I know Daddy voted for Al Smith. Did you vote for Hoover or Al Smith for President?" "Well, I had to vote for Al Smith," Emma replied. "First of all because he was against Prohibition, and he pointed out that it was being enforced to actually hurt the immigrants in the big cities. And I didn't like how people said they wouldn't vote for Smith since he was a Catholic and they didn't like his New York City accent. Can you believe it? There are so many prejudiced, small-minded people!" Then Jack asked, "Did you know those Prohibition laws are the reason so many gangs are operating with illegal activities in all the big cities? Look at that Al Capone in Chicago. He's making a fortune bootlegging, operating speakeasies—and he's not paying one cent to the government in taxes. Prohibition paved the way for all those Irish and Italian gangs to operate an assortment of illegal activities. Now, how has any of that helped our country?"

Dorothy chimed in. "President Hoover isn't doing anything to help anybody, especially the people who are unemployed. Look at those pictures in the newspaper of homeless people living in shacks. The politicians are totally out of touch—they're doing nothing. Daddy, I'm glad your job is secure. Thank goodness the city will always need plumbers, especially ones with years of experience." Her father nodded in agreement. "The city of Pittsburgh was built on the backs of immigrants…and all the politicians better remember that."

Emma was grateful her family was safe, and life was good again…
until it wasn't.

It was the first week of February on a Wednesday evening when Jack
received a telephone call from his sister Florence. She had debated with
Margaret and Alice Finnegan whether to tell him the news. Clare Murphy
had died that morning. She had been sick with a cold and bronchitis, which
had progressed to pneumonia. After being taken to the hospital, Clare had
slipped into a coma. She died the following morning. The funeral Mass
was scheduled for Saturday morning at St. Stephen's. Florence thought Jack
should know. Jack thanked his sister for the information; then he dutifully
reported the conversation to Emma. He was silent the rest of the evening,
lost in thought; and when they were in bed, Emma quietly said, "Jack, I don't
mind if you want to go to the funeral on Saturday."

Saturday morning was a clear cold day, and Jack decided to drive the
Ford to Hazelwood. Frigid air and storm clouds blew in from the north, but
Jack told Emma, "There's no snow on the roads, and it will be quicker to drive
instead of taking the streetcar. As soon as the church service is over, I'll drive
right back to Woodbridge." He informed the boys that he had to go visit his
sisters. "I'll be back by one o'clock," he promised. "Then we can spar for an
hour in the basement." Off he went, in his black suit, hat, and overcoat…
driving the black Ford. Looking as tall and handsome as ever, he appeared
somber. Emma remembered how much he hated funerals. As Emma busied
herself around the house, the weather gradually turned colder and overcast.
A light snow started to fall by noon. By two o'clock the snow was blowing
harder, accumulating in the front yard and the streets. Emma tried not to
worry, hoping the road from the city would not be slippery. She knew the hills
surrounding the Pittsburgh area could be challenging if snow covered, and
she also knew Jack had very little experience driving in wintry conditions.

By four o'clock, at least five inches of snow covered the streets and sidewalks. Emma sent the boys outside to shovel, reminding them to do the neighbors' walkways also. As she worried about Jack, she heard her sons outside hooting and hollering, having a good time throwing snowballs, slipping and sliding with Smokey on the slick sidewalks. Emma watched at the front door, laughing at Smokey as he romped through the snow, having as much fun as the boys.

At five o'clock, Emma, Dorothy, and Nan sat at the kitchen table peeling potatoes and drinking tea. "Try not to worry, Mother," Nan said. "Daddy will be fine. Although, to get home, he might have to park at the bottom of the hill, next to the streetcar tracks, and walk up." The boys were still out in the yard playing when the telephone rang. Emma answered it on the second ring. She heard her father's voice: "Emma, this is Papa. There's been an accident…Jack is fine but can't talk right now. He's in my dining room, talking to the police."

Emma gasped. "My God. What happened, why is he at your house?" Papa replied, "Jack didn't think he could make it to Woodbridge. It was snowing too hard. So, he turned off Steuben Street to come here. He started down the hill on Lorenz, and he says he was going slow; but the Ford started sliding, and he couldn't stop. It slid off the road, onto the sidewalk near where the tavern used to be."

Her father paused before continuing. "Emma, a group of children were playing in the snow on the sidewalk. Two of the children didn't move out of the way in time. Two young girls…sisters." Emma had to sit down. She kept repeating, "Oh my God, oh my God…Are they hurt bad? How's Jack? He must feel awful." She began trembling as she looked at the alarmed faces of her daughters. They both were staring at her.

"They were rushed to the hospital," Papa answered. "We haven't heard anything yet about their injuries. The police are questioning Jack to get all the details. He wasn't drinking…so that's a good thing. It was just the snow and the road conditions. But Jack is upset, Emma. I'll tell him that I talked to you, and hopefully he'll be able to call you soon. Don't worry; he is here with Mama, Monnie and Fred. Together we'll look after him. Just say a prayer for those two little girls." Emma had never said as many prayers as she did that evening and into the night. A book of short stories by Washington Irving sat next to her on the sofa in the living room; but "The Legend of Sleepy Hollow" just wasn't holding her interest. She finally set it down after she had read the same page three times. Eventually she fell asleep on the sofa, wanting to be close to the telephone, in case Jack or Papa called.

The snowfall stopped around midnight. Nearly a foot of snow blanketed Woodbridge and the surrounding communities. The boys were excited to play outside after breakfast; Johnny said he would finish the shoveling. Emma didn't like missing Sunday Mass, but she just couldn't gather the strength to get the boys ready. Neither did she feel like trudging half a mile through the snow to get to church. She knew owning an automobile had already spoiled her, and she was not about to walk anywhere.

Finally, at ten o'clock the phone rang. She quickly answered it. From the other end of the line, Papa told her he had sat up most of the night, talking with Jack. Emma's husband was very distraught. He had prayed with Papa and Mama then one of the priests had come over from church and offered prayers for the two little girls. "Jack is finally sleeping now," Papa told Emma near the end of the call. "We still haven't heard any reports about the injuries of the girls." Emma thanked her father then said to call her again as soon as they heard anything.

Several hours later, Papa called again. He exclaimed, "Oh Emma, I have great news! Our prayers have been answered! The older girl just had a broken leg, and the younger one had a head injury that the doctors were concerned about, but apparently, after being unconscious all night, she had woken up this morning complaining only about a headache. Apparently, the older girl had pushed her sister out of the way when she heard Jack honking his horn. That was when the younger sister hit her head, and the older girl slipped. Jack hadn't had enough control of the Ford to prevent the girl's leg from being run over."

Papa took a breath and paused for a moment. "Jack is still speaking to the policeman that came by to give us the news," he said. Emma breathed a sigh of relief. "Thank you, God," she whispered.

Her father told her that Fred and Jack were going to dig the Ford out of the snow and park it at his house. "Jack will be home this evening," Papa assured her. "He plans on taking the streetcar."

It was after eleven that night by the time Jack walked in the front door. The house was quiet, everyone asleep except Emma. Jack took off his coat and hat, his suit disheveled, his tie loosened, and his face in need of a shave. He glanced around, making sure he and Emma were alone. Then he walked right into Emma's awaiting arms, making a choking noise as he started to sob. She held him tight, not uttering a word, letting Jack weep softly, realizing she had never seen her husband so shaken.

Emma finally took Jack's hand and led him to the sofa, telling him to sit down and tell her everything about last night. Before she sat down, she brought over a glass of brandy, taking a sip from the glass before handing it to him. Jack was wiping his face with his handkerchief. "I'm so glad to be home. Yesterday was one of the worst days of my life." He took a sip of the brandy and shook his head regretfully. "Awful," he said. "Unbelievable, from start to finish."

"First, there was the funeral," he continued. "Funerals are always unpleasant…but you know what to expect. Then that damn snow started. I was trying to drive carefully but realized I couldn't make it home. I thought, well, I'll just go to your parents' house in Elliott. I turned onto Lorenz Avenue and slowly started down the hill. The tires must have hit a patch of ice—they just began sliding. The brakes weren't working. I tried to shift gears into neutral, but nothing helped. The Ford picked up speed and I couldn't steer it away from the girls. I kept pushing the horn, trying to get the group of children on the sidewalk to move out of the way."

Emma watched Jack nervously take another sip of brandy.

"The only thing I could do was honk the damn horn. There must have been five or six children, running and screaming. I kept honking. Then there were the two girls, the little one seemed frozen, just looking at me."

"God…I can still see those wide eyes staring—and I'm hollering at her, 'Move! Move!' The other girl yelled at her, then she finally ran over and pushed her out of the way. The Ford hit a pile of snow next to a telephone pole and stopped, pinning the older girl." Jack closed his eyes and put his face in his hands. "Oh Emma, the screams…I can still hear the screaming! I jumped out and saw the little girl lying on the ground, not moving, and the other girl was screaming and crying. And then people came running to help, and it took three men to lift the front end of the vehicle and push the tire off her leg."

"A woman was crouched down on the ground, holding the little girl who wasn't moving. I just stood there, not able to move or talk. I didn't know what to do. It was *awful*! All I could hear was the screaming. …Blood from the little girl's head spotted the snow. Awful!" Jack said again. "And it was my fault. I caused their pain and suffering."

"Then the police came. I remember Frank running over from the hardware store. The girls were taken to the hospital, and a policeman and Frank took me to your parents' house. I could barely walk, somebody said I was in shock. I remember your Mama holding my hand and telling me that she would help me pray. So that's what we did. We prayed and prayed. Your parents, and Monnie and Fred, and a priest from St. Martin's…I think your father called him and asked him to come to the house. We prayed for hours. Even me...*Especially* me."

Jack closed his eyes, took a deep breath, then exhaled slowly. Emma wrapped her arms around him, trying to comfort him. They sat side by side on their sofa in the living room. Emma understood all too well, bad things happen. We can have regrets, but in the end, after all is said and done... we must deal with the situation as best as we can. Resting her head on her husband's shoulder, holding his hands in hers, Emma closed her eyes. Her mind wandered back in time, back to that day years ago when her brother Eddie had died so suddenly...and then to the dark day when they received the news about Harry, that he had died overseas in the Great War, shot down on a battlefield thousands of miles away... and how her family had been devastated. No one, she realized, was immune from tragedy.

Someone had told her: you never really get over a death. You don't get over it, you get through it. And it changes you, it stays with you...always. Emma whispered to Jack, "Tomorrow will be a better day. You did all that you could do. God will handle the rest."

He turned toward her, patting her knee, and looked into her eyes. "I had time to think when I was on the streetcar riding home tonight, and I made a decision...I am never going to drive again. The Ford is yours now. I am finished driving. Forever."

That night as Emma replayed the events of the previous day in her head, she glanced at the book sitting next to her and thought about a famous passage by Washington Irving: *There is a sacredness in tears. They are not the mark of weakness, but of power. They are the messengers of overwhelming grief, of deep contrition, and of unspeakable love.* She was certain Jack had felt all those emotions.

CHAPTER 36

June 1931—Jack

Trrue to his word, Jack never drove again. He rode the streetcar to and from work, appreciating the swaying and rocking of the cars, the rumbling of the wheels along the tracks. He always found it soothing. His thoughts gravitated to events from the last few years; his sins, secrets, and dreams, as he gazed at the smokestacks along the river still spewing soot and grime.

More than a year had passed since his accident, and he still replayed the events in his mind, wondering if there was anything he could have done differently.

It troubled him that he had caused pain to two innocent little children. Henry had found out their names, and a few weeks after the incident, he reported that they were both doing well. He informed Jack and Emma that the girls belonged to one of the newer families in Elliott, a family that he did not know…a new generation. He wrote down their names so he could remember to tell Jack. Anna and Clara O'Malley. Jack vowed he would always remember their names, believing his Irish angels in heaven perhaps were looking out for him. He did not want to mention it to anyone, even Emma, since people might think it was a childish thought, but his mother's name was Annie…and Clare's funeral had been held the same day as the accident. Maybe the two women in heaven were trying to protect him…maybe they saved those little girls from serious injury. Jack thought the similarity of the names was very ironic…in fact, quite odd. And he couldn't banish the thought that perhaps Clare and his mother Annie had interceded, to spare the lives of two Irish girls. Anna and Clara O'Malley. Otherwise the useless tragedy would have destroyed Jack and permanently scarred his family. As the streetcar rumbled along its familiar path Jack reached for the metal flask in his jacket pocket. "Wake up," he chuckled to himself. "Jack Quinn, you must be getting soft in the head." Lost in thought, he took a welcome swig of whiskey.

Last fall in October, almost one year after the incident that had landed her in the hospital, Dorothy had finally decided what she wanted to do. Having fully recovered from her injuries, and not wanting to go back to work in Pittsburgh, she informed Emma and Jack she was moving to New York City. She had been invited by her friend Pauline, a former coworker at the hotel. They had kept in touch, writing letters to each other throughout the past year. Dorothy assured her parents she would be fine, and that Pauline had connections with people at several of the large hotels in New York. She was excited by the prospect of getting a fresh start and exploring a new city that offered opportunities beyond those she could find in Pittsburgh. Pauline had already moved to a small apartment she was willing to share.

Jack had checked with the city police department and verified that William Jones was still in jail. It was fortunate for Slick Willy that he would remain in prison for several years, since Jack would have found him and given him a painful punishment. No one hurts one of Jack Quinn's children and gets away with it. Jack was not above administering a bit of Irish retribution and that asshole would have deserved it.

Dorothy had sold her diamond jewelry. She now had enough money to help get situated in New York…to pay rent for two months and to buy some new clothes. She was confident she would find a job quickly.

Emma drove her oldest daughter to the train station in Pittsburgh on a bright autumn morning in 1930. She made Dorothy promise to come home for Christmas, which she did. Dorothy had instructed her brothers to take good care of Smokey for her. The boys of course were happy to accommodate Dorothy's request, since they were also fond of that dog.

Jack found it hard to believe the Quinn family had already celebrated four Christmas holidays in their sturdy red brick house in Woodbridge. But when Dorothy returned from New York City for five days at the end of December, Jack decided he enjoyed the Christmas of 1930 more than any other he could recall. Dorothy told the family all about New York and her new job at the front desk of a fine hotel near Times Square. During their daughter's stay, Emma and Jack each observed how Dorothy and Nan enjoyed each other's company, acting like friends instead of rivals. Both girls had good jobs, and both showered members of the family with gifts. Jack had done some Christmas shopping too, primarily at a jewelry store in the city. He bought Emma a blue sapphire necklace; the oval gemstone hung on a thin silver chain. She was overjoyed and commented that the stone was the same shade of blue as Jack's eyes. He gave each of his girls a gold wristwatch, to remind them to spend their time wisely. Then he went into a shoe store and bought Johnny sports shoes with cleats. He could use the new shoes for football and baseball. Jack purchased new baseballs for Paul, Michael, and Charlie, even though he was only five, since little Charlie always wanted to do what his older brothers did.

In the spring, Jack eagerly started digging and planting in the yard again; he savored his Saturdays and Sundays—the union had him working only five days a week now. There was not as much construction nowadays in the city, and many of the younger guys had been laid off. Jack felt fortunate he had years of experience and knew the right people. One bright Saturday morning, Jack took a break from pulling weeds in his garden and sat on the back porch, admiring the large pink blooms of the peony bushes. Earlier, he had finished planting a patch of lilies of the valley, which eventually would have small white flowers.

Jack rolled up the long sleeves of his cotton shirt so he could feel the warmth of the June sun on his arms. He breathed in the fresh clean air, appreciating the crispness more than anyone who had not grown up with sooty smoky air from nearby steel mills. Many of the men he worked with smoked cigarettes nowadays. Jack had spent his childhood years breathing soot and dirt; he couldn't see the point of paying money to breathe tobacco smoke. Some fellows rolled their own cigarettes, but if they had enough money, they smoked store-bought brands. At least that was one vice that had not tempted him.

The house was quiet. Emma was attending one of her club meetings. She was in her glory, relishing the various roles she played within their community. She seemed to have an inner calling to be of service to others. Jack admired that quality in her, even though he did not really understand it, as this was a character trait that he was lacking in. Earlier in the day Emma had delivered two jars of soup and a loaf of bread to an old friend from Elliott whose husband had recently lost his job at one of the steel mills. He had always admired women and their kind hearts. Kind perfect hearts. Forgiving hearts. Jack remembered his childhood days, how neighbors and relatives had always looked out for each other during any crisis: illness, tragedy, death, no job. Women were the heart of Hazelwood, trying to bring comfort to others while their husbands were busy laboring in the mill for meager wages....

His ears perked up—he could vaguely hear the voices of his sons. The sounds drifted from down the street, where the boys were playing with friends in a grassy vacant lot. Some days it was a football match, other times a baseball game. The boys were happy to have the lazy days of summer ahead of them, although Emma strictly enforced their chore duties. Jack was determined that his boys would never know the hard times like those he had experienced when he had been sent off to work in the mill as a young boy. He rarely discussed it. He had always wanted to forget about the fears and sorrows of those painful early years.

Jack was proud of Johnny. He had joined the high school football team and had good grades, as well as a lot of friends. Johnny had been in a squabble or two over a girl; but Jack was confident his son could defend himself if confronted, although he knew Johnny could smooth ruffled feathers with his words and persuasive personality...not having to use his fists. Jack figured it didn't hurt to have a back-up plan just in case words did not suffice. Emma often reminded Johnny, "Just use that Quinn charm you inherited from your father." That remark made Jack smile although he recognized that his children had learned diplomacy, patience, and forgiveness from their mother.

Jack's wife enjoyed being behind the wheel of the Ford. She never pushed for Jack to return to driving. She understood his reluctance and told him she supported his decision; she even helped him shop for Christmas presents for the two girls who had been injured in the accident. Jack thought perhaps Anna and Clara O'Malley would enjoy some new dolls. Secretly, he hoped they would play with the dolls inside their house, not in the street.

As Jack reflected on events from the past two years, he trusted Dorothy would find a suitable, loving husband someday, although he suspected that she would never return to Pittsburgh permanently. Nan was doing well in her job. She was working as a secretary in a big office in downtown Pittsburgh. So far, she had not gotten herself fired. Jack felt a sense of parental pride thinking about how much his daughter had matured since the Kennywood incident when she was fifteen. He and Emma were both glad Nan was still living at home—and that she had not brought home any undesirable suitors…no Slick Willies would survive around Nan. That feisty girl was no shrinking violet. She would never be dominated by any man.

Jack realized that having daughters was enough to give any man a few gray hairs, what with all the worrying about who they might be with and what they might be doing. Dorothy had never given him any reason to worry when she had still been living at home, but the events of the past two years had given him a different perspective. Jack hoped to keep Nan under his roof for as long as possible, although Nan's bold personality would perhaps serve her well: she would never put up with a condescending bastard who would raise a hand to her. Nan would be fearless in defending herself…never the victim. And pity to any man who crossed her or attempted to break her heart.

And then he thought about his third daughter, who did not even know he was her father. He figured Rose had recently turned thirteen. If he had to pick a man to be her father, he would have chosen Johnny Finnegan; and he knew that Alice was a wonderful mother. He was happy that at least Clare had been able to watch their daughter growing up for twelve years.

He remembered sitting in St. Stephen's Church at the funeral service for Clare, the same awful day of his accident. He had sat in the back, in the same pew where he had met with Clare when she had confirmed he was Rose's father.

Jack regretted causing so much pain for Clare. He was sorry for the times he had not been with her when she needed him…when she had been in the sanatorium, when she had given birth to his child, when she had been attacked by her brother Joe, and finally, when she had been sick, dying alone in a cold hospital bed.

Memories of Clare were filled with love, but also sorrow. And Jack felt guilt, ashamed of the lies, and the secrets. He realized he had never loved Clare Murphy *enough*… never loved her enough, or else he would have protected her and stayed with her so many years ago. His damn divided heart just had not been filled with enough love. His damaged, imperfect heart. Jack knew now, finally, that a man needs to love only *one* woman, and should love her with his entire heart. On the day of the funeral, he had watched young Rose crying softly, obviously missing her Auntie Clare. He observed how Alice comforted her, and then how Johnny, his old best friend, comforted his wife Alice. They were a perfect little family. After the Mass, when he had waited for them to come outside, he wanted to quickly convey a few words of sympathy to Alice and Johnny. As he looked at Rose, she smiled at him with her beautiful blue-green eyes, and he remembered Clare saying that Rose possessed the best of each of them. He had agreed…yes, she was a beautiful girl. She seemed intelligent and kind. He imagined—he hoped—Rose had been blessed with Clare's loving heart.

Standing in the cold as the snowflakes swirled around them, he had recalled how he had been taken aback when he noticed that Rose was wearing the gold locket. The gift he had given Clare many years ago. There, right in front of him, were the two entwined hearts engraved on the face of the locket. Rose noticed him staring at the necklace, and she reached up and touched it. She explained that her aunt had given it to her before she was taken to the hospital. "Auntie Clare told me that it was her most prized possession," she told Jack. "She said it was very old and very special to her. She asked me to take good care of it." Then she buttoned her coat and walked away with Alice and Johnny, her loving parents. Jack knew they would shield her from the truth, at least until the day they died. Jack resigned himself to the thought that he probably would never see the three of them again. Everything about that day in February, over a year ago, had saddened him to the bone. He reminisced about his dear departed father and how Dad would drink his whiskey and laugh, saying, "Jackie, remember to forget the things that made you sad, but never forget the things that made you glad." Thoughts of Dad always made him smile—and he was determined to appreciate Henry, Emma's wise father, for as long as that man walked the earth. Jack had learned how to be a husband and father from both of those gentle, content men. Whispering to himself, he said, "Jack Quinn, you are a lucky man indeed, as not every man gets to survive the bad times that are his lot in this world…to finally achieve his dreams, the dreams that never died. Forget the sad times and remember the good…just like Dad said."

He realized that now that he had survived for fifty years and learned how to live, and love, he had earned the right to sit on his porch and reflect. Now, he understood how Dad and Henry were able to sit for hours lost in thought….

Jack reached down and petted Smokey, who had curled up by his feet, rubbing his thick, warm fur. Not everyone reaches fifty years, and even Jack Quinn, who had given up on prayer so many years ago, thanked God for his blessings. In the last two years Jack had learned to pray again, which surprised him almost as much as it had surprised Emma. "Miracles do happen," he said. "But don't expect me to start coming to Mass anytime soon. That door is closed forever." Emma had just nodded, responding: "Never say never… Stranger things have happened in our lives!"

And then Jack closed his eyes, picturing Dad handing him a glass of whiskey, and Dad saying: "A life making mistakes is more honorable, and far more useful, than doing nothing at all…So drink up and learn from those mistakes, my boy!"

Jack stood up and admired his gardens, deeply breathing in the clean air…never tired of that privilege. He went into the kitchen to make a cheese sandwich, Limberger on rye, then carried the plate through the front hallway of the house and paused to look at a framed quotation from the Bible. Emma had recently hung the quotation on the wall. She had used black ink and fancy handwriting on thick paper; then she had placed it in a gold frame. He read the words:

Love never gives up, never loses faith, is always hopeful, and endures through every circumstance. —1 Corinthians 13:7 Jack continued his way out to the front porch. He would wait in the shade provided by the awning until his wife came home.

EPILOGUE

September 1953—Jack

The summer had been cooler than normal, with a good amount of rain, so this was going to be a good year for apples, Jack thought. He finished picking two apples off the ground then put them into his basket. He carried the heavy straw basket of ripened fruit into the kitchen, setting it on the table. Over the years, Emma had become an expert at making applesauce, apple strudel, apple pie. Today, she planned to begin baking as soon as she returned home from her club meeting.

Emma had informed him that this year she also intended to make jam from all those grapes ripening on his grapevine. Jack chuckled to himself, wondering if his wife would be able to find the time to make jam on top of all the traveling she planned to do: Emma had just returned from one convention in Harrisburg, and at the end of the month she was going to a national convention for the ladies auxiliary of the veterans group she had belonged to since before they were married. She was excited to be on the ballot for the organization's national office. Jack remembered she had told him this convention was being held in Baltimore, Maryland. She loved to travel, ride the train, make new friends. "I'll soon have pen pals from almost all of the forty-eight states," she told him. She loved writing letters and keeping in touch with a long list of friends and acquaintances she had met at conventions throughout the years. Jack never pretended to understand why, but he was happy that *she* was happy. Meanwhile, he had his friends and acquaintances who he enjoyed having a shot and a beer with during his occasional visits to the South Side taverns. He shared memories with fellows from his old plumbing crews, especially Jimmy Kennedy and Joe Sullivan. The trio could still spend an entire afternoon debating which drink they preferred: straight whiskey, blended whiskey, rye whiskey, or bourbon. Irish whiskey or Scotch whisky? Irish whiskey, of course. They all vowed to never drink wine, gin, or vodka; spirits favored by some of the younger generation. These men were hard-core, old-school whiskey lovers.

Twenty years ago, after the Prohibition laws had been repealed, the bars and saloons had gradually started gaining back their customers. He knew Emma was glad he had mellowed over the last few years and wasn't drinking as hard as when he was a younger man.

His drinking had always been a contentious issue between them, causing a fair number of arguments during their forty-five years of marriage. He readily admitted he was grateful Emma had been forgiving, and that they had always managed to compromise and rise above their disagreements. Jack really couldn't keep up with all his wife's activities, but he knew her proudest accomplishment was assisting in the establishment of the Woodbridge Community Library, which finally opened in 1946, right after World War II had ended. Her club activities had turned into a blessing in disguise: her duties had kept her busy during the war…when all four sons were overseas. He still did not like to think about those dark years, which had been filled with uncertainty. Jack finished drinking a glass of water as he sat at the kitchen table. He reached down and patted the brown and white Collie sleeping at his feet.

It occurred to Jack Quinn that he spent a good bit of time thinking and reminiscing. He gazed at his hands, picturing them when he was a young boy…working in the mill, where the heat caused blisters and scars. Then later, when he learned how to use the tools of his trade, and how his hands had held all sorts of wrenches, pliers, saws…tools that had enabled him to earn a living and feed a family. Tools that had helped him make money and pursue his dreams. A few of those tools were now kept in his basement, above his workbench. Looking at the scars on his hands, he remembered stories that went with each mark, a few that were reminders of the occasional fistfight….

Jack had finally retired from the Plumbers Union two years ago, when he turned seventy. He was content receiving Social Security benefits and his small pension from the union. He was now free to spend every day working in his gardens and the yard. There was always a tree or a flowerbed that needed his attention.

Glancing at the clock on the kitchen wall, he realized he had better change his clothes, put on his suit, and get on the next streetcar headed into the city. He had to be in Hazelwood by ten to attend yet another funeral. He still hated them.

His sister Margaret Quinn had passed away after a long illness, some sort of lung disease. Florence had died three years earlier, also after suffering for years from breathing issues. The damn smoke and soot from the steel mills had always caused lung issues for the residents of communities close to the rivers….

Luckily, his oldest sister, Mary, was still alive. She was a widow, eighty-one years old; her stepdaughter, Jane, was living with her. They had invited a few friends from church over to their house for lunch after the funeral Mass at St. Stephen's.

When he stepped off the streetcar on Second Avenue, he planned to walk the two blocks to St. Stephen's. He passed various storefronts then stopped in front of the clothing shop where Clare and his sisters, Margaret and Florence, used to work. His sisters had both quit there—when, exactly? Probably fifteen years ago, Jack guessed. He noticed a sign on the door informing patrons the store was closed today: the owner was attending a funeral. In the large shop window, another sign read—

Under New Ownership

The store had a new name also, painted on the glass in large letters:

ROSE MARY'S DRESS SHOP

Jack paused a moment, considering the name; then he hurried down the street and up the steps into the church. After taking off his hat and quietly walking down the main aisle, he slid in the front pew, next to his sister Mary. He reached over and patted her hand.

He remembered years ago, when he was a young boy, he would sit next to Mary in church, and she would pinch his arm whenever he started to fall asleep. He made a mental note to ask her if she recalled how she had tried to keep him awake in church more than sixty years ago....

Later, after the service and the ride to the cemetery with Mary, her stepdaughter, the funeral director, and the parish priest, Jack entered Mary's house and finally had a chance to have a conversation with his sister. Mary hugged him. "Well, Jackie, we are the last ones left," she said. "Margaret is in Heaven with Florence, Mum, and Dad. I'll probably be the next one." Jack returned his sister's heartfelt hug then finally said: "Mary, I don't know if I ever properly thanked you for everything you did for me when we were young...after Mum died. I don't know what I would have done without you."

Mary wiped her eyes with a handkerchief and smiled at him. "It was a hard time for all of us, but we got through it together. What choice did we have? You do what you have to do."

Jack followed Mary's eyes as she looked at a woman in a fashionable dress and high heels who was walking toward them. Mary took the woman's hands in her own and said to Jack, "You probably don't recognize this lovely lady, Jack. This is Rose Finnegan, Alice and Johnny's daughter." Just then, one of the neighbors asked if she could speak to his sister. Mary excused herself, leaving Jack and Rose staring at each. Rose immediately said, "Well hello, Mr. Quinn, it's been a long time since I've seen you...since I was a young girl."

Not waiting for him to speak, Rose continued: "I suppose you know that both of my parents are gone now. Dad died from a sudden heart attack eight years ago, and Mother was sick for a while with heart issues, and then her kidneys failed. She passed away just last year."

Jack tried not to stare as Rose spoke, but he kept thinking how much she resembled his daughter Dorothy. Of course, he understood why. To this day he was still grateful Clare had finally told him her secret. After all this time, there had still been only five people who had ever known…Clare, Alice and Johnny Finnegan, and then, later, Jack and Emma.

Rose was extremely attractive. She wore her wavy dark hair just above her shoulders, cut in a stylish bob. Her eyes were beautiful, with a touch of green. She flashed Jack a smile, and he noticed her lipstick and gold earrings. Then he saw the gold locket on a thin gold chain, hanging several inches below the neckline of her dark blue dress. The locket. That symbol of his devotion and love he had given Clare so many years ago. He looked away for a moment, thoughts swirling in his head, then finally found his voice.

"Yes, my sister Margaret had told me about my old friend passing away. Johnny and I were the same age… I was saddened to hear that he died so suddenly. I'm sorry, it must have been such a shock. And then, last year when Margaret took sick, my sister Mary told me about Alice, and how you had cared for her right up until the end. Again…I am so sorry. They were good people."

He noticed Rose was studying his face as he spoke, and then he thought maybe it was just his imagination. Glancing past her, he decided to ask about the clothing shop. "When I was walking on Second Avenue this morning, I passed the old clothing store where my sisters used to work and noticed that it's now called Rose Mary's Dress Shop. Would that by any chance be your business?"

Again, Rose smiled, and proudly said, "It is indeed. When I was young my Aunt Clare taught me to sew, and I became interested in dress design.

After high school, I worked for a good fifteen years at Kaufmann's department store, in their women's clothing section. I did a lot of alterations there; and after the war I even traveled to New York City several times with their buyers. Anyway, long story short, I lived at home with my parents, and I was able to save most of my pay, so when the old clothing store went up for sale I bought the business and the building, shortly after Mother passed away last year."

Out of curiosity, Jack asked, "I suppose you're not married?" Rose looked away. Softly, she replied: "Twelve years ago I was engaged to a wonderful man. He was over in the Pacific during the war. He was killed during the attack on Pearl Harbor."

"I'm sorry," Jack said, not wanting to ask any other questions. After an awkward moment, Rose commented, "I need to spend all my time and energy working at the store, making my business successful."

Jack couldn't help being impressed with this young woman's ambition—not to mention her poise and her charm. He complimented her. "That's quite an achievement, your family would be proud." And of course, he was thinking about Clare.

Rose touched the locket as she spoke: "When I leave here, I'm going back to the shop. Would you like to stop and see what I've done with the place, before you head back to your home? There's something I'd like to show you. I found it in my mother's personal belongings. Please." She smiled. For a moment it looked as if her confidence was melting away.

"Of course," Jack replied. "I'll be there in an hour."

After Jack left Mary's house, he walked slowly in the cool air. A few dry leaves swirled around his black shoes, as he turned and headed up the hill, past St. Stephen's school; then two more blocks, to where the gardens used to be. The entire area had been abandoned: it was now wooded and overgrown, suffering from more than twenty years of neglect. Even the willow tree was no longer standing. Once majestic, it lay in pieces on the ground, apparently struck by lightning and left to rot. The lilac bushes and apple trees had all been overrun with vines, weeds, and thick, wild growth. The old large houses had been demolished, their owners moving on to better neighborhoods.

Jack turned around, leaving the playground of his youth, now just a forest that had gone wild. The overgrown area no longer held any resemblance to the place that lived in his memories.

Slowly strolling back down the hill, he gazed in the direction of the aging mill, still spewing smoke that clouded the horizon and hung like a shroud over the town. He crossed Second Avenue then stepped carefully across the railroad tracks where the familiar streets of run-down row houses were located. Structures that had seen better days, waiting for their final demise, along with the mill and the whole damn town. Turning the corner, walking a block, he stopped in front of his old house. It felt as if he had come to say goodbye to an old friend.

A "For Sale" sign had been stuck in the yard; Margaret had spent her last few months of life at Mary's home. He observed the peeling paint on the porch, and a cracked window upstairs…The place had seen better days. Dad's old wooden rocking chair still sat on the porch. Jack pictured the old man sitting there, glass in hand. Jack nodded and touched the brim of his hat. For a moment he thought he saw Dad raise his glass to Jack in greeting, and Mum, Florence, and Margaret standing on the porch behind Dad's chair. He blinked—and then they were gone…. Back on Second Avenue, he could see the sign: ROSE MARY'S DRESS SHOP. A small bell attached to the top of the door rang gently as he entered the store. Rose appeared from the back, her high-heeled shoes clicking on the hardwood floor that gleamed in the light. Jack scanned the freshly painted walls, the new light fixtures, and the racks of dresses…everything from day dresses, to office attire, and even a wedding gown. "This is remarkable," he said. "So bright, and modern." He smiled at Rose. "I'm sure you will do well."

Rose nodded appreciatively. "Thank you. I design and sew some of the dresses. The rest I purchase from my contacts in New York. I find it all so exciting. Mother encouraged me to do it...to follow my dreams." Rose suddenly became serious, taking a deep breath. The color drained from her face, and Jack thought he noticed a slight quiver in her voice. He had been around women his entire life; he sensed she had not invited him here to just discuss her business.

"Speaking of Mother, this is what I wanted to show you." She held up a long white envelope. On the front, Alice had handwritten in black ink, *Rose, Do Not Open Until After My Funeral.* "I found this with her personal papers about a month ago when I was cleaning out the closet in her room. It was sealed, and of course I was curious...and I certainly was shocked when I read the letter and looked at my birth certificate." Her hands trembled as she pulled two folded papers from the envelope.

Jack swallowed hard. He realized where this conversation was heading. He was at a loss for words as he watched Rose and listened. He just needed to listen, and not interrupt.

Rose pointed to two upholstered armchairs by a full-length mirror on the opposite wall, next to what appeared to be a dressing room. "Please, sit down, so we can talk. I want you to read the letter and look carefully at the birth certificate." Jack took a seat and stared at the piece of paper then unfolded it. He started to read silently, slowly wrapping his mind around each hand-written sentence.

The letter was dated May 1952—about six months before Alice Finnegan had died.

Dearest Rose,

Years ago, in 1918 to be exact, I promised my sister Clare that I would keep her secret safe forever. After Clare died, your father and I agreed that we would continue to keep our promise to my sister. However, my dear Rose, you have grown into such an intelligent, accomplished woman, and I love you so much that I felt you should know the truth. When Clare was sick with tuberculosis back in 1917, and was confined to a sanatorium, she was told she was carrying a child. She had the baby, which had been conceived in love, and was going to give her up for adoption, since she could not marry the child's father. The father did not even know about the baby since Clare was not allowed to have contact with outsiders. He had always been her one true love, but he was committed to another. Dad and I were never able to have children, so we ended up adopting the child—which of course was you, my darling Rose. You were our gift from God and such a blessing for us. I was always grateful that we were able to raise you as our own. And my sister, your Aunt Clare, was thankful she was able to watch you grow surrounded by our love. Now you will see on your birth certificate that your biological father is our friend, Mr. Jack Quinn. About two years before she passed away, Clare finally told Mr. Quinn about you. So, when you read this letter, I want you to be aware that he does know that you are his daughter. What you do with this information is entirely up to you, but I felt that you need to know the truth of your origin. Just always remember that you were loved since the day you were born by Dad and me, and by your Aunt Clare.

Your Loving Mother,

Alice Finnegan

Jack examined the birth certificate and saw that Clare Murphy was listed as the mother and Jack Quinn was listed as the father. The child's name was Rose Mary Finnegan, legally adopted by Alice and Johnny Finnegan on May 20, 1918.

"Well…Rose, what do you think about this?" Jack inquired, not really knowing what else to say. Rose was sitting with her hands folded in her lap, looking directly at him. Jack saw that she was biting her lower lip, which made him remember how Clare used to do the same thing.

She quietly answered: "When I first read this…of course, I was in shock, not believing it. But after several days of feeling angry, I finally realized that it made sense. I think everyone did what they thought was best. After all, I always knew that I had been adopted as a newborn infant, so of course Mother and Dad are the only real parents that I ever knew. And they were wonderful."

"The only real question I have for you is…what were the circumstances around the relationship between you and Aunt Clare? I knew you had been friends with her and my parents since you were all very young. Why did you not marry her then?"

Leaning forward, his elbows on his thighs and his hands folded, Jack replied, "It's a long, complicated story. We had been best friends since we were fourteen, and we did love each other, but sometimes love just isn't enough."

Pausing thoughtfully, he continued: "I had known for many years that I wanted to leave Hazelwood and the smoke and dirt of the steel mills, which is why I became a union plumber. I had always told Clare that I couldn't live here, but she refused to even consider having a life elsewhere. She always thought I would change my mind, even though I kept telling her that I wouldn't. We never discussed marriage, and as we got older…we just grew apart. I eventually married Emma, my wife, and moved to Elliott."

Rose listened quietly as he told her about his marriage to Emma, and the tumultuous period when he had a falling out with his wife and had come back and lived with his father and sisters. This is when he had become friendly with Clare again, secretly, after years apart. Their affair had lasted for about a year, and no one in their families had known about it. Then he described Clare's illness, and how she was sent away.

Jack said, "For the sake of my children, I patched things up with my wife and stayed away from Hazelwood. Even after my sisters told me that Clare had returned, I thought it best to not see her at all, and that's how things remained for many years. I never knew about you until two years before Clare died. She didn't want you to know, and she had made Alice and Johnny promise to keep the secret. When she told me…I confessed the whole story to my wife Emma, and Clare insisted that we keep it a secret."

Rose smiled slightly in reply. "You know, I'm actually grateful Mother left that letter for me. I always had unanswered questions, wondering who my birth parents were…and the circumstances around my birth. And now I realize that I was quite lucky…being raised by two mothers, and of course my wonderful father, who I loved so much. I had more than most children. Being raised by three parents, instead of two."

Jack nodded in agreement. "They were three of the finest people I ever knew. And I believe that they were lucky to have you too."

Rose inquired about Jack's six children and asked him to bring photographs of them the next time he came to Hazelwood. She smiled and said, "I'm glad we had the opportunity to talk, and I hope you come to Hazelwood more often, and stop in my shop. You are always welcome."

As they both stood and faced each other, she stepped forward. "Do you mind if I give you a hug?" she asked.

Jack opened his arms. She embraced him tightly then stepped back, saying, "That was from me, my parents, and Aunt Clare."

As the streetcar rumbled across the river, Jack mulled over the events of the day. He pulled a silver flask from the pocket of his suit jacket. He took a long drink, and as he returned the flask to his pocket, he thought about his relationship with God: his inner turmoil, anger, and the battles that had raged inside of him when he was young. He still did not attend Mass, perhaps now from stubbornness and years of absence; but he was proud of the fact that he had started reading the Bible recently…when he was at home by himself. In the Book of Isaiah, he remembered reading a passage that stated: The grass withers, the flower fades, but the word of God stands forever. I am not alone, for my God is with me.

After all these years, Jack finally understood why Dad had always seemed so content. He mused that there was a truth to the fact that we are not alone, that God is indeed with us.

He thought about his conversation with Rose. He would have quite a story to tell Emma tonight, about his extraordinary day.

The streets were already dark as he stepped off the streetcar. He gazed up at the clear sky, at the full moon and the stars shining above him and wondered whether the stars were truly openings in the heavens, so the ones we love might watch over us. Walking up the hill, still looking at the star-filled sky, he pictured Dad and Mum. Florence and Margaret. Emma's brothers, Harry and Eddie. Alice and Johnny Finnegan. And of course, Clare. Their souls all safe with God.

Jack hurried toward home. Emma would be waiting.